THE
HORSEMAN'S
SONG

Ben Pastor

BITTER LEMON PRESS
LONDON

BITTER LEMON PRESS

First published in the United Kingdom in 2019 by

Bitter Lemon Press, 47 Wilmington Square, London WC1X OET

www.bitterlemonpress.com

Copyright © 2004 by Ben Pastor

This edition published in agreement with the Author through

Piergiorgio Nicolazzini Literary Agency (PNLA)

A CIP record for this book is available from the British Library

ISBN 978–1–912242–11-5

EBook ISBN 978–1–912242–12-2

Typeset by Tetragon, London

Printed and bound in Great Britain by Clays Ltd, Elcograf S.p.A.

To all those who struggle for bread, land and liberty.
In the black moonlight
Of the highwaymen,
Tinkle the spurs.

Little black horse,
Where are you taking
Your dead horseman?

FEDERICO GARCÍA LORCA, "CANCIÓN DE JÍNETE"

MAIN CHARACTERS

NATIONALISTS

Martin Bora, German volunteer, Tercio of the Spanish Foreign Legion
Indalecio Fuentes, Former policeman, Guardia Civil
Jacinto Costa y Serrano, Colonel, Spanish army
Josep Aixala, Volunteer from Catalonia
Niceto, Stage actor
Tomé, Guitar player
Paradís, Former sailor
Alfonso, University student
Mendez Roig, Captain, Francisco Franco's secret service (SIFNE)
Cziffra, Officer, Abwehr

INTERNATIONALISTS

Philip ("Felipe") Walton, American volunteer
Henri ("Mosko") Brissot, Physician and French volunteer
Marypaz, Walton's girlfriend
Chernik, American journalist
Iñaki Maetzu, Former convict from the Basque region
Valentin, Gypsy
Bernat, Volunteer from Catalonia
Rafael, Teenage volunteer

Almagro, Dispatch rider
Marroquí, Dispatch rider

SPANISH CIVILIANS

Federico García Lorca, Poet
Remedios, *Bruja* (witch)
Luisa Cadena, Lorca's cousin
Antonio Cadena, Luisa's husband
Francisco ("Paco") Soler, Stage designer
Vargas, Music teacher
Don Millares, Pharmacist
Consuelo Costa y Serrano, Colonel Serrano's wife
Soleá Yarza, Midwife and meddler

HISTORICAL TERMS

Abwehr German secret service.

Carlists Monarchist troops, named after their support for Don Carlos, brother of King Ferdinand VII, against the French in 1934.

CNT National Confederation of Labour, an anarchosyndicalist organization, and the largest Spanish labour union at the beginning of the Civil War.

FAI Spanish Anarchist Federation, an extreme Left political entity which, however, resisted growing Soviet intervention in Spain.

Falange Fascist-inspired extreme nationalist movement, founded by José Antonio Primo de Rivera in 1933.

Guardia Civil Militarized police force in Spain.

NKVD People's Commissariat for International Affairs; the Soviet secret police and espionage agency.

POUM Worker's Party of Marxist Unification. Formed by former exiled Spanish Marxists, it supported Trotsky's concept of "permanent revolution" and opposed Stalin.

PSUC United Socialist Party of Catalonia. Dominated by Communist elements and opposed to Anarchists.

SIFNE Technically, the Spanish Information Service for the North-East; in fact, the main information-gathering service for the Nationalists.

Tercio Name commonly given to the Spanish Foreign Legion, based in Morocco. It supported Franco's rebellion against the Republican government of Spain.

1

CAÑADA DE LOS ZAGALES, TERUEL
PROVINCE, ARAGON REGION,
NORTH-WESTERN SPAIN, 13 JULY 1937

The tall canes gave a rustle like rain, but it hadn't rained in a month, and down the bank the brook ran low.

From where he stood, Martin Bora knew death at once. Lately the inertia of death had grown familiar to him, and he recognized it in what he saw at the curve of the mule track, where trees clustered and a bundle of leafy canes swished like rain. He couldn't make out the shape from the bank of the brook, where he'd bathed and was now putting his uniform back on. In a time of civil war, these days did not call for inquisitiveness. Yet Bora was curious about life and the point when life ceases. Staring at the slumped dark mass, he finally managed to struggle into his wet clothes, quickly lacing and buttoning his uniform. The stiff riding boots and gun belt were next.

Overhead, the air was scented and moist. The summer sky would soon turn white like paper, but at this hour, it had the tender tinge of bruised flesh. Bora started up the incline, steadying his boots on the shifting pebbles, and reached the mule track to take a better look. He could see now that it was a human body. As he took out his gun, his arm and torso adjusted to the heft of steel, hardening immediately, almost aggressively. Shoulders hunched, he crossed the track, straining for sounds around him, but a lull had fallen over trees, brook and leafy canes. The sierra, its crude face of granite rising above, was silence itself.

The body lay twisted on the edge of the track, face down. Bora drew near, lowering his gun. *I shouldn't be turning my back to the trees, but look, look ...* A small hole gaped black and round at the base of the man's head; the dark fleece of the neck appeared sticky, matted. *I should not feel safe. Anyone could shoot me right now.* Yet the tension slackened in him. Bora's armed hand sank to his side. Not much blood on the ground, although the man's white shirt was deeply stained – a dark triangle between his shoulders. *No, no. No danger.* Bora looked down. *There's no danger.* He stood at the rim of the bloody puddle, a crisp lacy edge that gravelly dirt had absorbed and sunlight would dry soon. It marked a boundary at his feet, curving sharply where a twig had stopped it from flowing. *No danger.* Bora glanced up. A young ash tree stood smooth and tall, alone on the curve. How telling that a twig should be born from it and grow and fall to the ground to stop a man's lifeblood; that a man should live unaware that a bit of ash wood awaits him on a lonely road. Bora holstered the gun, wondering what kind of wood, which road, what sky, what morning waited for his dead body and would grow into the fullness of day without him.

He could smell blood as he crouched down, virtually tasting it when he turned the body to check if the bullet had destroyed the face. But it was intact. Handsome in a southern or gypsy way, with a broad forehead and eyebrows joined at the bridge of the nose, the man's face appeared serene, the eyelids lowered and the mouth slightly open. The lashes were like a woman's, dark and long. The body felt cold to the touch, sweaty with dew. *Like mashed lilies,* Bora thought, an unfamiliar image to him. *This dead man has the crushed pallor of white flowers that have been torn up and stepped on.*

Never in the past weeks of war had he looked at the dead, those of the Reds or of his companions, without pity of flesh for flesh, blood for blood. Yet he could kill without forsaking this pity. He handled the body with slow care, and when his fingers became smeared with blood, he wiped them on his own clothes.

The dead man's hands were narrow, square-fingered. No calluses, no wedding ring. Bora looked for a weapon, and found none. A brief examination of the clothes followed – small gestures, quick judgements. The man's shoes were missing, but the socks were good socks, white and unspotted. Bora touched something in the pocket that felt like a small photograph.

He stopped, holding his breath. Suddenly, he could hear the canes' whisper and watery sound again. Down the bank, eddies around the pebbles gave voice to the invisible brook. Even as he knelt there, he realized the absolute centrality of his position. Somehow this was a hub, a point from which radiated an intensifying sense of reality. He perceived in his mind's eye, as if from a high vantage point, the curve on the mule track, the brook in the dry land, the dizzying reaches of the sierra, Aragon and Spain around it, the sense of holding firm and yet being lost, in the presence of this death. Everything revolved around this, and he did not know why. The small photograph in the dead man's pocket felt smooth, hard-edged. Bora ran his fingers along its scalloped contours and the touch reconnected him to the here and now, a quick sinking back into reality. *Tuesday, 13 July 1937. The password for the day is "España una, y grande." What will Sergeant Fuentes say? My uniform is drenched and smells of silt.* Time to go. Behind him, the canes caught the last of the pre-dawn breeze, and soon his men and the Reds would be up. Bora pulled the photograph out, glanced at it, and slipped it into his own pocket.

SIERRA DE SAN MARTÍN, LOYALIST "REPUBLICAN" CAMP AT EL PALO DE LA VIRGEN

Twenty minutes up the mountainside, Major Philip Walton hadn't slept well. He'd slept very little, in fact, and had had the same recurring dream. That's all it was, not even a nightmare. A yellow wall in Guadalajara. Cornbread yellow, shit yellow. What the hell did a yellow plaster wall mean? Walton had a throbbing headache, but at least he knew where *that* came from, so he rinsed his mouth with more brandy before leaving his sweaty bed.

It was warm outside, too, but it smelled cleaner than indoors. Walking into the early sunlight, all Walton could think of was the shit-yellow wall, and how he'd like to kick it down in his next dream. Behind him, the squat, whitewashed house that served as observation post and refuge was real enough. Men still snored inside, sprawled on its ground floor. Ahead, on the bare expanse of rocky soil, Iñaki Maetzu's scarecrow silhouette was the only one in sight.

"He isn't here yet." Maetzu anticipated the question without raising his eyes from his work. He'd taken his rifle apart and was oiling each piece. He was a raw-boned shaggy Basque, mean-looking, big-eared, tanned to a leathery brown. "I'd have called you if he'd come."

"What time is it?"

"Don't know." Maetzu turned his seamed face eastward. "Maybe six, maybe earlier. Don't you wear a watch any more?"

"I can't remember where I put it."

Maetzu snorted derisively. "You were drunk enough when you got back from visiting Remedios."

With his back to the sun, fingers hooked, Walton combed back long strands of hair from his forehead and yawned. "I wonder why Lorca isn't here yet. He should have arrived by now."

"Maybe he isn't coming. As far as I'm concerned, anyone travelling this way just draws attention to us."

Walton found himself waking up rapidly now. "Have you seen Marypaz?" he asked, walking off to the fountain. It was free-standing, like a headstone spouting water from a pipe into a cement trough. Walton had wondered from his first day in the sierra where the water came from, how it snaked its way through immense plates of granite. He put his head under the flow, thinking how its hidden voyage through the rock made this water more precious than ever before in his life.

Maetzu answered the question at last. "No, but I know she's still mad. She was crying last night, and she said she'll kill you."

Walton dipped his brawny forearms in the water. "At least she's showing some initiative."

He felt fully alert by the time he left the fountain for the zigzagging path leading from the ledge down to the valley. Below, the ravine resembled a wild crystallized landslide. From the foot of the mountain, left of where he stood, El Baluarte rose almost vertically, jutting out and dividing the ledge. Beetling and humped, the cliff's stony prow hid the Fascist lookout on the other side without obstructing the view of the valley. Eastward, a milder, scruffy ascent rose from the ledge to the chapel of San Martín.

At this hour there seemed to be no war in Spain. The air, dry and almost unbearably clear, tricked men into thinking they could see forever, into distances too great for Walton to care about. It was a long way from poverty-stricken, winter-ravaged rural Vermont. Even further from working-class Pittsburgh, its smokestacks belching on the tight bend of the river. That was another life already, or a series of lifetimes.

Walton turned back towards the camp. The camp. He'd known *camps* in the Great War. Real army camps in France and Flanders, in places with unpronounceable names and long rows of barbed wire, trenches, sandbags. Battlegrounds where men measured up, or came up short. This was a joke of a camp. No artillery, no radio. A hollow in the rocky dirt for ammunition and that run-down squat house covered in peeling whitewash. Part of the roof had caved in and been replaced by sheet iron. Out the back, a ramshackle wall had once safely penned in flocks and fodder. Now horses grazed in it and chased flies from their manes. His men couldn't agree whether to fly the red flag of the communist PSUC or the anarchist red and black over the roof, so they'd stuck both by the door.

A hundred or so yards behind the house, past a fenced almond grove, a steep climb led deep into the sierra among naked granite crags. Inferior granite, Walton thought. Back in Vermont it would end up as grout, on the waste pile. The only good thing was that the Fascists, on the other side of El Baluarte, were sitting on a similar piece of lousy rock. Where the ledge sloped up the mountain, Walton's comrades were stirring, two of them making coffee on an open fire. He recognized Brissot's black beret and Chernik's bald head. Chernik saw him and waved. "G'd mawnin', Felipe!" Despite his Russian battle name he was from the Old South, and "morning" was always "mawnin'" to him. Walton nodded in return.

Henri Brissot – "Mosko" to everyone here – spooned out coffee grains with the spare motions learned during his medical training, without looking up. In his fifties, with a grizzled bushy moustache, he wore on his beret the badge he'd earned among the Bolsheviks in 1919. Walton had more than once felt the value of the little red star. Over a glass of wine, Mosko had spoken of the self-serving value of history, in his proficient school English. "A Brissot de Warville was Robespierre's comrade and lost his head to the guillotine in 1793," he'd said. "That's the likely end of all moderates in a revolution. *I* learned my lesson."

Rafael and Valentin, little more than boys, squatted playing cards by the stone fence of the almond grove. Rafael acted surly and proletarian but wore around his neck the silver rosary his mother had given him. As for Valentin, he was laughing, his square horsey teeth showing in a row. A nervous twitch made him blink when he was angry. "*Zape!*" he cried out now, slapping the cards down while the shy Rafael laid his on the ground with reluctance.

Walton turned to Maetzu, busy peering through the clean barrel of his rifle. "Iñaki, I don't like the fact that he hasn't shown up. I'm going down to see what the hell happened to him."

"It's not like we asked him to come," Maetzu grumbled. But he buckled a belt and holster around his waist and followed Walton down the ravine.

Rafael and Valentin looked up when Walton cried out, "Keep your eyes open while we're gone!" before resuming their game by the orchard wall. On it, a hand-painted sign read in bold red letters, LONG LIVE THE PEOPLE'S ARMY AND THE INTERNATIONAL BRIGADES. DEATH TO THE NATIONALISTS. DEATH TO THE FASCISTS. *No PASARÁN!*

SIERRA DE SAN MARTÍN, THE REBEL
"NATIONALIST" ARMY OUTPOST
AT RISCAL AMARGO

On the other side of El Baluarte, the men were just now getting up. As he gained the rim of the ledge, Bora saw a couple of them amble to the left, where a skinny grove of cedars served as a latrine. Barking playfully, Alfonso's three-legged dog came to meet him. Dead ahead, Sergeant Indalecio Fuentes waited with rifle in hand.

"No weapons, his hands were not tied," Bora was soon explaining. "The man had been shot once, in the nape of the neck. I found this in his shirt pocket." He produced the snapshot.

Fuentes ran his eyes over the photo and gave it back. Stocky, bearish, wide-jawed and eternally in need of a shave, he grunted out the words like the policeman that he was. "No identification, nothing? Could you tell if he was one of ours?"

"Nothing. He wore no uniform, ours or Red."

Fuentes drove his thumbs into his weathered army belt, repeating to himself what Bora had said in his clipped German accent. "Civilians get killed too," was his concise wisdom.

A former Guardia Civil non-com who didn't believe in the goodness or even the value of man, he carried his forty years, proud peasant face and wrestler's build well. Bora averted his eyes. Despite the steep climb from the brook, he was careful to keep his breathing under control because Fuentes was always alert to anything that would give away a man's physical condition and training. "I *think* he was a civilian," Bora said, tucking his army shirt in his breeches.

Against the mountain, on the ledge where they stood talking, a stone farmhouse faced the valley due north, with the red and yellow Spanish flag hoisted high on a pole. Set against Riscal Amargo, whose name meaning "bitterly rough ascent" fit all too well, the lines of the two-storeyed *caserón* had a parched nobility. In his sketchbook, Bora had tried to capture its bareness and strength. There were six external windows on the upper level, but only one small opening and a doorway on the fortified ground floor. Square buttresses reinforced the *caserón* at the corners. *The type of stronghold used since the days of El Cid,* Bora had noted in his diary, *probably against the Moors of Albarracín. Time-blackened rafters mark the ancient ceiling. A stable occupies its eastern wing, where the men often sleep.*

Niceto and Tomé returned from the cedar grove, yawning and stretching. Next to the lean-to where supplies were stacked, another volunteer, Josep Aixala, was keeping the last watch of the night.

"I didn't even know you were gone, *teniente,*" Fuentes told Bora, grinding his jaw. "Did anyone see you?"

Bora registered the emphasis. "I don't know."

"It isn't as if the Reds hadn't blown off the head of the lieutenant before you."

"Yes, you told me. I walk by the bloodstain every time I go down to the brook. But as long as the well is dry, I plan to go for a bath every morning."

Fuentes critically eyed Bora's wet Spanish Foreign Legion uniform. Bora imagined him thinking *These Germans and their obsession with washing and scrubbing. What good does it do when the heat makes men smell and sweat like horses within an hour?* Still, Bora felt his clean-shaven chin with a small surge of pride for keeping up appearances even in a place like this.

Fuentes snorted. "It'd be better if you kept me informed, *teniente.*" As the rusty weathervane on the house's roof caught a wisp of wind and made a jarring, plaintive sound, he added, "I'm going to shoot it off one of these days."

Just then, followed by a billow of fine silt, a mounted officer rode down the steep trail winding from the heights to the army post. Fuentes nodded. "Well, *mi teniente*, you had better show the snapshot to Colonel Serrano. There he is."

Bora finished buttoning his shirt, but didn't have time to roll down his sleeves before meeting the colonel.

Jacinto Costa y Serrano glowered at Bora from the saddle, and Bora snapped to attention. "At ease," Serrano said. A tall, sad-looking man, he resembled a careworn dead Christ. Stiff, inflexible and lacking in patience, his elegant Nationalist Army uniform displayed the finicky impracticality of starched shirt, tie and leather gaiters. On principle, he refused to address foreigners in his own language. Having attended army school in Potsdam thirty years earlier, Serrano spoke a heavily accented German and expected Bora to keep to his own tongue.

"*Herr Oberst,*" Bora said, addressing the colonel.

Although this was one of his hurried routine visits to the front, Serrano seemed to be making an effort to listen. "And where did you find this corpse?" he asked, dismounting. Tomé, a slim volunteer who loved horses, came to take his gelding and lead it to the shade. Even though it was only just past six, the temperature was quickly rising.

Bora pointed out the place on a map the colonel handed him. "Here. Thirty or so yards south of the bridge, where the mule track follows the brook and a cane grove conceals it on the east bank. The man was lying on his side, and though his legs were on the road, his torso was stretched on its side over the verge."

"What difference does it make?" Serrano snapped irritably.

"I think he was dumped there from a car."

A few feet away Tomé led the gelding to the scant shade of a small tree and squatted there. Niceto, who had been reading from a book with his back against the same tree, made a face and asked, "Did you have to tie the horse right under my nose?" And because Tomé didn't reply – wide-eyed, he was busy taking in the sight of the officers speaking to each other – Niceto added, "What are you looking at?"

"Nothing."

Following Tomé's gaze, Niceto saw the lieutenant. All he could see from that distance was how the blonde fuzz on Bora's arms gave his skin a sheen when the sun struck it. Next to him in the shade, screwing up his eyes in the sun, Tomé gaped. "A dark-haired *rubio*, that's what he is," he mumbled. And then he hugged his knees, breathing deeply the horse's animal smell.

"So?" Niceto stood up and walked away from the tree.

Stiffly, Serrano removed his gloves by turning the leather cuffs inside out. "The Reds are renowned for their 'night rides', Lieutenant. You've been in Spain enough weeks to know. It's clearly a Red murder. I hope you had the good sense to leave the corpse where it was. We have no need of bodies that don't belong to us."

Bora took the snapshot out of his breast pocket. "I really don't know which side he belongs to."

"What's this?" Serrano asked. When Bora said, "It's a photo of the dead man," the colonel tucked the gloves into his belt and looked. His gaunt face drained into a pallor that made him appear grey. "Do you realize who this is?" He stared at the likeness. "Describe him to me, quickly!" he urged, unaware that he'd switched into Spanish. "Don't you understand who the man was?" he hissed when Bora did so, as if it were the German's fault for not knowing to begin with. "We must retrieve the body at once!" Serrano turned around to call the sergeant. "Fuentes! Take two men and ride quickly to where the *teniente* tells you. Bring the body back here."

Fuentes gestured for a couple of the men to join him. "With the colonel's permission, we'll chance it down the ravine. By the ridge road it'll take us three times as long."

"Colonel," Bora asked with polite inquisitiveness, "may I know who the man was?"

Serrano spoke in a hoarse, controlled tone. "If your description is accurate and this photograph truly belongs to him, it's best if you don't ask. I have every reason to believe the Reds are behind it. That is all for now."

Bora stared at the colonel. He wasn't surprised that Serrano was choosing not to give him more information, but because no one so far had seemed affected by a death during a war that seemed to butcher bystanders simply for the sake of butchering them. Then he recalled that when he'd knelt by the body, he'd felt like he had been at the centre of the world.

Serrano's agitation was in contrast to the rigidity of his shoulders. "This event is not what it appears on the surface; it transcends its immediate meaning." He took some energetic, aimless steps around. "And to think that ... well, enough. This time we must make sure, make *absolutely sure*, that the murder isn't appropriated and used for political propaganda by the Reds."

This time? Absolutely sure? Painfully aware of the screeching weathervane, Bora watched Serrano study the snapshot, turn it over and shake his head. All there was on the back, written in a vertical, minute hand, was the dedication A MI QUERIDO AMIGO PAQUITO. "Colonel, what sort of murder would the Reds commit and then use against us?"

Behind Serrano, the sierra rose naked, seamed, formidable. "You have much to learn about civil wars. They are intricate, loyalties are intertwined, allegiances are endlessly complex. Spain is a difficult country in peacetime; how can foreign volunteers expect to understand it in these trying days?" His pacing started and stopped, causing dust to gather on his shiny gaiters. "You're not Spanish, you can't begin to comprehend. Even the best of men may invite controversy. One can be praised by anarchists in Bilbao and at the same time censored by political commissars in Catalonia." Serrano placed the snapshot in the map case at his belt. "We must retrieve the body to avoid rumours that we're responsible for his death. And under no circumstances do I want anyone here to ask about the man's identity."

Meanwhile Fuentes had chosen Alfonso, the college student, and a round-headed man called Paradís. They were scrambling down the ravine, shrubs releasing clouds of dust like gold spray. Bora didn't understand how Serrano could be sure that the Nationalists hadn't killed the man. "Sir," he said at last, "the description I gave you fits many Spaniards, and the photograph is so small, it doesn't seem enough to identify anyone."

"It's more than enough, Bora."

The way Serrano pronounced his surname was entirely Spanish, neither a V nor a B sound, but something in between. Bora was getting used to it. In the Moroccan training camp he'd been given the battle name Douglas, but no one here called him that, even though it was his Scottish grandmother's surname and his own middle name. His men addressed him by rank or simply as *Alemán*. When Serrano had first asked for his real name, Bora had told him. Now he followed the colonel in silence as he walked to the rim of the ledge.

"Believe me, Lieutenant, it'd be easy for me to ignore that CNT claimed him as one of its own, but not everyone thinks the same way I do."

Bora didn't understand how the anarchist trade union related to the matter at hand. "Will we bury him here?" he asked instead, realizing it'd be useless to inquire now.

"While it's imperative not to divulge the body's identity now, later on people will want to know, so you must remember its location."

"What if I get killed?" Bora asked in an offhand tone, as if it were an inconvenience worthy of consideration. "Shouldn't we tell someone else the location?"

"You will tell *me*. If we're both killed, then it's destiny that his final resting place should remain unknown. Let's go inside."

The ground floor of the army post felt comfortable compared to the outside. A chalky odour of freshly whitewashed walls filled the vaulted space. Serrano closed the door, and soon he was lighting a thin cigar by the solitary window, which afforded a view of ledge and sky. The colonel, who had a son Bora's age being held hostage by the Reds in Madrid and a daughter pregnant by her dead officer husband living in the same city, paid too much attention to the great tragedies of his life and country: sometimes he ignored the practical things. Bora, facing a wall map of the region, wasn't paying attention to the symbols on it. Instead, he was trying to understand why the men here, Fuentes included, accepted *him*, although it was difficult to say to what extent. His eyes wandered across the map, following the web of narrow mountain trails. Fuentes would obey an officer unquestioningly, while men like Josep Aixala disliked him because he was a foreigner and this was a Spanish war. As for the others … Bora didn't know them well enough yet. He hoped that heading this mountain outpost would help him learn more about them, and Spain in general.

In front of him, a fly was diligently tracking the course of the Alfambra River. Bora admitted to himself that he was here partly because it seemed the right place for a young politicized officer to be: a great dust-lined battlefield where rebellious Fascist officers called themselves Nationalists in order to confront a republic that referred to itself as Loyalist and Red. He chased the fly from the map. It was true, Serrano's passion was not Bora's own. But politics alone would have never brought him here, nor made him willing to die in the fly-spotted reticle of mountain trails. There were other reasons, like religion and the desire to prove himself, and something else which was dark and unnamed and like blood already spilled.

Less than an hour later, Tomé came to announce that the detail was returning from the valley. Fuentes' wide face was running with sweat when he regained the ledge. The others were still struggling up the sun-baked ravine. "*Coronel,*" he said slowly, so that the officers wouldn't notice he was panting. "*Teniente.* The body isn't there any more."

"Are you sure you went to the right spot?"

"Yes, sir." As he could see that Serrano was growing angry, Fuentes turned to Bora, who hadn't visibly reacted. "We found some blood, just where the *teniente* said, by the cane grove. Looks like the body was taken away on foot, because we couldn't find any traces of wheels."

"I bet the American did it," Bora said. "The Reds use the mule track more than we do."

Serrano threw the long-spent butt of his cigar off the ledge. "It's probably the American's men who committed the murder in the first place, Lieutenant."

Bora checked the time on his watch. "Whoever did it, the body must have been removed in the past hour, and there are only so many places on the sierra where it's possible to dig a grave. Did you search around, Fuentes?"

"They were clever, *mi teniente*. They carried off the body rather than dragging it. I couldn't even figure out the direction they took until I noticed a few drops of blood. It makes sense that it was the American and his men. From where the body was, it's a short hike up to their camp by way of San Martín."

"They couldn't bury a cat around San Martín, Fuentes. It's all solid rock."

Fuentes nodded. "There are the terraces at the back of the chapel, though. There's enough dirt there."

"Well, San Martín isn't their territory any more than it is ours. If Colonel Serrano permits us, I'm all for going there now."

"And do what?" Serrano had been listening, growing increasingly angry, and now flared up at Bora in German. "Have a gunfight over the body, assuming that you find it, or find the Reds? It'd be tantamount to confessing we killed the man. The damage is done."

"Whoever he is, sir, the Reds might not have recognized him."

"No? Why would they rush to bury him, then? No. Someone in the American's camp knew him, killed him, then decided to bury him and will try to blame us for it."

Fuentes, who understood no German, stood waiting for permission to leave. Serrano dismissed him with a snap of his fingers. Turning to Bora, he added, "I'm not through briefing you. Let's go to your office."

Once in Bora's small, well-kept room, the colonel said, "I realize I instructed you not to hold the men day and night at this post. But were they all accounted for last night?"

"Fuentes and I were. Niceto kept watch from nine to twelve, Alfonso from twelve to three, and Aixala for the three subsequent hours. I can't vouch for the other two or for anyone past their watch; they often go to Castellar to spend the night. They have women there."

Serrano's lips stretched into a stern, unsympathetic grimace. "These are the disgusting realities of war. I understand you yourself were not without reproach after Bilbao was taken."

Like many fair-skinned men, Bora could not conceal the fact that he was blushing, and he knew it. The rise of blood might go unnoticed under a tan, but the darkening of his eyes – there was no hiding that. "It was the Spanish comrades who made us Germans drink and brought women in," he replied. "Otherwise I'm not exactly used to an excess of either."

Serrano seemed to lose interest in the subject. "It's really not relevant to the issue. What you must find out – and be subtle about it – is whether the men were all accounted for. After all, you *are* working for German intelligence these days. You can deny it all you want; I know an *Abwehr* operative when I see one. I'm sure you have an idea what to do next. Find out where they were, and report back to me." Serrano lit a new cigar. "Doubts begin at home. Solutions begin at home."

Bora looked away. He didn't dislike Serrano, but was uncomfortable around him in the way he grew uncomfortable in the presence of his Prussian stepfather. There were no places to hide from older men. The colonel spoke of Bilbao as if he knew what had happened in June after the Nationalists and legionnaires finally broke through and took the city from the Reds. *There wasn't much to it other than Spanish officers' gossip.* He had been thrown into action within hours of flying into Spain, following the abstinence and gruelling months of training at Dar Riffian, grim with a death-seeking recklessness that seemed silly to him even now. Ten weeks of intense fighting had followed, during which he'd crammed in a year's worth of Spanish lessons and hand-to-hand combat practice. In the face of it all, he'd done damn well in Bilbao. He'd been the one to whom the first Reds had surrendered. Spanish officers had congratulated him, and a pudgy Italian colonel had gone as far as kissing him on both cheeks on the steps of the church of St Nicholas.

He remembered little of the drinking after the victory. A private house somewhere, with mud-smeared fine rugs and an endless supply of heady southern wines. The night had been rainy outside and the men around the table high on bragging and laughter. He had said – or thought – something about Greek heroes, and how the self-possessed man should act in war. Someone else spoke German, too, a Condor Legion pilot with a broken arm and a store of barracks jokes. What else? Of the women, Bora recalled that they were clean and young, officers' women: he'd made love to the one who sang well and then to the other, who'd had slim ankles and who had been so eager that they'd ended up falling off the bed together. He remembered vaguely a third one called Inés. She must be the one with whom he'd spent the rest of the night naked and giggling, making love at the foot of the bed. In the morning, he had been very ashamed.

Within hours, orders had come for the Germans to join other posts. Bora had spent two weeks in the hellhole around Santander, ending up in southern Aragon after a pause at the German consulate in Saragossa where a patronizing *Abwehr* officer had spoken to him of intelligence matters for an hour and then handed him sealed orders. Now he was being forced to serve here, where mountains ran in broken chains like high shelves rimming the south of the Aragon region, steep and bare around the Teruel plain. Teruel was Serrano's headquarters whenever he wasn't touring the advanced Nationalist army posts.

Bora watched the colonel's austere face suck in the strong tobacco of the cigar. His attention was drawn to the crickets in the house. Their feeble voices rose from crannies and narrow crevices where the whitewashed plain walls met the floor.

EL PALO DE LA VIRGEN

Standing up from a crouching position, Brissot cursed. His English was better than his Spanish, so he addressed Walton in English while rinsing his hands in front of the body. "What do you expect me to do? There's nothing I can *do*! Calm yourself, Felipe. At least we found him. Anger isn't going to make him any less dead. You want to know what they did to him. What they did to him was shoot him once in the head, six or seven hours ago." He nodded for Walton to pour more water into a dented metal basin. "The rigidity hasn't spread to his lower body yet. He's starting to show some hypostatic stains on his left side, which means he's been lying on that side since he died."

Water splashed about as Walton waved the pitcher in his hand. "They fooled with the body, though!"

Brissot shrugged. He began to dry his hands by turning his wrists vigorously. "It depends on what you mean by 'fooling'. They stole his shoes and searched him. From the *medical* standpoint, there's no evidence of anything else. And emotion is a bourgeois response from you as far as I'm concerned." He squirted alcohol from a bottle on to his palms and rubbed them together.

Maetzu stood behind Walton in the sweltering kitchen, as did the others. Rafael embarrassed himself by quickly giving the sign of the cross.

Walton spat on the floor. The gathering of saliva felt slick in his mouth, bitter with the sourness of alcohol in his system. His eyes and head ached. He could not bear to look at the body, so he faced Brissot instead. "I don't see how you can fucking say we're not supposed to be emotional about this. He was unarmed and alone and the Fascists killed and dumped him like a dog by the wayside. He was my friend, and I fucking *feel* like caring that he was dumped by the wayside!"

"Well, isn't that just like the Fascists? Ask Maetzu. Ask Bernat. They know first-hand."

"Go fuck yourself."

Brissot clammed up. Walton fell into the doctor's silence and angrily forced himself out of it. "Cover him up!" Walton ordered Bernat. "Flies are getting into his fucking mouth!"

As Walton walked outside, Maetzu followed close behind. The morning brightness blinded them. Maetzu shielded his eyes. "Was he supposed to have anything on him?" he asked. Beaded with sweat, reddish stubble glistened on his big-boned, triangular face. It was a murderous face; Walton never looked at it without feeling an inward revulsion, despite his admiration for the man. "Do you figure they *took* anything from him, Felipe?"

Walton spat out the acid taste in his mouth, his tongue feeling like a dead slug. "How should I know? He might not have been carrying identification papers, though he'd have been a fool not to do so. I doubt he had nothing in his pockets. Shit. He might have carried letters, other things."

"Money?"

"Maybe. I don't know." Walton led Maetzu to the higher ground, between spiny bushes that caught their arms and sleeves and were gradually being broken off to nothing. He snapped a branch and threw it away. A green lizard that had been squatting in the sun slithered under a rock like a fast-moving comma.

"We've got to bury him, you know."

"What?"

"Bury him, Felipe. We've got to bury him somewhere. There are a couple of places up the sierra, unless you want to use the cemetery at Castellar."

"No." What did Maetzu know? Walton felt like he had more than six months earlier, on the day he'd first met Maetzu and the others near Madrid: he was trying to hold on to his anger and losing it. That day he'd seen himself mentally and physically for what he was, a man with political grudges that embittered him, but not enough to keep him angry. Long, lank, shaggy and black-haired enough to pass for a Spaniard except for his blue eyes, speaking good Spanish for an American. And everyone thought him angry. He kept stripping the spiny bushes as he climbed.

"Where are we going, Felipe?"

"Up."

They left the path that wormed up by twists and turns to the village of Castellar, sitting in a rocky bowl inside the sierra. As much a roaming ground to them as to the Fascists, had they gone straight through the village, past the mass of El Baluarte parting the mountain ledge, they'd have come dangerously close to the enemy post. The chapel of San Martín, perched as it seemed at the edge of the world, was already below them to the south-east. Ahead sat only the gun emplacement, a Lewis .303 machine gun and a mortar, manned day and night by two volunteers from Castellar.

Maetzu stopped. "Are you going to tell me what you've got in mind, or not?"

Walton scrambled the short distance to the gun emplacement. He said a few words to the men who squatted there, puffing on hand-rolled cigarettes. Soon one of them stood up to slip a shell into the metal cylinder.

"This," Walton told Maetzu.

The shell left the mortar with a dull, hollow pop. It rose straight upwards in the white sky and arched westwards, over El Baluarte.

RISCAL AMARGO

It fell so suddenly at the rim of the ledge in front of the *caserón* that Fuentes barely had the time to dive behind a low wall before the shell exploded. The blast lifted a column of debris just under the rim, shattered shrubs flying up with it; rocks, dirt and dust shot skyward, the wind catching them and blowing them back against the ledge. Bora had been standing on the threshold talking to Colonel Serrano and the blast's concussion slammed the door shut against him, knocking him to the floor. The window of his room, closed against the heat of the day, burst and rained down glass. Men scurried up the mountainside, seeking the shelter of terracing walls.

The second shell struck the middle of the ledge, and the impact against solid rock magnified the explosion. A storm of shattering metal and bright granite splinters jetted in all directions, smashing the upper-floor windows, embedding shrapnel in the ashlar and battering and studding the door. Rocks and steel pelted the roof with the hard sound of hail; tiles broke and came falling down. The gutter, unhooked, loosened itself from the eaves and slid down, bouncing off the ground. Echoes rolled back from the sierra; when Serrano cried out something, Bora couldn't understand what he said. He assumed it was an order. Back on his feet, Bora ran outside to check the damage.

Dust was settling here and there, still whirling where an airstream from the valley buoyed it in sparkling yellow spirals. A gouged star-shaped gash marked the place where the second shell had hit; jagged pieces of granite rent from the mountain littered the ground around it. Thick metal slivers lay everywhere. On the ledge's rim, the first shell had demolished the stone step where the path leading down began. It seemed as though a gigantic mouth had taken a bite out of it. The lonely tree had lost one of its main branches, and there was no sign of the colonel's well-harnessed gelding.

"Fuentes! Aixala!" Bora called out as the men emerged from their temporary shelter. The others, who'd crawled behind terracing walls, came down shaking dust and dirt off their clothes. Only now did the words Serrano had yelled at him in the house register with him. "You can see the Reds are already acting as though we were responsible for the killing."

The gelding had trotted off to safety a short distance up the mountain. Tomé led it back, caressing its neck, and then went to check on Bora's grey in the stable. Serrano insisted on examining the damage, with Bora in tow. "Poor aim," he said disparagingly. "Far too long."

Bora scanned El Baluarte through his field glasses. "All they need is a man up there to tell them how to adjust their aim. I expect it was meant as a warning."

Serrano turned sharply. "That's obvious. Any more brilliant observations?"

After years of family life and school training, Bora had learned to conceal his frustration well, and simply said no.

With a flip of his glove, Serrano called for Tomé. "I am off. Lieutenant, ride with me only as far as the crossroads." He placed his foot in the cradle of Tomé's hands to get in the saddle.

Already mounted, Bora waited until the colonel started up the trail before telling Fuentes, "I'll be back in forty-five minutes, *sargento*."

"*Y si el americano nos bombardea además?*"

"If he does, there's not much we can do about shells, is there?"

Once Bora and Serrano reached higher land, dwarf trees crowded the trail as it entered a narrow passage in the mountains. Ahead, the trail curved away from Castellar, the Red camp and the chapel of San Martín. Shaggy cedar-like trees let out an aromatic scent as the officers rode between them.

"We don't need an incident here now," Serrano said between his teeth, sitting up straight in the saddle as if impaled. "You will strike only if and when you're ordered to do so." Once they entered the pass, the blue sky in the cleft of the rock felt refreshing after the chalky whiteness of the ledge below. "Did you tell me everything about the body in your report, Lieutenant?"

Bora wondered how the colonel had seen through him, but didn't consider not telling him the truth. "Well, his trousers were undone."

Serrano's reins made a slapping noise on the saddle. "He'd probably stopped to relieve himself. What's so unusual about that?"

"Maybe."

"Of course! They might have told him to get out of the car – *if* they came in a car – or just told him he could have a minute to do what he needed. It's a merciful way of killing someone."

Bora led the horse without pulling on its reins, instead tightening his knees every now and again. "What if they took him from his home without giving him time to get dressed? He was in his stockinged feet, too."

"Good shoes are at a premium, even if taken from a dead body."

"Yes, but ... This *man*, Colonel, do we know where he lived?"

In his dark green uniform Serrano cut an old-fashioned, self-possessed figure. He paused before responding. "It appears he'd been in hiding for the past several months. I hadn't kept up with his career or movements ever since he made his political choice."

"Or the choice was made *for* him."

Serrano looked over his shoulder with a frown. "How old are you?" he asked.

"Twenty-three."

"Your judgement is flawed."

"Because I advance hypotheses?"

"Because you advance flawed hypotheses."

"I can't be sure they are flawed until I prove or disprove them, Colonel."

"University-educated officers make bad subalterns, and worse superiors. Your family should have never allowed you to seek higher schooling. A soldier ought to receive no more academic attention than is required to be civilized in society. You'll need very different skills from those you received at university. I hope the Legion broke you in at Dar Riffian and Tétouan, beyond teaching you how to ride in the desert and shout *Viva la muerte.*"

Bora knew better than to argue. His right shoulder was sore from the fall, and he balanced his weight on the saddle so that Serrano would not notice. He waited to speak until they left the pass and the trail started to plunge towards the crossroads below, three miles west of the mule track. "Was the dead man from Aragon, Colonel?"

"No, he was Andalusian, from a long line of small landowners and *conversos* ... Jews converted to Christianity."

"It's curious that a man in hiding should land in Aragon, the most divided of provinces."

"No more curious than you finding yourself here when you're not even Spanish."

Bora saw from the colonel's expression that he meant to embarrass him; still, he held his tongue.

"His cousins live in Teruel, Lieutenant. Retrieving the body will be risky, but I don't want you to take more than two men along."

"I'll start by having informants ask around the countryside. And while a search would be best done at night, we'll need daylight to make sure we have the right body."

"Act quickly; the season is hot. Although the saying goes 'The dead and departed have no friends,' one such as he will be missed. So, you see, I want his body. Besides, no body – no crime."

"Sir, you speak as if we're responsible for this death after all!"

Serrano's voice came in impeccable Castilian. "Just find me the body, Lieutenant."

EL PALO DE LA VIRGEN

Maria Paz – Marypaz, he called her – came back to camp just before noon, when Walton had begun to hope she'd stay in Castellar for the day, moping.

But there she was, stirring dust from the bushes along the mountain trail, behind the drover and the donkey heavily laden with supplies. She was talking to the young man in a loud forced tone and paid no attention when Walton waved, which was a confirmation that she *knew*.

How she always knew, he couldn't figure out. Sitting by the fountain, Walton had been patching up his map of Aragon with the last of the paper tape he'd bought in Barcelona. Now he watched her help unload the donkey and send the drover on his way, ignoring *him*. Carefully he folded the map and put it back in his pocket. He reached for the tin cup hanging from a nail by the water pipe, filled it and began drinking. *Three gulps is all she'll let me take before she comes charging,* he thought. He waited.

Standing two yards away, trying to control the trembling in her voice, Marypaz said, "You went to see her yesterday. You're lying if you tell me that you didn't."

Walton rounded his lips to take another sip of water. Now that she was facing him, he didn't feel like arguing at all. "Why don't you wear a skirt? I don't like you in dungarees."

Marypaz tossed back her head, arching her plump throat. "Why, does *she* wear a skirt? I thought she didn't even bother with clothes if there were men around."

Despite her attempts at control, the tears came, and a sudden stupid need to laugh rose in Walton. He reached out his arm and grabbed her round the waist, making her lose her balance and fall into his lap. "Why, you're jealous!"

"I'm not jealous, I'm angry at you." She struggled in his grip, making him spill water from the tin. His left hand felt the soft bulges of her breasts under the blouse. "*Her* tits aren't anywhere near as big as these, Marypaz. What are you jealous of?"

"See? You're still sleeping with her! I knew it!" He let go and she scrambled to her feet. "*Eres un putero, Felipe!*" she wept, furiously pinning her sleek coil of dark hair into a bun.

A whore-chaser? Walton didn't move. *I guess that's what Remedios is,* he thought. *A whore, and sure as hell I'll chase her.* He watched Marypaz march off, admiring her short roundness. *Hey,* he ought to say to her, *there's a dead man inside. If you go inside, you'll find a body on the floor.* But there was a measure of spite in letting her walk in unawares. "Look on the bright side," he called to her. "At least you walked away from the fish stalls before you turned twenty, unlike your sisters."

She looked back. "It was Mosko who got me out of Cartagena. If it was up to you, I'd still be slaving in the marketplace. Remember? You had a girl from the big city in those days."

"So? You had Mosko." Walton filled the tin again. "Come now, we've been together six months, haven't we? I'd never spend six months with someone I don't like."

"Ha! Is that the way they do it in America?"

Walton's hand tightened around the tin. "Don't annoy me, Marypaz."

"I'm going to kill you, Felipe."

"Why don't you try to kill *her*?"

She stomped back over to him. "No, you. I'm going to kill *you*, because it's you who's going to her."

"*Pobrecita!*" The foolish need to laugh came back to him, and he laughed. "You're not skinny and mean enough to be that angry." She picked up a rock and threw it at him. It hit Walton on the shin and suddenly he was no longer amused. He tossed the tin at her feet. "Goddamn, Marypaz, you're getting on my nerves. I got divorced once already because my skinny bitch of a wife kept giving me grief. What in God's name do you want from me? You've had your fun. Mosko wasn't the only one you were having fun with when I met you. But that's OK, because that's the way it is in the People's Army. We all have a right to have fun, even me."

"I hate you. I hope a bomb falls on your head."

Walton turned away from her. Maetzu and Chernik were back from a scouting trip to climb El Baluarte and check on the effects of the mortar attack. "Get lost, Marypaz," he said flatly, before turning to the men.

"So, how did it go?"

Chernik answered, in his makeshift Spanish, "We hit the ledge, but you told us to do no more than scare them off. Iñaki here wanted to keep at it." Wiping sweat off his neck with a frayed handkerchief, he glanced over at Maetzu. "Didn't you?"

"I don't believe in warning Fascists."

Next to the Basque, Chernik seemed diminutive. Sparrow-necked and hairy all over except his head, Walton didn't know much about him. Nor did anyone else. He was always amiable, but his drawling speech and amiability were an armour over his true self. "Folks in Castellar report there's a German leading the Fascists at Riscal Amargo," he added.

Walton found himself grinning again, and began to worry that it might be his nervous reaction from the days of the Great War, masking very different feelings. Nothing to do with pleasure. "A *whole* German," he said. "You don't say. Should I worry?"

"He's new, and an officer." Maetzu lowered his voice, and spoke through his teeth. "It'd take me fifteen minutes to slip over and kill him."

Walton wished he could stop smiling, but he had no control over the grimace which had frozen on his face. He cut through the air with a broad wave of his hand. "You killed the last sonofabitch army lieutenant at Riscal and now we've got a German in his place. Too many Fascists in Teruel to risk them coming after our asses right now. Let it go, Iñaki. We have our own dead to bury. Mosko says there's a good place at Muralla del Rojo. Go as soon as it gets dark. By that time the grave will have been dug."

Maetzu said nothing, but Chernik nodded. He greeted Brissot, who had joined them, and then, as his eyes wandered to the place where Marypaz had stalked off to, added, "Well, if that don't beat it all. What's wrong with her, Felipe?"

"I don't know, she keeps giving me grief."

"Seems to me she's tearing your clothes apart."

Walton wheeled around in the dust. He'd washed his shorts this morning and put them out to dry on a saddle-shaped granite outcrop by the fountain. Marypaz was furiously ripping them to white shreds. Chernik laughed, and Maetzu walked away from the scene with a face of gloomy disgust. Walton felt Brissot's grip on his arm, stopping him from flying at Marypaz. "*What?*" he shouted.

"The trouble with you Americans is that you have no sense of history." Brissot scowled. "Every event, every crime has historical implications. Forget about Marypaz, and think about what's important. We're not dealing with a simple murder, Felipe. If you just bury the body or knock the Fascists over with mortar fire, you're not looking at his death in terms of propaganda. Lorca is dead. He was killed by the Fascists. A hundred years from now, all this shitty fighting on mountainsides won't mean a tinker's damn to anyone, but this one death will. If we use it well, his murder will show his enemies have no sense or understanding of history." Pulling on his tobacco-stained moustache, Brissot still scowled, but there was earnest concern in his voice. "I say we try to find out as much as possible about how he died."

Walton wearily passed both hands over his cheeks, feeling the calluses on his fingertips and palms. It was like Guadalajara. The thought sickened him. Entrapment. Maybe that's what the dream of the yellow wall meant. He felt trapped. Yet his anger was ebbing quickly, leaving him numb and forgetting about Marypaz, as Brissot had advised, but without any conscious effort on his part. Even the news of this recent death did nothing but weary him.

Facing Walton, Brissot spoke like a Soviet commissar, which was probably the closest thing to his political stance. "You forget that rumours of his death have been circulated before, Mosko. Besides, that's not my job."

"Well, *you* were the angry one. What else do you have to do? We can't move, same as the Fascists and their whole goddamned rebel army can't move. We sit on two sides of a rock close enough to spit and take potshots at each other, waiting for the moment when the civil war blows Aragon to bits. I say we try to find out. It's only then that the burial place will have any meaning."

"I have to think about it."

"Well, *think about it.*"

Out of habit, Walton glanced at his left wrist, where his watch had been until the day before. "You haven't seen my watch, have you?" he asked, walking away from Brissot.

RISCAL AMARGO

The afternoon brought stunning heat with it. Bora walked to the well, dug between the stable and the steep face of the mountain. Leaning over the ring of cemented stones, he looked down the shaft, where the sun high overhead showed a circle of silty dirt at the bottom. After the well had dried up two days earlier, Fuentes had held a rope for Bora to go down the musty hole. His footprints still formed a pattern in the silt, and the shaft already didn't smell damp any more. Behind the army post there was still a trickle of water oozing from the heights, enough to drink and shave, but the dry well felt like a rejection. Bora watched dusty loam crumble from the ring of the well as he leaned on it. Dust became a sparkling nothing as it floated down the shaft.

Despite his back-breaking months spent with the Tercio de la Legion near Tétouan, the heat here bothered him more than it had in North Africa. The welts under his arms ached. Cloth chafed the skin of his groin raw. His only relief was going down to the brook to swim in a waterhole that was growing muddy as it evaporated. At least it wouldn't dry up altogether, according to Tomé.

Tomé was an unknown quantity, slippery, shifting, unfathomable; and although the man meant nothing to him, it irked Bora that he couldn't get the measure of him. He'd been coming along to the brook for security, squatting with a rifle across his thighs in the shade of a fat evergreen bush. A slight, supple man with pointed ears and attentive eyes, he had a soft way of moving, like a deceitful cat … but many Spaniards were like that, in Bora's opinion. Tomé never said much. He normally chewed on a blade of grass, eyes on the shimmer of the water. Now, he unhesitatingly followed Bora down the hill for the second time that day.

At one point on the steep descent, they passed a flat rock marked by a ragged wide stain. There, Lieutenant Jover had been shot in the head a month earlier. The men said that insects had come for days to suck bits of brain from the drying blood. Bora stopped, staring at the dark outline on the rock. "Tomé," he said, "go back. Tell Sergeant Fuentes we're going down to the bottom."

"As the lieutenant wishes." Tomé turned around and started up the ravine again.

Fifteen minutes later, they reached the foot of the sierra together. Where the stones gave way to reddish earth, the heat rising from the parched sod took their breath. Shadows were negligible under the scant bushes. The brook, in its wide shingle bed, trembled like a mirage, canes and rushes forming a *cañada* that fanned fine wattled roots into the sluggish water. Where the watercourse twisted and grew deeper, Tomé sat on the bank to keep an eye on the sierra, but soon he was watching Bora slip into the hole and pour water over his head. Bora took it to be a sentinel's precaution, and did not resent the other man's attention. When he dipped his hands into the brook, tremulous shields and crescents of glitter broke the copper sheen of the water surface. He said, "Did you hear any noise last night, Tomé?"

"What kind of noise?"

"A motor car, or a shot."

"No. I never wake up at night."

"Well, you're lucky you can sleep, in this heat."

"I like the heat." Slouched against a sturdy bush, Tomé twirled a grass stalk between his lips. His dark, monkey-like hands gripped the rifle, and Bora saw how deceptive his quiescence really was. The inertia of things, he thought. Matter *is* potentiality.

"Why don't you ask Josep Aixala?" Tomé continued. "He's been out half the night. He has a girl in Castellar."

Bora was careful not to show any overt interest. He dived into the deep centre of the hole and then emerged head first. "He does, does he?"

"Fuentes does too."

"I thought Fuentes was married."

Tomé sneered. "Even Alfonso has got himself somebody. A widow."

"And you?"

"I don't. Women are a nuisance."

Bora laughed. The pain in his shoulder was worsening, but the water felt good. He plunged in again, tasting the cool siltiness. So, Aixala had been out part of the night. He knew already that Paradís, the wall-eyed sailor, might have been gone between twelve and three. The actor from

Cartagena, Niceto, would have had time to be away from his post for at least three hours, from three to six. Bora touched the bottom of the waterhole with his fingers before straightening up suddenly, emerging into the incandescent light of day. Everything seemed red and veiled in the glare. The cane grove hid the nearby bridge and the curving mule track from sight, but he glanced that way automatically. In his mind, it was from now on a place of death, altered and redefined by the presence of the dead man whose name he still did not know.

Cicadas chirred from every shrub and withering head of grass as Bora climbed onto the bank. He sat down where the pebbles touched the water's edge, because those farther away burned like coals. "Is Aixala serious about this girl?" He spoke idly, his feet still in the water.

Tomé watched him, stalk limp in his mouth. "Possibly."

"He must be, if he sneaks out to see her at night." Bora began gathering the pieces of his uniform one by one. He was in no hurry to leave. This line of inquiry was important, and gave him a reason to take his time. When he started dressing, the drenched linen stuck to him like a second skin, and he derived a raw, basic pleasure from forcing the stiff dry cloth of the uniform over that moisture.

Tomé swallowed hard. "Aixala didn't go to see his girl last night."

"How do you know?"

"He told me."

Turned away from Tomé, Bora buttoned his army shorts. Reaching for his pistol belt awoke a sequence of small throbs of pain from his shoulder muscle, like electrical impulses. The pain, too, was oddly pleasurable. He secured the belt around his hips. "There's something we must do before we go back."

Tomé leaned forward eagerly, without rising from his crouch. "I'll do anything you want, *mi teniente*," he said, not meeting Bora's eyes.

"It's not what I want, it's what needs to be done."

"Anything you want."

Bora found the alacrity annoying. "Well, that's good, because we're climbing the sierra by way of San Martín, to see if the Reds have dug a grave yet."

EL PALO DE LA VIRGEN

"It's more practical to bury him this way. Coffins require time." Brissot handed the mattress cover to Rafael, who was skulking in a corner of the kitchen. Rafael hadn't yet turned nineteen, and everyone knew he hadn't yet seen a dead man close-up. Chernik volunteered him for the job of sewing the body inside the cover, and now he was hesitating, needle and thread in his hands, stiff-jawed. He didn't move when Brissot held the cloth out to him.

"This is from my own pallet," Brissot grumbled, "so I'm being generous about this, considering I can't abide ceremonies. Take it. Come on, take it. Get started. After you've been handling a dead body for a while you get used to it."

Walton had so far been listening without any desire to intervene. Now he wiped his mouth after drinking from his bottle, took the needle and thread from Rafael's hands and told him, "Here, have a swig and get started. I want to see it when you're done."

"Aren't you going to stay?"

Walton turned to Brissot, who had asked the question and was now filling his pipe with tobacco, as he always did when he was running low on cigarettes.

Bernat looked in through the open window. "Are we done yet?" A freckled anarchist with a skin condition that made his ears and neck flake and shed continuously, he tried not to scratch himself, but it was second nature to him. As everyone ignored the question, he leaned over the sill to make conversation. "Strapping son of a bitch, wasn't he."

Brissot shrugged. "He'd have grown stout, had he lived."

"I think he looks like Tyrone Power," Chernik said. "When are we taking him up, Mosko?"

"Ask Felipe."

"When I say so," Walton said, walking out of the kitchen and scattering across the floor the almonds that had been set to dry along the wall. "I'm going to see Marypaz."

This was a lie. He longed to be alone. To get out, walk out, listen to no one. Marypaz spent her time away from the camp in the village of Castellar, but Walton had no idea whether she'd gone there after their row, and he didn't particularly care. Ever since that morning, the thought of death had been troubling him as he'd hoped it never would again. His thoughts were packed with guilt and sickness and the need to get away from death, yet he felt compelled to go sniffing for it, and find it. It might have something to do with Guadalajara. Damn and fuck Guadalajara: it was a stupid name for a stupid place and still he couldn't get it out of his system. No matter what he did, he ended up thinking of it. Even in his dreams, though he didn't remember a yellow wall in Guadalajara.

Walton went to the higher ground behind the house, whose north wall was peeling like Bernat's skin and where the pen smelled of horses. There, the grove of gnarled almond trees huddled, sheltered from the wind by a ruined fence of stacked stones. Entering the copse, Walton awoke a storm of green flies as he stepped over human dung. Shit and refuse were everywhere, as they had been during the Great War. There had been garlands of shit all around the embattled positions near Soissons, but here the soil was as hard as clay, grass growing on it only to wilt again in the July sun. He rested his shoulders against the fissured bark of an almond tree. Grasshoppers jumped around, then settled down again.

Maybe he shouldn't have gone to see *her*, as Marypaz had said. Things had grown confused after he'd seen Remedios, up there. She muddled him; the little construction of reasons for being here that underpinned his existence grew weak each time, but he'd gone twice in the last week. He'd go again, whatever Marypaz said. There were doors behind him, which he had to keep carefully shut. One was called Soissons. Another, Pittsburgh. Another, Guadalajara.

Walton thought of Lorca's body on the floor, with Rafael afraid to touch him. All the beauty, the wit, the kindness and love of words that had belonged to the poet lay dead, blood settled in his flesh to form Brissot's hypostatic stains. The recollection made him nauseous. How could he ever have thought he'd been done with death nineteen years ago? The old soul-sickness came back. Those closed doors, opened again. A wide circle, passing twice through the same point in the curve. How had he got here? Through choice, the need for money, the desire to leave things and people behind to find other, stranger things and people. Doors opening onto doors. Lorca, who had been his friend, had died. *He* was killing again, in this country with dry walls and gnarled trees and strange people. Death followed him, or he was following Death.

With its back to the valley, San Martín de la Sierra was no more than a box of rubble cemented together. It sat on a spur of rock reachable from both camps, but was so remote and irrelevant that neither side claimed it as its own.

Bora knew the chapel. Through its rickety grate, you could see a low altar under the faded fresco of a doll-like Roman soldier on horseback. The soldier saint held a stubby sword, and the square in his left hand must represent the cape he cut in two for the divine beggar. Dry flowers had been tossed in through the gate by occasional pilgrims, and small pebbles too.

When Bora and Tomé reached the rocky spur, there was no one in sight around the chapel. Tomé covered him while Bora ran across the open space to the terraced land ahead. As he vaulted over the first terrace, delicate spirals of loam flew up around him; a thin earth-coloured snake uncoiled and disappeared into a hole no wider than a thumb. Bora scrambled up the three terraces above, looking around.

"Did you find the grave?" Tomé asked Bora when he dropped back down at his side.

"No. Either they haven't dug it out yet, or they chose another spot. Anyway, they can't go too deep, the dirt is as hard as rock."

"If you want I'll go and check the cemetery at Castellar, *mi teniente.*"

They crouched close to each other, and it seemed to Bora that Tomé's lips were trembling. "Not now." He moved away from him. "Later. When you go, get one of the usual informants to come see me after dark."

"If the Reds dug a grave in the cemetery, they'll have someone guarding it."

"We'll take care of it when the time comes."

They didn't speak on their way back to Riscal Amargo, taking a perilous shortcut through grey outcrops studded with measly shrubs. In front of the army post, Alfonso's dog was the only thing moving about in the swelter of the hour. Crouching as he scanned the horizon through field glasses, Josep Aixala heard Bora approaching and got to his feet.

After being questioned by Bora, his glance grew morose. A few steps away from the officer, Aixala looked tall, although Bora stood nearly a head above everyone at Riscal. Aixala's broad torso, attached to overlong thin legs, fit loosely into the washed-out stirrup breeches of his green Legion uniform. The rows of buttons studding the breeches gave his calves the strange outline of an overgrown insect. According to Fuentes, he'd travelled on foot from San Feliu months earlier; he hadn't yet found his place in the unit nor made up his mind about Bora, who had only been here two weeks. "People like Aixala don't make up their minds quickly," Fuentes had said. "It troubles them to have to think things over, but once they do, ideas stick. Whatever he decides about you, it's how it's going to be."

Bora knew Aixala was taking his time deciding even now. "Well?" he prodded him.

Aixala stared at his feet. "I didn't know I had to report to an officer about where I spend the night. I wasn't on guard duty until three o'clock."

"And you didn't hear a gunshot, a cry, or the noise of an engine?"

"No." Aixala grimaced in the full sun, still avoiding Bora's eyes. "But I don't pay attention to gunshots much nowadays."

"Good enough. Depending on the informant's account, I might want you and Fuentes to be ready for action from midnight onwards."

Brissot's beret-clad head appeared over the wall of the almond grove, followed by his folded arms. "What's your decision?"

Walton had nearly succeeded in letting go and falling asleep. Brissot's arrival had worked him up to a terrific anger, short-lived and useless like so many of his emotions these days. "I haven't taken one." He didn't warn Brissot about the dung in the orchard, preferring to hear him curse as he stepped into it.

"If you don't, I will." Clad as always in dark coveralls, Brissot wiped the sole of his boot against the exposed root of the tree under which Walton sat. "Castellar is a good place to inquire about last night. There are mule drovers, there are shepherds. They might have seen and heard things. What's with you, anyway?"

"Nothing."

"Nothing? You drink too much, you pick fights with Marypaz, and there's no talking straight to you any more. You've changed since the days outside Madrid."

"Maybe I'm getting too old."

"At forty-five?"

"At forty-five, why not? White lung disease got my father at thirty-seven. Forty-five feels fucking old to me. Or maybe I don't know what I'm doing here. How's that?" Walton stood up to leave the orchard. "Chew on that one from an ideological standpoint."

"Well, the body is ready for burial," Brissot called after him. "You have to say something to the men about the importance of Lorca's death."

Lorca's death. You know nothing about him, Walton wanted to protest, but didn't. *You never even spoke to him. You have no idea of what his friendship meant to me, what his writings did for me when no one else cared to feed Philip Walton's soul, whatever his soul is, whatever the word soul means to one born and raised in Eden, Vermont, and who like Adam was chased from it to earn his bread.* "Let's go," he said.

On the ledge, the long afternoon was ending in a glow that made everything look weary; the valley sank, pale with haze. The body lay on the ground at the men's feet, where its cloth-bound shape made Walton think of a monstrous white grub.

"Stop scratching," an irritable Mosko scolded Bernat. "With chronic prurigo, scratching isn't going to help. Get a hold of yourself or take a bath."

"Right!" Bernat snapped back. "You want me to go down to the brook and get my head blown off by the Fascists. Isn't that just what a Third International apparatchik would say: get a hold of yourself or else?"

Brissot laughed a spiteful laugh, wiping his glasses with a grimy handkerchief. "No. It's what a physician would say to keep a Trotskyist from sclerodermic degeneration of the skin."

"Bernat, Mosko," Walton said, "I want you to cover Chernik and Maetzu as they carry the body for burial."

Brissot put his glasses back on. "Does one of us have to stay by the grave overnight?"

"No. If anyone's spying, I don't want them to think there's anybody important in the grave. Whether the Fascist who killed him knew who he was or not, let's just keep it simple." Walton hunched forward, feeling awkward. "And since we're here, I thought we ought to say a word or two over him before we put him away." He glanced at Valentin, who stood among the others looking sly. "It's not a prayer," he premised. Out of his pocket, Walton took a small book with a worn paper cover and opened it. "These are Lorca's own words …"

13 July. Evening.

It's been a long day. Not much in terms of information, but I wasn't expecting answers so soon. I'm curious about this entire thing, though I can never tell if my curiosity is justified. I often overanalyse things, which God knows serves none of my aims here. As for the colonel, I trust he'll come to appreciate my training with the Spanish Foreign Legion if we ever get a chance to engage in battle. Not that I hope it'll happen any time soon: this place is dead. With all the talk about how Lieutenant Jover 'got himself shot', the only action I've seen in two weeks amounts to the miserable mortar attack today.

Fuentes and I were talking – again – about the American in the Red camp. He speaks about him as if I should care, or else he wants to point out it's no business of any foreigner to be here. But unlike me, whoever he is, the American is a mercenary. Call him Red, Loyalist, Republican, member of the International Brigades: it all comes down to a thousand dollars' premium if he shoots down an enemy plane. The Legion is a regular army in all respects, and Fuentes ought to know better. But at least, out of everyone here, Fuentes appreciates my drilling the men every day, insisting on a password, sending out details for firewood, and so on. I know the men don't.

Second trip to the brook, with that odd Tomé fellow in tow. Halfway down I sent him back with an excuse because I wanted to stop where Jover was killed and the bloodstain still marks the place.

I'd promised myself that I'd do it. It wasn't nearly as strange as I'd expected. I scraped a bit of the dry crust with my nail, just a thin dark brown flake – blood? brains? – and

licked it off my fingertip. It had no flavour. Only a mild salti-
ness from the rock and the sweat on my hand. I'd just been
reading in Aristotle that pleasure perfects the work. Was I
expecting pleasure out of tasting Jover's blood? No. But I
thought there was goodness in the act, somehow. There was
value to my sitting there tasting a companion's blood, an
archaic holiness to the act itself, like a communion. More
than yesterday, I'm a part of something now.

Bora closed the cloth-bound diary. Writing in minute Gothic
cursive spared paper and gave him a measure of privacy, even
though he didn't expect Colonel Serrano to go through his
papers. He placed the diary under a pile of maps in his room
and went downstairs. On the ledge, Paradís and Alfonso were
re-stacking the terracing wall collapsed by the mortar blast.
High above, lost in the muted whiteness of the sky, a small
airplane made a long, slow banking curve. Bora looked at it
until it veered off to the south.

"How long has the plane been flying around?" he asked
the men.

Alfonso shrugged. "I didn't even hear it." Paradís looked
up, his moon-face flushed with the labour of moving stones.
"What plane?"

Bora made a mental note to tell Serrano about it as he
walked to the ledge's rim, where the evening breeze brought
relief to the sierra. From there, he saw how the front of
the post had been pockmarked by the mortar attack. On
the upper floor, like blind eyes, five of the six windows had
broken panes.

"Do you mind if I join you?" From a polite distance, Niceto
addressed him in his stage-trained voice.

Bora couldn't think of a reason to say no. For the next
ten minutes or so he paid little attention to Niceto's chatter

about playwrights and the stage. The words floated to him, but he was distracted, thinking in German about other things. Only when he perceived a change in pitch, a resentful edge in Niceto's voice, did Bora begin to listen.

"He died in Granada last year; still, he was a good example of what I was telling you, *mi teniente.* I met him in '35 at an audition in Granada."

Bora glanced at the veiled colours of the valley below. He had no idea what Niceto had been telling him. A touchy young stage actor who'd been trying until the start of the civil war to break into cinema, he would talk to whatever audience was at hand.

"Naturally there was no way a conservative like myself could make it; the industry is in the hands of Jews and communists," he was complaining. "Were you aware that in 1929 Spain and Portugal produced the fifth largest number of motion pictures in the world, over three hundred?"

"I believe Germany produced three thousand," Bora observed.

"Unfortunately I'm not a German actor."

"What happened at the audition?"

"The one with García Lorca? Oh, there was no chance of my working with Lorca, I knew that from the start." Niceto's nervous, strong hands moved with elegance, following his words. "He was an invert, you know."

Bora made no effort to look disinterested. The name Lorca meant little to him. "No," he said, "I didn't know."

"I could see that only a certain type of people were going to be accepted for his play *El Jínete Milagroso,* though I'd memorized the monologue from the first scene of the second act. I had the *presencia,* you know – the physique and voice of the Miraculous Horseman. I could feel the texture of the part, the tension and depth of it. I *was* El Jínete."

"So, how did you do?"

"He found somebody else for the part, a totally unsuitable oaf from León. But the oaf was willing to give what I wasn't." Niceto lowered his voice to a hiss. "And to think I'd been told Lorca didn't like *maricas*! He liked gypsies and *maricas*, and that's a fact."

Bora drove his hands deep into his pockets, nodding. They stood by the dishevelled lonely tree, close to the spot where the second mortar shell had landed. The valley ahead was a dull, violet bowl. Alfonso's dog sat at Bora's feet, balancing on its one front leg.

"I'm not saying Lorca wasn't a great poet, *mi teniente*. He was the best. He was genial. He had *duende*, really."

Bora didn't know what the word *duende* meant, but there were plenty of Spanish words he could only guess at. He bent to caress the dog's back. "Well, there isn't much theatrical activity for anyone right now."

Niceto's eyes followed the slow flight of hawks wheeling back to their nests in the mountains. "It's all precious time lost for me." He stepped away from the ledge. "Would you like to read something by Lorca? I have a selection of his poems in my bag."

"Sure." Bora showed the actor a small book he carried in his pocket. "I'm down to my last reading."

Niceto looked. "What is it?"

"*The Nicomachean Ethics.*"

"Is it a Greek tragedy?"

"No. Greek philosophy."

At dusk, the men gathered inside the post to eat what a dark little woman brought from Castellar. Bora heard their voices drifting now and then through the open windows and door. Like a long-held breath, the breeze exhausted itself in one gust and died down. The silence of the valley brimmed with shadows from here to the dim distance where Teruel lay. And there was hardly any light left by which to read Lorca's words:

> ... *I do not want to see it!My memory burns.*
> *Let the jasmines know,*
> *With their minute whiteness.*
> *I do not want to see it!*
> *The heifer of the old world*
> *Dragged her sad tongue*
> *Across a fearful snout of blood*
> *Spilled in the ring,*
> *And the Bulls of Guisando,*
> *Nearly death and nearly stone,*
> *Bellowed like two centuries*
> *Weary of pawing the earth ...*

The subject was blood. Earnestly Bora stole each line from the growing dark. He understood the motif well enough, but emotionally he didn't know what to make of it. It was like no poetry he'd ever read. It moved him, despite him taking pride these days in dispassion. His mind went to Lieutenant Jover, killed by the Reds just below this ledge. To the murdered man with the deep red stain on his shirt. To his own blood – how it, too, might soon be spilled, and someone might come and taste it, or curse it, or let the rain wash it from the earth.

> *But now he sleeps forever.*
> *Now grasses and moss*
> *Pry with knowing fingers*
> *The flower of his skull.*
> *And his blood comes forth, singing ...*

Fuentes came out to look for him. "*Señor teniente, algo que comer?*"

"I'm not hungry."

Fuentes left.

When it turned too dark to read, Bora put the book away. He could smell the dry dusty air of the valley. Small lights trembled in the swimming shadow below, from lonely farms and shepherds' fires. Lorca's words spoke of flesh and young death as if flesh longed for death and were in sad love with it. Bora sensed the hidden truth: the seductive dread, the danger of closing his eyes and saying "yes" to it. He kept his eyes on the shadow below, where solitude itself could be given a shape by connecting those trembling dots. And all the time he envied older men, who were not cocky one moment and vulnerable the next, and well beyond this hard communion with themselves.

"*Hola! Quien vive?*" Alfonso's call announced Tomé's return from the higher sierra. Bora shoved the poetry book into his pocket and left the ledge.

Tomé brought along a jittery old man who spoke fast and low. Bora saw him in the wedge of kerosene light shining from the open window. There were no fresh graves in the cemetery at Castellar, Tomé reported. Bora was disappointed. Still he said, "*Bueno,*" and dismissed him. Then he sat down with the old man and Fuentes, whose help he needed to understand the dialect.

EL PALO DE LA VIRGEN

"We did it."

Walton stretched out his legs on the dirt floor, relaxing his shoulders against the kitchen's end wall. The aroma of his American cigarettes gave him away in the dark, but he wouldn't answer Brissot's words.

"We couldn't reach much deeper than three feet, it's like digging through limestone," the Frenchman added, taking a groping step forward. Walton let him fumble towards the flickering light of his cigarette and sit on the floor somewhere. "We had to pile rocks on top of it. Hopefully it'll keep the animals away."

"That's good."

"I met Marypaz on the way down, Felipe. She's like a cat in heat, rubbing herself against anything that goes by. If I didn't respect you as a a comrade, I'd have bedded her tonight."

Walton shut his eyes, as if it'd keep him from hearing. "She'll get over it."

"I told her to look out for the Fascists, and she gave me the finger."

Walton swallowed a mouthful of smoke. In the dark, he could pretend he wasn't even here, though for the life of him he couldn't think of another place he might want to be. He flicked the cigarette butt across the room.

"Do you want her? Take her."

"No, thank you." Brissot was taking off his coveralls. A rustle of heavy cloth and a whiff of sweat accompanied the motions, the odour of fresh sweat on old sweat. "No, thank you. I have no intention of arguing with you about it tomorrow. I just thought you'd like to know."

RISCAL AMARGO

After the informant left, Fuentes and Bora sat outside the post in the dusty darkness.

Bora said, "The way we're going, we might not find out

where the grave is for some time yet. And with this heat to boot."

"At least we're pretty sure it didn't leave the mountains. And since they didn't bury it at San Martín, it can only be in one or two other places." Fuentes looked up to the star-crowded sky. "If the old man does his asking in the right way, you could have the news by morning."

"I hope so. Who has the first watch of the night?"

"I do."

"Excellent. Make sure no one leaves the post."

Fuentes stood up, his bulky figure squaring itself against a haze of small stars. "If you're going to stay out here, *teniente*, I'll fetch your sleeping bag."

While Bora waited for Fuentes, Tomé came out of the post with a blanket bunched under his arm. Dimly Bora saw him step with care, mincing around the stones and bits of shrapnel still lying around. "Good night," he said into the shadow where Bora was, and went around the corner to the stable. He kept his guitar there, and soon a few loose notes, like liquid, came from that direction. Through an open window Paradís' amused voice said, "He's serenading the horse," and someone else said something else and laughed, and then everyone stopped laughing because Fuentes was coming down the stairs.

Bora had stretched himself out by the well, where the mortar blast had caused no damage. Fuentes handed him the tightly rolled bundle of the sleeping bag.

"Fuentes, what's your definition of *maricas*?"

A thick, short silence preceded the answer. "Why, sir, they're men who act queer. Girl-like faggots, you'd say."

"I thought so. You throw the word around a great deal in this country."

Fuentes cleared his throat. "Anything else, *mi teniente*?"

"No. If I'm not awake, call me at the end of your watch."

Within an hour, the kerosene lamp was turned off inside the post. The ledge seemed to sink and vanish, then the clean margin between dull and starry dark, earth and sky, drew itself again. Eastward, on the ridgeline of the roof, a waning moon climbed over the scaly edge of the tiles. A black thread, like a seam, appeared to be running through its bright graceful curve, and Bora had to focus on the image before realizing that the moon was rising behind the weathervane.

Twenty-four hours earlier, the blood had still been alive in the veins of the nameless body by the roadside, and now he – Martin Bora from Edinburgh, Leipzig and Dar Riffian, just granted the rank of *teniente* in an army that wasn't his own – would have to find his grave. *I wonder if the nameless dead man wants to be found, if he wanted to be buried by us in the first place. I wonder if his blood will come forth singing, and reveal itself. And the poet García Lorca, who died last year in Granada ... well, he liked* maricas. *He must have very much feared and longed for death, judging by the way he wrote.* Bora lay back. Rifle at hand, Fuentes stood still in the starlight like the last picket of a vanished fence. According to him, there'd been fighting across the sierra until the end of May; whole units had passed through, then the lines had withdrawn. "Like the sides of a gash," Fuentes had said. Only small outposts had been left behind, harmless but for the meaning of their presence. Matter *was* equal to potentiality. From here to the valley, it was friendly territory; from Palo de la Virgen on, the whole mountain range was Red. A dull time of keeping watch lay ahead, poised for the next offensive. When Bora had first climbed El Baluarte to observe the enemy camp, he'd been surprised by how similar it was to the army post, a staged symmetry on two shelves of the same mountain ledge. How, in the end, the camps led parallel lives. It had a quality of suspended reality, this closeness, watching, killing one man at a time.

Sleep would not come. The hard ground had less to do with it, he knew, than his recurrent fantasies about Benedikta Coennewitz back home. It was another world already. His interest in her had begun in April, at an army reception he didn't even want to attend. When the breathtaking blonde smiled at him across the dance floor, Bora – who'd fleetingly met her the day he and her brother hadn't qualified for the German equestrian Olympic team – couldn't imagine why he hadn't flirted with her back then. Whatever military courtesy and his orders to mingle required, he danced and talked with her alone. Holding Bora's hand, his arm around her waist, the not-so-casual brushing of hips: Dikta flirted well. Humming the slow American swing tunes, she invited more closeness than even the crowded dance floor justified. "How come you're so tanned?"

"From the joint manoeuvres in Italy." It wasn't true, of course, though he'd told his mother the same.

She laughed. "That's not an Italian tan. Not in April."

"South of Rome, it is." He responded aggressively to her nearness, and when a second lieutenant insisted on asking Dikta for a dance, Bora pulled rank.

"How far south of Rome?" Sliding up from his shoulder, her thumb began grazing his neck in little spirals. Dikta was a girl of his class, his sport, his size. A well-spoken girl growing up to be like his mother and aunts, who had scented hair and bought clothes in Berlin and Paris and went to Red Cross benefits and expected their men to change for dinner and smoke in the other room. Slowly her thumb inched up to his mouth, and he wetted it with his tongue.

"Not very far."

Like other couples, during a pause in the music they'd taken their turn in the garden, kissing hard and groping each other in the complicit dark. He remembered the slack curve of a curl seeking the hollow of her neck, and feeling thrown off, hopeful, the blue and red Moroccan months without women suddenly like an immense injustice he had to remedy in the few hours left before going back. They went riding together the following day, and on the way back ended up in the bedroom of her parents' country house, where things went much too far to stop. Only after they had showered and dressed again did she tell him she had a fiancé in Hamburg.

"Will you keep him now?" he'd asked. She smiled the same smile he'd first seen on the dance floor. "That depends." And tonight Bora wondered where he stood in that regard, although he ached for her often and was more than a little lovesick. The girls in Bilbao came in between, but these days Bora was alone, not quite willing to find himself a widow in Castellar, like Alfonso had. He turned away from the moon, and closed his eyes.

EL PALO DE LA VIRGEN

Walton recognized Marypaz's warm fragrance even before she lay beside him in the narrow bed. Her round knees and shoulders, the moist sponginess of her breasts sought the length of his body, and for a time he was tempted to turn around and climb on top of her. But it was a mental, not a physical struggle with himself, which he won easily. Her nearness in the heat reminded him of everything he found oppressive in life and had tried to escape from. He chose not to move, breathing deeply and slowly with his face to the wall.

2

"Neighbours," I asked,
"Where is my grave?"
"In my tail," said the sun.
"In my throat," said the moon.

FEDERICO GARCÍA LORCA,
"IX: CASÍDA OF THE DARK DOVES"

RISCAL AMARGO

Before dawn, the sky had turned narrow with haze when Fuentes came to awaken Bora at the end of his watch. Bora was already standing by the well. "Has the informant returned?"

"No, sir."

The mugginess was resilient, palpable. Bora felt it on his face like a moist web. He walked away from the well. Past the rickety shadow of the lean-to, the mountain formed a ghostly wall. He had to grope for the stingy trickle of water still oozing from the cleft in the rock, hardly gathering enough on his fingers to wet his face. The men kept a barrel by the spring that was always full. Bora lifted the tarpaulin hooding it and reached inside to splash water on his head and shoulders.

It was nearly an hour before the informant picked his way down the rock-strewn incline from the sierra. "*Quien vive?*" came a call from Paradís, whose watch it was. The three-legged dog twitched in its sleep, but did not growl. "*Quien vive?*"

Bora came to meet the informant at the foot of the trail, followed by Fuentes, who balanced a brimming tin of coffee he'd made for him.

"Well, *viejo*," Bora asked, "did you find out where the body was buried?"

"Not yet." The old man stood just close enough to avoid having to raise his voice. "They didn't come anywhere close to the village to do it. The Widow Yarza has one of the Reds for a lover, and she didn't hear anything about it either. But I don't know if you can trust her; I think she's growing fond of the man."

"So, how long is it going to take you to find out?"

"Another day, maybe two. You can't rush these things, *señor teniente*, as Fuentes knows. There's a couple of boys I can send out to look for a fresh hole in the dirt. No one pays attention to boys."

"Go back, then. Come in person or send your wife if you hear anything."

Bora was just turning away when the informant held him back.

"There's something else you ought to know. A complaint has been made about one of yours molesting a young girl in Castellar. You'll hear from the priest tomorrow."

He jerked his arm free. "The priest? Why the priest? Fuentes, what is he talking about?"

Fuentes made a throaty sound which meant he was taking advantage of the half-dark to spit. "*Mierda*, I bet it's Paradís again. Damn him, he can't keep his hands to himself. He'll get us in trouble yet."

Bora felt a trickle of sweat running from under his sore right arm and down his side, and for an odd moment its tacky meandering on his skin kept him in suspense. Paradís was the quiet ex-sailor who didn't relate much to anyone; not even to Aixala, who came from the same province. The men teased him and called him *coño*, which seemed to be what one ended up being called here whenever one didn't qualify as a *marica*. Once Bora had caught sight of him masturbating behind the house, but he'd seen plenty of that at Tétouan and Dar Riffian and had just turned away in embarrassment. Suddenly, he was anxious to dismiss the informant. As soon as the old man was out of earshot, he turned to Fuentes. "Why wasn't I told about this before?"

Fuentes' silence lasted long enough for the feeble unison of crickets to rise from the gloom around them. Increasingly distant clinking noises of stones rolling down the trail betrayed the informant's laborious climb back to Castellar.

"I'm talking to you, Sergeant. What's the story, and why haven't I been told?"

"Men will be men, *teniente*. They'll go after women, young or not. You can't expect discipline from this mishmash."

Angrily Bora turned down the offer of coffee. "We'll see about that at sunrise."

EL PALO DE LA VIRGEN

At sunrise, the heat was still oppressive in Walton's room. He'd been tossing and turning all night, and now even getting out of bed seemed like an undeserved chore. Tangled in the sweaty sheet, he saw that Marypaz was leaning out of the window, making faces.

"Mosko. *Hola*, Mosko!" She blew down a kiss, and then stuck her tongue out.

Walton joined her. A wave of musk rose from her body as she brushed past him. She'd just put on the lacy slip he'd bought her in Barcelona, and her perspiration was already letting out a scent as thick as liquor and forming two yellow crescents where her armpits met the cloth. She went to sit cross-legged on the bed to comb her hair.

Under the window, Chernik had just joined Brissot after the last watch of the night. "Sure hope it rains before long," Chernik groaned.

Shielding his eyes with cupped hands, Brissot turned his black-clad self to the valley. "When it does, it'll pour. I've seen it happen before. I thought the shitty mountain was going to dissolve on us, but at least the air became breathable for a while."

"Throw me my pants, Marypaz," Walton called, and started dressing.

Thunder came from the hazy brightness to the southeast a few minutes later, when he reached Brissot on the ledge. He'd freshened up at the fountain and carried his shirt draped over his shoulder. Skinny bundles of muscle, broken in two places by coin-sized whitish bullet scars, roped themselves up and down his torso. Walton liked showing his muscles and scars. The most recent wound had nearly killed him at Guadalajara. "I swear I don't know why I get so angry at Marypaz; she's an excellent piece when she wants to be."

Brissot smirked. "I'm aware. You took her from me, remember?"

"She came willingly. Well, what's the forecast? Are we going to get any rain?"

"Seems like it." Brissot pulled at the grizzled brush of his moustache, where sweat hung in minute drops. "And while you're here, there's something we must discuss."

Walton hardened, the wiry muscles on his spare frame distending. "I know what it is, and I'm trying my damn best to put it out of my mind. Drop the propaganda."

"It's not as easy as that. I still believe we should try to find out more about his death. I was thinking —"

Walton flung the bundled shirt into Brissot's face, a reaction so uncalled for that he felt he should justify it by showing anger. "What do you expect to find? I warned him it was a bad idea to hide in Teruel, that Fascist bunghole of a small town! He assured me he had a safe escort, and now it's clear that he didn't, or else he tried to come alone. Shit, I should have gone out looking for him last night! Now he's dead, and I don't want to think about it any more."

Calmly Brissot used the shirt's threadbare fabric to wipe his sweaty face. "What else did he tell you?"

"When we met in Valdecebro last week he said someone had been following him, and he'd barely managed to give him the slip."

"Civilian? Soldier? Guardia Civil?"

"Dunno." Without showing it, Walton regretted his fit of temper. "One of those. Christ, most people believed he'd died in Granada a year ago. I told him that he was crazy to room with a socialist, even if he was a family member."

"When you met in Valdecebro, do you know for a fact that he got back safely that day?"

"Yes, yes." Restlessly Walton glanced to his right, where a remote swelling of clouds was now discernible in the eastern sky. "I waited by the public phone until he called to assure me he'd made it back to Teruel. Give me back the shirt."

Brissot handed it over. "And Valdecebro is where he told you he was working on an anthem for the Loyalist volunteers."

"No. He'd been working on it since before Barcelona. He first told me when I was at the hospital. In Valdecebro he said it was complete and he'd bring it over."

"'Bring it over'? It's not like any of us can move freely around the country. Travelling some twenty-three miles overnight! I don't believe for a minute he did it for a music score. Not for you, not for any of us. And not on foot, that's for sure. There must have been a car. So, where did the car go? It makes no sense."

Walton was in the mood for an argument. Brissot's self-control was now making him feel at fault, and he loathed the feeling. "You don't know shit. About him, about the way things went in Granada. You don't know shit."

"Suppose you told me."

"You don't even like people like him, so I can't begin to explain what kind of man he was." Walton suddenly noticed, as Brissot no doubt had, that the tension had gone out of his shoulders. "His idealism was … I don't know, a kind of hot coal inside, like a black fire. He burned too deep to show the flame, but the flame was there." He found himself searching for words, aware that Brissot had somehow opened a sluice and information would roll out of him whether he wanted or not.

"When he visited America back in '29, he came to Vermont, of all places. Of all places in Vermont, eight years ago next month he landed in Eden." Walton spoke with his eyes low. "What a laugh that we have a place called *Eden*, and I was born in it. Eden. Eden Mills. Eden Lake. If that's Eden, there's no way to know what hell is. Seed potatoes, that's what it's known for. A fork in the road, a house here and a house there, and the lake ahead. The rich own cabins on the lake, though. He was a guest of the Cummingses, but *I* got to show him around the woods." Walton glanced up at Brissot. "It's mind-boggling what you learn about a man when he sees things for the first time. Scrawny red bushes they don't have here in Spain, or a dinky flower I'd never noticed, even though I'd been running around the woods searching for the talc mine since I was five. The way the lake reaches out like a wing and changes colour when the clouds pass over it … Who knew? He pointed those things out and I *saw* them. Maybe Eden wasn't as desperate and hopeless as I thought, for all that my wife hated it as much as I did and we spent our days arguing about getting out of there. Afterwards he told me he wrote about that visit, the woods and the old mill and the lake, and all that." Walton began to massage his neck with slow twists of his right hand. "And who the hell was I in 1929? A foreman at the Woodbury Granite Company, which floundered after the stock market crash that year. No money, no security, and then Washington quits ordering stone for its monuments altogether. I was nobody, with no idea of who this Spaniard was. He spoke only this much English." Walton removed his hand from his neck and pinched his fingers together. "And I spoke what Spanish I'd learned from the Peña boys in the granite shed. I showed him around, that's all. Before leaving, he invited me to attend his lecture. Me? A lecture, in New York? I was on my way to Pittsburgh to find real work, not to attend a lecture in New York. All I had was unemployment and a wife I couldn't get rid of." With his hand back on his neck, Walton pulled himself up straight. "It was eight years before I met him again in Barcelona and told him what it'd meant to me to walk behind him and watch him appreciate life. And yesterday it took some bastard a second to put a bullet into the kind of brain that's made once every hundred years. The valley is Fascist land. Ask, and they won't tell you anything and you might end up the same way he did."

Brissot paused, watching the billowy clouds come from the east, a melancholy cast on his earnest face. "Will you at least come along and look around the spot with Maetzu and myself?"

"If it makes you shut up. Not now, though. Tell Maetzu we'll go in an hour or two."

As they spoke, Marypaz came out of the house. She'd put on a dress and plaited her hair in a long braid that swung at every step, like the glossy tail of a healthy cat.

The trickle of mountain water behind the lean-to had dried up sometime before dawn. At eight o'clock, when Fuentes came upstairs with the news, Bora couldn't find a curse word in Spanish. He swore in German, shoving his sketchbook into a field-grey canvas bag.

"Are you sure you want to go now, *teniente*?"

"Yes." Bora grabbed a handful of pencils from his table and thrust those into the bag as well. He preceded Fuentes down the airless stairs, and when he stepped out of the door, a stunning blast of heat met him. Hemmed in by towering clouds, the sun burned on the ledge as though through the focus of a lens. The men kept to the shade. Alfonso's dog lay looking dead, its spotted tongue limp, its mangy sides showing its ribcage.

"This is a mean sun," Fuentes said. "One who isn't used to it is liable to get sunstroke."

Bora slung the bag across his shoulder and headed for the stone edge struck by the mortar shell. He hadn't gone ten steps when Fuentes called him back.

"*Hay el cura, teniente.*"

Annoyed, Bora stopped. Halfway up the zigzag trail descending from the sierra, the priest was riding a big-headed donkey. A boy led the animal by a short rope, holding a white handkerchief in his left hand. Once on flat ground the priest took off his wide-brimmed hat and removed a cloth he'd been wearing on his head, tied at the corners. Bora's men, idling in every sliver of shade available, watched. Paradís had the grin of an idiot. Aixala, who'd been drinking from the water barrel, put down the ladle and went indoors.

Bora saluted the priest. With a gesture, he ordered Fuentes to help him down from his mount. "Tell Aixala to get out," he said, adding, "I want no one inside while I'm talking to the *reverendo padre.*"

Having preceded the priest to his office, Bora heard him stumble up the stairs. "*Siéntese.* How may I help?" he asked, encouraging his visitor to speak. For several minutes, all that was heard in the room was the monotonous speech coming from the priest's mouth.

"These are good women, you must understand. Churchgoing, respectable. Sadly, it isn't as though there aren't shameless ones in Castellar who would accommodate your men. When fathers and husbands leave the house, women are left to fend for themselves. Strange men come by, strangers: they assume that because women live alone ... You understand." Across the table from him, Bora was well aware he looked foreign, unsympathetic. He meant to. He meant for the priest to realize that he wasn't a Spanish officer, and not even a Spaniard. He meant to appear – what? – irreligious or, worse for a Catholic priest, a Protestant.

"You must understand," the old man blabbed on, "that when everything else fails, the Church must defend the weak. It's my Christian duty to ensure that those whom the Scriptures refer to as 'widows and virgins' aren't put to the test by those under your command."

Bora listened with his shoulders back, frowning, wanting to hear none of this. "Is there a description of the man in question?" he asked.

"The little girl, only fourteen, was walking home after sunset from the public fountain when a man in a light-green shirt and black braces accosted her." The priest interrupted himself, given that Bora wore a similar uniform. "Well, the soldier made an indecent proposal to her, and when she demurred, he tried to grab hold of her. She was so frightened that she dropped her pail, fled to the house, and doesn't want to go out now even during the daytime. She can't give a more accurate description than the one I just gave you. If that weren't enough, someone even tried to enter her house at night."

Bora turned to the drumming of thunder across the valley. "I will speak to the men." Like an invisible dragon, the choking heat breathed through the window.

The priest blotted his forehead. Sweat sullied the white collar emerging from his cassock, and he looked out of sorts. "I'm thirsty," he whined. Lost in the greasy collar, the turtle-like skin of his neck hung in folds under his chin. "May I have a glass of water?"

Bora stepped to the window and called out to Fuentes below to bring up a drink.

"It's bad enough," the priest added, "that there are harlots like that godless Remedios woman who lives up the sierra: why molest honest women? It makes caring for my people impossible and forces me to pay visits like this one, which I assure you I didn't need at my age and with my poor health."

Fuentes brought a tin full of water, handed it to the priest and left. Surely the water was warm, sour from sitting in the barrel. The priest twisted his mouth as he drank.

"*Usted es inglés?*" he asked.

"No."

Afterwards, when Fuentes came back up, Bora was sitting with his elbows on the table, chin resting on his clasped hands and his eyes low. "*Teniente —*"

Bora looked up. "I'm not listening, so spare your breath. Have the men assemble outside when I come back. Afterwards, have Paradís and Aixala come and see me here alone, one at a time."

And all the while he wondered who Remedios might be.

CAÑADA DE LOS ZAGALES

Fifteen minutes later, the scent of rain was already in the air. Birds vacated the sky. Insects made a continuous high-pitched noise in the shrubs and wilted grass. Behind the cane grove, a dancing hem of rain drew close, although the blanched stony bed of the brook still took in and reflected the full sun.

Walton had to shade his eyes to look at the pebbles edging the water. The wind had fallen since he'd reached the brook with Maetzu and Brissot; even the narrow shade created by the canes at the curve of the mule track was stifling. Walton couldn't wait for the gap in the clouds to close over the sun. Leaving his map case on a rock, he crouched to wash his hands and face in the worming current.

There was no evidence to be found at the place of death. No visible tyre tracks, no hoof prints. No dried blood. On the bank, a few resilient bushes with bright green leaves stood watch but offered no clues. You'd think Brissot would be satisfied. Still crouching, Walton dried his hands on his shirt. He thought he recognized Maetzu's careful step behind him. "Iñaki," he said, "pass me the map case."

The case was handed to him from behind.

"The pencil, too."

The pencil followed. Immediately afterwards, he felt a hard steel-like prod on the back of his head.

"Please do not rise."

Walton felt the muscles in his torso stiffen and his thighs grow hard in his squatting position. It was almost noon: the shadows were too short to betray who was standing behind him. The urge to reach for his holster crossed his mind even as the newcomer unlatched it to take his gun.

"Now stand."

Without turning his head, Walton tried to glance left and right for Maetzu and Brissot. He knew they were not far away. Their voices could be heard beyond the tallest cane grove That's how the murder had been committed the night before, a shot from the same angle; for all he knew from the same pistol. Despite the overwhelming heat before the storm, he broke into a cold sweat. When he stood up, the steel prod followed his motion, flush against his skull. It took Walton this long, perhaps ten seconds in all, to register that the voice had not spoken in Spanish but in English. On an impulse he turned, at the risk of the trigger being released.

A young man stood there, right arm outstretched, pointing a hefty automatic pistol at him.

Browning High Power was Walton's alarmed evaluation. *Brand new, a gun for an experienced shooter. Might have fourteen shots in it. It'd blow my head to a pulp.* His own gun sat wedged in the stranger's belt.

Bareheaded, the young man was tall and lean. In the blaze of the sun Walton could discern little, other than that he seemed to wear the shirt and riding breeches of a Tercio uniform. He was alone, which struck Walton as foolhardy when his comrades were within earshot. Still holding his pencil and map case, he tried to calculate how quickly his men would be here if he shouted for help.

"You could attempt to call your cohorts, but it wouldn't make good military sense, because I would shoot you."

The accent. Clipped and precise, not readily identifiable. Certainly not Spanish. Walton relaxed a little. He'd been frightened, but now annoyance replaced fear. If the man had meant to shoot him in cold blood, he'd have done it already. "What do you want me to do?" he asked.

Bora hadn't planned on meeting anyone, nor had he been sure that it was the American he was facing until he'd heard him answer. But he suspected what the three men might be looking for, and it was too late because he'd already been fortunate in his search. His only regret was that he'd have to leave quickly, before the others returned … their voices were growing nearer by the minute. "I wanted to see you up close," he decided to say. Carefully backing up, with his gun still pointed at the American, he was soon far enough away for Walton to dive for cover and call out, but by then Bora had scrambled up the mountainside and was out of sight. The clouds closed in on the sun.

Thunder rolling overhead drowned out the report of Maetzu's rifle. Sparse, heavy drops of rain had begun to fall and curdle the dust as Brissot ran out of the cane grove. "Are you all right?" he called. "Who was it, Felipe?"

Maetzu was still firing, and a couple of warning rifle shots rang down in response from the high ledge of the Riscal. Walton shouted at Brissot. "Fuck, I don't know!" Walton shouted. "He spoke English. The way he said the word 'military'… he pronounced it 'militree', like the British."

"There's a handful of Englishmen fighting with the Fascists."

"He took my fucking gun."

Ten yards away, Maetzu wasted bullets against the rocky wall. Brissot grinned at Walton. "Let's take it as a lesson not to separate when we leave camp. Next time we'll be ready. We have plenty of guns on hand, Felipe. Let's head back before it comes pouring down on us like a flood."

RISCAL AMARGO

By the time Bora was midway up the ravine, the dams of heaven had split open. Whips of hot stinging rain lashed the rocks and dirt, lifting vapours out of the dust, braiding into gushes around his feet. He looked for the stain from Jover's blood and could see nothing but splashes. He was soaked when he regained the ledge, sliding in the mud. All the while, Fuentes had been firing with a carbine into the valley, waiting for him.

"It's all right. Go inside!" Bora shouted. As for him, he needed the rage of the water, the drenching, so he slowed down, with his face upturned, to catch the rain in his mouth. Yellow streams already frothed among the rocks on the upper reaches of the sierra, angrily snaking down the sides of the army post. Like a solid ark, the building seemed to float on a river of mud. Bora walked slowly, head tilted back. No doubt the spring that had dried up overnight would have revived in its cleft, and the brook would be running full again.

"*Ándale, Pardo!*" Followed by the halting dog, Tomé led Bora's horse to cover in the stable. Lightning blinded the sky and thunder followed immediately with a burst overhead as Bora reached the doorstep. The men gathered in the vaulted room of the ground floor. Unlike Fuentes and Bora, and Tomé, who came running after them, their shirts were dry and still bore haloes of sweat at their armpits.

"I put two buckets out to fill," Tomé announced as he walked to the end wall, where a soot-mouthed fireplace was always lit. Bora saw him hang his shirt to dry from a nail in the mantel and turn his bony back to the room.

On his way upstairs, Bora showed the pistol to Fuentes. "It's the American's," he said. "Send Paradís in a few minutes, and when I'm done with him, send Aixala."

Rain poured into his room from the broken window. A puddle ran across the brick floor to the door. Bora straddled it to place his canvas bag in a dry corner. He pulled out of the bag the map he'd taken from the American's case, and ran his eyes over it. It was patched with paper tape and disappointingly unmarked. Whatever else he'd found by the brook, he chose to leave inside the bag.

Soon Paradís appeared on the threshold, his dull blue eyes immediately fixing on the pool of water at his feet. He didn't move from there until he was told to enter. It took a direct order for him to approach and stand across the desk from Bora.

"Did you go to Castellar the night before last?" Bora asked the question expecting to see a change come over Paradís.

The sailor's round face remained impassive instead, and his eyes – bulging, clear as glass marbles – stared back. "Not me, *teniente*. I haven't been to Castellar in over a week. I was here all night. You can ask Alfonso."

"But you have been to Castellar in the past. There are reports."

"Of course I have. I'm not a *marica* like Tomé."

Bora felt an unexpected wave of blood rise to his face at the words. A *marica* like Tomé. The way Paradís said it … it wasn't the usual bantering tone. Bora sat stock-still, but his mind went nervously to the image of Tomé slumped by the waterhole with a grain stalk in his mouth: one day after another, watching him bathe. A *marica* like Tomé. His slowness in understanding, his naivety were for a moment unbearable to him, and Bora was abjectly grateful to have his back to the window so that Paradís didn't see him blush.

Paradís continued to look stupid. "We've all gone to Castellar. There's whores there, and you won't find a real man among us who hasn't visited them at one time or another. Besides, I know the difference between whores and the other kind of women, *teniente*."

Bora tried, not very successfully, to hide his anger. "Make sure you keep the difference in mind, because I have orders to deal very severely with anyone accused of rape." That wasn't strictly true, and no one had spoken of rape. Paradís just sat, with his moon-face and inexpressive eyes.

"I don't know what the *teniente* is saying. Me, I haven't been to Castellar in a week."

CAÑADA DE LOS ZAGALES

It was Brissot's idea to find shelter from the storm at the foot of the mountain. There, a mule drover waited under a rock overhang that barely protected him and left his animal in the open. He moved over when the new arrivals came. His face was averted, and only the quick throbbing of his jaw muscles revealed his anxiety.

"*Salud,*" Maetzu said.

The choice of greeting in itself was political. Warily the *mulero* turned. Walton felt the scrutiny. He knew that Maetzu's red neckcloth gave him away, as Brissot's coveralls probably did. As for himself, he judged that he simply looked foreign. At length, the *mulero* stretched out a slow, calloused hand to the Basque. "*Salud.*"

Nothing else was said for a time. Muddy rain streamed from the overhang as if from many spouts, striking the hard dirt below. It poured straight down; provided the men kept their backs against the stone wall, they were only exposed to the foggy spray that flew about.

After Brissot and Walton questioned him, the *mulero* accepted a cigarette, but didn't answer at once. "Look," he finally said, "I stop over at Albarracín most of the time, though I often go as far as Caminreal and Cosa, but I learned to mind my own business from my mule, who's smart enough to wear blinkers. What I see and what I hear goes right through me, and it's kept me healthy so far." He puffed on the cigarette, seemingly judging the effect of his words out of the corner of his eye. Under Maetzu's ominous staring silence he added, reluctantly, "Things happen at night, I don't deny it. I guess I could tell you what I heard ... of course I don't know if it's true." His gaunt face had the colour of wet bricks, and a stubble of many hours. He sucked hard on Walton's cigarette. "A friend of mine was passing through two nights ago. You recall how hot it was; the night air was as thick as honey. My friend headed home to Campillo, and found himself on the little bridge over the brook, on the other side of the cane grove. There's a curve there."

Walton played along. "What time was it? Did your 'friend' say?"

"No. But when *I* go that way I reach the bridge around midnight."

"Well, what did he see?" Maetzu hounded him.

The *mulero* spat out some tobacco that had stuck to his lips. "He didn't see much. It'd been so hot all day that the mule took it into its head to drink from the brook, so he let it, and walked ahead a little. *Bueno*, there was enough moonlight for him to make out a car sitting near the curve with its lights and engine off." Picking shreds of tobacco from his lower lip, the *mulero* spat again. "He got curious and walked up a little, quietly, to see what it was all about. There wasn't much more to see. He thought he saw three people in the car, but who knows what you see at night. Those three heads, well, he could make them out, that's all."

Brissot frowned. Maetzu growled, "What else, what else?" and Walton lifted his hand to signal him to be patient before he too added, "What else?"

The *mulero* took a deep drag and swallowed the smoke. "My friend didn't get involved. What would a car be doing at night in the middle of nowhere? Nothing good, I say. He went back to fetch the mule and led it along the brook, so they wouldn't hear its hoofs from the car if the windows were open." Another drag, more smoke swallowed. "Then he thought he was far enough away to get back on the track, so he did. *Pan*! It sounded like a pistol shot from the car, kind of muffled. In a little while, *pan!* Another shot, closer in." Walton stared questioningly at Brissot, who was facing the *mulero*. "By this time my friend knew he wasn't about to get involved *at all*. He didn't even move for a good spell, waiting for the car to go by. It never did. After he heard it go off in the other direction, the one it'd come from, he hurried away."

"Without checking what had happened?"

The *mulero* had a quick, nervous grin. "What for? It wouldn't take a professor to figure out what had happened. There are times to be curious and times to follow your nose." He extended his forefinger and little finger from his closed right fist in a superstitious gesture. "A man ought to keep away from trouble whenever he can. That's what my friend did."

RISCAL AMARGO

Aixala's eyes searched Bora's room. An old scar on his left cheek showed, pale where the skin stretched. His shock of thick chestnut hair stood up in the humid air like a weed on his head. "It's a lie," he said. "Is that what the priest came here to say? It's a filthy lie. I wish he'd told me to my face! It's nothing like what happened, and I don't know why you have to ask me about it, because it's my business."

"If it's reported to me, I make it my business." Sitting across from Aixala, Bora had to make an effort to remain self-possessed after what Paradís had said about Tomé.

"There's nothing to say. First she agreed to kiss me, and as soon as I started kissing she got scared and ran off."

"And then?"

"Blood of Christ, that's all there is! I kissed her with my tongue, and she got scared."

"I thought you already had a woman in Castellar."

Aixala's small eyes sank into their orbits when he squinted hard. "Who told you about that? Anyway, I couldn't do with this girl what I do with the other. I just wanted to kiss this one. What's wrong with that? She's old enough." Shoulders hunched, elbows close to his sides, he took a defensive stance. "Later that night I went back because I wanted to talk to her. I knocked on the door but the mother woke up and they both started screaming. Now the girl is telling lies because she doesn't want her mother to know she kissed a man."

Bora sat back. "And what did you do after the women screamed?"

"I left. I went towards San Martín. I was so furious, I didn't care if I got a bullet in my head from the Reds. Anyway, I was back here in time for my watch."

Leaning back, Bora sat moodily in the thin aura of steam that rose from his drying clothes. He was thinking how women had taught him to kiss when he was fifteen, and kissing had never held such sweet terror since. He said, "You're confined to the post for the next two weeks."

"Two weeks!"

"You heard me."

Aixala turned around in a passion, splashing his way to the door.

Under the overhang, Walton whispered to Brissot. Brissot, who didn't hear him over the rushing sound of the water, turned to him. Next to them, Maetzu hadn't said a word for the last ten minutes. He rolled a cigarette and stuck it into his mouth, squeezing it unlit between his lips.

"Well, it's easing off a little," the *mulero* said. "I'd better get going." He stepped away from the shelter to reach the mule that waited with ears low. "*Salud.*"

What followed was unforeseeable and absurd to Walton, even though it happened before him as if in slow motion. One moment he was talking to Brissot; the next, Maetzu's gun rose from the holster, found the *mulero*'s skull and fired point-blank into it.

The top of the man's head seemed to explode. A crown of blood spurted from it and brightly mixed with the rain as he fell in a heap. Maetzu put the gun away.

Dumbly Walton looked down. The dead man lay with arms outstretched and that red fountain still gushing out of his skull. The mule had scampered off into the shrubs; Maetzu was now walking towards it to lead it back.

"What did he do that for?"

Brissot looked at Walton without answering. Maetzu returned, pulling the mule by its rope. Stepping in the pool of watery blood, he lifted the body and slung it across the double saddle of braided straw, then pushed the mule towards the track. Soon he was rinsing the blood off his hands under the rain. "It knows the road. It'll reach Campillo on its own."

"Jesus," Walton groaned.

Maetzu shrugged. He tapped Brissot on the shoulder. "Give me some tobacco." After the tobacco was handed to him, he reacted angrily. "What are you staring at, both of you? He'd have blabbed just as much to the first Fascist he met on the way, and added the three of us to his tale!"

RISCAL AMARGO

14 July. Afternoon, at the post.

I can't deny, as Aristotle insists, that shame is a feeling rather than a virtue. There's nothing virtuous about it, other than it means men fear dishonour. Thank God he says that it becomes youth, but only because young men 'live by feeling and commit many errors'. Little consolation there.

Bora raised his eyes to the window. It thundered less and less frequently, but rain still pelted the roof tiles. Downstairs the men whiled the time away playing cards. Paradis bet and swore and Tomé swore back over the noise of other voices not so recognizable. Bora sat on his cot to change into dry clothes. He lay down eventually, because he'd slept little the night before and could do with some rest now. Agonizing over the men's opinions of his trips to the brook with Tomé served no purpose, but he indulged in his thoughts gloomily until the rain distracted him from the voices below, from his lack of privacy and his general sense of being out of place.

When he closed his eyes, the way the American had turned upon hearing him speak English came to his mind, along with the memory of the sunny gravel bed around them. *There* was someone who'd faced death today. Maybe he should have fired; who knows? There hadn't been enough time to judge him, but at first sight the American fit the role of an older male, with all the detail that implied for Bora. Insecurity, swagger, a need to prove himself.

Sitting up, he wrote,

Fuentes had told me the American is a *feissimo hideputa*, when he's actually a common, rugged-looking fellow, such as we see in American motion pictures. Weathered, in his forties. I wager he's a veteran, which means he's fought Germans before. A hard, horsey face. His teeth are discoloured – he smokes, probably. Hair unkempt, shabbily dressed, no uniform. But of course smartness of uniform is difficult here. My stepfather the general wouldn't be impressed with my own perfunctory attention to detail: khaki shorts and an open-necked army shirt is often the best I can do here. Since Morocco the nattiness of peacetime soldiering has fallen by the wayside, too. There's a dull brutality in living under these primitive conditions, and yet a provisional quality to life, because at any moment open war could erupt and then this boredom and wearing down of one's idealism will explode; into what, it remains to be seen. I'm anxious and desirous and feel alive because there's a risk ahead of me. How can I explain to my stepfather (or to the colonel, for that matter) that the reason why I chose to attend university before army school was that I wasn't sure that Germany would commit to an army after all, and that the army would commit to *something*? Nation-building is well and good for some; but for those like myself, who have heard nothing else but retribution and bitterness for Versailles, there has to be something more than nation-building. A holy goal, a course sanctified by necessity and God's own injunction that we must protect civilization. As a German, I need to feel civilized, and civilizing wars provide a shortcut to that comfortable feeling of superiority. God keep me from being wrong about any of this, or else show me the way before it's too late.

Bora put away the diary. He was tired. Eventually, the sound of falling water obliterated all other sounds, echoing the priest's tedious talk of widows and virgins and of the harlot Remedios, who lived up the mountainside. Remedios. Shouldn't every man know a woman by that name? At one point he thought he heard a woman's voice whispering to him, "*Besame con tu lengua, aquí,*" but he was already asleep.

Fuentes came to wake him up. Judging by the lacklustre light coming through the window, the afternoon had worn off. "It's past seven, *teniente,* and there's news about the burial."

MURALLA DEL ROJO, SIERRA DE SAN MARTÍN

The place where the Reds had dug the grave lay beyond Castellar, almost an hour's climb away from either camp. During the storm, a torrent of rainwater had overrun the place and carved rambling furrows all around the grave, displacing rocks and uprooting bushes weakened by drought. Facing the valley, Bora could see the rain-washed roof of San Martín de la Sierra on its rocky spur, lost far below. The air smelled of dirt and broken twigs, and it was starting to rain again.

Fuentes put down a folded stretcher. "What a mess."

Bora turned. "It's a good thing," he said. "They won't be able to tell we tampered with the grave. Let's get on with it; we have half an hour of light left."

If his men had any doubts about moving a nameless body from one place to another, they didn't ask about it. Alfonso was a myopic mathematics student from Salamanca with an unimaginative mind; Fuentes simply didn't ask questions. One by one Alfonso removed the stones from the grave. In a short while the pile had been cleared and placed to one side with care. Below, the soil felt wet, but hadn't turned to mud like the surrounding ground. Fuentes dug systematically and placed each shovelful on a square piece of tarpaulin. Alfonso promptly covered the growing pile with the canvas sheet's hem to keep the loose soil from running off under the rain.

Kneeling over the grave, Bora gathered dirt with his cupped hands and placed it under the tarpaulin. His bare knees sank into the mud and met with bits of grit beneath. Before long, a winding sheet emerged from the grimy, sloshy soup. Fuentes joined Bora in digging and scooping by hand. Little by little, the full length of the bundled corpse appeared in the shallow pit. Fuentes pulled back, muddy hands spread across his knees. Alfonso stared.

Bora sensed the men were suddenly hesitant, and he wasn't sure himself that it didn't somehow amount to sacrilege. Still, Fuentes made a quick sign of the cross and clasped the corpse's feet. Bora reached under the dead man's torso; dirt forced its way under his nails as he found the hollow under his arms and lifted him. Together they raised the heavy load from its dirt bed and laid it on the stretcher.

Bora held his breath, using a penknife to cut the stitches in the cloth and expose the dead man's head. Alfonso looked away, and Fuentes simply waited for the officer to cover the man's face again.

"Now we have to fill the hole," Bora said.

They'd taken along bundles of wood to stack in the grave, and gathered pebbles to fill the hollow, packing them closely. Alfonso and Fuentes poured back the dirt from under the tarpaulin, stamped it down and re-stacked the stones above the barrow.

Alfonso was too short to help Fuentes with the stretcher, so Bora took his place. Slipping, cursing and rearranging the corpse's weight, they negotiated the steep climb and then the twisting track that led to Castellar. Darkness was coming fast. Tongues of fog licked the rock walls and sat in the hollows;

the width of the valley brimmed with it already. A drop in the temperature made the men's labour less grievous. On their way back, the only struggle was with their drenched clothes, and the gloom of the hour.

MAS DEL AIRE, SIERRA DE SAN MARTÍN

Walton buttoned his corduroy trousers, turning his back to the bed. Sharp pains travelled up and down his thighs and buttocks, and he couldn't understand why that should be. He said, "I don't understand. I hump Marypaz all night and it doesn't hurt. With you it always hurts."

Remedios crouched at the foot of the bed watching him, arms folded around her knees, dead-white and smooth. "I'm not Marypaz. I'm not like anyone you know."

He looked over at the knot of her small body. As always after they'd made love, melancholy was welling up from a deep place within, a darkness of mood that made him dislike himself for coming here. "You suck up my life." The words came out of him half-meant, half-believed.

Remedios smiled at him, not with him. Her amusement was silent and inward, and he'd never seen her laugh. She lay back so that her head hung down from the bed, and like a decapitated corpse she stretched, her sex showing red, the tips of her breasts like blood against the pallor of her skin. The fleshiness in the handful of fleece between her thighs caught his eye and he felt it like a stab in his belly, a need he couldn't satisfy now because his body was too tired. But he leaned over to take her ankles and part them, eager to see more.

"Some men need their lives sucked out of them." When she spoke, the fragility of her neck arching over the edge of the bed was apparent. He found resistance in her ankles, and

89

removed his hands. She lifted herself onto her elbows, pulling up her knees and opening them for him to see. "You only have to be careful if life hangs loose in you like a spiderweb."

Walton pulled back and stared at her. He stood up uneasily, suddenly anxious to leave and forget about Remedios until the next time.

When he walked out into the open, the air was cool and moist. High above the thorny bushes that grew in the rubble around her house, daylight would come soon. Stars sank into a milky washed-out sky, trembling in the endless space as if the storm had swept away most of them and these were the frightened survivors. The clouds had rolled back. There was a scent of mint, of plants torn and broken by rain.

The green odour reminded him of the forbidding winter's end back home, when the woods between Eden and Hardwick still harboured frosty puddles of melting snow. With his back to Remedios' doorway, he faced the wind-beaten plateau of weeds and pale rock, thrust like a wedge over the void below. He took a deep breath, feeling lonely. *Sucking up his life.* What did Remedios know? There were worse things than soreness after lovemaking. Regrets. Last night, after turning his back to her, he'd cowered in a cold sweat as if the dark were water, as if he were still climbing in the rain to her impossible mountain lair. Under the pinprick stars sinking and fading, Walton suspected what the truth was. The yellow wall of his dream – a forgotten memory? A sign of things to come? – was new and ominous, but the cold sweat was like in Guadalajara before he'd been wounded during the spring. Like in Soissons a generation ago, when he'd lain rigid in his foxhole at the bloody foot of Hill 205 for days and days, until he turned thin and yellow with fear. There was no denying it any more. Fear is fear is fear. *That* door was open again, and he'd walked straight into it at the brook yesterday noon.

Behind him, Remedios came naked to the doorstep, and locked him out.

SIERRA DE SAN MARTÍN, OVERLOOKING CASTELLAR

Not far from the canting trail Walton would soon follow to regain lower ground, Fuentes was holding a handkerchief to his nose.

"It begins at the sides of the belly," he mumbled, looking away from the body. "When it's as hot as it's been, flesh rots all the more quickly. We must bury him while the dirt is still moist."

Bora replaced his drawing pad and pencils in his canvas bag. "I'm done."

Daybreak found them halfway to Riscal, trudging along the barren ridge above Castellar. Set in its stony bowl, the handful of houses occupied a terraced, arid knoll. The high south rim of the bowl was what they'd have to climb back over in order to reach camp. To their right, spotted with broom and thorny shrubs, the soaring wedge of Mas del Aire crowned El Baluarte. The men were working in a gully, where a few bushes smelling of cedar protected them from view. In the gully, sheltered from the wind, loam had heaped over the years to form a long bed.

Alfonso had been digging a trench in the soil. "See if it's deep enough, will you?" he called to Fuentes. Bora came over to look as well. "One more foot," he said. "Get to the rock bottom if you can."

It didn't take long for Alfonso to strike stone. Fuentes joined him in the gully and widened the trench by hand.

Next to the bundled corpse, Bora waited, his face to the capricious wind that rose from Castellar. There had been bodies when they entered Bilbao and during the battle for Santander, but he'd never remained near them long enough to smell decay. He didn't like the experience of putrefaction now, and found the thought of it entirely different from any past intellectual musing over it. Sobering, that was the word. He glanced at the cuts and bruises on his hands, aware that the warlike rhetoric of family and army school talks, aseptic and firmly set in the pale frame of history, had no odour to compare to this.

Coming to take his end of the stretcher, Fuentes announced, "We're ready." He backed up into the gully, straining, while Bora carried his end. Together, they tilted the stretcher to let the body drop inside the trench, and began to push dirt over it from the sides. "Pack it down, Fuentes."

Afterwards, they strewed rocks and gravel up and down the gully, along with rain-torn branches and leaves.

"Looks like nothing ever happened here except yesterday's storm," Fuentes said approvingly.

Bora said nothing. Carrying the load up the mountain had reawakened the soreness in his shoulder. As for emotions, he couldn't identify clearly what he was feeling; perhaps it was just tiredness. While the men weren't looking, he'd torn a corner from his drawing pad, fashioned it into a small paper cross and slipped it inside the sheet. He felt foolish about it, but would have felt worse if he had done nothing.

EL PALO DE LA VIRGEN

Seated on the granite outcrop near the fountain, Brissot continued to trim his toenails even though Walton was calling out to him.

Walton knew that nonchalance was Brissot's way of disguising that he'd been worried. He made straight for the Frenchman, relieved to hear no mention of his leaving the camp drunk the night before. He squatted in the dirt and sipped cold coffee from the mug Brissot had next to him.

"Watch out, there might be pieces of toenail in it."

Greedily Walton kept drinking. The walk down from Mas del Aire had done him good. "I'm sure you noticed the airplane," he said.

"Yes. The same one that came buzzing around the other day. No markings. Circles the sierra and then leaves." Brissot lifted his eyes to the mountainside where the gun was emplaced. "We're ready for it if it tries anything."

"Where's everybody?"

"Off to gather kindling."

After yesterday's rain, the thin topsoil of the ledge had dried up and hardened again. Next, weeds would begin to grow in the pen, and the horses would have to fight ticks and fat flies. Walton returned his attention to Brissot. "Is Maetzu around?"

Brissot shrugged. "You know what *buscar sangre* means. Maetzu is out looking for blood." Reaching for his sandals, he knocked them against the granite to shake the dirt off them. "Right now he could be breaking into a Guardia Civil post to slit everyone's throat in it."

"Well, I was against letting ex-convicts into our group. I'll have a talk with him when he comes back."

Brissot put on his sandals without buckling them. "I expect the mule has brought his master's body to Campillo by now."

"Right." Walton tilted his head from side to side to relax, half-closing his eyes. "Mosko, what do you make of the story of the two shots?"

"I'd say the first was fired inside the car. That's why it sounded muffled to the *mulero*. The second was likely the killing shot."

"But Lorca was shot only once. We can't be sure the *mulero* was telling the truth. Maybe there weren't two shots fired, or even a car with people in it."

Brissot took a couple of shuffling steps around. "We found no evidence of shells near the body, although they shot him point-blank. That his shoes should be stolen ... that makes sense, as does the theft of any money or identification. But what about the music score – if, as you say, he had it on him? Who'd steal that?"

"Whoever took his things and fooled with the body, that's who."

"His *things*? So he was coming to stay. Why didn't you tell us?"

"There was no telling what his plans might be once he got here."

Stumbling in his unbuckled sandals, Brissot paced around, flustered. "Look, Felipe, the least you can do now is to exploit his death for propaganda purposes. The rumour that he died a year ago bought Lorca a few more months, but it's for real now: send word to Barcelona at once. From Barcelona the news will reach the foreign press, and we'll win a moral victory if nothing else."

"No."

"Why not? The Fascists would exploit his death if they were in your place!"

"No. We won't know what the party line is until we hear from our contacts in Teruel. I'm not going to circulate the news yet."

"You're dead wrong. Silence on our part would be a tactical error. I question your ability to decide —"

Walton didn't let him finish. He grabbed Brissot by the collar, shoving him backwards. "I'll talk about Lorca's death when I'm good and ready, Mosko. This isn't Russia, and I don't take orders from commissars. So don't you fucking bring up the murder again until I give you permission to do it!"

They angrily avoided each other until mid-morning, Walton busy making up with Marypaz and Brissot preparing his political lesson for the week.

Just before eleven, Maetzu's return brought them back together. The Basque was alone, brooding. "I just went off to be alone," he grumbled. "To work things out by myself without breaking Felipe's neck." When Walton grinned and stretched his hand out to him, Maetzu took it without returning the smile. "I also visited the grave," he added. "The storm had knocked some stones off overnight, so I put them back."

RISCAL AMARGO

There were two fine army horses tied outside the stable when Bora returned from the burial. Without waiting for instructions, Fuentes put the stretcher out of sight in the shed behind the house, and Alfonso tossed the shovel after it. Tomé, who was clearing up the last fragments from the mortar blast, was quick to respond to Bora's summons: "*A sus ordines, teniente.*"

"Whose mounts are those?"

"Two artillery captains'. They rode in ten minutes ago." Tomé ran his eyes over Bora's uniform. "I can run in and bring the *teniente* some clean clothes."

Bora turned his back to him. "It's not necessary."

On the ground floor, Aixala, Niceto and Paradís were peeling potatoes by the fireplace. In a rare show of discipline, they stood when Bora entered. Upstairs, the two captains were busy rummaging through maps and papers. They turned as Bora entered the room, slowly putting down the objects they'd been handling. Fussily taking in the sad state of his uniform, the shortest of the pair, a thirtyish, rotund man with the complexion of a Moor, pointed out Niceto's poetry book. "I hope you can explain why you've been indulging in the writings of a leftist author, *teniente.*"

Bora swallowed a spiteful comment. "To improve my Spanish, which I'm sure is a better explanation than the one you gentlemen will give me for digging through my papers." In fact, he was only pretending not to feel vulnerable. Thank God he'd taken along the canvas bag with his diary in it, and the evidence he'd found by the brook.

The chubby captain tossed the poetry book into a corner of the room. "What do you know about Red anti-aircraft guns on this mountain?"

"I reported on it. It consists of a mortar and a Lewis machine gun of the type used against planes in the Great War. Colonel Serrano has not ordered me to destroy it, and accordingly I have not." Bora walked around the desk to reclaim his space. "I'm First Lieutenant Douglas, Second Company, Third Legionary Regiment: may I ask who you captains are?"

The taller officer, whose striking grey eyes sat in a pock-marked face, said, "I'm Captain Mendez Roig, and this is Captain Olivares. We come from General Dávila Arrondo, and that should be enough for you." Neither of them would say more. Within minutes they were gone, bound, as Fuentes suggested, for the north-western heights of the Sierra de Albarracín.

"They've been here once before, *teniente.* The top brass sends them up and down the line, but I don't know that they ever accomplish anything. I bet they're SIFNE. The area is within their operating range."

SIFNE? Yes. There was no doubt in Bora's mind that the officers belonged to Spanish Intelligence, but he kept his counsel. "Has the water risen in the well?"

"No, sir. It's going to take more than one storm."

Together, they walked outside to the cleft in the rocky wall. Bora took a razor out of his pocket and started shaving under the rain-enriched trickle of mountain water. He stood with his feet in the mossy slush where moisture had found its way into the rock again. "You seem to know plenty about what goes on in the region, Fuentes."

"When a man serves in the Guardia Civil he'd better know his countryside. That's how we kept order in Spain the last hundred years."

"You should have told me about Tomé."

Wisps of air twisted the weathervane on the rooftop. Round and round it went, making a grating sound like an old hinge. Bora scraped off the stubble around his mouth in little downward strokes, eyeing Fuentes' shadow nearby. Soon he was rinsing the blade, his thumb and forefinger carefully running the flat of the flexible metal leaf under the trickle.

"I thought you knew, *teniente*."

Bora pocketed the razor. "It should have been obvious to you that I did not know."

15 July. Evening, at the post.

Tomorrow is the great Feast of the Carmel, *Virgo et Genitrix singulari titulo Carmeli*. Niceto knows I'm Catholic, and asked me for permission to attend mass at Castellar. I haven't answered him yet. I don't want to seem lax to the men, but the real choice is between knowing when they leave the post, and not being told that they do. I'd rather be told, and let them go. Fuentes has nothing but contempt for the lot of them.

The day remained cool, with a steady westerly that Fuentes calls *poniente*. The horizon is mirror-clear, though it will haze over as soon as the temperature rises again. There have been times today when I've distinctly heard the sound of church bells ringing God knows where. Teruel is much too far away from here; perhaps from Libros or Tramacastiel.

The rain has entirely cleansed the flat rock of Lieutenant Jover's blood. Fuentes says they took him to Teruel the same day he died and shipped him to his mother from there. I told him to use gasoline on my body, just in case. But I wonder if Fuentes even listens to what I say. He's been preaching about the risk I took facing the American alone, and I don't seem able to put into words how necessary it was for me to do something exciting for a change.

The American. I don't think he was a bit afraid, though it must have smarted that I took his gun. I was incredibly curious to hear him talk, but ran out of time. As it was, a couple of bullets whipped right over my head. During the race uphill in that deluge, I kept wondering what he thought of me, although the 'Man of Perfected Self-Mastery' doesn't depend on the judgement of others!

Speaking of judgement, I really don't believe any of mine shot the man on the mule track. Why would they not admit it (or even brag about it) if they had? On the other hand, why has Colonel Serrano hushed things up? I rather think he believes some here would recognize the body – which probably means the dead man was a political or military figure. Well, he's buried now, and the rain must have washed away his blood like Lieutenant Jover's.

The following morning, the brook ran deeper and was frothy with silt. Bora went down to bathe alone, very early. When he climbed back, he saw that Fuentes had been keeping watch from afar in the dull light before sunrise. "Fuentes," he said, "today I'm going to ride to Teruel. Where does Colonel Serrano live?"

Bora could tell that the sergeant had been just about to impart some good advice about going to the brook alone; the question caught him off guard. "He has a country house just out of town, on the way to Concud. It's called the Huerta de Santa Olalla, you can't miss it. Will you stay there overnight, *teniente?*"

"No, I'll be back before dark." Bora glanced at his watch, and then at the east. In the pallor of the sky, a coralline glow marked and set off a point on the horizon where light would soon burst out. Leaving now, he'd arrive in Teruel by nine.

"I could easily fetch a horse in Castellar and ride with you as far as Libros," Fuentes said.

"You could, but you won't." Bora knew he needed to change out of his well-worn colonials into full uniform in order to ride the blistering distance to Teruel, where he expected to meet Colonel Serrano. One step behind him, Fuentes began saying something else, and suddenly his insistence ruffled him. "Why don't you shut up, Fuentes? I'm not Jover."

Fuentes fell back, with an apologetic nod. "I'll saddle the *teniente*'s horse."

Bora waited outside the stable, breathing the bone-dry air deeply. High above, the tallest crags of the sierra were starting to look flushed against the white sky. Hawks circled and called to one another near the top. Fuentes led Pardo out, and placed the saddle blanket on his dappled back.

Bora glanced down from the mountain. "Fuentes," he said, "who is Remedios?"

"Remedios?" Peering at him from under the horse's belly while he secured the blanket, Fuentes ground his jaw before answering, "*Es una bruja.*"

Bora laughed. "What do you mean, a witch? Come, tell me: who is she?"

"Just as I told you, *teniente*. She lives way up the face of the sierra, at Mas del Aire. Even the goats have a hard time climbing that far." With a pull, Fuentes checked the blanket's buckle. "Mas del Aire is the right name for the place, too: air is what she must live on. You never see her in Castellar or around here. Never."

Bora ran his eyes up the rocky wall, bright pink now and verging on orange at the top. Forehead of the sierra, Mas del Aire grazed the sky. "Have you ever met her?"

"No." Fuentes adjusted the saddle on Pardo's back and buckled it. "Don't want to, either."

"Do men go to see her?"

Fuentes looked straight at him this time. Bora kept his eyes on the mountain, careful to sound non-committal. *I've got you this time, Fuentes. It's hard to tell with us northerners. Our faces don't give us away, and we know how to stay in control. You can't tell what's on my mind.*

"The American has gone to see her."

Bora returned his eyes to Fuentes. "How would you know?"

"Before you came, we were posted closer to Castellar. To reach her place the American had to cross a stretch in the open between the two camps. In the moonlight we could see him as plain as day."

"And you let him? You didn't shoot at him?"

"He was just going to get himself a lay, *teniente*. He's entitled to that like the rest of us. We shot at him, you can be sure of that. It happened twice during my watch, and we gave him a hell of fire when he went up, but on the way down, we let him pass. There's nothing else but Remedios' place up that way."

As the sun rose, the angle of ruddy light came down the Riscal like a curtain rippling against the rocky face. Bora let the colour wash over him, feeling warmth escape the earth as it lost moisture under his feet. The light and warmth might graze Fuentes and the horse and everything on the ledge, but they were meant to envelop and search *him*. He found unforeseen and troubling intimacy in the mountain this morning, and it was best to get away from Fuentes' stare. "Give Niceto a three-hour pass to go to Castellar for High Mass."

"High Mass, my foot!" Fuentes burst into unrehearsed deep laughter. "He's going to get himself a piece, not religion!"

"Well, whether he gets one or the other, I'm sure God will know the difference."

TERUEL, CAPITAL OF TERUEL PROVINCE

Just before nine, from a distance the Moorish towers of the churches of San Martín and El Salvador stood out like stubby masts over the outline of Teruel. After Bora entered the town from the south, however, he lost sight of them entirely in the narrow streets. He rode past massive public buildings – the council offices, the hospital – and then he had to ask a Guardia Civil officer for directions.

"That way. If you reach the church of San Pedro, you've gone too far."

Despite this, Bora rode twice past the address given to him by German intelligence in Saragossa because the sign on the house's front read FÀBRICA DE AZULEJOS VALERA Y PASTOR and no one had mentioned anything about a tile factory. He dismounted and tied up his horse nearby. The door was unmarked, unlocked. Through it, he entered a spacious office with no windows. The light was on, and the air smelled of new furniture. Samples of floor tiles, some hand-painted in watery green, lined the walls. A young woman with short brown hair sat at a desk, typing in the breeze of an electric fan. "May I help you?" she said in Spanish, without interrupting her work.

"I'm here to see Herr Cziffra."

She looked up, taking a brief inventory of Bora's appearance. "For what reason?"

"I have news to report to him."

The young woman pointed to a corridor at the back of the office. Her German, like her Spanish, was impeccable. "Second door on the right. Leave the door open as you go in."

Bora did as he was told. The back room had walls covered in egg-yellow wallpaper. The framed poster of a Hamburg Line ship hung opposite the door, next to a poster advertising Riquet Cocoa, the silhouette of a mammoth with immense curved tusks. There was no significant amount of paperwork anywhere. An ugly red vase sat in a niche to the left of the desk. The carpet was a faded imitation of a Persian prayer rug. The typing of the short-haired woman outside came in rapid spurts, punctuated by the bell at each return.

"Lieutenant 'Douglas', I take it?"

Bora turned in a smart military fashion. "At your orders."

"That you are." The Abwehr officer – Herr Cziffra, as Bora knew him – wore horn-rimmed glasses and his sandy hair parted in the middle. The flexing of the muscles in his jaw was evident on his hairless stony face when he spoke. Bora was reminded of teachers he had known, dogmatic and devoid of creativity, but the similarity might only be physical. "So, you're the young man without whom Germany had to manage in order to win Olympic gold. I was wondering what made you pull out at the last minute. Now I can see that Spain did."

Bora relaxed from attention. "Lieutenant Pollay did very well, and we won all the equestrian gold anyway."

"But you'd have made it under 15 points."

The crumpled linen suit contrasted absurdly with the starchy whiteness of Cziffra's shirt; Bora thought it a German attempt at looking unassuming. This address and the agent's name were the sole information he'd been given in Saragossa. What was expected of him was unclear.

"I understand you have news," Cziffra said.

Bora reported in detail on the finding of the body and all that had transpired since. From memory, he'd made sketches of the location of the grave and of the dead man's face before the second burial. He took them out of the canvas bag and handed them to Cziffra. "Tell me more," the Abwehr officer said placidly. While he listened, his eyes never left Bora. Only when Bora finished speaking did he glance at the drawings. "Of course, you know who he was."

"On the contrary, I have no idea."

"Serrano didn't tell you?"

"No."

Cziffra gave the drawings back. "A good likeness. It's Federico García Lorca."

Bora clumsily dropped the sheets he had in his hands. His own voice sounded strange to his ears, as if coming from somewhere else in the room. "The poet?"

"The poet. We assumed that's what had happened. He'd been gone two days."

Bora was unable to hide his surprise. "You knew!"

"Knew? I had arranged an escort for him." Cziffra shrugged. "Win a few, lose a few. Had Serrano cared to enlighten you, he'd have informed you that Lorca was involved with leftist propaganda. Especially the anarchists, as late as last April in Barcelona."

"But I thought he'd died last year in —"

"Granada? No. Well-placed rumours. It suited all parties concerned not to correct them."

Bora had no doubt that he looked stupid for not know-ing more, but there was no time to worry about details now. "And you provided an escort for someone who wrote enemy propaganda?"

"I had my reasons, and it was the safest of arrangements. But then again, people are killed all the time these days for much less than being a poet, a spy or a queer. Even you and I could be dead ten minutes from now." Cziffra's inexpressive face turned to Bora. "You seem confused."

"Forgive me, but I am."

"Confusion is an unforgivable failing in my view. *Unconfuse* yourself."

"I still don't see what Lorca was doing on the road at night, with or without your escort."

"The answer is getting out of Teruel, although he disap-peared the night before his appointment with the escort I secured. We know he befriended a former member of the International Brigades on your mountain. An American who calls himself Felipe, likely the same fellow you surprised by the brook. Of him, we only know that he was among the first to arrive in Spain – on the now infamous December '36 *Normandie* shipment – but parted ways with his colleagues at Albacete as early as January. He's to receive from us a false report on the defences around Teruel, since we have reason to believe that in a few weeks the Reds will attempt a major offensive north of here."

Bora thought of the captains rummaging through his papers. "Is SIFNE involved?"

"Not in *our* business. As for Felipe, he's a clever free-lancer who operates through couriers and will undoubtedly communicate the fabricated intelligence to his comrades in Valencia and Barcelona. All we can assume for the time being," Cziffra continued, "is that Lorca must have decided to leave Teruel before the appointed time, and met with trouble on the way."

Bora swallowed. "Is it possible that he drove himself? There was no car near the body."

"Correction: *you* found no car by the body. Whether or not there was a car, or even more than one car, is another matter."

Bora dropped the subject. He said, sheepishly, "I found these at the edge of the brook. They were underwater, and the ink has nearly washed off. They seem to be a musical score. Should I not have gathered them?"

Cziffra glanced at the sheets and returned them. "No matter. What else did you find?"

"This."

Nestled in the palm of Bora's hand, a brass shell attracted Cziffra's attention for a moment. "Were there more around?"

"I only found this one."

Cziffra brought the shell close to his face to examine it. "Bergmann-Bayard." He put the casing in the breast pocket of his linen suit. A hint of a smile crimped his lips. "Well, that's that. Anything else?"

"I found a pair of canvas shoes in the cane grove. I brought them along too."

"Let's have them." Cziffra examined the shoes quickly and tossed them into a wastebasket. "A naive attempt to make it appear as if those who killed him needed supplies. It's a botched-up job."

Facing him, Bora stared at the frayed carpet's design. He felt as if someone had struck him unawares and he couldn't work out the source of the pain. "I happened to read some of Lorca's works. I must admit, it seems out of character for the man to be a double agent."

"A double agent? That's your inference, although there are ways of nudging people into accepting uncharacteristic roles. All you need to know for now is that I had arranged for him to leave Teruel. Had you not run into his body, you wouldn't have been told that much." Cziffra wrote something in a log which he then slipped into the top drawer of his desk.

Bora watched him pace from his desk to the window, which looked onto a dismal inner courtyard. "Colonel Serrano seems interested in knowing whether our men committed the murder."

Coolly Cziffra turned from the window. "Has he given you a motive for his concern?"

"No. At first I thought it was because he believed the Reds had done it; now I'm not sure. Certainly, he appears to want to conceal the body or the death somehow. He might know more than he is choosing to share with me. He suspects I work for the Abwehr."

"Did he tell you that? Ha! He's a horse's ass."

"When I mentioned to him the state of Lorca's clothing, he also seemed to discount the issue of homosexuality, although it doesn't exactly seem to have been a secret."

"There are lots of queers in Spain. It's typical of intellectuals everywhere to be sexual deviants. Lorca was a self-indulgent pervert."

"Then why did you use him?"

Cziffra let the hint of a smile cross his face again. "One uses what is available, most promising and most unlikely. As for Serrano, there's no need for the old monarchist to know more than any of his colleagues. You'll refrain from sharing that we met, and report to Serrano as you have been doing. The only real change is that now you'll do some investigating for me. *I* am curious to know who killed Lorca."

"Herr Cziffra, my primary goal in Spain —"

Cziffra's jaw muscles tightened under his hairless skin. "Are you telling *me* what your primary goal in Spain is? Your goal is to develop the 'handmaiden of the Lord' response. All you have to say is 'yes'. And as in Mary's case, it will be done with you according to our word. It was you who showed an interest in intelligence work in army school." He walked to the middle of the room and pointed at the niche in the wall. "Tell me, what's the object in front of you?"

Bora found the question pointless. "A vase. A red vase."

"Are you sure? Try again."

"It's a vase, about eight inches tall, made of red ceramic."

Cziffra reached into the niche and turned the vase around. The back of it was painted blue. "Report only on the things you know, Lieutenant, not on the things you do not know. You majored in philosophy, did you not? Well, your purview in Spain is observational judgement. Leave the analysis and synthesis to us." Replacing the vase in its original position, Cziffra seemed satisfied with his cleverness. "Now be off to Serrano. On your way back from his house, stop by Teruel again. If there are any further instructions for you, you'll receive them within fifteen minutes of arriving at this address." A card materialized from Cziffra's pocket only long enough for Bora to read the words scribbled on it. "Take the drawings and papers along with you. Serrano can have them. The shoes and the spent shell will stay here."

Bora replaced the music score in his canvas bag. "Did Lorca have a code name?"

"He did. We called him 'Reiter'. *Jínete* in Spanish."

"'Horseman'. Why?"

Cziffra ignored the question. He reached into the second drawer of his desk. "You might need a camera," he said. "Here's a Leica. There's already film in it. Now report to Colonel Serrano's residence. He doesn't know yet – and do not tell him – that his son was executed by the Reds in Madrid two days ago."

HUERTA DE SANTA OLALLA, NEAR CONCUD

Concud lay less than five miles north-west of Teruel, in a dry undulating wilderness of reddish land. Midway between the two towns the Huerta de Santa Olalla formed a green island along the sun-baked lane. The olive groves across the road looked bleached in comparison. Bora found a shady spot to tie Pardo away from the sun, and before ringing the bell of the forbidding garden gate, he carefully dusted off his uniform and boots.

The first impression he had upon being introduced was that Señora Consuelo Costa y Serrano, Condesa de Almondral, had been beautiful once. The life-size Zuloaga portrait above the sofa showed her in traditional garb, black lace on black, unsmiling, with a view of her native Toledo in the background.

She said, "My husband will come down shortly, *teniente.* He has instructed me to receive you in the meantime. Please sit." She studied his manners closely, without indulgence. "He tells me you are Catholic. And you are my son Alejandro's age. I also have a daughter. She recently lost her husband of twenty weeks."

The thick walls and the greenery outside kept the house cool, the first cool interior Bora had sat in since coming to Spain. Señora Serrano's tall figure recalled an expensive wax candle wrapped in black crepe. He looked again at her portrait, wondering where beauty goes.

"At a Red Cross benefit three years ago in Barcelona I met Marina Ashworth-Douglas, married to a von Bora, once the German consul in Edinburgh. Are you related to her?"

"She's my grandmother."

"My husband was right in judging you of *casta pura.* Your hands give you away."

His hands. Bora slowly closed his right fist to hide the blisters on his palm from digging Lorca's grave. "Today we recognize German birthright as our only aristocracy."

"Nonsense. Virtue may be acquired, but noble blood is inherited. My children have it, as yours will." His children? Bora paid sudden attention. He never thought of having children of his own, of being anything but the next generation. It gave him a strange feeling to be reminded that he carried the ready-made potential of fatherhood within him. "Of course," Señora Serrano pointed out, "as Catholics we must be merciful to the lower classes, as Our Lord taught us."

Colonel Serrano's booted step accompanied his perfectly attired, austere image to the threshold. Bora stood at attention while the colonel paused to kiss his wife's hand. Next, Serrano invited his visitor to follow him into the study, beyond a glass-panelled door. "I was listening to a broadcast from Madrid. There is encouraging news. It appears the leftist factions are in disagreement as to what to do with their hostages, and all threatened reprisals are on hold."

Impassively, Bora carried the weight of Cziffra's unspeakable tidings as best he could. "I found and reburied the body, Colonel."

Stark against the white wall above an unlit fireplace, Moroccan textiles and hooked blades created exotic patterns, stains of colour. The pale greenness filtering through louvred shutters gave Serrano the look of a drowned saint. He took the sketches and music score Bora handed him and laid them on a massive carved table.

The faded score (Bora had found it in a manila folder held together by a rubber band) was penned on lightweight sheets. One of them fell to the floor while the colonel perused them. Bora bent to retrieve it, and as he did he heard the sound of paper being shredded. Standing by his desk, Serrano had torn the sketch of Lorca's face in half, and was now tearing it crosswise. Bora hesitated, not wanting to hand over the music. Serrano noticed and solicited the sheets with a wave of his fingers.

Just then, they heard women's voices in the parlour where Bora had first been received. Serrano took no notice until his wife opened the glass door, accompanied by a distraught younger woman. "*Perdóneme*, Jacinto. You need to hear this at once."

Bora motioned to leave, but Serrano indicated that he should stay. "Señora Cadena, what happened?" the colonel asked. As she was holding back, he gestured towards Bora. "One of my young officers, Don Martín. He is a safe listener." Coolly he gathered the paper fragments, walked to the fireplace and tossed them behind the screen. "How can I be of assistance?"

Don Martín? Bora understood why Serrano was playing on his first name to conceal his identity as a foreign volunteer. He kept alert and still.

"Speak up, my dear," Señora Serrano encouraged the young woman. "Tell the colonel what you told me, how your cousin left Teruel two days ago and you haven't heard from him since."

Bora's mouth went dry. He recognized Lorca's gypsy looks in the girl, the same large eyes and delicate hands. With an unobtrusive gesture, he returned the music score to his canvas bag.

The young woman began to cry. "I called on friends, acquaintances; I went to the Guardia Civil. No one knows. No one has seen him. I've just come from the bishop's palace: His Eminence suggested I ask for your help. Don Jacinto, for God's sake do what you can to find out where Federico is! Mother would have come to beg you, but she's in a terrible state."

"Are you sure he left Teruel?"

"He told us he'd spend the night at a friend's house, but it seems he wasn't even expected there."

Bora heard Serrano observe that there was no reason for premature worry. She could rest assured he would do everything within the bounds of his authority, and beyond. "I suggest that you return home," he was saying now. "Sit quietly there and wait until you hear news from your cousin. He is sure to call soon. Be confident and let me look into this at my own pace."

Señora Serrano embraced the young woman, gently leading her out of the study. "Let us leave the men alone to talk, my dear," she said. "Didn't I tell you the colonel would take charge? You must trust in God, as I do, and all will be well."

Afterwards, they sat in silence, the only audible sound a piece of torn paper rustling in the fireplace. Facing Bora, Serrano said, "These are the lessons you are given neither at the university nor at the army school. See that you benefit from what you just saw and heard."

Bora didn't care that Serrano would judge him to be lacking in confidence. Just now, he couldn't look the colonel in the face. He understood every pragmatic reason for profiting from what he had just heard and learning from it, but the untruth disgusted him. This unease at lying and hearing people lied to obviously demonstrated his lack of adjustment to active service.

EL PALO DE LA VIRGEN

The airplane was back. Little more than a dot, it came in from the east. Walton couldn't judge whether it had taken off from friendly or enemy territory. Even through the field glasses, it was an indeterminate single-winged silhouette – not a German dive-bomber, at any rate. From the doorstep, he watched it bank widely, disappear behind the sierra and return at an even higher altitude.

"Felipe, I've got to talk to you."

Hearing Rafael's voice, Walton was tempted to shout him down. Of all of them, he was the one he couldn't abide, a snivelling youngster who didn't know shit about life and shouldn't be here in the first place. "We already discussed it," he said, cutting him short, and lifted the field glasses to his face again.

"It's not the religious value of the thing, Felipe: it's the sentimental principle."

Aimlessly studying the mountainside, Walton refused to engage. "I understand it's the principle. What I don't understand is carrying around a superstitious trinket. I thought you left all that church crap behind."

"I did! It's just that my mother gave it to me."

Given that Rafael was bent on complaining, Walton decided to listen. "What of it?" He stepped indoors and from a wooden crate in the corner which smelled of oiled guns packed in straw, he lifted out one revolver, then another, weighing each in turn.

"It's made of silver, Felipe."

Walton put back the first revolver. "What do you expect me to do, ask the comrades here about your silver rosary? You probably lost it."

"How?" Rafael whined. "How could I have lost it if I wore it around my neck?"

Walton was satisfied with his choice of guns. He checked the cylinder for dirt, and one by one he slipped cartridges into its chambers. "And how could anyone steal it from around your neck?"

"I take it off at night. Look, all I want is for you to mention it to the others." Rafael lowered his eyes, rubbing the toe of his boot back and forth on the ground like a fidgety schoolboy. "Of course, I have my suspicions, but it's better if you do the asking."

"Sure, OK." Walton drove the revolver into his holster and walked out. The airplane was nowhere in sight. Brissot, however, was just returning from his rounds on the heights. "Hey, Mosko!" he called.

"Why, it's true," Brissot agreed a moment later. "For once he isn't just bellyaching. Things have been disappearing; witness your watch. My lighter's gone, though it was cheap metal and worth nothing."

Irritably Walton raked back a limp strand of hair from his forehead. "*Now* what do we do, search each other's bedding for keepsakes or go ask the whores in Castellar if any of us in this egalitarian army paid them in kind?"

Brissot acted suspiciously calm, preceding Walton to the privacy of the almond grove. "Excluding the two of us, Felipe, we can't discount Rafael, because he might be claiming a loss to remove suspicion from himself."

"That's just swell! We do nothing but sit on our asses, with the Fascists next door, and now we have to purge ourselves of thieves. What kind of a commissar are you anyway, keeping dirty little secrets to yourself?"

For a month Brissot had treasured his one pack of ready-made cigarettes, and now he handed Walton the last one. "If I felt that you really wanted to hear the truth, I could report more than idle gossip about stolen rosaries."

"Out with it." Walton brought the cigarette to his mouth and lit it. "What do you know?"

Brissot signalled to wait. He walked to the orchard wall and looked over it right and left, then came back with his physician's stoop. "On the night Lorca was killed, Maetzu left camp after his watch. I was next, and thought at first he was just looking for a place to piss. In fact, he headed for the valley. You told me not to harass the men with useless discipline, so after making sure that everyone else was in place I went back to my watch."

Walton licked his lips. A drop of sweat hung from his nose like a tear, but he didn't bother to wipe it off. "What are you telling me?"

"That Maetzu was gone for at least three hours. I'm not sure what I'm telling you. It troubles me, that's all. Ever since Maetzu killed the *mulero* it's been on my mind."

The drop of sweat fell from Walton's nose. "So you wanted to trouble me, too."

3

I say your name,
In this dark night,
And your name sounds to me
Farther than ever.
Farther away than all the stars
And sadder than the tame rain.

FEDERICO GARCÍA LORCA,
"IF MY HANDS COULD PLUCK"

HUERTA DE SANTA OLALLA, NEAR CONCUD

The olive grove around the *huerta* cast a tenuous grey shade across the grass. When Bora looked back at the house from outside the gate, the dark lustrous green of the laurel trees peering over the high wall renewed his impression of an enclosed, exclusive Eden compared to the dry light of the road. Stretched over mild undulations and billowy hills, the landscape ahead reminded him of the windswept Moroccan *bled*: scented argan oil, the darkness of a doorway, carpets of morning shadows under the feet of marching men. He wondered if Africa and Spain would come back to him at the end of his life, splinters of images and smells, whether he'd regret or feel nostalgia for them. This or that shape, a shifting leaf that let the sun through, the old Arab in a forgotten marketplace saying, "*Mezian, mezian,*" to extol the value of his trinkets. Women from the Moroccan south, wrists stained blue with the dye of their robes, sitting wide-kneed. Bora turned to Pardo and waved the flies away from him before mounting.

"May I speak to you, Don Martín?"

Bora stopped, his left foot in the stirrup and his hand on the saddle. Luisa Cadena had been waiting around the corner of the garden wall and was approaching him. Of course, she'd be able to tell he wasn't Spanish once she heard him speak. It was unavoidable, and he braced himself for it.

"Don Martín, I told the cab driver to wait because I needed to ask a question I couldn't ask in front of Colonel Serrano." She stood before him as women often did in this country, arms folded across her chest in a sexually protective stance. "My husband was arrested in Alfambra the same night my cousin Federico disappeared. Has Colonel Serrano told you anything about him? I beg you to tell me if you know. I can't stand being frightened for both of them!"

She was about to cry again but kept herself under control, perhaps fearful that he'd grow annoyed. Bora glanced through the garden gate at the patio where Serrano's ornate door was closed against the heat of the day. "The colonel has told me nothing," he replied. "*Pero lo siento.*"

It was an acceptable formula of sympathy. She didn't seem to notice his accent, nor that he was relieved at not having to lie to her. "Here is our phone number. If you have news, call any time, day or night. Any time. The colonel is a busy man. Tell me you'll call us if he can't. Please."

Without saying yes or no, Bora took the folded piece of paper she handed him. "What time did your cousin leave the house?" he asked, leading Pardo by the bridle towards the olive grove. She followed him there with a furtive, disquieted glance at the cab parked a few feet away. The driver seemed to be dozing, cap lowered over his eyes. "At about eight in the evening, Don Martín. My husband was still out, we hadn't even started supper. The children were already in bed, so it must have been just after eight."

Bora looked away from the cab, at the bleak, wavy horizon, and then at Luisa Cadena's face. Her pallor made the melancholy depth of her eyes appear sunken in her skull, and despite her youth there were sorrowful lines at the sides of her mouth. He said, "Did your cousin tell you when he expected to be back?"

"We didn't ask. Sometimes he spent the night out, as bachelors do." The way she said it, a little defensively, made him wonder if she wanted him to believe that Lorca had women. "We expected him to show up sometime in the morning, or for lunch. Federico often read his work in private homes, and this month he'd started revising *El Jínete Milagroso* with the intention of making it into a trilogy. His next play is to be called *La Casida de la Muerte Olvidada.*" Her voice grew dim, unsteady. "The day he left he asked me to sew him a puppet of 'The Forgotten Death' to use in the prologue. I thought ... I thought he'd surely be at a friend's house. In the morning we heard that Antonio had been arrested, and now I don't know what's happened to either of them."

Bora let her weep, because she needed to. But he was embarrassed by her reaction and stepped away. This was his big opportunity, one which not even the Abwehr could have planned so well. To avoid showing his eagerness, he waited at the edge of the olive grove for her to stop crying. All around, in the merciless heat of midday, the haze created trembling double images of the slanting horizon – fictitious pools of water and phantom hills in the air. False perspectives, Bora thought, matched everything else in this matter.

"I wonder if I could come and see you about your cousin sometime," he cautiously asked.

"Will you have news of my husband?"

"I don't know."

"But will you try to find out about my husband? His name is Antonio Cadena, he was mayor of Teruel twice. Will you ask about him?"

"If I can."

"We live on Calle Temprado, across from the nuns." Luisa Cadena pressed a handkerchief to her eyes: stoically, like Bora's mother had in April after he'd told her that he was leaving again. "You must forgive me for weeping. I shouldn't be weeping but trust in God, because God will take care of both Federico and Antonio. When will you come?"

"I can't say. I'm not even sure that I'll have any information. I'll try."

EL PALO DE LA VIRGEN

By the orchard wall, Valentin stood up and waved. "Felipe!" he shouted. "There's people coming up!"

Walton had been expecting couriers from Barcelona and quickly reached the ledge, from where he could see three men trudging up the sweltering ascent. The two men in front wore black berets like Brissot. *Boinas negras*, Walton thought. From afar, you might mistake them for Italian Fascists. Rifles hung from their shoulders. The third man, who was dressed in a collarless shirt and a wide-brimmed hat, he couldn't identify.

The black berets drew closer, bobbing along the granite crags with the straw hat trailing several feet behind. One of the couriers waved. "*Salud!*"

Walton waited until the three drew closer to decide whether he'd take out the gun or not. After he recognized both couriers he relaxed. "*Salud*, Almagro." Marypaz had joined him to watch, and although her presence annoyed him, he didn't send her away.

The men negotiated the last hard footings of the climb. "Hello, Felipe. We brought somebody to meet you."

The stranger was thirtyish, lean-jawed. He wore city shoes and a pair of expensive trousers; the shirtsleeves rolled up on his forearms showed an abundance of dark body hair against his pale flesh. When Almagro was standing before him, Walton grabbed him by the wrist. "Who's *he*?"

"Take it easy, Felipe. He's harmless."

The stranger remained awkwardly to one side. As no one made an effort to acknowledge him, he extended his right hand to Walton. "My name is Paco Soler. I'm from Teruel."

Walton took the hand impulsively. You could tell a man's character from a handshake, at least in America. Soler's hand was sweaty but firm; Walton couldn't glean much else from it other than that the weather was hot.

"Let me explain, Felipe." Almagro took him aside while the other courier, Marroquí, threw an admiring look at Marypaz. "He was roaming around when the truck dropped us at the foot of the mountain, so we decided to bring him in." Almagro grinned. He had a salesman's smile, and Walton disliked him for it. "Says he's looking for a friend of his. A poet, he says. See what you can make of him." Almagro lowered his voice to a whisper, widening his grin as he said it. "*Creo que es un maricón.* Limp as a noodle. Anyhow, we brought him along with us."

Soler had not moved from his place when Walton rejoined him. Blotting his forehead with a blue handkerchief, he seemed tired from the climb, but tried to smile. "I wasn't really heading up here," he began, "but your friends thought I should follow them. You might be able to help me. A friend of mine may have come this way, perhaps to visit San Martín de la Sierra. It's a chapel somewhere around here." When Soler crushed the handkerchief in his fists, Walton noticed how white and hairy they were. "He's been gone longer than I thought. I'm worried. I'd like to go to San Martín, so I'd be grateful if you told me the way from here."

Through the brim of his straw hat, the sun threw diminutive pocks of light onto Soler's colourless face. Walton knew of him. When they'd last met in Valdecebro, Lorca had mentioned him. Still, Walton was leery. "What reason did your friend have to go to San Martín?"

"He didn't say. We're working on a new play, and he's been researching the peasant art of the region. I understand there's an old fresco in the chapel, and perhaps that's what Federico wanted to see." Soler clumsily replaced the handkerchief in the back pocket of his well-cut trousers. "He's been gone since Monday night. As I said, I'm worried, and so is his family."

"This is not exactly peaceful territory. How did you get here, and why did you come alone?"

"I got a lift to Libros, and then started to walk: I had to come alone. My friend is the poet García Lorca. He's had trouble with the authorities before. He … was not safe in Teruel."

TERUEL

Bora rode back to Teruel from the north-west, up the ramp along the brooding ramparts of the twin-steepled seminary, under the squat crusader arch of the Andaquilla Gate. There the flagstoned climb grew steeper, and he had to direct Pardo sideways so that he wouldn't lose his footing. A madness of swallows clamoured overhead, and the streets were empty.

The address given him by Cziffra was on Calle Santiago. Arching above the alley that led in from the gate, the Mudejar tower of Our Saviour stood with its intricate brickwork, a lattice of jutting false arches inset with green ceramic discs. Bora rode past it and took a right turn. Pardo's neck was running with sweat and he tried to keep to the shade, but there was no shade, only swallows, and the sun cutting straight down. Yet behind these lowered blinds, carved doors and window grids someone here knew about Lorca and Luisa's husband. The sleepiness of the noon hour was as deceptive as the false horizons near Concud.

The address corresponded to a dingy barbershop with a curtain of linked tin chains hanging across the open doorway. However unlikely, it must be the place, because Bora didn't know of any Spanish business that ran during holidays and the lunch hour. He tied Pardo in the shade of an overhang, slung the canvas bag across his shoulder and parted the chains to walk in. An odd mixture of odours – hair tonic and fried garlic – met him, along with the blink of an electric bulb slowly materializing out of the dimness. A barber's chair and mirror emerged next, and on the end wall was an ugly set of orange drapes, past which a clatter of dishes was audible. The barber himself stepped out from behind the orange cloth. "*Sí?*"

Aside from a full head of wavy bluish hair, Bora could have sworn he was facing Francisco Franco, pudgy, smiling and shifty-eyed. He advanced no theory as to whether this was his contact, or if someone else would bring him instructions in the next fifteen minutes. The vase might be a completely different colour on the other side. Bora glanced at his watch and inquired about a haircut.

The barber took a puzzled look at Bora's army crop. "A cut? Forgive me, but a cut to what? You don't need a cut."

"Trim back and sides, then."

Seeing that Bora gave no sign of parting with the canvas

bag, the barber invited him to sit in the only chair. Bora laid the bag in his lap.

"How much shorter?"

"Shorter."

"*Más corto de esto*, and I'll have to shave it!"

"Then shave it."

Just as the barber arranged a cloth over his shoulders, the tin chains across the door opened, letting in light and flies. Bora glanced over expectantly.

A tanned, fleshy man in a wrinkled coat and tie was looking in from the street. His hooded, round eyes drifted from the barber to Bora and back again. "How long before you're free?" he asked the barber, and without waiting for an answer he added, "I'll be back later," and was gone. If he was the messenger, it was hardly a message. With an ear on the rattle of dishes coming from beyond the orange curtains, Bora settled in the chair.

Choosing from several pairs of scissors, the barber smiled at his reflection in the mirror. "We finally had some good rain, didn't we?" More trivialities about the weather followed, even though Bora had indicated his disinterest early on by not answering the initial question.

Ahead of him, the mirror was bolted to the wall. Spidery stains dulled it at the corners, and on the right side two hand-tinted postcards sat between the wall and the mirror's frameless edge. On one of them Bora recognized the square minaret of the great mosque in Marrakesh, limned against an improbable alizarin sky. The other was a blue-grey aerial view of St Peter's Square. The sight of the Roman cathedral unexpectedly moved him. *As I wrote in my diary last night*, he thought, *this is the reason I'm here. All ideologies aside, this is what Spain is – intramurum Christianitatis, a bulwark of Christendom for so many: the anti-Bolsheviks and the monarchists, the Italians spoiling for a fight after Libya, and us, young Germans carrying the shame of a lost war we took no part in. I still find it hard to comprehend how neatly this civil war serves my desire to redeem Germany, serve my country and allows me to break at least some rules. Damn, I never knew before how free you are in the face of death. I wish Colonel Serrano would ask me again why I am really here.* It all sounded self-conscious in the face of Cziffra's contempt about his mission in Spain.

The barber had been talking over the sound of the scissors snipping and sliding along the teeth of his comb when a Spanish army captain walked in, followed by a stout man in shirtsleeves. Bora paid close attention this time. The officer was one of the two artillery captains who had come "from General Dávila Arrondo", the tall, pockmarked man who'd given his name as Mendez Roig. Despite the heat, he was faultlessly attired, down to his kid gloves and the spruce red tassel on his side cap. As for the stout man, he was sweating buckets despite the fluttering motion of a small paper fan. Despite the fact that they'd walked in together, it was soon obvious to Bora that they had nothing to do with each other.

The barber greeted them, "*Señor capitán;* Don Millares."

"I didn't expect you to be open today," Roig remarked, taking a folded newspaper from under his arm. Exchanging a nod of acknowledgement with Bora, he went to sit in a varnished chair against the side wall, where he faced the mirror and, indirectly, Bora himself.

There is my contact. Roig removed his gloves and cap. Fair, thin-nosed, with nostrils that seemed to open only enough to grant the passage of air, he had an intelligent, intellectual mien. Bora thought that his mouth, downturned and giving him a slightly bitter expression, made him seem older than he was – thirty or so, in his judgement. He opened the newspaper and ostensibly began to read.

Millares had meanwhile sprawled in the armchair closest to the door. "God help us," he moaned. "How hot it is."

Bora ignored him. Keeping Cziffra's bicolour vase in mind, he surmised from Roig's dustless boots and lack of spurs that he was quartered in town, probably at the Comandancia Militar. Roig glanced up at Bora over the edge of his newspaper and looked away again, perhaps aware the German had been watching him. *What is he going to say, and when?*

"Lower your head, please," the barber told him, razor in hand.

"Have you heard the latest?" Millares addressed the room from his armchair, flapping his fan. "They say that the Bank of France will not return the gold treasury to the Azaña ministry, because most Spaniards live in nationalist areas."

"If only that was true," Roig commented.

"They also say that General Franco may receive supreme military honours, of the kind only reserved for kings and such."

Bora listened to the political gossip, alert for anything relevant to him. Roig didn't participate in the conversation, so it was largely Millares' monologue, occasionally interrupted by the barber's emphatic yes or no. Then Roig put down the newspaper and looked at Bora in the mirror. A cool, probing, judging look. Singularly direct, it discriminated and evaluated but was neither friendly nor unfriendly. It promised nothing. Bora returned the stare at first, but when no exchange followed, he looked away. *Maybe he's keeping quiet because of the fat man. Perhaps he'll leave and wait for me outside.*

"What else do they say, Don Millares?" the barber asked, starting to shave around Bora's ears.

The stout man rolled his eyes. "Not much. Locally, I hear that Antonio Cadena left for Alfambra four days ago and hasn't returned."

With a jerk, the barber pulled back the razor from Bora's head. "Careful! If you move like that I'll take a piece of your ear off!"

Bora could have kicked himself for reacting. Roig's grey eyes rested on him for a moment, no more. Millares only repeated, "How hot it is", and gave his useless fan a rest. The barber started shaving Bora's temples. On his lap, around the chair, a dust-like residue of shaven dark hair wafted down. Moments later, Millares was walking heavily across the room and past the orange curtains, where he began in his slow voice to discuss with someone the right way to serve garlic soup.

Roig simply glanced at his watch. "It's getting late," he said. Folding the newspaper under his arm again, he stiffly left his chair. "I'll come back tomorrow." He walked outside. A tinkle of flimsy tin chains followed. More flies entered the shop.

Bora checked the time. *It's been seventeen minutes. He's got tired of waiting, or thinks I'm not his contact because I didn't make myself known.* Forgetting he had the canvas bag in his lap, he surged from the barber's chair, freeing his neck and shoulders from the cloth. He shoved money into the barber's hand. "Keep the change." Beyond the swinging metal chains, he made out Roig's silhouette against the brightness of the street. As he watched, a small Fiat pulled up and the officer climbed into it. Suddenly there was no point in rushing out of the shop. Disappointed, Bora slung the canvas bag across his shoulder. Perhaps there was no message.

"May I?" the barber said, and standing on tiptoes finished brushing hair off his neck. Bora let him. Behind the curtains, Millares was still jabbering about soup. Flies had settled on the minaret and St Peter's alike.

Bora thought he might as well try to get *some* answers, at least. "Who is this Cadena they talk about?" he asked.

The barber started sweeping Bora's hair from the floor. "He was city mayor until three years ago, and he teaches at the school now. Married an Andalusian girl. They just had a second child. It'd be too bad if something happened to him. But that's life, isn't it?"

There was nothing judgemental in his words. If anything, there was a prudent lack of opinion. Still, the barber's Spanish fatalism came across so clearly that Bora felt like it was a warning of personal danger, as if he'd walked to the brink of something without knowing and were being reminded of the risks of falling off. "Why, what *should* have happened to him?"

Leaning on the broom, the barber fixed his small, beady eyes on Bora's dusty uniform. "God knows." When the last of the clippings had been swept into a corner, he added pleasantly, "You wouldn't by any chance need supplies? I don't know where you quarter, and I'm not asking, mind you. But should you need supplies, my wife runs the general store next door. She can open up for you."

The mention of supplies distracted Bora from his foreboding. He drew back from the brink, and life was trite again. He'd actually drawn up a list. "I do need toothpaste and some other things," he said.

The barber stuck his head between the orange drapes. "Emilia, stop talking to Don Millares ... there's business to take care of!"

EL PALO DE LA VIRGEN

Soler removed his straw hat before accepting a shot of whisky and water. He swallowed his drink straight away, while Walton only rinsed his mouth with his. Brissot sat back from the table, staring at the flat tortoiseshell case from which Soler had just taken out cigarettes. Walton accepted a smoke, but Brissot said he preferred his pipe.

Soft-spoken, with a cleft chin, Soler looked younger than his thinning hair suggested.

"The other night," he said, "Federico came by at about 8.15 or 8.20. I was speechless when I heard he was planning to travel to the sierra, but when working on a new play he always becomes obsessed with details. Otherwise, he never wanders off any further than his cousin's house or the *huerta* of his old music teacher. They're the only places where he feels safe."

Walton had heard about the music teacher from Lorca, but gave nothing away. "How long did your friend stay at your house?" he asked.

"Just over an hour. I wanted him to spend the night, it was safer than walking the streets, even in a town as small as Teruel. He has enemies there." Under Walton's scrutiny, Soler looked for a place to snuff his cigarette. When Brissot pointed to the floor, he smothered the butt with the sole of his shoe. "Not only political enemies," he specified. "People envious of his success, moral hypocrites from the upper classes. Federico doesn't talk about it, but I worry for him."

Brissot puffed on his pipe, and Walton had the impression that he was wondering when the news of Lorca's death would be shared. "If you're getting bored," he told him in English, "you can wait outside." Brissot took the pipe out of his mouth and stayed. Seeing Soler's eyes wander uneasily to the door, where Maetzu briefly appeared with a marksman's rifle in the crook of his arm, Walton resumed his questioning. "What happened next?"

Soler looked away from the door. "I assumed that he'd returned to his relatives'. It'd be unthinkable for him to head out of Teruel at that hour. There are checkpoints on the major roads, and even if you could manage to slip past them … Well, how would he reach the sierra? He had no hiking gear with him, just a portfolio of his papers." Walton glanced at Brissot, and Brissot at Soler. Soler took out the blue handkerchief and wiped his neck through the open collar of his shirt. "A day later, his cousin Luisa Cadena phoned to ask if I knew where Federico was. I inquired at his teacher's *huerta*, since he owns no telephone, but he hadn't seen him either. Supposing he'd found his way into the mountains after all, I waited two more days to hear from him." Soler let his shoulders slump, avoiding everyone's eyes. "Luisa thinks he's been arrested, but *I* know he's dead."

Again Brissot exchanged a glance with Walton, who then walked over to the door and leaned on the jamb in a watchful attitude. "What makes you think so?"

Soler wouldn't raise his eyes. "I don't *think* so. I *know*. For three days I've struggled with the godawful certainty that he's been killed." Steadily he planted his hands on the table, palms flat on the surface. The hairiness of his wrists drew a fine dark tangle against the weave of his cuffs. "He never spoke about any of you," he continued, "and I don't presume to inquire. These are difficult times, people make complicated choices. I won't even ask if he planned to meet you at any point on his errand. All I wish to hear from you is whether he's dead or alive. Surely, as anti-Fascists, you won't withhold the information if you have any to give."

Walton sucked all he could out of the cigarette and dropped it before it burned his lips. Shoulders against the door frame, he eyed the lilting dance of flies over the table. The sound of Marypaz's laughter came from outside, where she'd gone to sit with the couriers by the fountain. "Unfortunately we have no information about Señor Lorca to give you or the family." Walton used his shoulders to push himself away from the doorway as Brissot turned towards him. "We'll accompany you to San Martín if you think it might be useful. If not, one of us will escort you back after dark."

Soler straightened up. He nodded – Walton couldn't tell to which of the two proposals. His only overt sign of emotion was the way his right hand contracted around the cigarette case. Replacing it in his shirt pocket, he mumbled, "I would like to go to San Martín."

EL CABEZO BLANCO, OFF THE TERUEL–VILLASPESA ROAD

Bora had left the highway over a mile behind. He had a good sense of direction, an affinity for landmarks, shapes and distances freed him from having to check his map. The road he travelled rose moderately through the countryside, edged on the right by a continuous wall of stacked stones. On top of the wall, flat stones sat vertically, leaning on one another at an angle. Beyond, saffron fields and fallow land lay higher than the road, exposing a blaze of poppies here and there. The rain had brought about a burst of plant life. Pardo could smell the green odour from the fields, and though Bora had fed him in Teruel, he showed a stubborn tendency to graze. It was now half past two in the afternoon, and frenzied cicadas lent a hoarse voice to the land. Bora clicked his tongue, tightening his knees to keep the horse going. "Come on, Pardo, it's too hot to stop."

Ever since leaving Teruel he'd been thinking of Lorca, who had died, and of Serrano, who wouldn't admit that he'd died and who was ignoring his own son's death. There was some morbid justice in it, but no gratification. Bora kept his eyes on the land. No houses, no people in sight anywhere.

Ahead of him, a ghostly pond shivered in every dip and rise of the dirt road, unreachable. Farther out, where the horizon flattened after a climb, the road was a white ribbon cut short. "Pardo, move." Borderless splashes of brilliant red widened beyond the wall and merged into uninterrupted ruddiness. Soon the wall resembled a spotted dam set against a bloody surge. The fields hadn't seemed so red early in the morning, or so lonely. Just before dismissing him, Cziffra had told him, "Owing to your stepfather's high military rank, it's been impossible to keep the true nature of your assignment from him. He wired you a message."

"May I see it?"

"You don't need to see it. All it says is, 'Do well.'"

Do well. Of course he'd do well. He had been raised to do well. The stone walls broke and started up again. A haemorrhage of poppies. Bora reached inside his saddlebag, where he'd placed the supplies bought from the barber's wife, and pulled out a tin of mints. They tasted chalky but relieved the thirst somewhat.

Just beyond the top of the rise, he expected to see a solitary oak tree at the juncture of two walls. He remembered from his morning ride how past the climb the road straightened for a long stretch, followed by a curve rising smoothly to the left and soon branching like a tuning fork. A small post of the Guardia Civil sat in the eye of the bend a few miles off, seemingly lost in the wilderness although maps showed it to be halfway between the hamlets of Cunia and Cascante del Rio. "Come *on*, Pardo. What's with you? Move."

Again Bora clicked his tongue, and when the horse did not respond, he gave a light touch of the spurs. Pardo bucked and shied, holding back wide-eyed. One ear bent nervously, and then alarm turned to fright, both ears pulling back against the long animal skull.

"*Qué pasa*, Pardo?"

Like whiplash in front of his face, rifle shots came in quick succession, one-two-three, from two different angles. The horse reared up and would have thrown him had Bora not left the saddle. His boots struck the ground hard, as if the earth were flying at him. Pardo sprinted off and was gone.

Dust rose, and at once the wall was a race of stones askew. Dust, wall. He ran. Shots barely missed him. Stones askew. Grass. Bora vaulted over the wall, throwing his weight forward. Bullets struck stone and rang back or lodged in the cracks. He smelled the rank mash of poppies under his elbow while he unlatched the holster.

Across the road there were other walls, intersecting at odd angles, parting the countryside from here to Cascante del Rio; they protected those who had shot at him. Bora got his heartbeat under control enough to reason that he was facing at least two attackers, stationed right and left at ten or fifteen paces apart. They could safely steal away and cross over unseen, and then it'd be impossible for him to defend himself. Edging the field some thirty paces behind him, a third wall ran perpendicular to the one behind which he crouched now. From there, anyone aiming in his direction could fire on his back from a forty-five-degree angle.

Pardo was gone. Bora thought of crawling in the direction he'd been riding, but the stonework just ahead was dilapidated and he'd have to run several feet in the open before reaching cover again. Still, he began to creep that way, knees and elbows dragging in the dry grass. A turmoil of brown crickets accompanied his motions. And so did every stain and grainy patch of lichen on the wall, each threadlike delicate stalk and trembling insect antenna, the scent of leaves and stems trod upon: all followed him and mapped his crawl to the breach in the stonework. He'd nearly reached the place where he'd have to make a run for it when a shot came from a distant vantage point across the way, on the curve ahead. Bora felt it miss his jaw by a hair, and sank back.

Without lifting his head, cautiously he removed a stone from the top of the wall to look. A bullet smashed at once through the narrow gap. Bora grew so outraged, he rose to his knees and fired twice. Arm stretched forward, gripping the hefty American pistol, he fired twice at the wall across the street, doing nothing more than chipping the stone. A crossfire ensued, several angry shots that forced him to crouch and turn back. Someone reached the perpendicular third wall behind him and began aiming from there. A bullet fell short of him and embedded itself three feet away, with a thud that lifted a spurt of dust. Promptly Bora dropped face down into the grass. He could taste crackling loam under his teeth, and what remained of the chalky mint. *For Christ's sake*, he thought. *What's the name of this place? Shouldn't I know the name of this place?* He felt futile anger and shame at being trapped in a place he didn't know the name of. And with it, hard and clear as glass, the most absolute perception that he was about to die. It would happen here and now, and there were countless things he should and shouldn't have done and said in his life, like not taking communion or bedding the girls in Bilbao or refusing to turn around to look at his mother at the train station, or not telling Dikta that he hoped she loved him. *O good God, I'm heartily sorry …*

From where he lay on his stomach, thirty paces across the turfy, uneven field, the third wall ran in a straight line. Bora scanned its toothed ridge against the blazing sky. Behind it, the marksman waited for the right moment to shoot again, and could not possibly miss this time. *Now the man of valour will resist fear with all he has. And though he may be afraid even of things not above human strength, he'll face them as he should ...* What did Aristotle have to do with any of this? Bora kept his torso, head and legs dead still, all the while trying to move his right arm slowly up his side to bring his own gun in line with the new target. From his forced ground-level perspective, a scarlet cluster of poppies framed the centre of the third wall. If he focused his eyes on the stonework, the flowers blurred into red stains. *He'll face them as he should and as it is right he should. Because it is proper, and for the sake of honour ...*

For the longest time Bora felt like his eyes focusing and unfocusing were the only parts of him that were moving. But all along, so slowly as to be hardly a motion at all, his right arm was bending closer to his side, trailing in the grass so as not to create a visible angle. His wrist trembled with the effort of holding the Browning sideways, low but not in contact with the dirt. A cricket jumped on his hand, then off it. Slow, slow. *Because it is proper, and for the sake of honour ...*

The men across the road were holding their fire. The marksman, Bora knew, was debating whether to stand up and aim a last shot at his motionless body. His hands, face, every part of him was bathed in mucky sweat. Bora was afraid of losing his grip on the pistol when he began rotating his wrist to aim. He passed his thumb over the rear sight to assure himself it was free of dirt. Ants crawled over him, labouring on his sweaty skin.

Across the road men's voices called to each other. Brief, harsh words, distorted by his tension; Bora couldn't make them out. They were like sounds in a dream.

Then it came to him in a flash that the voices were drawing closer, that the men were crossing the street and would reach the wall right at the point where he lay, look over it where he was helplessly lying and empty their rifles into the back of his head. Revulsion rose into his throat like vomit. He'd die, there was no preventing it. He'd be shot and die. He was about to die. His wrist trembled hard with the weight of steel. *And for the sake of honour ...*

The marksman behind the third wall stood up. Past the red stains of the field, in a split second he was fully visible from the thighs up, aiming. Bora's hands met with a jolt around the Browning and fired. The standing figure swayed, arms open wide – the rifle was like a third upper limb flung off – and fell forward. Stones slid, tumbled with him. Frantic for time, in a storm of insects Bora jumped to his feet, wheeled his torso around and kept firing.

... And for the sake of honour. For such is the end of virtue.

One man was already so close, Bora's shots felled him in a spray of blood. His companion dived back into cover across the road. Farther off, a third attacker fired and missed. But there were more coming. Out of his peripheral vision, Bora saw three men riding on horseback around the curve, aiming and shooting as they did so. He had never thought stoicism would feel numb. All he knew was that he didn't want to sink back and wait to be gunned down like a rabbit, with ants crawling over him. He pushed another magazine in and remained on his feet, ready to answer the horsemen's fire.

But the horsemen did not shoot at him. Riding with the ease of gypsies on their shiny bays, they were speeding at a gallop in the direction of the wall across the road. Their strange black leather hats and green uniforms made them look like puppet soldiers, and Bora remembered Lorca had called them such in his poems against the Guardia Civil.

Sitting between the couriers, Marypaz was squealing with laughter when Walton left the house, followed by Brissot. "What do you make of him, Mosko?" Walton asked.

"I don't know. We could keep him here if you're concerned about him."

Walton listened to Marypaz hoot in childish bursts. "I'm not concerned about Soler." He made an effort not to look towards the fountain. "Lorca showed me pictures of the two of them together. I'm sure he is who he says he is."

"Why ask my opinion, then?" Brissot's teeth clicked around the stem of his pipe as he turned it upside down to empty it of tobacco residue. "And would you listen to it anyway?"

"I might."

"Well, *I* think he's a high-strung bourgeois intellectual who would break under interrogation as soon as the Fascist authorities questioned him. And if the authorities did kill Lorca, can his lover be far behind?"

Still talking, they reached the midway point between the house and the fountain. Marypaz sat astride the cement wall of the trough, one leg in the water, the other dangling outside. Almagro sat behind her, and the other man, a big-eared, grinning chump, faced her, close enough to touch her bare knee. In the sun, a partly sheathed army knife hanging from his belt showed a mirror-bright inch of blade near its handle. Walton stopped walking. "I'm not arguing that point," he said irritably. "But how could anything Soler reports affect us? It's not like they don't know we're here. For Chrissake, we and the Fascists are sitting in each other's crotches."

"Well then, let's escort Soler to San Martín and be done with it." Brissot dug into the pipe's bowl with his forefinger, scraping all around. "Only, since he seems convinced of

Lorca's death I'd be damn careful not to let out anything about a grave. *That* is something I don't think you'd want the Fascists to find out from him."

"I'm not stupid." Walton took one more step towards the fountain. "Marypaz!" he called. "Come here, I want to talk to you!"

She pulled her leg out of the water. "In a minute. I'm talking."

Walton turned back to Brissot, who'd pocketed his clean pipe. "Mosko, I want you to pump Soler for information when you take him to San Martín. Find out who drove him to Libros, and if it's true that Lorca never told him about us. I can't believe he wouldn't mention the fact that he knew me."

"Why? Do you think Soler was lying about it, or that Lorca didn't think enough of your friendship to mention you to Soler?"

Walton didn't answer.

Marypaz trotted over from the fountain, barefooted. "What did you want, Felipe?"

Passively he let her lean against him to rub grit from between her wet toes. "Nothing."

"Nothing? What did you call me for, then?"

EL CABEZO BLANCO, OFF THE
TERUEL–VILLASPESA ROAD

The men of the Guardia Civil were curious about Bora's accent. They asked him to repeat his words, as if they didn't understand him, but were friendly enough. Grabbing at their crotches, they remarked admiringly on the size of his *cojones*, which he found curious because he'd been quite scared. The highest-ranking among them, a sergeant, helped him look for the cap he'd lost somewhere in the grass. "First we heard the shots," he said. "We heard rifle shots and pistol shots, but what convinced us was seeing a riderless army horse pass by our post. There was no telling what we'd find; we thought you'd have a pound of lead in you already."

Bora continued to search the grass. He didn't particularly care about finding his cap, but he needed somehow to relieve the tension he was feeling, and the exercise of looking where minutes earlier he'd nearly died helped. "Who were they?"

The sergeant made a face. He was a big grey-haired man packed into his cheap uniform, with wrists as thick as a child's leg. He nodded towards the road, where deep pools of blood were forming meandering traceries in the dirt and three bodies were lined up side by side. An ooze looking like burnt sugar trickled from their mouths and ears, and flies were already clustered on it. "Call them what you please. *Rojos*. Reds, is what they are. They were shooting at a Legion officer, and that's reason enough to kill them." The sergeant parted the grass with his beefy hands. "I patrol as far as Campillo, and the other morning I was rolling myself a cigarette when I saw a mule come down the street with its dead *mulero* on its back, tied down so he wouldn't fall off. Now, who in his right mind would kill someone like Vasquez? He was poor as Job, didn't know his right hand from his left, and all he ever did was carry his load from Albarracín to Cosa by way of Castellar."

Bora straightened up, suddenly intrigued. "How had he been killed?"

"A shot in the head, right back here." The sergeant pointed at the base of his own skull. "So close the shot had burned his hair around the hole. Poor bastard. On top of that, I had to tell his wife and kids. *Hola*, here is your cap." Holding it by the visor, the sergeant stretched the cap over to Bora, who

137

had already straddled the wall to regain the road. One of the guardsmen was leading a wide-eyed, skittish Pardo back. Bora made sure the canvas bag and its contents were untouched before patting and scratching the horse. Next, he dug out the camera Cziffra had given him and took some pictures of the bodies, his back to the sun.

"Wait," the sergeant said. "There's also the one you shot back there. Go and pick him up, Galindo."

It took Galindo some time to drag the marksman from the wall across the field. Although he could clearly have used some help, his companions remained squatting by the side of the road, glancing at the bodies and cracking jokes. Finally Bora passed the camera strap around his neck and helped Galindo haul the body over.

"Watch the blood, *teniente*," Galindo said. "He's got blood and shit coming out of him."

The sergeant immediately showed an interest again. "Any papers on him?"

A bloodstained document passed from hand to hand until it reached Bora. Bound in cardboard, the top left corner of the first page had a photograph of the dead man glued to it. All the information – his name, date of birth, city of origin, profession – was printed in French, but someone had used a pen to write over it in Spanish.

"No telling where these Red volunteers come from any more," the sergeant said. "Seems this shooter of yours was a German. You'd think the Germans would be on our side."

Bora felt slightly sick. The dead man gave as his residence the Leipzig suburb of Mockau, across town from his parents' city house. Mockau was where he'd gone riding with Dikta and they'd found a place to kiss behind the airplane factory.

He leaned over the man's body, mildly curious to see his face. It was a blonde, wide-eyed, anonymous dead face, and there was a stench of faeces and blood on him. In Mockau, Dikta had unbuttoned her blouse to let him reach inside her riding jacket, and, not knowing she had a lover, Bora had thought it a humbling privilege. "I want this document," he said. "Is there any reason why I shouldn't take it?"

The sergeant shook his head. "He was shooting at you, *teniente*. Keep it. Aren't you going to take a picture of him?"

Bora had to photograph the body twice, with and without the guards posing alongside it with grins and cigarettes. He parted ways from them at the post on the sharp curve of the road, and made sure he was out of sight before dismounting to throw up in the ditch.

EL PALO DE LA VIRGEN

There had been summer evenings in Eden when dust in the air had made the horizon look like yellow gauze, but not often. Walton looked at the dry band of haze across the valley and felt a renewed sense of safety in being away from home and those who knew him well. All his life he'd resented closeness, and the explanations that it required. *Things happen. Things happen and there is nothing written anywhere that says you should haul around the responsibility forever for people to stare at, like a wart on your face.*

Brissot and Soler had been gone for over three hours; they would return from San Martín any time. *I'm cutting myself off from this, too. If I don't look back, there is no camp. No Soler, no dead Lorca. There's no Spain. What happened at Guadalajara is not important and no one knows about it, which means that it didn't happen unless I talk about it. The same as Soissons. They're like thoughts: there's no substance to them if I don't speak them out. And if I don't look back, there's no wife, no Pittsburgh, no Eden. There's no Walton, either.*

Funny, though, that the band of haze reminded him of the yellow wall in his dreams. Maybe the wall meant that he ought to forget Guadalajara, block it off. Walls were what he needed inside, not doors. He shouldn't let any of the doors open again on the past, or else – here he remembered the anxiety of the morning, leaving Remedios' house – he ought to ignore them.

He rolled a cigarette and lit it. The first drag released a pungent curl of smoke in his mouth, and Walton swallowed it even though a conscientious young doctor at the Maurin Sanatorium had advised him against it just yet. Why? One of the most practical lessons learned in Spain was how to roll cigarettes firm and tight, Andalusian style. Even tobacco with the texture of wood shavings is acceptable if the cigarette is rolled tight. Walton sucked on it. *Yes, I'm cutting myself off.* With a sort of pleasure in the pit of his stomach, he recalled his relief at leaving the Brigade volunteers, mostly war veterans, at Albacete. None had served with him in France, but he didn't want them to get too close. Going to Madrid on his own as a militiaman had been his plan since stepping on board the *Normandie*. As for Guadalajara, the confusion of battle had been such that not even Brissot, who'd fought in it, had heard anything other than Walton's account of how things had gone. And man, the cigarette was good.

"Mosko is back." Valentin's voice reached him from behind. "And the faggot's with him."

"I'm coming," Walton said, but didn't move. Eyes wandering back to the dimming haze, he tried to prolong the acquisitive pleasure of owning his thoughts. The term was "avarice", a word he'd always liked the sound of. Keeping things to yourself, hoarding them where others couldn't get to them. He saw clearly, almost like a picture, his poverty-stricken boyhood in Eden, the long summer evenings after

140

school when his father had already died and his mother had grown tired of calling him for supper. He'd rolled his first cigarette then, a moist lump that had fallen apart in his mouth like sawdust. He remembered the grit of dirt and ice-ground pebbles under his feet. And nobody around except the woods, drawn like curtains behind him. How he'd enjoyed hiding things from others even then. Worn, unreadable coins, pieces of chipped Indian flint so thin its edges were transparent, hand-forged nails bent double. There had to be some of those possessions still buried somewhere along Eden Lake, where frost and mud and rank grass would keep layering over them and deepen their safety.

Marypaz's laughter, so much like the clucking of a young chicken, reached him from further back on the ledge. The courier with the flashy knife had been talking since his arrival about the changes in Barcelona, how shops had opened again after the riots and you could find butter and women's fancy underwear for sale. Walton couldn't hear what he was saying now, but imagined the empty chatter.

When he turned towards the camp, Brissot was drinking from the fountain. Soler, unused to riding, was still saddled, and only when Valentin gave him a hand did he dismount. In a rare show of domesticity, Marypaz announced she was going to prepare supper, which prompted the couriers to follow her inside the house.

Walton nodded to Soler, whose pale face was a blur in the evening light, and, taking Brissot aside, said, "I'm escorting him back as soon as it grows dark. What happened at San Martín?"

"Nothing. Soler didn't expect to find anything."

Walton watched Soler gather water in his hand and drink greedily. In his mind, there was effeminacy in the way he scooped the water to his lips. "What did he tell you?"

"He's either too smart or too scared to talk beyond generalities. According to him, Lorca had been nervous before his disappearance but unwilling to give explicit reasons for it. It seems he felt guilty about staying with his relatives, and at least once in the past month had spoken of moving into a place of his own. Soler offered to share his apartment with him, but he refused."

Soler stepped back from the fountain as Valentin brought the horses to water them. His weariness and grief were obvious, but not enough for Walton to feel sympathy. "Mosko, did he explain how he got to Libros?"

"He was driven by a wholesale grocer who's friends with his father and delivers goods in and around Teruel. He admits he had no plans for his trip back. Says he discouraged Lorca from travelling outside Teruel, and that Lorca had all but quit discussing his movements with him. I don't know if we ought to believe this detail. Claiming ignorance is a safe alternative for people like Soler."

"OK. What about politics? Where does he stand politically?"

Brissot tilted his hand in a flutter that expressed ambivalence. "He concedes that his father owns a chocolate factory in Montalbán, and that the old man's very much the conservative king-loving Carlist. Wants us to believe he hasn't become politically involved so far, even though, of course, his heart 'is with the forces of democracy'. Little does he know how the term is being tossed around these days and how many of us feel about it. He says his old man cut him off years ago due to his decision to be an artist."

"And a queer."

"Maybe. If his old man even knows about it. Anyway, it's a bad idea for you to take him back by yourself, even if you have a mind to leave him on this side of Teruel. He may very well be who he says he is, but riding with him into Fascist territory is another matter."

"I'm not letting him go alone, and there's no point in having more than one of us accompany him," Walton retorted. "Relax, he *is* Lorca's close friend. I told you, I saw a snapshot of the two of them in his billfold when Lorca showed me a Workers' Union card."

"What?" For the first time in their conversation, Brissot raised his voice. "Lorca carried a CNT card in Teruel?"

"Take it easy, it wasn't even his. He picked it up from a gutter in Barcelona after the riots, when PSUC guardsmen started confiscating weapons and tearing up syndicalist cards. It still amazes me how he was afraid and yet would take risks for nothing, for a lark. I convinced him to tear it up when we met at Castralvo. I burned it myself." Ignoring Brissot's scowl, Walton started for the house. "Tell comrade Soler he can take a nap, and in good time he and I will go for a night ride." He grinned at the ambiguity of his words. "I mean that literally, of course."

RISCAL AMARGO

Grabrelief eines jungen Mannes mit Militärinsignien. Bora could not imagine why the sentence, scribbled in his diary when he was first listing the antiquities and oddities of Spain, had accompanied him for the last stretch of his journey back to the sierra. It described the weathered Roman headstone he'd seen embedded in the foundation of an orchard wall: a vacuous young face, snub-nosed and chinless with the rain of centuries and the injuries of reuse, and a mutilated funeral inscription. Nothing but a schoolboy interest in the past, but this evening, as Pardo wearily entered the mountain pass,

Bora felt kinship for the dead. The ancient and the new, the long buried and the exposed, those over whom people wept, and the dead whose name or gravesite no one knew. All of them claimed brotherhood with him tonight. It might be the balmy scent of the evergreens brushing against his boots, or the day closing like an eye, or knowing that Lorca was dead, as was Colonel Serrano's son. The man from Mockau, too, was as dead "as all the dead of the earth", in Lorca's own words. It might be any of those things, but his narrow escape only made him kin to the bones of Spain. Bora guided Pardo into the descent to Riscal with his knees and voice, breathing the green odour of the bushes. Ahead of him, the sky opened up its fleshy paleness, and the valley was a boundless cup. A tendril of smoke rose straight up from the yet invisible chimney of the army post.

Life. Tomorrow it'd make him hungry and thirsty and aroused: in need of cleansing his body, sleeping, fighting, making love, explaining himself to himself and others. Tonight, having nearly died on Spanish soil, a gut-rending love of Spain was beginning to take shape. Bora savoured the evening air as if his whole body were an organ of taste and vision.

Life? The intricacy of delicate stems, blurring poppies, the stacked stones of the wall and nameless fields and waysides claimed him, owned him now. The ambush had been life. And for all his intention to keep to his role as a foreigner, Bora knew that he could never fight for his own country so selflessly. Spain's greatness and cruelty and divided passions all owned him ... his side *and* the enemy side, because it is the crusader's lot to mirror his foe. It surprised him that he had begun to love Spain, and that of all the losses today, Lorca's death was his one deep grief.

When Pardo floundered on the steepest point of the way down, Bora only remained saddled due to skill and luck. At the edge of the camp, he couldn't remember the password he'd given out this morning. Luckily there was enough light left, and Niceto let him through without asking for it.

Bora dismounted and handed Pardo's reins to Tomé, who'd come with his solicitous catlike sidling walk. Standing after the long ride made him unsteady and nauseous again. For a moment the few steps to the door seemed an insurmountable distance which Bora faced with a curious sense of astonishment and forgetfulness. This was … what? Home? Fuentes advanced, hitching his trousers from the grove, dark head bobbing like a cork in a pond. Behind him, El Baluarte stood like Böcklin's *Island of the Dead*.

Home? Spain. Bora walked inside, and upstairs, and to the narrow shelter of his cot.

EL PALO DE LA VIRGEN

It was turning out to be the kind of summer night Walton liked. Moonless, temperate. In the pen behind the house, the odour of trampled grass and horse urine was strong, nearly aromatic. Walton walked outside, leaving the back door ajar so that the glare of the oil lamp cast a wedge of light: in the middle of it Valentin was saddling the horses, and didn't turn or say a word. A lazy shuffle of hoofs came from the other mounts, a gelding and two mules grouped in the dark ahead. He only realized Maetzu was behind him when his grudging voice came from close to his ear.

"Mosko told me you're going. It's a bad idea. Which way are you travelling?"

"The long way. Castellar, then down. I won't follow the mule track."

145

The wedge of light darkened when Soler appeared at the back door. Whatever Maetzu was about to add, he kept it to himself. Standing so that a ripple of light ran down his face and right shoulder, Soler spoke. "I haven't done much riding until now," he apologized. "I'm sure you noticed. I hope the horse will find his way in the dark without my help."

"He will." Walton vaulted into the saddle. "Valentin, help him mount."

Outside the pen the wind increased, carrying spicy whiffs of wild rosemary from the sierra.

"From now on we don't speak until I give permission," Walton said, and rode ahead. His horse instinctively sought the trail on the obscure face of the mountain, and Soler's horse followed.

Only the clicking of stones under hoofs was heard during the climb towards the dark houses of Castellar, which the riders skirted and left behind. Dim shapes and uncertain depths cushioned their field of vision, and a vast silence surrounded them. The haze of sundown had turned the sky into a dome of cottony gloom, like a blind urban sky. On the night his train had reached Pittsburgh nine years before, Walton had looked up from the platform at the lurid glare of the sky and sensed the city trap. Shivering in her thin coat, his wife had hung on his arm. He'd pulled away from her, but the trap had snapped shut already, and it would be seven years before he could tear himself loose again.

When they began the descent to the valley, Walton let Soler ride ahead, and as the incline levelled gradually, he unlatched his pistol holster.

There was no wind in the valley. A shrill, grating sound of insects came from the denser darkness of the cane groves alongside the mule track. Like sinking stars, shepherds' fires dotted the dark towards Riodeva and Camarena de la Sierra.

"Now we can talk," Walton said, and riding alongside Soler led both horses away from the track. Soon they were heading north across dry pastures and untended fields. Invisible on their right, the brook also wound north past the mule track. Along its curving banks, the clamour of frogs, like rusted wheels, rose and sank.

When Soler's voice came, it was no longer apologetic. "Look, I'm not good at lying. I might as well tell you that Federico speaks of you often."

Walton straightened in his saddle. The words captured his attention and flattered him, though he wasn't about to admit that. He felt vindicated and not even curious to hear why Soler hadn't admitted it earlier.

But Soler was confessing, his voice made uneven by the jolts of riding on hard terrain. "I've been wanting to meet this Felipe 'whose heart is like an Aragon drum'. The reason why I didn't speak up at your camp is that ... well, I saw both the anarchist black and the red flag flying outside the door, and I didn't know if I should mention it in mixed company. I'm not politically astute."

It made sense. Walton ignored the self-serving clumsiness of the last sentence and asked, careful to use the present tense, "*I* never told you I knew him. What does Lorca say about me?"

"He told me how you met in America. How you were poor, self-educated, risen from the ranks in wartime: *el hombre de Edem*. He spoke of you as of a picturesque character from a book. He understood you were crushed by the menial nature of your job and pay after proving yourself by fighting overseas." Through the dark, the sound of an isolated, faraway gunshot reached them, and Soler paused until Walton said it was nothing and urged him to go on. "He thought he'd never meet you again, but he did. He was thrilled like a boy and melancholy about it, too. He told me that you have a wife, which made me feel better."

Again Walton pretended the last sentence didn't apply, whatever Soler meant by it. He got his bearings by glancing at the dim outlines of the landscape. "This way," he said. "Try to keep up." He slowed down to a pace because Soler was falling behind. "I met Lorca again in the spring," he added, no longer seeing the wisdom of keeping Lorca's death from Soler but vexed that the other man expected the truth and was only speaking to get it out of him. "That's when he came to read poetry to the wounded from Jarama and Guadalajara at the sanatorium in Barcelona. Like everybody else, I assumed he'd been killed months before. Next thing I know, he shows up at my bedside." Walton couldn't help embellishing the next detail. "I told him – I had a bullet through my lungs, and speaking was a major effort – how rumours of his assassination had led me to volunteer." It was true that it'd been *part* of his motivation, but he hadn't told Lorca that. In fact, he'd been too ill to say much. "He gave us an account of how CNT agents were behind his fortunate escape in Granada. He even joked and asked me if I was disappointed to find him alive. Disappointed? His showing up was the best news I'd had in weeks. If anything, it helped me get better."

Soler took his time to agree. "He enjoyed his visits to the Maurin Sanatorium, but it became dangerous because there were so many foreigners there and he didn't want to be recognized. Soon after the Guardia Civil seized the telephone exchange, he left Barcelona altogether."

"I was too caught up in the riots to pay attention, but by 9 May I was out of Barcelona too." Walton felt the old acquisitive pleasure of choosing what to say, and what to leave unsaid. Bent nails, buried flint. What had really happened at Guadalajara. He added, "Hearing that Lorca had made it to this province, I tried my best to contact him."

When the echo of another, even more remote gunshot rolled in from the night across the brook, Soler simply opened his mouth again. "He said he met you in Castralvo, though he didn't mention why. It was difficult to understand Federico's real motivations at times, but in Barcelona he'd become more politicized, and now he had to watch himself closely."

Hearing Soler's voice lose energy under the weight of grief, Walton could imagine him crumpling in the saddle. He began to say, "We shouldn't assume —" but the Spaniard would no longer play the game.

"He's dead, isn't he?" He sounded firm, unwilling to let Walton get away with untruths. In the windless dark, his voice was controlled and hoarse. "I love him, and am asking you because you were his friend. I'll answer any question you ask. Anything. Just answer this: is Federico dead?"

Walton overcame the impulse to spur ahead. The terrain dipped as they crossed a dry gravel bed, and he knew by it that they were on the right path, heading for the low land around Villel. He hung on to silence by a thread, and Soler snapped it.

"Is he dead?"

"He is."

"*O Jesús!*"

Walton spoke angrily now. "That's all I know, there's no more to say. He's dead, and you're forbidden to tell his family or anyone. It's not the right time to talk about it yet, and if I hear that the news is being spread in Teruel I swear to God I'll kill you." He couldn't tell why he was threatening Soler, other than that he was acting out of a belated, testy desire for control over what he'd already said.

Up high and down low, in barren fields, insects sang and peeped and chirped all around. Like in Eden, nature couldn't care less if anyone was hurting. Alongside him in the night, Walton saw the outline of his companion hunch over as he buried his face in his hands.

RISCAL AMARGO

16 July. Night, at the post.

Now that I know the body was Lorca, I can't get over feeling diminished by his death, and am grateful that the first reading of his poetry unsettled me. I needed unsettling. The poem of the Unfaithful Bride, which I like most of all and have nearly memorized, challenges my sense of what honourable conduct is. How I'd love to lie with her in the dry riverbed! It's this desire to break rules (fraught with sexuality as far as I'm concerned, by my teachers' and my dear mother's leave) that keeps men alive in battle, I think, more than any skill learned during army training. After today I can vouch for Aristotle's statement – "Those acting out of anger only appear to be brave" – and make no claims about my courage. But I'm beginning to understand that war is not a *possibility* for some of us: rather, it's a way of clarifying things to ourselves by seeking someone to oppose, a shamelessly primitive dualism I'm too inexperienced or dense to go beyond just now.

That's why I keep mentally comparing myself to the American – Felipe, as they call him. Is he a better soldier than I? Does he "believe" as much (or more) than I do, and is he readier to die for it than I was today? I hate the thought that we might end up killing one another, and the comparison will stay unresolved for all times. So, to quote

Father, I try to "do well". But something connects the two of us, other than the fact that we both buried Lorca. Why was he by the brook, anyway? Is he, too, trying to discover who committed the murder? If we didn't kill the poet, and he didn't either, then who did? I wish I knew why I keep thinking of the worn-out Roman headstone.

The first, distant rifle shot – the one towards Riodeva and Camarena de la Sierra – startled Bora awake with the certainty that someone had walked into his room.

The narrow cot was uncomfortable and damp under his body. Drowsiness and sweat wove a limp net ensnaring him, and he couldn't move enough to reach for his gun under the bed. Someone in the room? It only took a glance across the murky twilight from the broken window to see that the small space was empty. Bora lay there wide-eyed until his mind convinced his spine and back muscles to function, and then lifted himself up on his elbows. He didn't remember hearing the shot. Only that something had jolted him from sleep and it felt like a presence. *Grabrelief eines jungen* ... The Roman headstone had belonged to a horseman.

Bora sat up. That's why the sentence had floated to the edges of his weariness last night. *Reiter, Jínete,* Horseman ... What Cziffra and Niceto and Luisa Cadena had spoken of. It all fit together into a strange composite image, and it had something to do with Lorca and his death. The Miraculous Horseman. For a moment, the room seemed to shrink around him, imploding into a nucleus of darkness where Bora stared and held his breath. He couldn't get the image to cohere, but the Miraculous Horseman – half Spaniard, half Roman soldier – was at the centre, and darkness seemed to drain slowly around it. It had no shape really, only a name and denser darkness, like a sinkhole whose bottom reached the other side of the universe. Bora found himself holding on to the sides of his cot, lest the shrinking dark would swallow him, too. Cautiously he let the air out of his lungs. When he took another breath, and another, the dark began to settle, neither shrinking nor growing, like water in a well. The shadowy Horseman sank into it. Within seconds, Bora's muscles had loosened enough for him to swallow and relax his neck, and then there was nothing around him but the dimness of the small room. Time and space were familiar again.

I'm awake. I may have been dreaming until a moment ago, but I'm awake now. Quickly he assessed sounds, images. In the next room, Fuentes snored a bizarre intermittent snore. As always, the beams across the ceiling stood out against the whitewash. The broken window let in a blurry starless sky.

Despite the mildness of the night, Bora was cold. He felt around for his discarded shirt and put it on to stop his teeth from chattering. *It was a strange dream, and I'm only cold because I'm soaking wet.* It had better be that he was sweating because he had had a nightmare, and not because he was afraid, if what Fuentes said was true: that Aragon winters turned so bitter that beggars and farm animals caught out in the open froze to death.

Cziffra kept speaking of a rabid year's-end battle for Teruel that might last through the spring and help decide the war. "You'll be in it." He'd reinforced the statement in a professorial tone. "So keep your eyes open now. You're here for us as much as for Spain. Before you get your guts spilled this winter, look around; learn your business in the field. Ask, talk. Meet people. Try to figure out the American. The post is just the base you work from."

The base he worked from. Bora could see how loving Spain would only complicate matters. He got off the cot and sat cross-legged on the floor with his back to the wall. Already it seemed impossible that he'd ever been afraid or would be again, ever. All he'd taken away from the scramble of the ambush was the arousal, the stunned feeling of potency he'd experienced for a sensual split second between the end of the shoot-out and any consideration of it. Which is why the Civil Guard had said *cojones* and not *coraje*, although both meant the same.

Bora smiled. The girls in Bilbao had danced on the dinner table, wrists slowly twisting, backs arched, heels tapping hard. And then there was the *bruja* Remedios, whom he'd never seen. Death in Spain was female, he was suddenly and blissfully sure: you watch her dance and come closer step by step, relishing her odour and noise and the flash of motion, and in the end you lie down with her. *Besame con tu lengua, aquí.*

10 July. Night, continued at the post.

On the verge of elation, or rather well into it. Sweaty, cold. As for the somewhat immature warring sentiments expressed above, I can't help them. I don't deny the cruel stupidity of combat, nor am I unafraid: I'm unwilling to stay away from it. Call it the cheapening or the sublimation of my soldiery if you will; I'm all but looking forward to 'spilling my guts' if I must, though hopefully not in an ambush. I only wish I were in the line of battle and had to measure up every day.

More soberly, my accomplishments since coming to Spain have been: 1. The first Red unit surrendered to me in Bilbao; 2. I wasn't killed in the battle for 1.; 3. I didn't get a venereal disease from the victory party; 4. I've managed to avoid lice so far. Not much to brag about, considering that less than ten hours ago I killed a man from Leipzig. Matthias Braun, labourer, from the Mockau district past the railroad junction. The place where Dikta asked me to go home with her! The blood soaked black into his shirt as we dragged him to the road. Lorca writes that "blood comes forth singing", which is what Lieutenant Jover's blood did.

I heard a rifle shot just now, so distant and muffled that it could have been fired as far away as the next province. So much for excitement on the Teruel front.

EL PALO DE LA VIRGEN

As if by appointment, the small airplane returned in the morning. From the orchard, Walton could see that it was a flimsy machine, circling like a moth around the flame. Through his field glasses, he tried to identify its markings in the low sun (the three stick-like Italian *fasci* or the German crossbars), but saw none.

All the men looked up at the swaying dot in the sky. Even Rafael, who'd just accused Valentin of stealing his silver rosary and come close to exchanging blows with him over it. Squatting by the open fire on the terraced ground, Chernik burned his fingers on the coffee pot and cursed.

Walton slipped back into the orchard, where the coolness of the night had not yet evaporated. Soon Brissot joined him there. "How did it go last night?"

"Fine. On the way back I spotted a patrol at Cabezo Blanco. Guardsmen, I think."

"Where did you end up leaving Soler?"

"At a place outside Valdecebro. The *huerta* of a man called Vargas." Walton swallowed a yawn, crossing the orchard on his way to get coffee from Chernik. "Two old people living alone. Vargas is the music teacher Soler mentioned."

Brissot stayed at heel like a swarthy terrier. "You were supposed to use the trip to gather information from Soler. Let's hear it."

On the terraced ground, Chernik's small fire made with green sticks reminded Walton that they were once more running low on fuel. "Time to send the youngsters to gather wood," he said.

The other man passed him a tin of steaming coffee. "I told Rafael, but he's in a downright foul mood. As if he's the only one who's lost anything. I can't find my friggin' fountain pen."

Walton avoided Brissot's meaningful look. "Well," he answered him at last, "Soler explained in detail why Lorca left Barcelona when he did."

"Ha! It doesn't take a wizard to figure *that* out." Brissot spat the words in contempt. "If he was even remotely connected with CNT or FAI anarchists, we all know how it went with the *cenetistas* and other moderates during the spring. They and the communist POUM got what was coming to them. But I forget that you have Marxist Unification sympathies yourself."

Walton ignored Chernik's visible amusement at the sally. "And we all know where you stand, Mosko, don't we?"

Brissot rose to the bait. "I never advocated the harsh measures adopted by the PSUC after the riots. But executions are necessary, sometimes, and purging is a time-honoured medical practice."

"Yes. It does make for a lot of shit." Walton said so knowingly, but wondered where his allegiances really were. Cutting oneself off was not as easy as it had seemed yesterday evening. "In any case, Soler says that Lorca felt physically in danger. PSUC members associated with the NKVD —"

"So now it's the Soviet Secret Service that drove Lorca out of Barcelona!"

Walton tried to grin, but his lips stretched humourlessly. "Mosko, it isn't as if they hadn't bumped off a few hundred lately, including Andrés Nin."

"We don't know what happened to Andrés Nin."

Walton yawned. "It's too fucking early in the day to argue. Look, all I'm saying is that Lorca was afraid of the NKVD."

"Because Soler says so?"

"Because he has nothing to gain from making accusations about a left-wing organization to us." Walton succeeded in grinning this time, sure that would gall Brissot. "I mean, how does he know I don't belong to the NKVD? Why, I don't even know that *you* don't."

"You'd never find out, either. If you're prepared to accuse anyone on our side of killing Lorca, you've lost your critical sense altogether."

"I keep an open mind, that's all." Walton knew there was no point in searching his pockets for cigarette paper or matches, but he still went through the motions. "I did tell Soler that Lorca is dead. I added nothing, explained nothing. He knows no more than he suspected before coming here."

"Well, isn't that grand!" Brissot looked exasperated. "No attempt to frame the message and exploit it! You have no sense of history, none whatsoever!"

Rafael had been approaching, but hearing the altercation he drew back. Walton caught sight of his gangling figure in retreat and felt free to shout back. "And what the hell is history? You said yourself no one is going to care in a hundred years' time. Who's going to care who told Lorca's queer friend that he was killed? All I told Soler is that he's dead, and forbade him to pass it on to anyone."

Brissot made a grandiose, angry wave with his open hands. "And you went out of your way, at your own risk, to take him to a hiding place! Why? There's more to this and to Lorca than you've been sharing. Yesterday I heard you tell Almagro that there was 'no news'. No news about what? I think Lorca must have been carrying more than a piece of sheet music.

Otherwise you'd never have agreed to come down to the mule track and look for clues."

"Don't be a fool."

"I'm not. But I expect you to share all you know."

They approached the fountain. "It's about the deployment of Fascist units around Teruel," Walton grudgingly admitted. "Every courier who hikes up here tells us how in Valencia they insist on obtaining that information. When I heard from Lorca that he'd secured an escort to leave Teruel, I figured he was in touch with CNT-FAI agents in town: they're the only ones active there and likely to offer help at this point. I assumed he'd bring the intelligence with him."

Brissot frowned. Before speaking, he wiped his glasses with his dirty handkerchief. "And why would the *cenetistas* use as a courier a famous writer in hiding who was too terrified to leave his own house?"

"I don't mean that." Walton lowered his eyes to the ground, where a line of ants were travelling busily from a dead locust to a dainty mound of chewed dust. Packing food in their mandibles, one by one they clambered up the mound and crawled into their hole. "Maybe the *cenetistas* would bring the information at the same time they escorted Lorca."

"And where does Soler fit into all this?"

"Nowhere." Walton watched the ants dismember the locust, each of them tearing a bit from the carcass. "After I told him about Lorca's death, he opened up like a faucet. I could have gotten anything out of him. He hasn't a clue about what really went on, and Lorca wouldn't deliberately endanger him. I promise you, Soler won't get over his very physical fear of death any time soon, and the last place where he'll want to be seen is Teruel."

Brissot stomped his foot, coming close to crushing the dead locust and the labourers toiling inside it. "So, if what you say is true, and what the *mulero* said is true, then we can assume Lorca's escort abandoned him to his fate. In addition, *someone* stripped his body of all he had." One more step, and Brissot would destroy a month's supply of collective insect food. Caught in the turmoil of sandal-churned dust, the line of ants became disarrayed. Some fled.

Walton stared at Brissot's feet. The argument was getting on his nerves. Memories of the day he and Brissot had gone looking for clues clicked before him like a series of snapshots. The chalky gravel bed, the Browning pointed at his face. The English-speaking legionnaire who had relieved him of his gun and scrambled off.

The German. Of course. Whatever language he spoke, he had to be the German in the next camp. His accent, his build … he was the one Maetzu had spoken of. Why hadn't he realized it earlier? Either the German had killed Lorca, or he had at least reached his body before anyone else. *He* had been looking for clues by the brook. Eyes on the ants' disciplined attempt to line up again, Walton confronted the new knowledge and paid careful attention to Brissot as he would another, oversized insect. The German had been looking for papers. Or clues. Why? In order to conceal them, or to destroy them. So why hadn't he gone the full distance and disposed of Lorca's body? Had he tried to? How much did he know? Questions spawned fast in Walton's head, Brissot scolding him all the while. "You have no sense of history and no political acumen. From now on you'll keep me informed of every single thing that goes on."

"Ooh. Is that commissar talk?"

"It is commissar and security talk, Felipe."

4

I come to devour your mouth
And drag you by your hair
Into a shell-coloured dawn.
Because I want to,
And because I can.

FEDERICO GARCÍA LORCA, "EROS WITH A CANE"

RISCAL AMARGO

Colonel Serrano rode in shortly after 7.30 in the morning, as the flag was being raised in front of the army post. Two brightly attired Requetés came behind him on long-maned horses, followed by an army mule loaded with supplies.

It was a credit to his disciplinary efforts, Bora thought, that his men didn't break ranks immediately to run to unload the sacks, though the final words of the anthem they were singing wavered considerably. Soon, with Paradís and Aixala in the lead, they gathered around the mule, hopeful for tobacco and coffee.

Serrano glanced at them with disdain. "Were your men singing 'Cara al Sol'?" he asked Bora, though it was obvious that they had been. "Why not the national royal anthem?"

Bora found no better answer than the truth. Focusing on Serrano's figure, the Requetés were blurs of red and blue behind him. "Because not all of them are royalists, sir."

"And what about yourself?"

"I'm not a monarchist either, but I wouldn't keep the men from singing 'La Granadera' if they wanted to."

Serrano tightened his mouth, and for a moment his drawn features resembled the embalmed face of a mummy. By contrast, the young royalist horsemen behind him, mounted with the slouching ease of landowners, had boyish unlined faces. In blue shirts and blood-red berets, they looked at Bora from their ornate saddles and neither saluted nor seemed openly hostile. Serrano handed the reins to Tomé, who stood at attention with his shirt pockets full of cigarettes. Fastidiously removing his riding gloves, the colonel eyed the field glasses hanging around Bora's neck. "Have you seen the plane?"

"Yes, sir. No markings, but it's a German machine. I think it may be photographing the unsurveyed parts of the sierra."

Serrano seemed annoyed by the men crowding to receive their rations from Fuentes: Canaries tobacco, canned meat, bars of soap and chocolate. "You shaved your temples," he said, with a critical look at Bora. "Did you fear you might not look German enough?" He nodded towards the young men, who had just dismounted. "Those are my wife's nephews, just in from their parents' *estancia*. They need to be exposed to the front, which is the reason I brought them along: you needn't be introduced to them yet. What I want you to do now is to show me the gravesite. In case you should be killed."

Bora was tempted to tell Serrano about the ambush and to brag a little, but since another German had been involved in the incident, he decided against it. He entrusted the young men to Fuentes' care, and with the colonel took the winding climb from Riscal to Castellar.

Before long, their horses were scrambling to the top of the ridge. Its crest was narrow except where it joined El Baluarte, and ran along the rim of the hollow where Castellar sat on its own parched knoll. The riders cast infinite, deep blue shadows against the sunlit shrubbery or moved, shadowless, in the shade. Lizards sluggish with the cool of night were slow in seeking cover from the hoofs. A skinny hare took off from a tuft of grass in a scamper of ears and legs. When they made it to the top of the ridge and came in sight of Castellar, the sunbeams only reached its bell tower, like a torch fired at the tip.

"Where to from here?" Serrano asked.

"We follow the ridge to the north-east."

The ravine yawned to their left as they travelled the rim. Below, the view of Castellar changed with every step the horses took on the shifting pebbles. Bora rode with assurance, enjoying the risk, waiting for the right moment to ask appropriately indirect questions. What about Luisa Cadena's husband, for example?

Just then, the colonel said, "You could have told me that you belong to our class." He stared ahead, as if the listener were not essential to the dialogue. "It makes a difference."

"Why?"

"*Porqué los hidalgos se entienden el uno al otro.*"

Bora wasn't sure that being a gentleman involved understanding others of his class. He found Serrano's argument hollow in view of the difference in rank between them. He said, cautiously, "I can't imagine why yesterday Señora Cadena had to come in person to ask you about her cousin. Wouldn't that be a husband's responsibility? I wouldn't let my wife —"

Slapping the reins against his horse's neck, Serrano interrupted sharply. "You're not married. What do you care about what Cadena does with his wife, Lieutenant?"

"Nothing, I'm sure. I just thought —"

The colonel stared him down. "You only need to think about matters that concern you militarily."

And that was how gentlemen understood each other in Serrano's mind.

As the sun crested over the ridge, cicadas began their grating call. From their perches on bushes and blades of grass, they kept a rhythmic pitch, piercing, constant in volume. Once in a while, they held the note longer. Ahead, Bora could already see the sunny spur where they had buried Lorca. He deliberately approached it by a meandering route, in case anyone was looking on from Castellar. With Serrano still looking at him sternly, he remained silent, worried that the colonel suspected he'd spoken to Luisa Cadena. Or worse still, that he was planning to visit her in Teruel.

"There's nothing more incestuous than a civil war," Serrano said instead, ramrod straight in his saddle. "It is obscene in nature and none involved in it are free of the taint unless idealism overrides the filth." He led the bay onwards with expert prods of his calves. "Do you understand what it means?"

Unexpectedly Bora resented the colonel's stare and words. "I understand perfectly," he said.

"So, are you idealistic?"

"I am."

"But not for Spain."

"For Spain and for more than Spain, hopefully."

Despite the unsafe terrain, the colonel stopped the horse in mid-stride. "Most idealists are also unaware of their own inner workings. How long do you think you'll remain idealistic or ignorant of yourself?"

"As long as God wills, Colonel."

Loose stones rolled down the ravine when the army bay started moving again. Serrano's demeanour changed almost imperceptibly, like hard metal bending a little. He nodded, his lean profile drawn against the brightening sky. "It is good to fear God." A moment later, he added, "Since you're bound to find out sooner or later, you might as well know that the murdered man was the poet García Lorca."

Quickly wetting his lips, Bora chose silence. He was sure that the colonel would take his lack of reaction as proof of his insensitivity or ignorance and become self-righteous.

"I suppose you've never heard of him and that this tragedy means nothing to you," Serrano continued accusingly.

"I've heard of him, Colonel, but my feelings are of no relevance in the matter."

"And you call yourself an idealist?"

When they reached the lonely rock spur, Bora pointed out the sandy gulch where Lorca had been buried. Serrano dismounted and walked over to the tangle of desiccated branches Alfonso and Fuentes had piled on the grave.

Bora stayed saddled. From this vantage point, Castellar was fully visible below, and so was the rocky saddle joining El Baluarte to the sierra. Mas del Aire was the highest point of the massif, Fuentes had said, a climb mostly barren but spotted with yellow growth here and there. Despite Serrano's obvious contempt for him, Bora felt remarkably well, and his curiosity led him to notice small details: the lack of trails leading to Mas del Aire, the fact that he'd never heard bells ringing from Castellar. Church bells were forbidden in Red-controlled areas, and Castellar had been fought over. But it was neutral ground now. Bora could see the bells in the arched window of the tower and wondered about their silence.

"The heart of Spain is buried here." From the edge of the gully, Serrano spoke in a low, rancorous voice. "It was a wild heart and had to be cut out, but the body won't live without it. What do you say to that, Don Martín?"

Bora spoke before thinking. "That I am glad I wasn't the one who cut it out."

Serrano nodded. Whether in agreement or mere acceptance, it was impossible to say. He promptly mounted his horse, turning away from the grave. "My son was killed in Madrid three days ago."

EL PALO DE LA VIRGEN

Marypaz was complaining that she couldn't find a gilded bracelet of hers. She was refusing to eat, and was still in bed past midday. She'd got all she could from looking at the pictures in *Life*, brought by Almagro for Walton, and now Brissot was engrossed in the magazine. Sandalled feet propped on the kitchen table, he sat oblivious to the dance of flies over the oily dishes, reading about the strike in Flint, Michigan.

From the doorway Walton said, "Will you hand it over when you're done? I haven't even had a chance to finish reading the damn thing."

Brissot stretched the magazine across the table. "Take it. I don't particularly care about the photos, especially the insider view of a Fascist plane bombing one of our trains." He glanced at his watch and took his feet off the table. "I thought we were supposed to start our friendly questioning about the theft."

"We are." Walton crossed the kitchen on his way to the stairs. "I'm going up to check on Marypaz. Broach the subject with Valentin, he'll be in any time."

Moments later, Brissot's dark expression told Walton that talking to Valentin would lead nowhere. The gypsy walked in and sat down, but that was as far as his collaboration would go. Like cocky youngsters anywhere, he listened with his head low, as if the subject were only marginally interesting to him and the effort of listening made his neck weary. When Brissot paused, he rolled his eyes, following the dancing flies.

"Rafael had better have more than a hunch if he's going to accuse me of taking anything of his," he said at last. "Without proof I don't have to take any lip from him or you or anyone else." He drawled his words defiantly, his bony young face motionless except for a nervous blink.

Walton was no diplomat. "Bragging about having served time sure succeeded in making Rafael suspicious. Neither Mosko nor I are accusing you of anything. We just want to hear your side of the story."

Valentin bared his teeth in a grimace. One of his front teeth was broken, and its white triangular stump reinforced the impression of an animal sneer. "I've been to jail, same as the others who were sent to jail in this country. Lenin did time, too. I haven't heard Rafael saying that Lenin was a thief, but I'm not even sure Rafael knows who Lenin was. Proof is what counts. Without proof I don't give a damn about Rafael's hunches or any committee supposed to find out who's been stealing around here."

"Well, has anything been stolen from you?"

Valentin looked at Walton, who'd asked the question. His eyelids began to twitch in earnest. "I haven't got anything to steal."

"Four of us have had things disappear."

"Disappear is not the same as stolen." Valentin tossed back a wave of black hair. The twitching of his lids was becoming spasmodic, but his defiance was undimmed. "All I can say is that you'd better grill everyone in this unit, because you can't talk equality the way you do and single me out." He stood up, tipping the chair. "Ask Maetzu, who takes off any time he feels like it, and no one knows where he goes. In the meantime, keep Rafael away from me."

Walton scowled. "Or else?"

"Just keep him away from me, that's all."

After Valentin had walked outdoors, Brissot took out his pipe and passed his forefinger around inside the empty bowl. "I don't know, Felipe."

"About what?" Walton was angry at Valentin and unwilling to listen to recriminations. "It's you who said someone stole your lighter and Chernik's pen and now Marypaz's whatever it was. It's you who wants to find out. Don't you fucking go back on it now."

Brissot stuck the pipe randomly into one of his many pockets, without looking. "We may have got carried away. Any of those objects could have been lost."

"Where would Rafael have lost a rosary he constantly wore around his neck?"

"Chains break; watch straps and bracelets break. Even if there *is* a thief, we acted along bourgeois lines by confronting Valentin before everyone else just because we knew he'd served time."

Walton couldn't help sounding sour. "And what would be the appropriate Soviet model? Abolishing private property altogether so there's no theft?"

"Actually, no. That's something your Marxist Union chums advocated in Barcelona. I stick by the Third International. The appropriate model would be for Valentin to have a chance to confront us with the same accusation. It may come down to openly examining what each of us has in his duffel bag or trunk."

Walton attempted to slam his hand down on a fly, and missed. "As if a thief would keep evidence in his backpack. If you want, I can stop this right now and tell Rafael to stuff his rosary. It'd be easier."

"Easier but not fair. No. We must question everyone else, including Maetzu and Marypaz."

Walton shut his eyes. *What the fuck do I care about any of this?* A short, trembling seizure stiffened his jaw, drove a spike of pain up his sore neck. He'd felt caught before and sprung the trap: coming to Spain had been part of the escape, and he hadn't fucking come to Spain to get caught. *Christ, I can no more make myself care about finding out who the thief is than finding out who killed Lorca, and Lorca was my friend.*

I don't want to, he thought. *I don't want to.* He didn't want to feel trapped by duty or Marypaz or Brissot or anything else. "I'll tell you what, Mosko. Be a worthy comrade and apply all the politically appropriate pressure until someone confesses he stole from his friends. While you're at it, try your hand at making Maetzu tell where he was on the night they killed Lorca. That is, if he doesn't blow your head off first."

"It's your responsibility, not mine."

Walton stood. "Is it? *Is it mine?*" He found anger a waste of energy just now. "Then I choose to take a full week before I bring up the matter of theft again with any of you. Put up or keep your mouth shut, and stick the Third International up your ass."

RISCAL AMARGO

Bora realized by the amount of equipment deposited on the ground floor of the post that the Requetés might be staying for some time. The boys had been sitting by the door drinking from their canteens, and stood up simultaneously at their uncle's approach. They exchanged glances and a terse salute with Bora, who passed in front of them to lead Serrano to his room upstairs.

The colonel glanced at the neatly folded clothes in the trunk Bora was hastily closing. He said, "I wish to show my nephews the ragged line of our front, Lieutenant. We will use the camp as our base for the next few days."

Bora started gathering books and maps from the table. "My room and Fuentes' room next door are at your disposal."

"I expect it. I won't be needing you again until later this evening, when I'll want to be shown the enemy gun emplacement. Tell the men they are free to carry out their usual duties, and have Fuentes fetch my nephews." Last on Bora's table sat the book of Lorca's poetry. It caught Serrano's eye, but he touched it with his glove without opening it.

After telling Fuentes to fetch the two young men, Bora walked to the stable, and was giving Tomé a hard time when the sergeant joined him. A few feet away, Aixala and Paradís were scrubbing down the Requetés' sweaty mounts, making faces and exchanging jokes in Catalan. It was Alfonso's turn to cook, and the odour of fried onions reached the ledge. Niceto was invisible, but his voice could be heard singing a *zarzuela* tune behind the house, where he usually sat in the shade to clean his rifle.

"*Teniente*," Fuentes said, "the colonel's nephews are set up. Have you by any chance spoken to them?"

"No."

"They asked about you while you were out with the colonel."

"So?" Bora stepped out of Tomé's earshot. "It's not your place to gossip about officers."

"That's not it, sir." Fuentes kept his policeman's stolid resolve, staring and unmoved, but lowered his voice to a whisper. "They wanted to know if you left the post on the night the man was killed."

Bora stared back. "And what did you tell them?"

"I said that as far as I knew you didn't leave until daybreak, and that there wasn't anything unusual in that. The way they asked, it's like they'd been *told* to ask. They didn't rightly know why they were asking, it seemed to me."

Paradís' laughter came from the place nearby, where

he and Aixala were still taking care of the horses. Bora was annoyed by it. "Did they say anything about the dead man?"

"No. They didn't even mention him directly. It's because they said 'Monday night' that I understood they were talking about the twelfth." Fuentes' bearlike head lolled in stubborn denial. "Me and Alfonso haven't said a word about the burial, not even to anyone here."

It was clear Serrano had made the boys ask. Bora kept any comment to himself. He told Fuentes that the colonel and his nephews would be studying maps until lunch. "This afternoon I'm off to Castellar to talk to the priest. If anyone asks for more information, you're to tell the truth."

CASTELLAR VILLAGE, SIERRA DE SAN MARTÍN

Castellar numbered maybe thirty houses, set on its whalebone-like knoll. After entering the bowl-like depression around it, anyone arriving on foot faced a short laborious climb to the village. It wouldn't take a good walker long, but there was no cover anywhere, not even enough shade to crouch in if one came under fire.

That's how Lieutenant Jover got it. But that place midway down the ravine was destined to be his killing place since forever. Since before Jover was born, since the antiquity and tumult of creation, that flat rock was made for Jover to die on. None of these rocks are my place of death.

Bora reached the edge of town, where fig trees twisted like thick wire. Evidence of past battles stared out of disarrayed stone fences, pockmarked houses and tightly shuttered balconies. A faded, sagging roof, leaning inwards, formed a dragon's back against the colourless sky. On the way, Bora had met no one except two malicious goats that had butted him to keep him away from a bush they were stripping bare. In the searing heat of the afternoon, the pebble-strewn track through town was empty, too.

In the scorching small square, the church was a shrivelled building three or four hundred years old, with an ugly baroque facade and a shabbily whitewashed bell tower. Bora shielded his eyes to look up at the tall shaft. Through the years, pigeons and martins had deposited conical piles of silvery droppings on the high windowsills. Shavings of flimsy excrement must fly off every time the bells rang; but did they ever ring?

From the doorway of the church, looking left, Bora could discern the rocky spur behind which Lorca lay. It stood high, lonely, like the edge of a forlorn world. He knew something about the difficulty of hauling a dead body up to it. Poor Lorca, sealed in the mute, withering matrix of dirt and stone.

The church door was locked. Bora walked around the building accompanied by the mournful cooing of pigeons from the eaves. He found a smaller door on the north side, but this, too, was shut and bolted. So he rounded the base of the bell tower, stepping momentarily into the shade of a house. The shade seemed red to his sun-filled eyes. He continued to the opposite side of the church, where a third, low door responded to his touch and opened. A tepid breath of dankness came from within, as it had when he'd looked into the well at Riscal. He had to duck to pass under the lintel.

When his eyes grew used to the twilight, he saw a long vaulted room, old cracks whitewashed over. He smelled the odour of must-filled corners and dusty cloth, of tapers and incense. Up and down the nave, chalk reliefs in lurid colours illustrated the Stations of the Cross. Jesus Falls the First Time, Jesus Speaks to the Women of Jerusalem, Jesus is Laid in the Sepulchre. It was unlikely, Bora thought from recent experience, that the apostles could so effortlessly have lowered the Master's body into the grave. Four pews and a sparse arrangement of empty chairs took up the floor. The priest was nowhere in sight. Bora had taken his gun out but now holstered it again as he walked up the aisle.

Set off by glass vases containing neither water nor flowers, the main altar was covered by a starched cloth like cut paper and dwarfed by a life-size statue of the Madonna. Draped in black damask, the statue stood with one hand outstretched and the other on her exposed heart, pierced by seven thin daggers. Her face and hands were modelled out of polished, fine wax the heat of day had caused to bead and glow, the sheen on her skin's surface emerging from the heavy cloth: hands, face, and a childlike small foot.

Bora drew closer. A wig of human hair, black and rich like horsehair, was piled up under a dusty, complicated head-dress of silver filigree and gauze. Startlingly true to life, the Madonna's upturned glass eyes stared from the sweet, pained feminine face at the grimy rafters of the ceiling. The daggers spilled carmine blood. To the right of the statue hung the framed print of another Madonna, flanked by angels carrying the instruments of the Passion. Above the altar, in gilded tin letters nailed to the wall, it read, VIVA LA PURÍSIMA VIRGEN MARIA, NUESTRA SEÑORA DE LOS REMEDIOS.

"What are you doing here?"

Bora wheeled back at the priest's words. As he did, he knocked over one of the empty vases and had to snatch at it to keep it from crashing to the floor.

The old man wheezed, buttoning the top of his cassock with his tobacco-stained fingers. "I never suggested that you should come. It's not a good idea, coming here. The church is no place for politics."

Bora understood the old man was afraid for himself. "There's no one out there," he said.

"No one? In the last five minutes, three different people have come to tell me they saw you entering the church. I was about to take a nap. I need a nap, I'm an old man. I don't need these aggravations." More flustered than the situation deserved, the priest turned in search of a place to sit, as if there weren't empty pews on both sides of the aisle.

"I talked to my men," Bora explained. "For whatever it's worth, I hope it helps."

The priest finally sat down, crumpling like a bat. "Is that all you came to say?"

"I also wanted to see the village."

"You could have seen it without entering the church."

Bora strode away from the altar, not caring if he sounded contemptuous. "I take it the American's men come to town more often than we do."

"Do they? I wouldn't know." Grudgingly the priest kept his eyes on him. "I never go out except to say Mass, and I say Mass only once a day, even on Sunday. I live next door. So you see it was a great sacrifice for me to travel to your camp." He bunched the worn cloth of the cassock between his knees, like a fussy housewife. "It was too hot, and I got diarrhoea from it. I'm an old man. You don't understand because you're a young man, and young men are foolish and full of sensuousness. It's their flesh that drives them, not courage."

Bora wouldn't argue the point: it was quite true as far as he was concerned. Still, he felt the need to comment. "Flesh and courage lead you to different things. The first drives you to what you want, and the second to what you fear."

"What you fear is always what you secretly want." Sluggishly the priest started for the low side door, shaking his head. "Don't follow me out. Stay another ten minutes before you go."

For half an hour or so Bora sat rereading the gilded letters on the wall. The priest might be right. It was a matter of flesh: everything was. Being here, exerting oneself, the war itself. Competing with other men, proving oneself. Seeking worn-out philosophical justifications for what his excess of energy demanded, which was a regular lancing. The gilded letters swayed if he stared at them too intensely, turning into a blur. VIVA LA PURÍSIMA VIRGEN MARIA, NUESTRA SEÑORA DE LOS REMEDIOS.

Next, he was standing in the front pew and looking for the door to the bell tower. He found it where the wall angled into a recessed area behind the altar, next to the door to the vestry. It was open.

A steep ramp of wooden steps rose from the limited floor space into the tall, light-gorged shaft of the tower. Heedless of the groaning planks Bora began the climb, only to find that the three top flights of wooden steps were missing. The frayed bell ropes hung useless at mid-shaft, and the bells themselves were invisible in the converging splendour of the sunlight shining through the top windows. Bora noticed that ladders had been precariously set at acute angles on what remained of the landings ahead. And the narrow platform under his feet was already some twenty feet from the ground.

The cooing of pigeons increased as he tried the strength of the first ladder and started up the shrunken rungs. He felt the wooden frame tremble under his weight, creak and give as his hobnailed boots gained footing, but didn't look down. The odour of powdery plaster, dust and guano filled his nostrils as he straddled the second landing. Here he nearly overturned the precariously balanced ladder set against the wall. In a storm of weightless down from the fleeing pigeons, he steadied it and climbed it quickly. The third landing was narrower than the rest, a square of time-weary mortar and stone. The last ladder rested on it as if by a miracle, two middle rungs broken. Bora hesitated. In the glare of afternoon light flooding into the belfry, it was impossible to judge whether it'd stand his weight. Below him, the rickety ladders and steps criss-crossing the plunging drop would not stop a fall. Above, the pigeons returned in a squall of wings and paced the sills amid ashen mounds of guano. Bora watched the delicate fluff waft down and stick to the dangling bell ropes, too far out of reach to grasp if he needed them. Bora passed the strap of his field glasses under his arm, so they wouldn't dangle in front of him, took firm hold of the ladder, and went up.

As soon as he set foot on the top landing, the pigeons whirred off for good. The tarnished bells were so close he could tap his fingers on them, but already he was focusing his field glasses on the sweeping view of the ridge past clustered roofs. Details of striped rocks appeared, squat bushes, the occasional blinding glare of the sky as he moved the lenses. He recognized the trail from Riscal Amargo, where goats were still ravaging the shrub. Framed by the northern window, the spur of Lorca's burial, flattened by perspective, seemed less forbidding from this height. Between the two points, El Baluarte dominated the sky with its formidable prow of barren rock.

Its top was Mas del Aire. Flashes and rainbows of refracted sunlight played across the lenses as Bora scanned the strange high place where Remedios lived. All he could see was the profile of an empty crest. He desperately searched for her house, knowing it to be there because both Fuentes and the American had said so.

Heedless of the chalky bird waste, Bora straddled the sill of the western window to take a better look, and when a scent of hardy grasses reached the tower from the sierra his blood pulsed through him. The priest, he admitted, was not only right about young men; he was also very wise.

In the evening the airplane banked high over Walton's camp. The sun, already below the horizon, still lit it up fully, making it look like a slowly circling star against the dim sky.

Walton crouched behind the anti-aircraft gun with the two men manning it, conscripts who had left their Madrid artillery barracks to come home to Castellar. It had taken him some time to convince them to join. Now they perched above their comrades on this wind-beaten rock, ate and slept and grew bored here, and their makeshift shelter of sticks and tarpaulin looked and smelled like an animal's lair. Only once a week did two men from the camp come to take their place. Refuse piled up in the crags, waiting to be washed away or else mark the spot long after the war and the men were gone.

Walton said, "If it ever comes lower ... as soon as it comes lower, open fire. We can't afford to wait and see. Knock it out of the sky and then we'll ask questions."

The two nodded. Walton saw they still had cigarettes, probably the same dried-up Italian ones he'd given them days before. They quietly puffed on the thin Macedonias, as if solitude had carved the need to communicate out of them. It was only pride that kept Walton from bumming one, because even cheap tobacco sounded good after hours of abstinence.

"Well," he added, "the pilot isn't going to try anything for tonight."

With the coming of darkness, the airplane went out like a shooting star in the north-west sky. Walton smelled the stale tobacco smoke, ashamed to admit to himself that, like Chernik, he might end up having to roll toasted onion pieces in cigarette paper.

When he walked down to camp under a mess of stars, past the spot where Bernat stood watch, the others sat munching their dinner between a small open fire and the fountain. Bernat anticipated Walton's question with a quick furtive scratch of his neck: "Beans. What else?"

Chernik, Brissot and Rafael were crouched smoking onion tobacco by the embers. Brissot nodded to Walton when he came to squat opposite to him.

"Let me take a drag, Mosko."

Brissot handed him his pipe. "You have to talk to Rafael. Things are getting out of hand." As an impatient Walton rose to leave, he clamped his hand on his shoulder. "Rafael doesn't want to hear reason, and has got everyone thinking that Valentin is a thief. A week from now will be too late. You have to talk to him tonight or we'll have trouble."

Walton spat twice to get rid of the onion taste. Valentin, sitting away from the others, was looking back at them, and though the conversation had been whispered in English, he must have understood what it was about. In the glimmer of the dying fire his lids twitched as if he were squinting at a source of unbearable light. Rafael stuffed himself with beans without looking up.

"OK, I will," Walton said.

"When?"

"Later tonight. Just tell Rafael I want to talk to him." As soon as Brissot left to carry out the order, Walton turned his back to the fire and to the men around it. The incident was annoying him more than he cared to show. He was, after all, the one who had quit his job as a foreman at the Union Switch and Signal Company when he couldn't exonerate a worker wrongly accused of theft. A move that seemed stupid now, because it had accomplished nothing. He'd even forgotten the details. So much about Pittsburgh, despite the years spent there, had gone from his memory. But it had happened at the end of April 1935, on his wife's birthday.

He remembered riding the bus home, the cold, smudge-filled city air spattered with hazy stars and thickening clouds. She'd become hysterical when he entered the room with a silver wristwatch wrapped in pink paper and news of his resignation. He recalled nothing of the argument other than that he'd left the house again to avoid hearing her weep and recriminate to her mother on the neighbours' phone. Until dawn, he'd walked the streets under a drizzle that could never rinse away the crowd of steel mills and belching smokestacks. Tonight he would give a year of his life for a cigarette and complete oblivion. It wasn't enough that his wife was merely an insect against the backdrop of factories and bridges lacing the confluence of Pittsburgh's rivers; insect and backdrop both had to be flicked away.

Later, when he was the only one left near the grey embers, Brissot returned.

"I told you I'll talk to Rafael," Walton said. "You don't need to remind me."

"I wasn't going to." Brissot spoke in bursts, in the conspiratorial voice he used sometimes. "I was thinking of the bloodstains on Lorca's shirt. Did you notice how blood had flowed down between his shoulders? He was shot sitting up."

Walton tossed a pebble into the coals, raising a spark. "Or standing, or kneeling."

"Anyhow, he maintained that position long enough for most of the blood to flow vertically. But how could that have been the case? I believe he was killed instantly."

"So there was a car, and they shot him inside it. We've been through that."

"Then ask yourself: whose car was it? The Fascists next door don't have one. And if Lorca was travelling under escort, where did they vanish to? Wouldn't there have been more shots fired? Wouldn't the *mulero* haven see them? I say there wasn't an escort at all."

177

"Or maybe there was, and they left without opening fire, and the *mulero* was lying."

Brissot shook his burly head. "Suppose he was telling the truth. If Lorca was shot inside a car at close range, why were there two shots fired? How could they have missed the first time? And why wouldn't they have taken off at once? The *mulero* didn't say the car left in haste."

In spite of himself, Walton began to pay attention. He poked the ashes with a stick, freeing more sparks.

When Valentin flitted past to his watch like a shadow, Brissot followed him with his eyes. "And supposing that the *cenetistas* did escort Lorca out of Teruel and lost him to a Fascist ambush, wouldn't they have come searching for him later?"

Walton said nothing. Rafael hurried past in Valentin's footsteps, misplacing rocks as he went, and Brissot nudged the American. "We'd better make sure we stop them from doing something stupid —"

He hadn't even finished the sentence when scuffling sounds came from the darkness. Brissot was already up and running. Walton didn't move. He heard thuds and stifled sounds, groans, Brissot's voice reproving Rafael and Valentin, but all he said was, "*Callaos.*" A short pause followed, as if the contenders were being restrained, then the voices grew loud and abusive again. From the dark, a piercing, high cry of physical pain caused him to bristle. Walton started out too, scattering embers under his feet.

RISCAL AMARGO

Fuentes, who was about to stand watch, carried the sleeping bag to the well, where the lieutenant wanted it. Bora dipped the ladle into the barrel, pouring water over his head and shoulders. "Everything in order, Fuentes?"

"Everything in order. *Buenas noches, mi teniente.*"

Three hours later, walking back from his watch, Fuentes noticed that the sleeping bag hadn't even been unrolled, and Bora was nowhere near it.

Bora didn't show up again until dawn. A damp clarity etched the looming prow of the sierra when he climbed, wringing wet, from the valley.

He found himself face to face with Fuentes, who'd been waiting a long time judging by the cramped way he stood to salute and his hard-eyed frown of concern. To avoid embarrassing both of them, Bora chose to ignore the other man's concern. "The password for today is *Coraje hasta la Victoria*," he said, adding, "Is the colonel up?" because Fuentes was still staring at him.

"Not yet, sir."

Blood was running from numerous cuts on Bora's legs, from the hem of the drenched khaki shorts above his knees to the rolled hems of his heavy army socks. He tried to look indifferent to Fuentes' attention. What would be the use? There was no hiding the wounds. They had stopped bleeding overnight but swimming had reopened them, and now the broken skin stung, itched, and blood was again starting to crawl across his skin in red trails. Fuentes was no doubt wondering how he could have blundered into barbed wire when there was no barbed wire on the sierra.

Bora waited for the sergeant to enter the post before recovering a straight, long thorn from his pocket. *I can't imagine where I went wrong. I went around from the Castellar side, just as I planned in the bell tower. The goat path leads up to Mas del Aire: there are no possible wrong turns. I took no wrong turns. I could even see the light of her window from below.* Yet at the foot of the last climb, by far the steepest, he had ended up entangling himself in a thick growth of bushes that seemed to have no leaves, only woody, sharp thorns, thin and straight as sailcloth needles. In the dark, he hadn't realized how far he'd gone into the spiny patch until he was in the middle of it. His good sense of direction hadn't kept him from gashing his arms and legs, and he never did regain the path. He had struggled just to free himself, tearing his skin as if struggling through razor wire. Each rip in the flesh had made him angrier, but the shrubs wouldn't give way. He'd fought the thorns until the tangle somehow spewed him out further down the mountainside. The golden light of her small window had no longer been visible above him. The worn, bare crags all around were unknown to him, and he had to watch his steps to avoid stumbling into the Red camp. Losing sight of her tempting window when it was nearly at hand had made him lonely and more fiercely eager to meet Remedios, who was perhaps, after all, a *bruja.*

For the first time since coming to the sierra, he'd really got lost afterwards. He'd wandered around gaunt granite faces and down steep narrow trails, where unexpected breaths of wind from below warned him that he'd come dangerously close to the abyss. Sudden wells of starry sky opened above him, shadowy figures glided overhead to hunt in the clefts of the earth. Bora had strayed as far as San Martín de la Sierra, the dark sentinel guarding the pit. As he had gone on, his blood had trickled to coat his broken skin. An intimate, heady odour had risen from it, and bringing his battered hands to his lips he'd tasted the blood on the tip of his tongue.

"Besame con tu lengua, aquí."

The sky had begun to pale by the time he had scrambled down the last slope to the brook. Sore and thick with blood and dust, Bora hadn't bothered to take his clothes off before getting into the water. Now he hoped to get changed before the men saw him.

The last thing he wanted to see was Serrano's immaculate shirt-clad torso at the windowsill of his room. Bora slipped the thorn into his chest pocket to execute a smart army salute. The colonel was putting on his tunic with the slow, measured gestures of a priest dressing for Mass. "Come up, Bora," he said. "I wish to speak to you."

The young Requetés were still asleep in Fuentes' narrow room. Bora glanced at them as he walked by the open door. They were about his age but he thought they looked much younger, almost like boys. He considered the possibility that he might look so hopelessly young himself.

Serrano had his back to the window. His left hand was closed in a fist, and the book of Lorca's poetry was in his right hand. "Close the door," he said. "How did you come to have this publication, Lieutenant?"

Bora answered that he had borrowed it, which wasn't apparently what Serrano wanted to know.

"I meant ideologically speaking: what made you wish to read these works?"

He's noticed the cuts, and that I haven't shaved. Bora tried to keep from worrying. *If he asks about the cuts, I'll have to make something up. I can't tell him the truth.*

"I heard about Lorca's poetry, Colonel, and was curious. There was no political curiosity on my part, only a literary interest."

Serrano's deep-set eyes slowly rose from the bloody marks on Bora's legs. "You said you didn't know who the man was when you found his body."

"It's true; I didn't."

"I happen to be familiar with this particular edition of Lorca's works. The frontispiece features a full-page photographic portrait of him."

Bora made an effort to slow down his breathing. "I don't recall seeing a photograph, Colonel Serrano."

"Of course not." Serrano opened the book wide, showing it to Bora. "It was ripped out of this copy."

Bora forgot about his breathing. "The photograph was already missing from the book when I borrowed it."

Serrano showed no interest in the book's provenance. "Is it your habit to spend nights away from this post?" he asked sharply.

"No, sir." So this was how Aixala and Paradís must have felt while he was questioning them. It was uncomfortable, and since Bora had no intention to lie as they had done, making comparisons didn't help. "I only spent one night away from the post."

"*Last* night, judging by your state. Doing what?"

"I went for a walk around the sierra, and I'm sorry to admit that I got lost."

Serrano placed the book on the table, face down. "Have the sergeant saddle our horses; my nephews and I are riding out for the morning."

Gloomily Bora walked to the water barrel to shave. It wasn't until he stared into the pinkish lather that he realized blood had run down his forearms to the palms of his hands.

EL PALO DE LA VIRGEN

"How's he doing?" Walton was waiting for Brissot at the foot of the stairs with Marypaz, whose cotton dress showed the plumpness of her thighs against the morning-lit door.

Brissot winked at Marypaz. "Oh, he's all right. The blade only glanced off his arm. It's a good thing that it was dark. Even so, gypsies seldom miss their mark, so we can assume that Valentin didn't want to hurt Rafael badly, only teach him a lesson. I can't say Rafael didn't deserve it, and you're partly responsible, because you didn't speak to him as I told you to. What about Valentin?"

"Looks like Maetzu broke his nose restraining him, but he won't let anybody get close. He won't let you take a look, even, unless you can get Rafael to apologize to him first."

RISCAL AMARGO

Sunday 18 July. Midday, at the post.

"Pleasure gives accuracy to the Workings," says Book 10 of the *Ethics*. It's true enough that the things I like doing come easiest. Twice as much effort has to go into doing the things I'm less interested in *as well*, but the result is the same. Their accuracy is the same. In any case, the life choice of a volunteer is damn revealing, especially in a war like this.

Herr C. is not telling me everything he knows about Lorca. Whether he wants me to find out on my own or doesn't think it worth his trouble to inform me, it matters little. What I *do* know is that Lorca didn't keep the appointment with his escort. This can only mean that: 1. he was kidnapped after leaving Herr C., driven off and killed; or, 2. he drove himself out of Teruel and was ambushed by the Reds. In either case, since there was no car near the body, somebody must have driven away with it.

I can only wonder why he didn't wait for his escort: did he mistrust them? I don't see why. According to Herr C. they saved him in Granada. But let's say Lorca left Teruel on his own and drove himself unarmed to the sierra. The Reds could have easily overtaken him on the mule track. Would they have taken the car afterwards, and where to? Surely not to this mountain.

I think he was more likely kidnapped in Teruel: but when? His family didn't see him after eight or so. He left Herr C.'s place an hour later. Three hours after that, he was dead at the foot of the sierra. Those are the facts. There's also the photograph: why would he carry a signed picture of himself if not to give it to that friend of his, Francisco, whom they called Paquito? It rankles with me that I know so little and can't figure out the rest.

The rest? He couldn't even find his way to Remedios'. Bora capped his pen. Sitting in the shady swelter of the lean-to, he left the diary open for the ink to dry on the page. He'd been careful to keep his right palm from bleeding onto the paper, and now studiously examined the cut.

The crisp, torn edges of gaping skin were translucent on both sides of the dark curdle of blood and plasma. If he pressed the edges together, the clot started oozing again; if he pressed harder, a gummy trickle beaded up, carrying red cells and minute bits of skin. If he pulled apart the sides of the cut, the tear bled and hurt more. Bora blotted his hand on his shirt before clasping the diary shut.

"You wanted to see me, *teniente*."

Niceto stood in the dazzle just outside the lean-to. The laxness of his attire and head of curls made him the perfect provincial Hamlet, but he was a good fighter from what Fuentes said, and Bora didn't dislike him. "I want you to escort me down to the brook at 05.00 sharp tomorrow," he said.

"*A sus ordines.*"

184

Bora stood up. He took Lorca's paperback out of his pocket. "Here. *Me ha gustado mucho.*" Niceto stretched out his hand to receive the book, but Bora held on to it. "I'm just curious about this missing page," he said.

"What missing page?" Niceto studied the margin of the frontispiece, where bits of torn paper betrayed the removal of the photograph. "I hadn't noticed there was a page missing." He snapped his fingers self-consciously. "The book was used when I bought it. Whoever owned it before me must have taken it out. Is it important?"

"It's a nice little edition. Where did you buy it?"

Niceto saw that Bora was handing him the book this time, and took it. "Good God, let me think ... it was in Madrid, more than two years ago. I also bought a collection of Rubén Darío and an illustrated Cervantes that day. It all cost very little." He made an artificial, proffering gesture with his right hand. "Feel welcome to keep it, *teniente.* You're not about to find Lorca's poems in the stores this summer."

Grateful that Niceto gave no sign of noticing the cuts, Bora would not accept the book as a gift, but said he'd keep it a few more days. "Does anyone know how Lorca died?" he added nonchalantly.

"Not really. He was killed in Granada last year, as I told you. Shot by firing squad, according to reports. He should have left Spain, or else remained holed up in Madrid where he could weather the storm."

Bora sneered. "We'll take Madrid soon enough."

"Not soon enough for me, *teniente.* My sister is a nun there, and I don't even know if she's still alive."

"We'll take Madrid soon, be sure of that." It sounded like a foreigner's glib confidence, but Bora could not come up with anything deeper right now. "I can't imagine who'd want to kill a poet."

Even in the shade, the heat made the men's lungs feel like leather pouches in their chests, and Niceto looked suddenly burdened by the sultriness. "Who, *teniente? How many*, you mean. Artists have their bitter conflicts. They say Buñuel couldn't stand him, and the painter Dali had his own grudges against him. I was so furious after he turned me down for that oaf from León, I could have strangled Lorca myself. It's just that strangling playwrights won't solve an actor's problems." Proudly Niceto tossed his head of dark hair. "It'd do no good whatever, in fact. Who knows who physically killed García Lorca, *teniente*. It might not even matter. What *really* killed him is something else."

Bora glanced past Niceto to the mutilated tree on the ledge, where Tomé was watering Pardo from a bucket. "What do you mean, something else? What else?"

"*Duende.*"

"*Duende.* You said that before. I don't know what the word means. What is *duende?*"

Niceto grinned politely. "*What* is it? It's not an answerable question."

"If it exists, it has to have a definition!"

"Yes, of course. But it's one of those things that are best described by what they lack. I can always judge who has no *duende*. But if one has it, then … it's hard to put it into words. 'Spirit' is a word for it. 'Soul' is another. But neither term does justice to what *duende* allows a man to do. Let me put it another way, *teniente*. I've seen you draw sketches. You read; I expect you like art. Do you by any chance play an instrument?"

Bora nodded, unsure of where the conversation was going. "Yes, the piano."

"And do you play well?"

"Sometimes I play quite well."

Niceto brought his hands together with a faint clapping sound. "Ah, but *so* well that it is as though God were in your fingers, and you were one with the piano, and music, and God himself?"

Bora hesitated.

"What I mean, *teniente*, is as if you and music —"

"At times, yes. There are such times."

"Beyond technique?"

"Beyond and outside of it, even."

"But is it a *fire*, a burning fire in the marrow and the gut?"

Bora understood. "Like love?" he surprised himself by saying, although the admission embarrassed him and seemed out of place. "Yes. But also like death. When I play as you say, no matter what or where, it is … like death, mostly."

"Yes!" Niceto lit up. "*That* – what you just said – that is *duende*. Whatever your field, music, poetry, war. When you do it so well that no one can compare with you, when the edge is too close to tell what is life and what isn't, there is *duende*. That's what Lorca had. Too much of it. Having too much is as bad as having none at all."

Bora worried at the cut on his hand, nodding. On the ledge, Tomé had finished watering Pardo, and as he walked back he stared at the lean-to and the two men in the shade. Bora resented the attention, and felt petty anger towards him.

"I get your point," he quickly told Niceto. "Perhaps it explains Lorca's artistry and fascination for death, but how could it have killed him?"

Niceto might have noticed Tomé's look, or he might not. In any case, he left the shade of the lean-to. "*Los enduendados se mueren jovenes, teniente.*" He stepped back into the sun. "Dying young is the price. Which is why I don't regret being just a slightly above average actor: it may guarantee me a longer life."

"I see." Bora had scraped the cut on his palm until it bled. "Was Lieutenant Jover *enduendado*?"

"Lieutenant Jover?" Niceto stepped away, grimacing in the sun. "No. No, he wasn't, *teniente*. But you … I don't know you well enough, but you might turn out to be."

Bora stayed behind, with his diary and Lorca's poems under his arm and his hand bleeding. He was startled when Fuentes approached with his heavy tread and saluted.

"*Teniente*, the colonel and his nephews are back from the sierra."

Even Serrano's fastidious figure was wilting in the oppressive swelter. The Requetés' youthful glowing faces were nearly as red as the Royalist berets they wore. The lathered horses were at once attended to and sheltered by Tomé.

"This is nothing compared to Morocco's *bled es siba*," the colonel was telling his nephews by way of consolation. "That borderland is where men prove themselves." While the boys went to greedily drink the barrel water they'd been shunning until this morning, Serrano slid his gloves into his belt and searched his breast pocket for a cigar. "Bora, I heard in Castellar that there's a vantage point higher than both camps. What do you know about it?"

Mas del Aire. Bora felt his heart thump suddenly. "The place is marked on the maps as little more than a ruin. I know" – he checked himself – "I more or less know how to get there."

Serrano struck a match. "And with all your wanderings through the sierra you haven't yet inspected the place?"

The glare of the sun on the ledge was unbearable; for a moment Bora saw nothing but a veil of blood lighting his entire body. When he managed clumsily to mumble, "I'm at the Colonel's orders," he was worried the huskiness in his voice might give him away.

"Well, there's no time like the present. Go."

He should be wondering why the order was coming now, but Bora wasn't about to question it. Soon he was stuffing map, sketchbook and camera in the canvas bag, where the bloody passbook of the man from Mockau was stashed away. So were the partially erased music sheets he'd found by the side of the brook after Lorca's death. Not even the key signature was recognizable on them; a few bars with semiquavers, a repeat sign and the runny dots of other notes smeared the first sheet. It was impossible to read them, and Bora understood why he had given up on the task. Standing in the full sun, however, he now made out a pencilled line that he managed to decipher by tilting the sheet so that the light hit it at an angle: the words CANCIÓN DE JÍNETE.

It was the title of two poems by Lorca, he recalled. One of them read, "In the black moonlight / of the highwaymen ..." Could it be a musical version of either poem? The blurred indication of a march tempo made it unlikely. Because Serrano was keeping an eye on him, he hastened to put the papers away and take the path up the sierra.

In less than twenty minutes, he reached Castellar. The climb to Mas del Aire looked moderately demanding from here, but the heat promised to make it brutal at this time of day. Bora started up at a steady pace.

Observing the small things around him in order to disregard his physical exertion worked for a time. Yellow and white crucifers bloomed in their clusters of bluish clover-like leaves. New thistles raised their barbed purple tufts, while old ones disintegrated to the touch into feathery bursts. Under the beating-down sunlight, rocks and shrubs had no shade; if he stopped to rest or look around for direction, Bora himself cast only the trace of a shadow, like a purple hem tucked beneath his feet. There was a moment when he mistook a swift cruciform silhouette on the ground for the airplane, but it was only a hawk swooping and soaring overhead.

Castellar appeared to shrink behind him. Ahead, the rise was steeper on this side of the sierra than it must be from the camp where the American known as Felipe climbed to see Remedios. Whatever his real name was – Philip, maybe? Philip what? – he was not someone Bora cared to think about now. He clambered up, using his hands at times when the grade became difficult, hampered by the canvas bag on his back, keeping on the lookout for the Reds.

It had been much easier in the cool of night. In front of him, small brown snakes slithered and shiny-eyed lizards darted into their holes or under the rocks. An invisible multitude of insects spoke a babel of clicking, ticking, grating voices. The crucifers became sparse and eventually disappeared from sight. Then there were only rocks, both safe and unsafe. Pebbles which escaped his grip clattered hollowly downhill. Dusty dirt came down with the sound of sifted wheat. Blanched, mirror-bright, the sky was too much to look at. Bora kept his face to the rock.

At one point he lost his footing. He thought he wasn't afraid of heights until he began to fall backwards and only a narrow shelf broke the fall as it met the sole of his boot and held his weight. Blood drummed in the veins of his neck. How had he done this in the dark? Bora clung to the rock wall to catch his breath. He smelled the stone's ancient dusty odour, dead and maternal. I'm sorry, he felt he ought to say, as though his slipping and then clinging on were clumsy and crude.

That's how he'd done it in the dark. At night, he hadn't fought the rock. He'd trusted it. This awareness made the climb less of a struggle, although the grade soon reached the limit of his ability to climb without equipment. No more insect noises, no more crumbling of pebbles into the void.

Suddenly, a brown ruffle of feathers alerted him that he'd caught up with the hawk. It balanced on a crag to his right, crouching over a young hare it was shredding with its beak and talons. Angry or disturbed, the bird flung a furry red scrap skyward before taking off with its broken prey. Stringy drops of blood fell, one of them landing on Bora's upturned, staring face.

Castellar had plunged into a cauldron of trembling haze by the time he wormed up El Baluarte, where it rose in wider, eroded shelves before the last strenuous climb to Mas del Aire. Bora reached a place wide enough to stand and catch his breath.

Here he had got lost the night before. Looking at it now, it seemed impossible. Only a few brambles clawed the inhospitable dryness. Bora recognized the thorns, but it was hardly the maze that had drawn blood from him hours earlier. Yet he'd been here; there was no other route he could have taken, even in the dark. It was right here, under Remedios' bright window, that the thorns had forced him back. Glancing up, only the blind corner of a rubble wall was visible from where he stood.

How strange. Even had he wanted to, he could not have followed a different path. Even the man called Felipe would eventually have to pass this way. But the wall had no windows.

EL PALO DE LA VIRGEN

Chernik walked to where Walton and Maetzu stood, at the edge of the camp. "Why is Marypaz crying?"

Walton said nothing. Maetzu, glued to the field glasses as if the valley had something to reveal today that yesterday or the day before had not been there, answered, "I didn't know she was crying. Ask Felipe."

Walton turned on his heel. "Not me. I'm going to the sierra."

"She's crying her heart out, Felipe."

"She'll get over it, Chernik. Let her cry."

Maetzu spat over his shoulder. "Going to see Remedios, eh? And Chernik wonders why Marypaz is crying."

"Mind your business, Iñaki."

"See if I don't."

Chernik followed Walton as he started out. "Well, Felipe, that's not good enough for me. She's miserable, and this time you can't just walk off."

MAS DEL AIRE

Standing at the edge of Mas del Aire, a bracing dry wind, like God's breath, gusted at him from the huge eastern sky. He felt a sense of exhilaration.

Remedios' house. *This* was Remedios' house. His heart sank pleasurably at the sight. Fifty paces away, the battered wing of an abandoned friary rose out of a circle of stone rubble. Its long side faced south-west towards the inner sierra, jutting out at the north end where a ramp of steps led up to a small three-arched porch. On the roof a scrolled iron cross, filed away by rust, leaned askew on the bleached bed of tiles. Shuttered windows marked the upper floor; martins flew back and forth from the eaves in front of them. Among tall weeds, a doorway opened on the long side, directly under the shuttling flight of birds.

All that separated him from an overwhelming silence was a dampened throb of blood in his ears if he turned his head to the valley. Bora kept still lest the rustle of his clothes break the hush.

But her door, Remedios' door, attracted him. With no plans about what he'd do or say if she came to open it, he knocked. No one answered. He knocked again, and a third time, and when he tried to push the wooden leaf inward, he met the obstacle of the lock. The door did not yield. Turning away from the door, Bora felt his way along the walls of the building through a growth of wild mint and nettles, searching for another opening. Leaving a trail of broken weeds, he found a small shuttered window on the south wall, and, coming around the back, he recognized the blank wall he'd seen from below. It belonged to the dilapidated enclosure of a chapel. Arched and more substantial, its double door did not budge, though Bora went as far as kicking it before leaving it be.

The porch, then. Around the corner, there was still the porch. Racing up the eroded steps, Bora found a door that had been left ajar. He unlatched his holster and went in. Inside, a stifling corridor divided two rows of empty low cells, where scented bundles of herbs hung from the rafters. No staircase led downwards, although Bora could look down into the chapel through an inner window.

It was a simple unfurnished space lit by windows set high under the eaves. No hangings, no altar cloth. No altar. Only heaps of drying grass on the floor, smelling like half-forgotten harvests and summers, and a faded fresco of the Holy Ghost as a clumsy dove blotching the sky-blue plaster wall. Bora walked out, feeling something between disappointment and anger. Remedios wasn't here, so what was the point of going inside? He moodily looked ahead, where the bright north rim of Mas del Aire seemed to mark the edge of the world. From there, martins sought their nests under the porch's eaves, slicing through the glare like slender skiffs.

The edge of the world. Bora started towards the rim, drawn by the silence and the hard, breathing heat. He found himself thinking, *If I reach the edge and look below, I might see all the kingdoms of this earth and their follies, swarms of warring peoples, towers and monuments and graves, rivers writhing into pocket-size oceans. I might see the end of all things and never be allowed to come back.* Crazy images scorched him like the fiery breeze. *It's the heat,* he reasoned. *It's the sun. What am I thinking of? I won't see all the kingdoms of this earth. God forbid I should see all the kingdoms of the earth. Fuentes was right; one shouldn't go bareheaded under this sun.*

The void at his feet lent him a dizzy view of the massif dividing the ledge far below, down to the remote valley floor where the brook wandered like strips of foil. Bora could imagine Teruel in the distance behind the haze. Not the kingdoms of the world: only Teruel, and a hawk sweeping in solemn circles on motionless wings, following the updraughts.

He had to crawl to look safely below. On his half of the ledge, the field glasses showed him the army post and the enemy camp. Here, where El Baluarte rose up less steeply than from Riscal, making it more manageable for scouts and sentinels, he saw a roof patched with sheet iron, an enclosure for horses and a terraced orchard. In front of the house, there was a trough full of water. Two men stood talking nearby, one of whom Bora recognized as the American. *At least he isn't with her,* he thought. The other was a small hairy man, balding on top, turned so that Bora couldn't make out his face.

Turning to the massif, he caught the glint of metal betraying at least two armed sentinels.

Searching the valley, Bora found the glimmering brook again, and the place where Lorca had been killed. The cane grove looked feathery from this height; the bridge past the curve a diminutive half-buried ring. Beyond it all, rock walls, sheepfolds, treacherous byways and hidden villages grew hazy until the land blurred into the northern sky.

Looking not at all the kingdoms of the earth but at Spain, lying under the haze with her war and blood and foreign hate, humbled him. He realized how irresponsibly, how shamelessly he had used his idealism to gain experience and learn. Closer in, Lorca's place of death – where, according to Serrano, the heart of Spain had been cut out – troubled him. *I carried the weight of his dead body and buried him with my hands. I laid the heart back in place. And, although I'm the foreigner from Leipzig, the flighty volunteer, the man who dared to cut him out of his country's breast.*

Precariously leaning over the edge, Bora took photographs of the valley and the camps below. The wind had fallen by the time he withdrew to safe ground and turned away from the rim. Remedios' house, huddled in its charmed circle of stone, brought him to his senses.

How had he been able to keep her out of his mind for so long? Whatever Serrano or Cziffra thought, she was the reason he'd scaled the mountain. Somehow seeking Remedios simplified everything. Although he had never seen her, he couldn't now bear to leave without meeting her. Young or old, dark or fair, handsome or not ... desire overtook his sense of discipline. To hell with duty, politeness, religion. It hadn't been so brutally simple even with the girls in Bilbao, when wine had made a difference.

Like an eager young dog, Bora crouched in the sun on her doorstep for an hour, waiting, but she did not return. When he finally, reluctantly decided to leave, he took the thorn from his pocket and stuck it in the wood of her door.

He'd gone some distance on the thistle-strewn path down from her house before he turned around on an impulse. Against the white sky, a girl stood there with a willow switch in her hand.

At first he mistook her for a child. Small, bare-legged, barefooted. In the sunlight, a crisp halo of red hair made her look like a slender torch. She'd seen him, of course, but did nothing other than flick the willow switch back and forth along her side. Bora's blood ran high. He had no doubt that this was Remedios, and he was overtaken by a clumsy, shameless desire for her to want him.

Remedios looked at him as if it were usual for a man in a Legion uniform to find himself there. They were not so close that they could plainly see each other's features, but he recognized that she was smiling.

"I came to see your house." Bora climbed back a few steps.

She whipped the willow through the air. "Well, have you seen it?"

"The door was locked." Bora spoke the next words in the hope that she would take them as he meant them, as a brazen hint. "I want to see inside."

"Why?"

"Because I want to."

She smiled. Her toes drew a small raking pattern in the silt when she turned to precede him uphill. "Let's go, then."

Bora watched her saunter up the path and nimbly climb the rise that took a fit man some effort. He followed, torn between looking at the strokes of the green switch and at the delicacy of her ankles. He preferred to stumble and stare rather than carefully choose his steps.

Past nettles and thistle blooms she led him, flicking her willow wand. Once in front of the door, she removed the thorn Bora had stuck in the wood, and instead of tossing it away, she put it between her lips. Under the pressure of her hands, the door gave way and opened.

"You didn't push hard enough," she said.

"I absolutely pushed hard enough."

"*Como te gusta.* It's open now." She smiled as he unholstered his gun before entering, the fullness of her lower lip arching, round and moist. "See what you want to see. I'll wait outside."

Coming from the rage of the afternoon, her house was as cool as a cave. Bora's eyes saw nothing but darkness at first. Then the dark turned into shapes, like night opening around him.

He stood in a vaulted space of plastered walls, festooned with aromatic bundles of dry flowers and thorny branches. Beyond a squat open arch was a second room, with an iron bed set against the wall. There, the brightness from the open door became muted like sunlight underwater. Bora drew near the wide, unmade bed. Plain linen sheets rippled across the mattress in eddies and loose spirals of cloth. Pillows were heaped at its head. Looking up from the bed, he recognized the pinched sweet face of Nuestra Señora de los Remedios in an unframed print nailed to the wall. A real butterfly wing was pinned onto the Child's dress.

Past a curtained doorway, the kitchen. Bora glanced in but wasn't interested. In the twilight of the bedroom, the scent of wild herbs – mint, dill, unnamed but familiar mountain flowers – was heady. The filigree of twigs and leaves drew a seductive spiderweb against the bare walls.

Outside, the heat felt like a blow to his chest, as painful and red as when he had emerged from the murky waterhole on the shingled bank of the brook. Remedios sat on a rock, drawing circles in the silt with the pointed end of the switch. Her amused expression hadn't changed, although she had now pinned the thorn to the breast of her cotton dress. "Have you found what you were looking for?"

"No." Bora put away his gun, feeling more than a little foolish.

"You didn't look hard enough."

"You're wrong. I do everything more than hard enough." Bora walked over to her and she laughed, but he didn't know why until he looked down at his feet and saw that he'd stepped into one of the circles. He erased the furrow with the hobnailed sole of his boot. "Do sounds from the valley carry up here?"

"At night, if the wind's right. When I'm alone."

Alone? Bora wondered how that could ever be, with sex-starved men up and down the sierra. Remedios was very beautiful, even under the severest scrutiny. She was what he'd always thought beautiful, and her fairness in a land of dark women, her whiteness attracted him, created an intimate kinship of colour and race. When she bent forward to draw another loop in the silt, the motion offered him a glimpse of her small breasts. It was an unrehearsed, fleeting movement, while her knees and ankles stayed tightly joined throughout.

Bora tasted salty dust on his tongue. "And in the daytime?"

"In the daytime I'm alone."

"Did you hear shooting a few nights ago?"

"No." Her small face shone like silver in the red halo of her hair. "I must not have been alone."

Bora looked at her grimly. His life seemed to have compressed itself into the area where his taut stomach muscles met his groin. Although a part of him was counting on the light summer uniform to hide nothing, the awareness of it distressed him. Half despairing, half hopeful, he stood there, silent and resentful and sure that she knew what he was thinking.

Without looking up, Remedios said, "At dawn, before the haze settles in the valley, I can see a long way down." She drew smaller circles now, one inside the other. "You go to the brook before sunrise."

Bora watched the circles reduce in size, as in a target that would soon find its centre mark. "How do you know who it is? It's too far away to tell."

"I have good eyes, and you look different from all your companions." She giggled at the cuts on his legs. "Especially now."

Bora felt the blood rush to his head. He felt such a crude ache that he couldn't condense it into anything simpler, so essential that it made him shiver and forget every other reason for being here – what his commanders had ordered and expected, why the country was at war, anything. He felt stupid and raw. "I don't know what you mean."

"No?"

Reaching out quickly, Bora took the sapling from her hand and threw it away.

Remedios let him do it. "*Hace mucho calor,*" she said, smoothing her dress with the palms of her hands. She stood from the rock and started towards the house. "I have a well inside. I'll give you to drink."

Just past the threshold, through the chink between the door and the frame, a fine blade of white light filtered in. There Remedios stopped. Bora held his breath as she leaned her shoulders against the corner where the sunbeam sliced through the darkness, blocking the light out for the length of her small body, trapping herself in the narrow space. Light and dark fusing. Heat and coolness. Outside became inside. She stood poised between opposites like a slender shuttle in the weave. He stood facing her, and couldn't begin to think of the right words to say.

Remedios pulled the thorn out of the cloth on her breast and touched her lower lip with it. "*Besame con tu lengua, aquí.*"

Bora did. He kissed her, cradling the nape of her neck without drawing too close, afraid that an embrace would make him lose control.

This is what men remember when they die. Holding a woman's face, seeking the first opening on offer because to enter her mouth is to be inside her for the first time, to slowly sink into a breathlessness of the body and soul. This is what I'll remember. All the kingdoms of the earth were in the curl of her tongue. Light, shadow, light knifing the dark and setting her hair afire. *Poor Jover, who never again can feel this exquisite pain.*

By the act of sliding buttons through cloth, Remedios turned all gleaming and white, darts of brilliant light etching a line along her shoulder and one small breast, lighting her pearlescent skin like an ember. Bora felt her nipple gather crisply under his fingertips as she slid out of her dress to the waist, like an almond clean from its hull. He could no longer bear to look at her face. The dazzle was unsustainable, his entire self singed by her brightness and touch. Still the dress clung husk-like to the moisture of her hips.

Oh, Remedios, you have the navel of a virgin. The cut on Bora's palm opened and bled. She sank down until he was crouching in front of her, and her knees parted under the cloth like knots of ivory. Everything that had ever opened before him, or been answered, revealed, given, had been preparation for this. The light was as sharp and white as steel, like God looking in at them. Bora folded the dress back.

Remedios, let me do it for the sake of God looking in, looking in – Remedios, let me do it for the sake of God looking in.

Remedios had a well inside. She would give him to drink.

5

What grief,
What grief,
What pain!

FEDERICO GARCÍA LORCA, "HOSPICE"

EL PALO DE LA VIRGEN

As it had the day before, the airplane returned towards evening, when Walton had finally succeeded in convincing Valentin to have his broken nose treated. Now Valentin was stamping his feet as Brissot disinfected the wound: Walton heard his groans while he stood at the door watching the sky. Like a thumbtack on light-blue cardboard, out of reach of the Lewis gun, the airplane sought the interior of the sierra. Minutes later, it was back. High above Remedios' house it banked slowly, glimmering as the sun struck the cockpit.

Remedios. Walton kneaded the back of his neck. He'd never been able to figure her out, although in recent days he'd been thinking about her more than ever before. Perhaps this change was in response to Marypaz's jealousy; or perhaps Remedios no longer occupied an important place in his life and was ready to pass into the realm of things he no longer cared about.

For all her flirting with Almagro's men, there was no denying Marypaz's love for him. Likewise, Lorca's death was certain and definitive. Walton didn't need confirmation of what was secure; vigilance was necessary only where there was doubt, when things could be taken away from him.

By her own admission, Remedios was like no one else. He liked her because she never spoke ill of other women, never asked about Marypaz, never talked politics. There was the lovemaking, too, but that alone didn't explain the way he felt about her. High overhead the metal tack flew past again, engine straining.

Walton didn't understand the way Remedios spoke, though, or else she didn't make sense. "Today the sky is laughing," she'd say. "What does that mean?" he'd ask, and Remedios would point at the sky: "Look. Can't you see?" she'd add, as though it were self-evident. And another one: "Some men need to have their lives sucked out of them." *Some* men. What kind of men? Men like him, obviously. And what do the other kind of men need?

"Are you done yet?" he heard Valentin complain from inside the house, followed by Brissot's irritable answer: "No, pig-head."

On the terraced ground, Rafael and Chernik had returned from gathering sticks to keep the fire going. Oblivious to the airplane, they now squatted by the embers, while Maetzu stood guard halfway up El Baluarte.

Remedios. Walton remembered how he'd once gone to her drunk and somehow they'd ended up arguing. In June, it had been. "You're just a whore," he'd said, and had believed it too, as he more or less did now. Anyway, it was close enough to the truth that there had been nothing wrong with saying so. But Remedios had withdrawn to one corner of the bed, squatting like a cat, white-faced, so shrunken into herself that she appeared diminutive.

"Then I'll give you a whore-gift tonight." It was all she had said. After returning to camp at daybreak, he'd learned that one of the men had accidentally killed himself while cleaning his gun. He told himself he didn't believe in coincidences, yet from that day on he chose his words carefully with her.

After a last round, the airplane veered to the north-west and disappeared for the night. For Walton it was a signal to go back inside, where Brissot was still scolding Valentin. He walked past them and up the stairs.

All afternoon Marypaz had been asleep in his bed, exhausted from crying. She still lay on her side on top of the sheets, beaded with perspiration, sucking her thumb. Walton contemplated her. She hadn't sucked her thumb since Barcelona but had gone back to it, teeth holding on to her knuckle and the rest of her hand half-closed against her chin. Arguing with Marypaz had forced him to open old doors, doors he'd closed on past aches and disappointments, on his reasons for trying to escape. Like the fact that in eight years and six months of marriage, his wife had proved barren. After five years they'd started the rounds of specialists as far away as Cleveland and Baltimore. They had thought about adopting, at one point, but there had never been enough money, or perhaps not even enough interest on his part. It had played a definite role in their divorce, and although he had told everyone that he'd left his wife, the truth was that she had been as sick of him as he'd been of her. *Man*, he thought, *the door's wide open now.*

Walton straightened himself up silently to avoid waking Marypaz, and went back over to the door. Just before coming to Spain he'd heard his ex-wife had married a drugstore manager with two grown sons and was living past the railroad tracks off Smallman Street. Smallman. How fitting. Life all seemed like that, small and useless like a pinch of dirt you have to put under a microscope to see if it's real. *Slam that door, Walton, and keep it shut.* The dimples and folds in Marypaz's flesh were pale green and sweaty. Walton took another step back, and another.

After his flare-up, he felt a sullen contempt for everyone. Contempt was what the edge of the floating scum at melting season left on the shores of Eden Lake. Scum and waste the snow covers in fake prettiness until the spring. Back in '29, Lorca had walked the foamy edge of the lake and called it beautiful.

Downstairs Brissot was alone, wiping his hands on a frayed towel. "I heard something interesting from Valentin," he said, with his conspiratorial owlish look.

Walton felt like spitting. "Well, isn't that grand."

"You know he has this widow in Castellar —"

"Yes, yes, the Yarza woman. A busybody midwife. What of it?"

Brissot led him outside, dumped the bloody water on the ground and stopped at the fountain to rinse the washbowl. "It seems someone from the Fascist camp has been asking about a burial on the sierra."

"Who?"

"We don't know yet." As Brissot headed for the almond orchard in the back, Walton followed. "It changes everything, Felipe! Maetzu was right to do away with the *mulero* and his lies. Why would the Fascists be interested in the burial if they hadn't killed Lorca?"

Walton sat in a cloud of gnats, finding that closing his eyes helped him to think. "All we know is that *someone* killed him. We've been over it a hundred times." When he looked, he realized how beautiful the sky was through the branches of the almond tree. "His shoes, his papers could have been taken by his killer or by someone unrelated. But I doubt a killer would have laid him on his back and folded his hands on his stomach."

"Is that what you meant by 'fooling with the body'?"

"Of course not. By that I meant that the fly of his pants was undone."

"Well, *that*!" Brissot waved away the gnats. "It could have happened while they were frisking him, although you know how intolerant the natives can be when it comes to sexual matters! Knowing of Lorca's leanings, maybe the killer meant to disgrace his body. I reckon the person who closed his eyes and folded his hands was someone else entirely. He'd been dead over six hours when we found him. Plenty could have happened in that time."

"The place is hardly a frequented highway, Mosko."

"No, but the *mulero* happened to be there that night. *He* could have stolen the shoes, for that matter. It's not a detail he'd have mentioned, even if Maetzu had given him more time."

Walton grumbled. "Back to the *mulero*, are we? Don't forget that when we returned to the brook looking for clues, the German was already there, damn him."

"Then it *was* the German. I thought you said he sounded British."

"Whatever he is, what else would he be doing there?" Pressing his thumbs into his eyelids, Walton could see nothing but a blind yellow glare like the wall in his dreams.

"He might have orders to dispose of any evidence left behind."

As he let his arms drop to his sides, bright green circles burst in front of Walton's eyes. "He acted curious, not surprised. Maybe he was looking for the body. Or maybe he'd gotten there before we did and was the one who went through Lorca's clothes. Or maybe he had no idea what the fuck *we* were doing down there, or that anyone had been killed." Walton's desire to argue fled from him like gnats chased by a piece of cloth. "Who's to tell if Lorca was killed by the German or his men? For Chrissake, Mosko. As if people need a reason for killing these days. It's only with murders that you've got to look for motives."

"This is a political assassination."

"You don't fucking know that. Can't you get it? None of us knows for sure why Lorca was killed, or why he wasn't killed in Granada the first time around!"

Brissot gave up for the time being. "I reported what the widow said: you take it from here. When I told Valentin to learn all that he can from her, he answered that he'll do us no favours until we stop treating him like a thief."

"Well, screw him too. Today, instead of going to the sierra, with Rafael's help I searched every pallet and sack – including yours, including mine – and turned up nothing."

RISCAL AMARGO

In the evening, Serrano listened indifferently to Bora's report on Mas del Aire. "It's of no use to us," he commented. "But sometimes intelligence is good by default."

Bora had been worried he'd have to supply details; now that he'd been asked for none, his only concern was that Serrano might notice his lips were raw. Would the colonel think the wind had caused it? Climbing *might* account for the reopening of the cuts on his limbs. "The plane," he said to keep the other's scrutiny away from his scruffy appearance, "is definitely surveying the inner sierra."

Serrano said nothing about Bora's lips or the plane or anything else. He looked beyond the lieutenant in an unfocused way. "It is fair for you to know that this afternoon my nephews and I rode to the place where you buried Lorca. Naturally I explained nothing to them whatsoever; young men are seldom worthy of confidence."

Did he suspect I might have moved the body since our first visit together? After leaving Remedios' house, Bora had euphorically wandered the deserted streets of Castellar, and anyone could have shot him dead ten times over. He sensed mistrust in Serrano's words, but right now he couldn't bring himself to give a damn about his opinion of young men in general, or of him as a representative of that group.

Sunday 18 July. 23.00, written by candlelight at the post.

I met Remedios today.

Since my visit, I need to reconsider, reorder, throw away or put so many of my previous assumptions aside somewhere I won't be able to find them in the near future. Everything is upside down, and intellectual patterns – even Kant's reason, *especially* Kant's reason – serve me nothing. To hell with universals, first principles and all that: the term "relative" meant nothing to me until now. Everything has become small, and small is immense.

How have I spent weeks in this place without knowing the *bruja*? When I die I'll think of her, I am sure. How many men have the privilege of knowing what their final thought will be? I may not be deserving of it, but the privilege is mine.

There's purity about her: her colour, her grace, the way she speaks. I thought about it, and that's the word: purity. I asked her, "Are you a gypsy?" And she said no. She asked me nothing. She didn't ask my name, even. I asked her, "Are you married?" And she said no. But she didn't ask if *I* was. As if I could envision being married to anyone after what happened today, after realizing how it can be. From now on, everything will have to compare to that.

As for me, my naivety was appalling. Not that I thought of myself as experienced, but still! Is it because I grew up Catholic, or half-English, or my stepfather's son? All the while I marvelled at how wise she is, how unlike anything, anybody else. Neither coarse nor jaded, wiser than her years (how old is she? Twenty-six at most, but you could believe her ten years younger, except for her wisdom).

Walking back I was reminded of Professor Hohmann quoting Aquinas to the class: there was *splendour of order* in what happened, nothing less. I can't sleep, I can't think, I can't write anything that makes sense. I read and reread Lorca's poem about the unfaithful bride. '... the rustle of her skirt sounded in my ear like silk torn by ten knives ...' It's all true, just as he says. I'm certain Niceto and Herr C. are only reporting malicious rumours about him. No one can write as Lorca did about women and not love them. As for me, I couldn't put today's experience into words if I wanted to: it is ineffable.

The colonel, who acted strangely all evening, wants me to go to Teruel tomorrow. Does he want me away from Riscal? In any case I'm glad of my orders, since the trip will give me a chance to see Herr C. and do some other things I promised I would do.

Bora was about to cap his pen, but hesitated. In a very small hand, at the bottom of the page, he added,

I don't want to believe that the American goes to her, that's all. She never mentioned him, and I was grateful for that.

Early on Monday morning Colonel Serrano was waiting on the ledge when Bora climbed back from the brook. The sierra was a giant cathedral, all ramparts and spires against the tender sky. Mas del Aire hovered suspended between earth and heaven, in the place where the pediment of the cathedral would be.

"Here are the papers I want you to deliver to Teruel, Lieutenant."

"Yes, sir."

"And here is a letter I want you to carry by hand to my wife." The sealed letter lay in his gloved hand. "Don't go just yet," Serrano added as Bora took it. His gaunt face, seamed and grey, promised no compassion to others or to himself.

Bora, who was anxious to set off, expected everything but the words that came next.

"There are some shadowy points in Lorca's death, Bora, beginning with the actual hour of death. Couldn't he have been killed much later than around midnight?"

Bora placed Serrano's documents and letter in the inner pocket of his tunic. "I'm not medically trained, but I believe I estimated the hour of death approximately enough."

"Well, all I have is your statement on it. *You* said he was killed by a gunshot to the head, and that he had no papers on him."

The gravity of the innuendo began to dawn on Bora. "Sir, I had no reason whatever to lie about García Lorca when I didn't even know who he was. Why would I have reported to you that I'd found his body in the first place, and show you the snapshot he had with him?"

"For one, because you didn't ask me whether I'd followed and had already seen the body on my way to the sierra."

Bora was reminded of a fencer, stock-still and deliberate as he readies to deal the winning blow.

"Accidents happen in civil wars, Lieutenant. There are times when we kill in haste, or by mistake."

What? Bora tensed up. He only managed to keep control of his posture and voice because Fuentes and Niceto were watching from afar. "I have not come to Spain to carry out indiscriminate killings. As a brother officer the colonel cannot possibly —"

A wave of the gloved hand interrupted him. "We're not in your national socialist army, Bora: I am your superior, not your brother officer. Hard though my words may seem to you, I must make sure. I do not trust young men. You must give me your word of honour as a Christian and a gentleman that you did not kill García Lorca."

Bora hated himself for blinking. He hated himself for feeling mortified. But he said, automatically, "You have my word of honour, Colonel Serrano."

TERUEL

He'd recovered part of his composure by the time he entered the unobtrusive Abwehr office and greeted the short-haired secretary. Cziffra had apparently overheard him, because he stuck his well-groomed head out of his office door down the hall. "Come in, come in, Lieutenant. If there's film in it, leave the camera on my secretary's desk."

The first thing Bora noticed stepping into Cziffra's space was that the ugly red vase was missing from its niche. Only shards remained; looking across the room in a straight line, he saw a large, ragged hole in the windowpane.

"Just a .22 calibre, nothing to worry about," Cziffra smirked. "It's better than being deadly bored in Düsseldorf."

Bora laid on the desk the bloodstained document found on the man called Matthias Braun, and while the operative glanced at it scornfully, he reported on the ambush, on the disappearance of Lorca's relative Antonio Cadena, and the unidentified airplane.

"The plane isn't ours," Cziffra said briefly. "Oh, I believe it's a German machine, as you say, but it isn't manned by us. Unless the Italians are sending it around, we'll have to live with the mystery unless it flies low enough to show its intentions."

Cziffra had a way of bringing up relevant subjects in a tone that put a safe, unemotional distance between himself and the matter at hand. Danger and politics sounded like small talk. "So, how are you getting along with the colonel?" he inquired now, carefully dabbing a starched handkerchief to his neck.

Bora's plans to keep his resentment to himself collapsed the moment he was asked. "He demanded my word of honour that I didn't kill Lorca."

Cziffra's jaw moved under his smooth skin like the well-oiled element of a vice. "He's only angry at you because, unlike his son, you're alive."

"He ought to impress his grief on his nephews, then. I'm nothing to him."

"He may see you as more promising than his nephews, and in need of the traditional hard whipping that goes with the perception of quality."

"With all due respect, that is an inference on your part. You do not know me well enough to say."

"Ah. Is that what you think?" With a scowl, Cziffra reached for a grey folder, which he waved like a teacher showing graded homework. "Just preliminary information, but there's more coming." He opened the folder and lifted out a typewritten sheet of onion paper. "Family: von Bora, or von Borna, of baronial Saxon stock, related to Martin Luther's wife but faithful to Romanism, which prompted your ancestors to adopt the motto *Fidem Servavi*. Paul's words, if I am not mistaken, for 'I kept the faith.' A family of landowning diplomats and career soldiers, but also, for the past two hundred years, publishers. The Bora Verlag dominates the scene at the Leipzig International Book Fair, specializing in books on philosophy, history and religion, having recently added a much-acclaimed line of foreign literature in translation. True?"

Bora found the question too academic to answer. Still, since Cziffra was glaring at him, waiting for a reply, he said, "True."

"I thought so. Let's see what else. Your mother Georgiana Alexandra, known as Nina, is Scots on her mother's side – a cadet branch of the Black Douglases, it says here – and a first cousin to your late father, the famous musician and friend of Richard Wagner. A gossiped romance between relatives, your parents', with a difference of thirty years between them. You were born 11 November 1913 in Edinburgh, and baptized Martin-Heinz Douglas Wilhelm Frederick in the Jesuit church there; a few months later your father died of throat cancer. In 1916 your mother married an Imperial Staff old-line Junker who'd wooed her unsuccessfully the first time around, namely Army Generaloberst Edwin von Sickingen, of the 1870 contingent. A Catholic convert, vegetarian, non-smoker and believer in homoeopathy, who two years ago left his post as commander of the Leipzig 14th Division of Gruppenkommando 3, Dresden, in a huff over some political disagreement we'd best not go into." At this point in the reading Cziffra smiled. His teeth, small and even like children's milk teeth, showed in the unkind crescent of his mouth. "At least you seem to have your ideological heart in the right place, even though you started by studying philosophy at the University of Leipzig. There you graduated summa cum laude, having already been awarded permission to lecture, the coveted *venia legendi*, in your first year. You then surprised everyone – including your stepfather, who had secretly hoped you would – by choosing a military career." Cziffra didn't look up from the page, but a vestige of the malicious smile was still on his face. "Cavalry school in Hanover, infantry school in Dresden, they gave you a special leave from the War

Academy to let you serve here. So far your superiors have had nothing but good things to say about you ... but then several of them are your stepfather's former colleagues. You consistently demonstrated – and I quote – 'strong will, lucidity of intellect, splendid resilience under stress, exceptional capacity for leadership, et cetera'." The smile widened, no kinder than before. "Traditional Feldherr qualities, although you haven't yet even held company command, and much can happen between the stages of diligent student and warlord. What else? You have a younger stepbrother; the family country house in Trakehnen is a shrine to your late father, whom both your parents mourn mawkishly. You spent several summers in Rome, a guest of Sickingen's Italian first wife; their marriage was annulled during the Great War. Raised with the customary trilingualism of your social class – German, English, French – you have added Greek, Latin, Italian and Spanish since." Here Cziffra did look up, over his glasses. "I suggest you turn your attention to Slavic tongues next; they might come in handy before you know it." The folder had more pages in it, but these remained unread. "Yes, you managed to do it all. Now you must only take care that you don't burn out before you're thirty. Or that you don't go off the rails."

Despite the heat of the closed room, Bora's perspiration felt clammy, and his clothes stuck to the cuts on his arms and legs. "I'd like to hear what you meant by 'political disagreement', as relates to the general."

"Naturally: the political disagreement about which you argued with your stepfather. The fact is that, unlike the old man, you believe in an intimate relationship between army and politics." Careful to pinch his trousers at the knees, Cziffra sat on the corner of his desk. "Philosophy seems to have done you good, unless it's plain ambition. Poor Lorca, the very thought that a German volunteer could have killed

213

him by mistake! It would lend credence to the belief that the Abwehr buries its blunders." Seeing Bora prick up his ears at these words, Cziffra changed the subject. "Is that the end of your report?"

"Yes, until I learn more about Lorca's last evening in Teruel."

"What if I told you that he had NKDV enemies in town?"

"You teach me that we all have communist enemies, Herr Cziffra. And your vase is shattered beyond my ability to tell which side is which colour."

Cziffra looked moderately amused. "You're not nearly as clever as you think, but it's fun watching you try. What else?"

"The hour of Lorca's arrival at your office might be helpful."

"That, I can supply to you." After dabbing again at his neck and face, Cziffra took a small notebook out of his pocket and leafed through it. "He arrived at my office at 9.25, stayed half an hour and said nothing about leaving that night. If he left his cousin's house shortly after eight, he must have been somewhere else during the intervening hour and more."

"Señora Cadena mentioned a stage designer friend."

"His lover, you mean. Francisco 'Paco' Soler, a Madrid faggot he met while preparing a play. He's a harmless cocksucker."

Bora felt a slight blush rise to his face at Cziffra's uncouthness. He recalled the writing behind the photograph: A MI QUERIDO AMIGO PAQUITO. "Is it possible that Lorca went to visit him?"

"It's possible, even though things had cooled off between them lately."

So maybe Soler returned the snapshot to Lorca, who carried it in his pocket. "Perhaps Lorca was worried, or had had a premonition."

Cziffra laughed this time around, a strange reaction on his unfriendly face. "Lorca had nothing but premonitions. Eighty per cent of what he produced deals with death one way or another. The only good thing about premonitions is that sooner or later one will prove you right."

"Given the circumstances, may I try to meet with Soler after I visit Señora Cadena?"

"You may. But what do you hope to learn, and how will you justify a visit? He won't think for a moment that you're Spanish."

Bora caught himself looking at the blue and red shards in the niche. "I'm an officer in the Foreign Legion, and as a member of the armed forces, I'm perfectly within my rights to inquire. After all, the family asked me about Lorca's disappearance. If Soler is unaware of the murder, he'll be anxious to have details. If he knows plenty, he'll likely clam up or evade questioning. My goal is to find out whether Lorca in fact visited him on the night he died, and if so, whether Soler saw him leave alone or with others, on foot, horseback or in a car."

Cziffra casually ran the folded handkerchief over his neck, above his immaculate shirt collar. "Lorca came here alone, on foot. As for his leaving Teruel, despite his codename he was no horse devotee, so scratch the possibility of his spontaneously riding to the mountains. If he did in fact die sometime after midnight, a motor vehicle must have been involved. Not ours, because he never met his escort. And the public car is still in the garage here in Teruel."

Carelessly, Cziffra crumpled the handkerchief in his breast pocket. "By the way, the deceptive information about our deployment in Aragon reached the Reds through another courier, in another sector. As for Antonio Cadena, it seems he was detained on the afternoon of the twelfth in the town of Alfambra, north of here. He reportedly lies half-dead in a prison camp, despite the fact that his family was forced by the police to pay an exorbitant sum against promises of a quick release. Today's newspapers list the Cadenas among the donors of money and personal jewels 'to the Cause'."

"How much may I tell Señora Cadena, sir?"

"As little as possible. Here's Soler's address, and the location of the public garage."

EL PALO DE LA VIRGEN

"If Marypaz asks where I am, just tell her I've gone to the sierra." Walton spoke to Bernat because he was the only one who would pass on the intelligence if needed. Brissot wasn't to be trusted in this matter, Maetzu and Chernik had gone deep into the mountains to hunt for meat, and neither Rafael nor Valentin was in a sociable mood.

Bernat said he would. "But you're really going to see Remedios, aren't you? You've never been in the daytime before."

"I'm going where I'm going. Unless Marypaz asks, keep your trap shut."

Halfway up the climb from the camp, Walton changed his mind. He intended to visit Remedios, but what was the hurry? There was something else in Castellar to clear up first.

CASTELLAR

In the village, shutters and doors were already closed to the mid-morning sun. A woman's scolding voice came muffled from a second floor, along with the monotonous click of a handloom. Walton walked on, to a whitewashed house in the middle of a fig orchard at the south edge of Castellar.

"Yes, yes. I know who you are," the Widow Yarza said without opening the door more than was needed. Her pasty face and ring-laden right hand stood out against her black clothes. She huffed as if she were doing him a favour. "Well, all right. Come in."

At first she only listened, hands on her generous hips, cocking her head. There was something absurdly provocative in her stance, but Walton chose to indulge her vanity. "Why, you're much younger than I thought! No wonder the men talk about you."

"Do they?" Self-consciously smoothing her hair, she sat down in front of him, under a framed picture of old King Alfonso and his queen. The hand-tinted postcard of a flamenco dancer was jammed between the frame and the glass, along with the photo of a much younger Yarza and her late husband: he seated, she standing at his side in a high-combed wedding mantilla.

Walton nodded, mumbling another flattery so that he could spring the question he had come for. Her small eyes searched him as if she were making up her mind about him. Her eyebrows were hairless; she must have plucked them, because there was fine black down on her upper lip. Watching her mull over an answer, Walton had the impression that one could deflate plump cheeks by poking them, like dough filled with yeast. Yes, she said at last, dragging her words. Someone had come probing about a recent burial; she didn't know who, but the query had come from the *Alemán* in the Fascist camp.

"The German, eh?" Walton concealed his irritation. "How much do you know about him?"

The bare eyebrows went up half an inch. "Not much. He's been to Castellar twice, maybe three times. Has no woman in the village."

That is, Walton thought, *he hasn't come to you.* Still, he asked, "Have you seen him?"

The widow picked at invisible lint on her black skirt. She had braided her sleek hair so tightly that, sitting opposite her, Walton could have sworn she'd gone bald and painted black shoe polish onto her scalp. "Through my bedroom shutters, just yesterday. I knew it was him because he's tall. Taller than you, even."

Walton resented the comparison. "Well, what else?"

"Army shorts, good-looking boy."

"I mean, what was he *doing*? Was he alone, walking?"

"Walking?" She threw up her hands. "He laid down a canvas bag, sprinted up and did *two cartwheels* right in front of my window."

The craziness of doing cartwheels in the streets of Castellar peeved him. There was something defiant or light-hearted or insane about it that made Walton resentful. It had to be the same man who had put a gun to his head to see him "up close" and barely escaped Maetzu's angry fire.

Leaving the village, he was still chewing over the news. No one in Castellar knew about the burial, so the German's asking was useless. One dust-kicking step after the other, he reached the place where the climb to Mas del Aire began. Yes, but how much did the German know? Why was he meddling?

Walton came to a halt, pressing his gathered fingers together to wipe the sweat from his forehead. The gravesite at Muralla del Rojo was easier to reach from where he stood than Remedios' house.

Still, it took him nearly an hour to get there. Across a flat pebble over the grave, a tailless lizard sunned itself, and scuttled out of sight when Walton chased it. During their last meeting in Castralvo, Lorca had half-jokingly stuck out the index and small finger of his right hand when mentioning death. He'd recited to Walton some incantation about a lizard, and here was the lizard again, sunning itself on his grave.

Women are lucky, who can cry. Walton squatted to remove windblown burrs and chalky traces of bird droppings from the mound. In the noon hour, the pebbles glared white, hiding more lizards and the body. *Damn*, he thought, *there's something about graves that separates. That's why men build them. They form an obstacle between us and the dead, giving a shape to grief, a name to it.* Grief without a place to grieve is more heart-rending: graves draw pain to themselves, and make it bearable.

In Valdecebro Lorca had showed him the anthem he was working on. "It's almost ready, Felipe. What do you want me to call it?"

Walton answered that he didn't know.

"Well, I'll call it 'Canción de Jínete', then." Lorca laughed his infectious laugh, a dark man's bright laughter.

"Why 'The Horseman's Song', Federico?"

"Because death comes riding to the enemy." Lorca was still smiling, but Walton felt an edge of fear in the words, and in himself.

"And to us?"

Lorca raised his hand in the superstitious two-fingered sign. "To us too, Felipe." Other than farewell, they were the last words Walton heard from him.

In front of him, the lizard felt confident enough to resume its place in the sun. After talking to the widow, the image of the German doing cartwheels had been replaced in Walton's mind by another. He could imagine him by the brook searching, spying, trying to make sense of things. Even folding Lorca's hands, which was just like something a man who does cartwheels in the street would do. That day, as with so many other days in his life, Walton had come second, too late.

Turning his back to the grave, he started to head for Mas del Aire from the side he was familiar with, less steep and wind-beaten.

TERUEL

The public garage opened on to a sloping square at the highest point of Teruel's hill. To the north of the square, limestone walls ran along both sides of a tower, facing the dry hollow that had once been the ancient Moorish town. As Bora walked in, a stench of oily rags weighed down the air. Four cars sat there. Two had their hoods lifted; the windshield was missing from the smallest one, an old Fiat. An engine rested on cement blocks. A grease-smeared door on the end wall led somewhere, but it was closed and no sounds came from within.

Cziffra had told him the car for hire was an Ansaldo, surely the dark green Model 10 with its windows rolled down. He walked around it in search of holes, scratches, dirt packed in the tyres, and any telltale marks of violence to the interior. He had time to lean in and read the odometer before someone approached slowly from behind.

"Anything I can help you with?"

Bora backed out of the car. "Yes."

An albino in dirty overalls stood with a wrench in his hand. "If you're looking to hire this car, it's already reserved for a wedding party in the afternoon. It'll be available again tomorrow morning."

Bora scribbled the numbers he'd read in a notebook. "I don't need it. I want to know when it was used last."

The man's cautious stare at the Legion uniform told Bora he'd meet no resistance. "We keep the records in the back," he said, heading with a stoop to the smudgy door.

Bora followed. Only when the albino used his stump to hold the door open for him did he notice that his left arm had been severed at the wrist. The rosy lump of freshly cicatrized flesh emerging from the sleeve surprised him like something private and obscene which a decent man should conceal or deny.

The office was a closet-sized storage room for inner tubes and boxes of spare parts. As he leafed through a ledger under a bare light bulb, the albino's head looked like a pale growth of winter wheat. "The car hasn't been taken out in over a week, *señor teniente.*"

"But when was it taken out last?"

"On 9 July."

"And when was it returned?"

"On the same day."

Three days before Lorca was killed. Bora curbed his disappointment. "Who hired it?" he asked.

"The Reinas. They were going to a funeral in Daroca." The albino put down the ledger on a bracketed worktable, resting his ugly stump on it. "Do you know the Reinas? The old man used to play the organ in the cathedral."

Bora pocketed the notebook. When he asked for the ledger, the albino handed it over. "Just leave it here when you're finished. I'll be in the garage if you need anything else."

Bora waited to be alone in the small room before leafing through the transactions of the past two months. In the weeks between mid-May and 12 July, nowhere did he read Lorca's name. He did come across a signature five times that was marked by minute lower case and tall capital letters, remarkably similar to the handwriting behind the snapshot he had found on the body. The signature read *F. García*, a name common in Spain yet too much of a coincidence given the circumstances.

Lorca might have used his middle name to do business. Surely, some people in Teruel knew who he was, and why he was lying low, but I expect people don't ask questions these days.

The distances travelled by the man who signed himself García varied, although twice they hovered around forty miles, a possible round trip to the sierra. Holding the lamp by the wire to direct its glare, Bora studied the wall map of Aragon above the worktable. Alternatively, an approximately forty-mile round trip from Teruel might lead to Perales del Alfambra, twenty-four miles away; Caminreal lay forty miles to the north-west; smaller lanes wormed due east and west to Albarracín, Bezas and Cedrillas. The road along the Turia River led to the south-west and to the sierra of San Martín. The last trip entered under the name of F. García, on Sunday 4 July, totalled less than twelve miles, enough for a round trip to nearby Valdecebro or Concud.

After jotting down the dates, Bora turned to 9 July, the Reina entry. On that day, the car had been out from seven in the morning to seven in the evening for a total of just under 125 miles, the distance to and from Daroca. Whoever the Reinas were, they had had enough time for a leisurely drive to a funeral and back. The biggest surprise, however, scrawled above Reina's signature, was the last recorded mileage of the car.

In the garage, Bora's question about it startled the albino. He'd been leaning under the hood of the old Fiat, and knocked his head as a result. "I was off sick for a week until yesterday," he explained defensively. "And the car wasn't taken out after the ninth. Let me double-check." After comparing the Ansaldo's odometer to the last number entered in the ledger, he seemed anxious to agree. "You're right. There's a difference of some forty-three miles." Grumpily, he added, "It's not like I run this place, *teniente*. If you want to, you can ask the owner when he returns from his honeymoon. He got married on Sunday, and should be back this Friday. Maybe it's a mistake. I don't know what else to tell you."

Bora did not press the matter. He stepped to the entrance to look at the ledger in full daylight. All transactions – repairs, tune-ups, rentals – were entered together, chronologically. He saw no evidence of corrections, erasures or tampering with the last few pages. He slammed the register down on the hood of the Fiat and stormed out.

MAS DEL AIRE

"Oh, it's you," Remedios said.

Walton stepped closer, hands in his pockets. "Why, who should it be?"

Remedios didn't answer. She sat on the rubble wall behind her house, sunning her legs with her cotton dress folded back over her knees to mid-thigh. Her head was tilted back so that the mass of red hair fell back over her shoulders, like an intricate net of fine metal strands. "What do you want?"

She'd never asked what he *wanted* before. Moodily Walton fumbled in his pockets. There had never been a need for words between them. But today all she did was glance at him through half-lowered lids, taking in the sun on her white face. From where Walton stood, the smooth length of her inner thighs was visible under the rolled-back dress. Deep between them, the handful of red fleece nestled safe and now troubled him, because it was exposed and yet no direct offer to him came from it. He moved his eyes up from her legs, trying to smile. "Let's go inside, Remedios."

"What for?" She sat with her eyes closed, the palms of her hands upturned on her knees. From a hole in the rubble wall, a dusty snake slithered out, leaving comma-like traces in the silt. It slid over her bare foot and around her ankle as it went seeking a rock.

Walton understood none of this. *What for?* He wondered if it had to do with his going to the Widow Yarza, and tried to explain, clumsily. Remedios' lids stayed low, but she came as close to laughing as he'd ever seen her. Walton was unexpectedly hurt by it. He searched himself for anger and found some, inadvisable at this time. "Damn it, will you look at me while I'm talking?"

"I can see you."

"And fucking close your legs. I can't think straight if you sit that way."

"I was sitting this way before you came. The sun loves me, so I need to sit this way. Move over if you have to."

Walton did, nearly turning his back to her. He could have asked what was wrong, but she had not refused him outright, so he felt wounded and dull, too proud to beg. Whatever he added – plainly, sincerely – brought about no change in Remedios' posture or expression. Her eyes remained closed; the white slack cradles of her hands did not move from her knees. She gave no outward sign to Walton that he'd be able to expect a spoken answer.

TERUEL

Bora recognized Luisa Cadena's house from her description: across from a convent one block away from the city hall, on a long alley with narrow sidewalks. Ornate details and ironwork showed a bygone elegance; the arched doorway, guarded by stone masks, was still impressive. When Bora rang the bell, he heard the barking of small dogs before a leathery housekeeper came to open up. Luisa Cadena was behind her at once, and invited Bora in: "*Sírvase usted entrar*, Don Martín." She preceded him across a paved court to a parlour, glancing back over her shoulder. "I hope to God you have some news."

Bora removed his army cap and followed her in silence, a distracted ear to the crying of a child upstairs.

The parlour was as he'd expected, from the crowd of potted plants to the upright piano covered by an embroidered shawl, good china and some silver. On the piano, Bora noticed the framed enlargement of a snapshot – a smiling dark man in cotton suit and white shoes against the background of an American skyscraper. He remembered the verses in Garcia Lorca's 1929 *Poeta en Nueva York*. In a wicker armchair by the window, with a rosary in her lap, sat an old woman to whom Luisa went to speak, leaning in close to her. All Bora understood was, "*Noticias de Antonio y Federico, Mamá.*"

He stood awkwardly, seeking enough confidence to lie. "I came with more questions than answers, Señora Cadena. And the news I have is not good."

Luisa turned to him. The eyes in her pallor – the complexion Lorca called "olive and lily" in his poems – were like holes. "*Siéntese.*" She indicated a much used, overstuffed sofa. "Please. You must be warm after riding." The polite artificiality of her conduct was something she needed to keep herself together, and Bora complied with her request. "Would you like something cold to drink?"

"Yes, please. Water would be fine."

Luisa summoned the housekeeper, whom she called Martirio. It struck Bora as the name for a sad dancer or a gypsy, and hung loosely around her spare frame. In the gauzy halo of the window, the old woman had resumed telling her beads. Was she senile, or hard of hearing? His first words had not alarmed her.

Luisa stood behind her, visibly seeking the courage before asking, "What is the news, Don Martín? Is it about Antonio or about my cousin?"

"I have news of your husband."

Her lips went tight, nearly disappearing. Bora wished she wouldn't stare at him so hard, so hopelessly in control. "My information is that your husband was relocated to a prison camp. I'm afraid he's very ill."

"Is he expected to live?"

Bora eyed the old woman, who stopped fingering the rosary and seemed to be straining to hear. "I don't know," he said, even though Cziffra had reported that Cadena had gangrene and was as good as dead.

"*Qué tiene Antonio?*" the old woman asked in a loud, distressed tone. Luisa repeated Bora's words, and the old woman began to weep.

"Do you have any details?" Luisa Cadena was trembling, but her eyes were dry.

Bora watched her tremble and felt unspeakably sorry for her. "*Lo siento.* I have no other news."

What else could he say? Martirio came to lay a tray on the low table in front of Bora. The water was cold enough to frost the sparkling sides of the crystal pitcher. His throat was parched, but he did not drink at once.

Tight-lipped, her back to the window, Luisa Cadena guarded her pain. Bora did no more than steal an embarrassed glance at the way the clasp of her hands formed an unflinching knot. Finally she said, nodding towards the pitcher, "Please help yourself, Don Martín. You have been very good in finding out and coming to tell us."

Bora had to make an effort not to drain the goblet in one long gulp. "I would like to help concerning your cousin," he said. "But I will need some information from you first."

Slowly Luisa unclasped her hands, and the desolate crucified motion that followed made Bora fear his own sadness. "Anything you need, Don Martín. Just allow me to check on the baby upstairs. Martirio will bring more water, if you wish."

In the time Luisa was gone Bora filled and emptied his goblet again. From the old woman came low moaning sounds, this side of weeping, and the link-by-link ticking of rosary beads.

The fussing of the infant upstairs lessened, then ceased. When Luisa Cadena returned, her eyes were red but tearless. "*Mamá.*" She went to the old woman. "Would you like to go and lie down?" And when the old woman shook her head she addressed Bora. "I'm ready to answer your questions. But please do sit down."

Bora would not, until she took her place at the other end of the sofa.

"Señora Cadena, I'm still trying to understand the context of your cousin's disappearance, and don't have much to go on. You said he left this house shortly after eight in the evening. I have information – from a source I cannot reveal now – that he was still in Teruel two hours later. What I need to hear is where he might have been between the time he left here and 9.30. It's very important that I find out."

Luisa looked at him for a long moment. "Does Colonel Serrano know you're here, Don Martín?"

"He does not."

"And you're not Spanish."

"No."

She sighed. "I believe Federico went from here to a friend's house, although I couldn't say how long he might have stayed there."

"Has this friend talked to you since we last met?"

"No. I can only surmise what I just told you."

It was Bora's turn to stare. "Haven't you tried to contact him?"

"Yes, but I've failed so far."

"I will need his name."

Luisa Cadena's shoulders stiffened. "I can't give it to you."

Bora tried unsuccessfully to hide his irritation. "It is Francisco Soler, is it not?"

She looked away with a fluttering lost look around the room, a second sign of dismay after she'd opened her arms, Christ-like.

"Señora Cadena," Bora whispered, "I will visit Señor Soler. Please simplify my task by answering me. Unlike others, I have no power to arrest or deport the citizens of Teruel, and Soler is safer with me than with anyone else now. Tell me if your cousin went to see him on that night."

"Yes, Don Martín. He did."

Francisco Soler owned a flat in the north-western Judería district. The street where he lived turned sharply near the entrance of Number 6, where a glazed tile read S. D. DE LOS PESCADORES.

Bora rang the doorbell, waited, rang again. When it was clear that no one would answer, he stepped back to look up at the shuttered windows of the second floor.

"Who are you looking for?" The question came from behind and above him. The visor of the army cap limited his view, so Bora removed it to look. A hefty woman in a yellow smock was watering geraniums on her balcony across the street.

"I'm looking for Señor Soler."

"Eh? What did you say?"

Bora didn't like raising his voice. He spelled out, no louder than before, "I'm looking for Señor Paco Soler."

"Ah, I get you now. He's gone."

"What do you mean, 'gone'?"

The woman looked down. From the street, Bora could see the black stockings under her skirt squeezing the flesh around her knees. "His windows have been shut since Saturday morning. He's probably out in the country. Who wouldn't be, in this heat?"

Another washout. Bora moodily returned to the town centre. In the main square, the Confitería y Pastelería Muñoz was open at this time of day (and had been for the past eighty-two years, if the sign over the entrance was telling the truth), so he walked into it to get something cold to drink. The room was crowded with idlers, a typical fixture of Spanish public places. They were the low-voiced, short and fair men of central Aragon, playing cards, chatting over fried snacks and small cups of thick coffee. All eyes trailed Bora as he neared the counter.

"Do you have anything cold to drink?"

The waiter lifted a bottle from a bucket of melting ice. "Horchata," he said, and though Bora didn't care for the almond drink, he said it was fine.

A portly customer with a distinct medicinal smell about him had been leaning with his elbows on the same counter. No paper fan this time, but Bora recognized the man whom the barber had called Don Millares. They exchanged a glance – Bora was about to nod a greeting but thought better of it – before Bora looked away. Millares said nothing, though he stayed turned towards him inquisitively.

Reflected in the mirror behind the counter, Bora could see the pillar and fountain in the square. On the pillar, framed by the door and the stone columns of the portico outside, stood the feisty, cat-sized bronze bull, symbol of Teruel. Even under the proud *torico* men sat idly on the rim of the fountain, curious about the stranger.

The buzz interrupted by his arrival began again. Bora caught a mention of the wheat crop having gone poorly, of the rainless month and someone's illness. Flies feasted on spilled beer across the counter, landing noiselessly on the suds. Now and then, with a sweep of his wet rag, the waiter chased them off.

Millares walked by Bora to join a table of card players. The medicinal smell, he guessed, identified him as a pharmacist or physician, and the only reason why he hadn't noticed it at the barber's was that the aroma of garlic and hair tonic had overpowered it. Offering his broad, shirt-clad back to the counter, Millares related something that made his listeners grin. Whatever the subject, it had a measure of spite judging by his tone and the expressions of those facing him.

"... Sure, and where else? The stage designer goes there every time it gets uncomfortable for him in Teruel." The way Millares raised his voice told Bora that the story was meant for a general laugh. "You all remember the same thing happened when there was that story of the seminarians. The cockhound! I'm only amazed at old Vargas, who calls himself a good Catholic."

There was open laughter, followed by some comment about "old Vargas' choirboys". That was it. As quickly as the gossip had its desired effect, another took its place. It revolved around a *campesino* called Luis, and there was a novice involved.

Bora took a last sip of almond drink, paid and walked out. He felt the stares follow him to the door, and could imagine the muted light of the portico broken by the shadow of his tall, spurred boots. From inside, he overhead Millares order-ing another cup of coffee.

He rode out of town by the viaduct that linked Teruel to the next hill with the perilous cement span of its arch. Ahead, the south-west road to Castralvo stretched, lonely and sun-cursed. Soon Pardo started to baulk, stopping to graze impossible tufts of dry grass and aiming for the meagre shade of each struggling tree along the way.

Before the railroad track, Bora reached the fork that split the road to Castralvo from a dirt trail leading to the Ermita de Santa Ana. He took the trail with a disheartened look at the grassless, treeless expanse studded by low hills. It was now close to one o'clock. A wilting heat scorched the land between the road and the knobbly hills and beyond, far into the remote haze of the sierra of San Martín. At a glance, Bora could embrace the low, broken crown of arid mountains circling the plain. Swallows flew high, almost invisible in the glitter of the sky. Bora hoped rain would come again, but it was unlikely it'd be any time soon.

Along the dry bed of a seasonal torrent, cane groves and struggling poplars reached no higher than a man's head. Faraway almond groves dotted the chalky land, and on both sides of the road funnels of dust spiralled upwards, only to fall again. Only the blistering sun seemed to remain.

Bora didn't know exactly where he was going, but he went there anyway.

EL PALO DE LA VIRGEN

When Walton returned from Mas del Aire, Bernat told him that Marypaz was not around. She'd gone off, to Castellar, maybe, sure that Remedios was the reason for his errand. "It's not like I told her, Felipe. She figured it out on her own, and she's furious at you now. Don't look at me that way and don't blame it on me, because I did as you told me. It's between you and Marypaz."

Walton felt something like vomit coming up. "OK," he said, and walked around Bernat.

"Remember, it's between you and Marypaz. I've got nothing to do with it."

The long trek in the heat and the meeting with Remedios had made him nauseous. Walton sought shelter from the sun past the threshold, where thick walls and the scent of dry figs created an illusion of coolness. There was always time later to argue with Marypaz.

"Damn hot, isn't it?"

The words came from nowhere. Walton's eyes detected Brissot by the table, his figure gradually appearing through slowly dissolving green and red stains from the sun. "Rafael seems to be doing better," he added. "I talked Valentin into some pride-saving form of apology, and they shook hands a little while ago."

Walton stared at the map laid out on the table. "It must have been your diplomatic touch."

"Diplomacy?" Brissot sneered. "I'm too honest to engage in that bourgeois art of lying. I merely lectured them on comradeship and good fighting spirit. Speaking of which, is it too much to ask what you were doing in the sierra?"

Walton sat astride a chair. "I went to the grave." How close everything seemed on the map. Mas del Aire, the unnamed spot where his men had been shot at, the camp. Lorca's grave, the brook. The Fascist post. "On my way back I kept trying to put two and two together about Lorca, but it still doesn't add up. I mean, what if he came alone? No escort, no *cenetistas*, no ambush … Only the men in the car the *mulero* spoke of."

"Yes. Well?"

Walton slumped back in his chair. Nausea was giving way to a sick headache, and pain had started to slur his speech. "The question is, when did they kidnap him? Let's say shortly after he visited Soler, although Soler said nothing about a car. All he knows is that Lorca left his house before half past nine."

Brissot gravely placed the empty pipe in his mouth. "Maybe he's lying. If two men waylaid Lorca in Teruel with the intention of shooting him, why drive all the way here? They could have killed him in any back alley in Teruel."

"It's a small town; you can't just bump people off in the street." Walton turned the chair around. His headache eased somewhat if he anchored his elbow on the table and rested his head on his open hand. "The open country is a better choice."

Brissot drove his forefinger into the map. "But why *here*, of all places, the foot of a mountain that borders Republican territory? Look, Felipe. They could have taken ten different directions! No executioner would travel an hour to shoot somebody and accidentally reach the sierra, Lorca's own destination."

"Dunno." Walton leaned heavily on the palm of his hand. "It made sense when I thought about it before, though I don't know why."

"That's because it doesn't make any sense. Besides, where does that leave the sierra Fascists?"

"They fit in somehow. I just can't figure out *how*."

Brissot bit the pipe stem with a clacking sound. He took off his glasses to study the map. "If the Fascists discovered the murder before we did, they're keeping mum because they're behind it and fear repercussions. They're involved, I say. The German wouldn't be asking questions if he didn't see the value of learning who buried Lorca, and where. Look at the distance between the mule track and the Fascist post ... Felipe, are you looking?"

"I'm looking."

"Suppose only one of them – let's say the German – arrived on the scene before you and Maetzu: he'd have to seek help in order to transport the body. By then we'd already hauled it away."

When Walton pulled back on the chair, a stab of pain travelled from the top of his head to his neck. He rose to his feet, unsteadily walked to the door and leaned against the jamb, away from the sun. "The Widow Yarza says he was in Castellar yesterday, and a few days back he met the priest in church."

"No one in Castellar, priest included, could tell him anything. And the German could be in town for any reason: maybe he was looking for a piece of tail."

"If that's the case, he's not getting it from the widow, and she seems sore about it. For Chrissake, have you seen her? I can't imagine anyone bedding *that*." Just as his headache improved, Walton saw Marypaz returning, picking her steps past the spiny bushes in the blistering midday, hands in the pockets of her cotton trousers, head low. Rafael, who was keeping watch, told her something, and she replied with a wave that meant, *Leave me alone.*

I don't want to talk to her, Walton thought. *Talking to her right now is the last thing I want to do.*

Having reached the ledge, Marypaz turned to the house, saw him and immediately made an about-face. The old desire to laugh at the wrong time tempted him, but Walton neither laughed nor pulled back. "You don't trust Soler, Mosko, but he's the one at risk now, even hiding out at Vargas' *huerta*. If the Fascists find out he came to us, I wouldn't give a penny for his life."

Bora could imagine the effect of an army horseman stopping at the gate of the lonely *huerta*. *Old* Vargas, as Millares had called him, was probably spying through the window, agonizing over the wisdom of answering the garden bell.

. At the end of a brick path, the house sat in perfect silence, shutters folded like praying hands. Freeing himself of the sweaty riding gloves, Bora stared through the iron bars. Vargas might not have heard the bell, though it'd rung long enough. He might be upstairs; being an old man, it would take him a while to reach the ground floor. He might not be in.

He'd run out of excuses and was about to scale the gate when the front door swung open just enough to let out a wispy-haired, petite old woman in an apron. Halfway along the brick path, a frail shirtsleeved man joined her, and stood by as she let Bora in.

"Señor Vargas? I'm looking for Francisco Soler."

Vargas blinked. He opened his lipless mouth and closed it again, a weak-jawed grimace on his bony face. Recognizing the two stars of lieutenancy on Bora's uniform, he said, "Francisco Soler lives in Teruel, *señor teniente*. You must be mistaken." Bora fought a sting of road-weary despair at the thought that Vargas might be telling the truth, but it passed quickly and he knew it was a lie. He courteously bowed his head to Señora Vargas and went past her towards the house. "Please fetch Soler. I'm in a hurry."

"I promise you, *teniente* —"

Bora ignored him. When Vargas tried to hold him back, he pushed him away. It wasn't hard enough to push him over and simply forced him into the flower bed, but Vargas gave up the attempt.

Inside, there was no stopping Bora. Followed by Vargas' pleading wife, he barged into the next room and back, crossed the floor, went to the kitchen and returned after a brief exchange with the lady. At the foot of the stairs, he paused with one hand on the banister. "Señor Vargas," he said, "kindly fetch Soler before I go up for him. The windows of the second floor are too high for jumping out of, and I don't think he'll be able to climb the garden wall." He showed them the key to the garden gate, which the embarrassed Señora Vargas admitted giving Soler.

"But I am telling you that Soler —"

Bora climbed the first step. He couldn't make up his mind whether the frustration was angering him or giving him an amusing sense of power. He slipped the key into his breast pocket and buttoned it, reaching to his left side for the pistol holster. "I'll search the house, then."

"There's no need." Soler's words reached him from the top of the stairs. A pale man in an open-collared shirt and house slippers, Bora saw him flinch in alarm, and slowly withdrew his hand from the holster.

"I was just visiting Señor Vargas, Lieutenant. What he says is true. Am I not allowed to visit friends?"

Bora unholstered the gun. "Precede me outside," he said, using his armed hand to direct Soler. Admittedly, the words sounded ominous to his own ears; God knows what the Vargases and Soler took from them. Señora Vargas' little face looked horrified as Soler went unprotestingly past her, tailed by Bora.

Outside the door, Bora halted. Soler took a couple more steps along the brick path and looked back at him.

"Are you here to kill me? If you have to kill me, I wish you'd do it outside the garden."

Cruelly Bora kept him hanging there before holstering the gun. "I want to talk to you about García Lorca."

The other man's expression went through a predictable change. The tension rearranged itself on his drawn face as grief took the place of physical fear. "What?"

"I want to know when you last saw him."

Soler was panting. He glanced over his shoulder, in case there were other soldiers outside the *huerta*. For a fleeting moment, Bora suspected he was about to attempt a dash for the gate.

But he didn't. He spoke, grasping his thighs to keep his hands from shaking. "He died last year in Granada."

"Not true. When did you last see him?"

The movement of Soler's throat signalled he'd just swallowed a mouthful of saliva. Was he wondering whether Luisa Cadena had betrayed him? Bora watched him try to steady himself in order to think, deny or tell the truth.

All around, the flower beds in the overgrown Vargas garden let out the bittersweet smell of wilting leaves. It was unbearably hot. Soler stood wide-eyed, ashen, a dark curl of chest hair showing through the opening of his shirt like the tip of a rat's tail. At last, he said, "I briefly saw him on the evening of 12 July, after eight. We discussed theatre matters for about an hour. That's all."

"At your house?"

"Yes."

Long strands of hair from the top of his head blew into Soler's eyes when a blistering breath of wind swept the *huerta*. Bora noticed how he kept from flicking the hair off his face, staring intently at him, as if staring would keep Bora from attacking.

"Was Lorca on foot when he came to see you?"

"He was."

"Did he leave on foot?"

"Yes."

"Do you *know* this?"

Here it came, the first trickle of sweat on Soler's face. It wormed down the side of his neck and followed the collarbone, becoming lost in the curl of chest hair. "I'm not sure. Maybe he took a car afterwards."

"To go where?"

Another trickle strayed down Soler's neck. "He didn't say."

That's a lie. In a show of self-possession, Bora kept from wiping his own sweaty face. *Does he think he can fool me? He's swallowing saliva again, and I can see the veins bulging in his temples from here. His heartbeat must be out of control.* "Let me jog your memory: is it possible he might have crossed into Red territory? I am told you often had disagreements."

Soler's limbs were starting to assume a corpse-like stiffness, yet his jaw twitched uncontrollably. "Disagreements? Who told you?" The haste with which he dug into his pocket for a handkerchief momentarily alarmed Bora, but not enough for him to touch the holster. "Teruel is gossipy and provincial."

"Nevertheless." Bora tasted a drop of sweat as it cleared his upper lip. "What did you argue about?"

"Not politics." Unlike Cziffra's fastidious dabbing of his neck, Soler dragged the handkerchief across his face and down to the shaggy hollow at the root of his throat. "A professional disagreement over the play we were working on, that's what it was. During the visit, I took back my sketches for *The Miraculous Horseman*, because he didn't like them. I'm redoing them now in my Teruel flat." The gesture of putting away the crumpled handkerchief was artificial, forcibly calm. He added, slyly, "Antonio Cadena disappeared the same day, surely you've heard *that*. Maybe the two of them left together."

"I doubt it. Antonio Cadena was in Alfambra that day. Tell me instead, does Señor Lorca have enemies in Teruel?"

Behind Bora, the creak of hinges alerted him that the door had opened. He wheeled around briskly enough that Señora Vargas hesitated on the threshold. Her eyes went from Bora to Soler and back, smiling and apologetic. "It's such a warm afternoon; I thought you gentlemen might want some cold water and lemon."

Why do women try to defuse men's anger? The offer of a drink at this point was grotesque but hard to resist. Bora moodily accepted a round-bellied glass and watched Soler do the same. "Please go back inside." He dismissed her.

In front of him, Soler held the glass with both hands to keep the drink from spilling. "No enemies, no." But there was no telling if he felt trapped beyond his ability to attempt an escape. "Why should he? He had no enemies."

Had. Had? Bora took a mental note of the slip, and of his own budding heartlessness. He felt indifferent to Soler's fear. "Well, do *you*?" he insisted, lowering his eyes to the lemon wedge in his glass.

"No." The answer came as if Soler's tongue had gone numb in his mouth. "No, no."

Bora picked the lemon wedge out of the water and started chewing on it. "That may be your impression. How do you think I found out you were here?"

Unsteady against the motley pattern of garden plants, Soler tilted his head back and emptied his glass in an open-mouthed gulp. Bora felt the change in the other man. Something like an invisible frenzy went through the Spaniard, an inner spasm of nerves and muscles that was not quite a shiver. A few steps away, Bora pensively chewed a tip of the lemon wedge, the water in his glass untouched.

"Please, *teniente* ... are we done?"

"No." Bora dropped the lemon wedge back in the water. He set down his glass at the edge of the brick path. Oddly, he recognized the twinge in Soler's muscles – was it time to run away, make a dash for it? – as if it were his own. He stared at the Spaniard to keep him in suspense, to make him cringe at the clipped politeness of his words. "Señor Soler, you place me in a quandary. Given your acquaintances, I cannot allow you to stay behind after I leave, free to escape, abscond, or do whatever else you see fit. I *could* take you to Teruel for further interrogation. There, however, I would have to hand you over to the Guardia Civil. It's a dilemma, and I'm struggling with it."

"That is, if you don't choose to shoot me."

Soler's spelling out how things were came as a surprise. Bora had judged him more impotent and afraid, and the words caught him off guard. He began to say, "If you give me a reason to shoot you —"

It came now. Just as he was off guard: now.

Soler sprinted from where he stood like a released metal spring, aiming not for the gate but the side of the house, straddling bushes, crushing flower beds on his frantic way around the corner and out of sight.

Bora blasphemed for the first and only time in his life. He started running a moment after Soler, leaves and branches whipping past and giving way, and reached the corner in time to see the Spaniard scramble up a ladder leaning against the garden wall, knock the ladder down and drop down to the other side. There was no time to go back and use the gate. Bora raised the unwieldy ladder from the tangle of bushes; he replaced it against the wall, climbed furiously and jumped off without thinking how high the wall might be. Leafy bushes below broke his fall and once more he was after Soler, who'd crossed the road and sent a cloud of dust into the air as he scampered down into a dry ditch.

Bora raced, lunged after him, missed him by a hair at the bottom of the trench, again stretched and missed him, but the other side of the hole was steep and Soler couldn't run uphill in his house slippers. Bora seized him by the waist and they both lost their footing, rolling back down to the dusty floor of the ditch. Immediately Soler tried to resume his flight, but Bora held him by the ankles and caused him to fall again.

The slide of the automatic pistol made a clacking sound as it drew back and locked in place.

Soler froze, with Bora standing over him in the colourless dust. They were both unhurt, although only Soler was out of breath. Bora's gun-wielding, outstretched arm was very firm.

"You do want to give me a reason to shoot you, Señor Soler."

EL PALO DE LA VIRGEN

Marypaz crouched in the almond grove, where the grass had wilted and the tree leaves were too sparse to offer any real shade.

The smell of horses drifted here from their enclosure when Walton came up the hill to join her. The heat was making the manure ferment and let out a powerful odour of ammonia, but he quashed the temptation to turn away. Turning away was what he'd done in his marriage and in his life so far, and it'd helped nothing.

Whatever pretence Marypaz was making of ignoring him, a small jerk of her shoulders proved that she'd seen him. She'd been using her nails to tear the papery, ashen leaves fallen from the thirsty branches above.

"You went to see Remedios," she hissed. "I can smell her on you. So turn your tail and leave, because I got here first and I want to stay here by myself."

"You've got it wrong."

Walton craned his neck to look at Marypaz, who was propped against the dilapidated orchard wall. She pouted at him and continued to tear the wilted leaves, stripping them and throwing them away. "I don't believe it, and I don't believe *you*."

"As true as God is, Marypaz —"

"As if *you* believed in God."

How different was this from the wearisome quarrels in the living room long ago, with the rain outside and the radio on? Walton made no effort to touch her.

"I don't trust you, Felipe. *Márchate!* Leave me alone. After all the times you've gone sniffing her doorpost! *Márchate, márchate!* Get away from here before I start screaming."

"Suit yourself." Walton turned to leave.

He'd gone a few steps from the orchard when Marypaz called him back, and her voice only made him pick up his pace. He'd also learned not to crawl back when women called him. In Pittsburgh or in Spain, it only made things worse. Loose gravel shifted under his boots, frightening small insects out of his way.

Maetzu, back from reconnoitring on El Baluarte, came towards him to report. On the ledge, Bernat pointed to invisible newcomers climbing to the camp. "Felipe, Almagro is here!"

Walton felt like sending everyone to hell.

No sooner had Maetzu joined him than Marypaz came too, interrupting what the Basque had started to say: "Wait, Iñaki. I was talking to him first. Felipe, swear you didn't go to her."

Walton spat in the dust. "I'm not going to fucking swear. If you want to believe it, believe it."

"Can you prove it to me, then? There's a way you can prove it to me."

"I don't feel like *proving it* to you, Marypaz."

"Is that because you don't want to, or because you can't?"

Walton regretted that he couldn't get as angry with her as he'd done even just a month ago. She irritated him, but it wasn't the same as real anger. Because Maetzu was staring, he reacted to Marypaz's words with a foolish need to boast sexually before another man. "Wait for me inside, Marypaz, I must talk to Almagro first. Silly cow. *Sabes que puedo siempre que quiero.* Any time I feel like it." He stooped to kiss her so that she'd leave. When he turned to Maetzu again, he saw him shake his head with a scowl of great contempt.

6

TERUEL

At sundown Bora returned to Teruel from Castralvo. The heat of day abated slowly, leaving behind a pale sky streaked with red pennants of clouds. Swallows clamoured above the roofs of the old town; among the tall ornate buildings of Calle Nueva, blankets of shadow filled the space that had blazed at midday. A small breeze unravelled, but Bora's overheated body required more than a wisp of air to cool off. Pardo needed watering, fodder and rest, which he found in the stables under the fortress-like barracks of the Guardia Civil.

"Don't take this animal out again tonight, *teniente*," the sergeant who came to take the horse said. "Leave it here overnight."

"Out of the question. I need to ride out shortly."

The Guardia Civil swept an assessing glance over him. "*Con permiso*, you don't look that good either."

"I don't need advice." Bora stepped back to the stable door. "If the Guardia Civil wants to be useful, get me another mount ready, and I'll come for it in an hour."

"*Como usted quiera.* But you'll have to ask for it upstairs at the office."

Bora did. A spiffy colonel who knew Serrano "like a brother" promised a good horse, graciously inquired about his health and sent him on his way without waiting for an answer.

Back in the street, Bora found that his muscles were starting to ache from a full day in the saddle, and the visit to Santa Olalla arranged with Serrano was still two hours away. In the main square, worshippers were heading for the church of San Pedro. Bora went the opposite way, in the direction of Luisa Cadena's house. There he stopped and unfastened the watch from his left wrist. He timed the walking distance from the Cadenas' to Cziffra's office: less than five minutes. Without stopping, he then continued to Soler's house. Six additional minutes, which he could have stretched to ten at most by keeping a slower pace.

Finding the door to the house ajar, Bora stepped inside. He met an elaborate, buckling floor of thin bricks and river pebbles, and a stairwell dank with the smell of cat urine. The glimmer from a high recessed window allowed him to stumble upstairs. In his chest pocket, the bulky key to Vargas' gate shared space with Soler's house key, which he'd managed to get in the end, although not without a struggle.

On the first landing, hardly readable in the twilight, a brass plate spelled out FRANCISCO HERAS SOLER, ARQUITECTO. Inside, the darkness had the peculiar opacity of shuttered, draped rooms. Bora groped for a switch on the wall, found it and closed the door behind him.

A papered vestibule opened on to three rooms. On the wall, like the intricate spoil of a great gilded insect, a bull-fighter's jacket hung spreadeagled. Sewn to the embroidery, a handwritten note bore the name Ignacio Sánchez Mejías. Of course. Mejías, the most accomplished matador of the last twenty years, the one praised by everyone who mentioned bullfighting. The same whose death in the arena Lorca had bitterly sung of. Bora looked for traces of blood on the jacket, but there were none, so this wasn't the splendid *traje de luces* Ignacio had worn in his last fight.

In Soler's bedroom, everything was tidy. Strangely, Bora felt himself go on alert, as if someone else were in the flat, hiding. The impression was strong enough for him to search every room at gunpoint, only to discover a subtler sense of intrusion.

Things had been moved and replaced on their shelves, as the disturbed veil of dust showed. Books stood in disorderly rows. The bedding looked indented as if someone's hand had reached under and around it. A portfolio of sketches leaning against the wall had been searched: some of the dividing sheets had been removed from the fresh pastels, and light blue smears had soiled their cardboard cover. The pastels were no more than abstract pairings of shaded nuances, perhaps a colour study for stage costumes.

When Bora opened the wardrobe, the full-length mirror inside its door swung back to reflect his own travel-worn self. The dark red stain on his sleeve was so obvious, no wonder the Guardia Civil officer had noticed. Soler's clothes hung crowded at one end of their wooden rod. Daubs of light blue pastel smeared the hem of a white shirt, and that was all. Bora uselessly searched the flat for the manuscript of *The Horseman's Song* and the sketches mentioned by Soler. But for the careless daub of blue on the white shirt, he'd have thought Lorca's friend had lied to him and removed all evidence of his work with the poet.

No. That's not what happened. Someone was here, found what he was looking for, and didn't take care to disguise that fact. Someone, someone ... why wouldn't they have tried to hide their tracks?

Leaving the stairs and cat smell behind, Bora timed himself from the *Judería* to the public garage, a leisurely five-minute walk.

In the garage, all cars except the dark green Ansaldo sat where he'd seen them at midday. The albino was still working on the old Fiat. He had his back to the street entrance, and didn't notice Bora.

"*Buenas tardes.*"

The man withdrew from under the hood. He tipped his head in recognition. "*Buenas tardes a usted.*"

Bora stood on the threshold, securing the watch to his wrist. "What are your opening hours during the week?"

"On paper, six in the morning to ten at night. The proprietor lives upstairs." The albino lifted his eyes to the ceiling. "When returning the car after hours, people ring his doorbell, and he lowers a basket for them to put the key in."

"And now that he's away?"

"His spinster aunt lives with him. She gives the key out after hours, and takes it back too. If you want to reserve the car in advance, you can."

"Not now."

"As you like, but remember that come Sunday people'll want to take their families out for the feast of St James."

Bora walked away. When he emerged from the archway of the Saviour's tower, the last daylight had left the horizon. He found a saddled, lively horse waiting in the Guardia Civil stables, and then it was time for him to take the solitary westward road that led to Concud.

Once he left Teruel, the sky turned endlessly high. Along the gravel road, bare hills stretched their rolling surfaces, parted by purple hollows and waterless ditches. Beyond them, the land rose again, slowly twisting towards the distant heights of Albarracín or to the north, where the sky sank deep and dark.

Slumping on the saddle eased the soreness in his thighs. Bora checked the mischievous horse by gentle squeezes of his knees, attentive to the simple sounds that rose from the earth. Insect sounds, the shift of dry grass on the verge of the road, the hard click of pebbles under the hoofs: he was ashamed of his lack of simplicity, of being tired and dirty. The day weighed upon him, and he was worried about the wrong things. *Maybe I will simply hand over the letter from Colonel Serrano and not go in at all.*

Silent sheet lightning flashed at the edge of the plain and died out. Invisible flocks were revealed by the faint tinkle of bells around a ram's neck, or a barking sheepdog. In the distance, the *huerta* of Santa Olalla waited like a dim island. The Northern Cross drew its brilliant pattern right above it, in the way Bora thought constellations must appear to lost sailors seeking a harbour.

Past the *huerta*'s gate, the flower beds had just been watered. After the scorching day, there was something almost sinful in the moisture lavished on the plants. Bora stretched his hand to touch the dripping leaves, thinking how he'd love to throw himself face down among the fortunate shrubs.

Señora Serrano, like the first time, sat on the divan under her portrait. Her sombre figure in the shadowy parlour had lost none of its righteous posture. "You are punctual," she said.

Bora stepped forward and presented the colonel's letter on the open palm of his right hand. "Señora Condesa."

She looked at his boots. Bora had dusted them as best he could before entering, and understood that his boots had nothing to do with it. Serrano's wife was avoiding looking at his face. She reached for the letter, which she laid on a side table without opening.

"My husband writes me a letter every day," she commented. "Every day since we met, no matter how near or far we are from one another. I thank you for bringing this one."

Bora bowed his head, clicking his heels. Riding here, he'd been debating if and how to bring up the death of Alejandro Serrano. Some expression of condolence was in order, but he felt awkward now that he had to put it into words. "Please accept my profound regrets for your loss," he said in the end, and given her lack of reaction he couldn't tell whether his words had affected her.

As if making up for the lack of courage that had kept her from looking a moment earlier, Señora Serrano stared in his direction. Still she said nothing. In the dusky room she only seemed to stare, inert on the divan, with the proud younger image of herself also gazing from the canvas above.

Bora understood. He knew what derelict shred of illusion his figure and uniform afforded her in this half-darkness even before she said, in a strangled voice, "Only a moment longer, Don Martin. Please let me look without turning the lights on."

All the same, it didn't take long for these signs of emotion to leave her. When she stood, stiffly walking to the light switch, the practicality of an army wife had returned. "Tell me, have you had dinner?"

Bora hadn't anticipated such a question. He'd gone from one errand to the next without even thinking of food. Aside from Señora Vargas' lemon wedge, a drink of water at the Cadenas' was all he'd had.

Señora Serrano noticed his hesitation. "You haven't had dinner, and it is unthinkable that you should leave without partaking of it. I will instruct the servants." Her motion to the door had something of a nun's self-control, energy or frustration harnessed to serve discipline. When she re-entered the parlour, she asked in a careful, dispassionate voice, "I see there is blood on your right sleeve. Are you hurt?"

Bora followed her stare to the stain. "No, no. It's nothing. It's less than nothing."

"'Less than nothing' does not bleed. Did you have a fall?"

"I did not. It's really irrelevant, Señora Condesa. It embarrasses me to speak of it."

"Well, soldiers aren't embarrassed by spilling enemy blood, so it must be something entirely different. Did you have a nosebleed, Don Martín?"

Bora knew he was looking blankly at her. "Yes. Yes. It just started bleeding this afternoon. I expect I'm not as used to the sun or the heat as I thought."

"So." Her eyes remained on the stain, sharply. "It must have bled a great deal."

"It did. I will apologize to the colonel for presenting myself to you in this state."

Standing by the sofa, Señora Serrano opened the envelope. "Sometimes not even gentlemen can help their state. You needn't be self-conscious." After scanning the letter, she added, "My husband informs me that you're to spend the night. Of course, you must say yes. Dinner is in an hour, so I hope you won't mind my taking a few decisions for you. My husband's attendant will show you upstairs for a bath and change."

Bora thought of the lush dripping plants outside, and his sore muscles tensed in anticipation. Whatever he said by confused way of thanks, Señora Serrano dismissed his words. "This is how things are done in our family. We are not used to hearing our offers rejected. I am certain your family is the same way. Had my son visited your mother, she would have extended him the same courtesy."

It was far beyond courtesy; it was absolute luxury to have running water, good soap and plenty of towels. By the time Bora left the tub, his boots had been shined and his breeches thoroughly brushed. Fresh linen waited, folded on the bed; it was Alejandro's room, and these were Alejandro's things, tailor-made, fine like the underwear his own mother had packed for him in Leipzig. The ageing, prim attendant was unbuttoning a well-cut military shirt on the bed. "This won't be likely to fit you, Don Martín, your shoulders are too wide. But the Condesa begs you to accept the linen at least. She finished sewing it for Lieutenant Serrano a week ago."

Bora looked at the minute, precise hand stitching on the white cloth, running with painstaking evenness like hope itself. It had meaning. It had meaning. This night had meaning.

Alejandro's shirt did not fit. Bora laid it on the bed, looking round for the rest of his uniform. "No matter what state they're in, I'll need my shirt and tunic back."

The attendant spoke from the threshold, one hand on the doorknob. "Your shirt was rinsed and is being ironed. As for the tunic, we have done our best to remove the stain."

Alone in the room Bora put on the dead man's linen, feeling that either great luck or great misfortune would come to him from accepting it.

EL PALO DE LA VIRGEN

Leaning forward, Walton laced his boots by candlelight. The wick made a hissing sound on top of the stearin cylinder; the flame widened, narrowed and grew short, and a breath of night wind from the open window smacked it and caused it to sway more.

Marypaz slept soundly. Her face was in the shade, while the tanned plumpness of her shoulder shone under the web of her black hair. Walton reached for his shirt across the bed, careful not to touch her because he didn't want to have to talk to her.

It was a sign of their relationship ending, he thought, that he wanted to avoid her mind. It always started that way. Then he'd start avoiding her body, too. He could have counted on the fingers of one hand the times he'd made love to his wife during the last six months of their marriage. Any sexual interest in her had simply died out, and he'd even felt resentful about sleeping in the same bed with her.

He'd told Lorca once, at the sanatorium in Barcelona, when the wound had made him feel sorry enough for himself to talk. Lorca listened, his handsome, wide face turned to the window and to Barcelona's springtime outside. "Were you afraid?"

The question had made him wince. Walton remembered feeling trapped, defensive. "*Afraid?* Afraid of what?"

Lorca had smiled with a kind of brotherly lenience, a friendly geniality. "Of her, I mean. There are good reasons to be afraid of women."

"I'm not afraid of anything."

And now? Tonight there was nothing to be afraid of. Marypaz slept. Walton trimmed the candle, thinking that he'd enjoyed being with her until some moment in time he couldn't pinpoint. He stood up by the bed to put on his shirt. His shadow danced a crazy dance against the wall, according to the swaying of the flame.

Only Remedios never asked for promises, never gave any. Maybe all he needed was Remedios, who sucked up his life but drew him back to her again and again.

Walton looked away from the bed and quietly left the room. Below, Maetzu and Brissot were talking, Maetzu sounding agitated. When he heard his name mentioned, Walton stopped at the head of the staircase to listen.

Brissot sounded as if he'd just scooped a spoonful into his mouth. Bluntly, he answered Maetzu's question. "He's upstairs screwing Marypaz."

"How long is he going to be?"

252

"They've been up there ever since they came in. Don't ask me."

"Chernik has gone out for women in Castellar, and the couriers too."

The laugh must have been Brissot's. "Well! I guess it's rutting time. Why didn't *you* go?"

"I'm here to kill Fascists, not to bed whores."

Walton had expected Maetzu's reply. He could also imagine the face that went with it, humourless and fixed. He heard the dragging of metal on metal as Brissot gathered up the last of his food from the plate while saying, "You could get both things done in Castellar. The Fascists get their pieces there, same as we do."

Maetzu's words came back fast and sour. "You all make me sick. You, Felipe, the others. You foreigners come to Spain to work out whatever you've got to work out for yourselves or to make money. All of you. I thought you and Felipe were different, but you're not. The so-called Spanish comrades are no better. You all squat around trying to convince one another that we shouldn't attack the Fascist camp, or waste time on a dead faggot who deserved a bullet in his head. You eat and sleep and then you go and find yourself a whore. I'm not that way: *I don't want* to go to Castellar. *I don't want* to chase whores. I had a wife, and the Fascists killed her. I'm not going to rest until I've killed enough to stop thinking about her death and the death of my children."

It was the longest sentence Walton had ever heard Maetzu speak.

"If that's your reason for killing Fascists" – Brissot grasped for words in his bad Spanish – "you're even more self-serving than the rest of us. Your motives are more pressing, but that's about it."

The exchange ended. When Walton reached the bottom of the stairs, Brissot was sitting at one end of the table with an empty plate in front of him. At the other end, Rafael and Valentin were deep in a card game. Valentin was dealing and had his back to Walton, but Rafael's frown was visible to him. The cards between them, which were rapidly put down on the table and picked up again immediately, looked oily and worn.

"I thought it was your turn to be on watch," Walton told Brissot in English.

"It is, but Maetzu wanted it. He's gone out just now."

The greasy smell of leftover beans was so tiresome, Walton grabbed a handful of dry figs instead. He stood munching their crunchy stringiness with an eye on the card players. Brissot also watched them, with the stern look of a scientist observing a potentially explosive experiment.

Valentin had been speaking under his breath, but the last words distinctly reached Walton's ear. "If it was me, that's what I'd do."

"I'm not you," Rafael replied, morosely gripping the bandage on his skinny arm. "How do I know you're not making it up?"

Valentin's slick black hair flipped back as he made a brusque, contemptuous chin-up motion. "'Cause if I was making it up, you'd never believe I was."

Only a few of the whispered words that followed stood out enough for Walton to understand: *Lost*, and *look for it*, and *stop blaming*.

So the topic was the same; Rafael had not given up on it. Walton exchanged a glance with Brissot, who said nothing. Rafael pursed his lip, poring over the cards and prudently laying them face down on the table. Valentin's eyelids twitched. He held the cards close to his chest, but when he slapped one down it was always to snatch one of the other man's cards with it. Rafael's pile grew small, until Valentin tossed the whole stack on the table between them. "See?" He laughed. "I'm cheatin'. I won 'cause I was cheatin', and you didn't even realize I was. You ought to listen to me, Rafael."

The last fig Walton put in his mouth, shrunken, overly sweet, satiated him. From the table, Valentin turned to address Brissot. "Want to play for money, Mosko? I need money to go to Castcllar."

"Not now."

Walton walked out. On the ledge, the same breeze that had caused the candle to flicker came in harmless puffs, just a shift of air from the valley that kept him from smelling the horses in their enclosure. Stars drew a busy curve across the sky above, like drops of curdling milk in a long, long spill.

Lorca, who'd asked, "Are you afraid?" and was closer to the truth than he knew, found inspiration in things like a night breeze and a mess of stars. Yet Walton knew that to most men, these things don't signify as much as being able to fill your stomach or find a job or get out of a small town. There was no poetry in any of that, and listening to Lorca at Eden Lake or in Barcelona was like glimpsing life through someone else's eyes and being dazzled. But life is real, danger is real. You can't stay dazzled.

He couldn't, and that's why he'd run away in Soissons.

The thought stopped him in the dark like a shouted revelation, although he'd carried the secret for twenty years and dealt with it as best he could, coming to Spain because of it as much as he'd come for Lorca's sake. He'd run away in Guadalajara too, though no one knew it and his wounds told the opposite story. If enemy bullets hadn't struck him in the soggy misery outside Brihuega, his absence from the battlefield would have been called desertion. He could smile at the thought now, without pride or shame.

As it was, with blood foaming out of him at every breath, the medics had believed him when they found him in a ditch under the chilling rain. Never mind that he'd been shot twice by accident, by a man who was lost or as much a runaway as himself; wounds are wounds. Walton remembered spitting red saliva and saying the word "scouting" over and again. The medics said, caringly, "Don't talk; we understand." Most of the men in his unit had died that day, and the rest had been scattered to fight elsewhere.

Did he regret it? Safe in the dark, Walton couldn't quite come as close as usual to comforting himself, though the good old arguments were intact: panic under fire meant no more than the unwillingness to be taken prisoner; it was an extension of his need for freedom. That others had died because of it was a coincidence, not a consequence; no one knew the truth. And the one who most recently could have figured him out – the German who had pointed a gun at his head – didn't know either.

Unchangeable, the stars had poured their bright spill over the trenches in France and through the haze in Pittsburgh; in Guadalajara too, and now here. Was that poetry? Pieces and pieces and pieces of rock in the sky, to which a man running away or a dead poet made no difference at all.

Maetzu stood guard at the edge of camp, a scraggy silhouette on the first terrace. When Walton started talking to him, he didn't fall for the diversion.

"If Mosko's sent you, you might as well know how sick I really am of things here, Felipe. We could blow the Fascists to hell and still have plenty of time to pull south before anyone came riding from Teruel. Nothing's going on in Teruel, and you keep us sitting on our asses watching the valley."

Walton took out a cigarette. The couriers had brought cheap packets captured from the Italians and good loose tobacco, and he intended to use the bad stuff first. "There'll be plenty happening soon. Our asses are sitting on a volcano. Do you know what Almagro said? He said that in a few weeks it's going to look like a butcher's holiday down Teruel way."

"I don't believe it."

"No? Comrade Hernández Saravia has orders to take up positions north and south of Teruel."

Maetzu made a strange sound, a strangled noise from his throat like a repressed shout or a moan. "*When?* What does it mean for us? When do *we* get to move?"

"We'll know soon."

At once Maetzu was trembling; Walton could hear the unsteadiness in his voice. "Felipe, if you're lying to me I'll cut your throat."

"It's the truth. As for cutting throats or any other part of the human body, Valentin has done all the knife work I'm going to take from this group."

A lazy shuffle of hoofs came from the enclosure behind the house. Maetzu lifted his rifle and called out. "It's just me," Valentin called back. "Can't a man take a piss in peace?"

Maetzu returned the rifle strap to his shoulder. "Damn gypsy. But we *will* get to move, Felipe, won't we? We'll get into it!"

"Yes, sure." The unlit cigarette stuck to his lower lip, and Walton moistened it with his tongue to remove it without stripping his skin. Sure. Reducing the Teruel salient from Saragossa, taking over the Sierra Palomera and the heights of Albarracín: the couriers believed the offensive would come soon, from Tarragona. He didn't tell Maetzu, but it'd be at the year's end, most likely, and up the Turia River from Castellón. In any case, it would pass through here, sweeping the valley to Caminreal and beyond. Walton could bring himself to look forward to the attack, but not beyond it: when

Almagro had told him, a void had gaped inside him like the false bottom of a box that hinges open. Death catching up with him, that's what it was. The yellow wall, Soissons and Guadalajara obscured the rest.

"Iñaki," he said slowly, "on the night Lorca was killed, someone heard you start down the mountain. Where did you go?"

Maetzu did not answer, featureless against the backdrop of the sierra as if the rock had absorbed him and made him its own. Walton waited, prepared for a shouting match or worse. Still, he insisted, "Where did you go?"

The reply was not new, but Walton's vulnerability was. He felt dread, physical dread and revulsion that had less to do with the words than with the voice speaking them. "I told you. I went looking for blood."

Walton had to force himself to speak. "And did you find it?"

"Blood's easy to find."

When he walked back to the house, Brissot was standing on the doorstep smoking. The bowl of his pipe gave out a faint glow every time he took a drag. "I was positive the Fascists had killed Lorca, but hearing Maetzu tonight ..." he told Walton.

"Right." Studiously Walton rolled himself a cigarette. "I asked him about the night of the twelfth. He killed somebody."

"What does 'somebody' mean? Where? Tonight he implied that men like Lorca deserve a bullet."

"I overheard your conversation. But for all that he's sore at anyone who's politically lukewarm, what real reason would he possibly have —"

"A real reason, Felipe? When did Maetzu ever need a reason? Wasn't he doing time for a senseless double murder when the anarchists sprung him in Bilbao? That crime had nothing to do with politics."

"But Maetzu acts on impulse, not in cold blood."

"Like when he killed the mule drover?"

In the dark, Walton could imagine that he was somewhere away from here, or nowhere at all. "I'll tell you what Maetzu is likely to do. He'll probably sneak over to the Fascist post and slit the German's throat one of these days: that's more in keeping with him."

"You talk as if you were opposed to it."

Walton reached for Brissot's pipe and lit his cigarette with its embers, carefully. "Why should I be opposed to slitting a German's throat? In Flanders I did it myself."

HUERTA DE SANTA OLALLA

By half past ten, dinner was over. Bora was not often asked about himself, and he felt flattered by Señora Serrano's attention.

"I'm actually Scots-born," he said. "Father was working as a conductor in Bayreuth, so Nina lived for a time with her parents at the German consulate in Edinburgh. Nina is my mother, yes. I always called her that. She went into early labour after seeing a worker's hand crushed during a factory visit with her father, and barely made it back to extraterritorial Germany: I was born in the lobby of the consulate." Bora smiled. "She says she was afraid to look at me when they first showed me to her. She thought the incident was an omen and maybe I'd be born missing a hand."

"You shouldn't smile. We never know what God has in store for us, Don Martín."

The image of the albino's maimed arm flashed uncomfortably through Bora's mind. "Of course not. I didn't mean to imply that we do."

"You're a soldier. You should believe in precognition."

Besame con tu lengua, aquí. Hadn't he heard the words in his sleep long before Remedios spoke them to him? Bora looked down at the table. "I don't know," he said. "I haven't been a soldier long enough. I am … intellectually disinclined to believe in it. Which again doesn't preclude a religious interpretation of the term. In that case, I think I would have to believe in it by faith, I think."

Señora Serrano removed the napkin from her lap and laid it on the elegant table. "I sensed that my son would die long before it happened. Just as I knew my daughter would be widowed."

"It may be down to intensity of love rather than precognition."

"Love? You're young and unmarried. How much do you know about love?"

Bora glanced across the old silver and crystal, not directly at Serrano's wife. "There are forms of love other than marital or family love."

"Are you speaking of the love of God?"

"That, too." He groped for the right words, but only because he was anxious that some of this conversation might get back to Colonel Serrano. "I had in mind … a more physical form of love."

"So you did." Señora Serrano sounded more indulgent than he had expected. "Do you have a fiancée in Germany?"

"Not yet." Bora couldn't tell why he was flushed. He felt gratified that she was curious about his opinion, but embarrassment, like drunkenness, made him speak more freely than he would otherwise. He thought of Dikta and blushed deeply, as if sex with a girl of his class were automatically binding, even though she had a lover in Hamburg. The army shirt was still damp under his arms from being washed, or else he was sweating. "I would like to find someone, naturally. Someone appropriate. Someone I love, who is also appropriate."

"You should rely on your mother for advice in these matters, Don Martín. She knows best what kind of wife you need. Young men, God love them, make mistakes at times, especially when they're off on their own, in their country or abroad."

"I have the greatest respect for Spanish ladies," Bora said clumsily, too quickly. Of course he respected Spanish *ladies*. But there were the giggling girls in Bilbao, the bed that had fallen apart under them when he and Inés had made love. Splendid in their contrast were the darkness and glowing blade of light behind Remedios' door, the unspeakable pleasure of bruising his knees on Remedios' floor, between Remedios' thighs. He stared at his plate so that Señora Serrano wouldn't see through him, since she seemed capable of doing so.

"Don Martín, do you recall Luisa Cadena, the young woman who was here during your last visit? Like me, she had a premonition. Now we shall see how accurate she was in her fears."

How accurate? Bora didn't know how much Serrano had shared with his wife about Lorca's death, or if Luisa Cadena had spoken to anyone about meeting *him*. He kept silent, even when Señora Serrano added, "My husband told me he discussed Don Federico's disappearance with you."

Had the colonel sent him to the *huerta* so that questions could be asked of him? He readied himself to mention something about not being at liberty to speak, but Señora Serrano didn't give him time.

"That Monday night was a dreadful night, not just for the Lorcas. I had dream after dream about Alejandro being shot. It was precognition, and Colonel Serrano wasn't even home to comfort me."

Colonel Serrano was away from home the night Lorca was killed. Bora went from unease to keen attention in the time it took him to blink. He said, casually, "Nina always regretted the lonely nights when my stepfather was on military duty."

"Well, it isn't like my husband to absent himself at night without apprising me of it beforehand. So you understand that I was worried for him, too."

He didn't tell her that he'd be away, either. Bora jumped from the chair and snapped to attention when Señora Serrano left her place at the table to dismiss him.

"You will have Alejandro's room, Don Martín. I attend church very early in the morning. Should you depart while I'm gone, make sure to pick up the reply to my husband's letter on your way out. It will be on the table in the library." She preceded Bora out of the dining room, and coolly gave him her hand to kiss. "I do feel for the Lorcas," she said, "even though Don Federico wasn't a very good Christian. And his 'Ode to the Most Holy Sacrament' … he should have been ashamed of writing it."

Tuesday, 20 July. Morning, Huerta de Santa Olalla.

A very vivid dream. The family place in Trakehnen. There is a war on in East Prussia. The house staff lines up along the garden path as when we first arrive for the summer, the women curtsying as I pass by. The housekeeper looks like Señora Serrano, but younger. There's piano music coming from the open windows of the third floor, and I know it is my father playing. I tell myself that he's long dead, so his music sounds very beautiful for a man who has been out of practice these many years. Accompanying me across the grounds there is a shadowy figure which I take to be a woman. In the stables, the horses are being groomed by the Guardia Civil.

"They'll give the horses Spanish names if you let them," my companion tells me. I look over, and realize that it isn't a woman at all, but Federico García Lorca. He's wearing the white shirt he had on when I found his body and carries a bundle of sheet music under his arm. I remember burying him, and shudder at the thought that he was obviously still alive; I'm about to say something about it, but he smiles and shakes his head. "Only the dead can bury the dead," he says. Then he remarks that my father is playing a Spanish piece of his composition, even though the music is actually Schubert's "Gretchen am Spinnrade" ("My peace is gone / my heart is heavy ..."). I point out the error, but Lorca smiles again and insists that such is the case.

We're still facing the stables. Lorca singles out Turnus – the horse I rode for the Olympics – and tells me he won't like Russia. I reply that I have no plans to ever go to Russia. "But you are already fighting the Russians," he informs me, indicating my braided epaulettes. I see on them the rank of major, and although I should feel overjoyed, I am in fact overcome by a great sense of sadness and loss. Lorca says that Russia will be my "white wall of grief", just as Spain was his own. I don't know what language we have been speaking until now, but he now says distinctly in Spanish that *los jinetes se entienden el uno al otro*. "If horsemen understand one another," I answer, "then tell me who killed you." "You already know," he says. I mean to protest that I don't, that I really have no idea, but the Guardia Civil is letting the horses out of the stable, and in the confusion I lose sight of Lorca. I wake up in frustration.

At sunrise, the Turia River resembled mirror shards behind the branches of the quaking young poplars. Bora followed the bank to Teruel, reaching the Guardia Civil stables from the low ground of the railway station.

Pardo looked much better than the night before, good-natured and bright-eyed. Bora rode to the square, tied him near the Confitería y Pastelería Muñoz and continued on foot towards the Valera y Pastor Factory front.

Someone followed him there. Bora sensed it at first, and then heard it. He listened. Without turning around, he sensed movement, in the same way he had perceived a lack of movement and recognized death the day he had found Lorca.

The street was long and balconied, with a row of prison-like barred windows and doorways. There where Bora was, the space turned into a brink. He stood there unsure of where the edge might be, how close, how deep. A razor's edge separated perception from reality, fear and confidence, and that hair's breadth contained a world of possibilities: women moving about in dark kitchens, armed men stalking, innocent passers-by; death close by or remote, life ahead of or behind him.

At once his body felt breakable. What Señora Serrano had said about premonition, what wearing Alejandro's things meant … they were sudden clues to this uncomfortable fragility. Having reached the corner of Cziffra's street, Bora reached for his gun. Turning so fast that his ability to aim would be hampered if he needed to shoot, he caught a quick blur: nothing but a trick of sun and shadows on the silent fugue of house fronts.

His gut told him he had been right. Even after he walked the length of the street to make sure, he was still convinced of it. Someone *had* watched him leave the square, and knew his route. Someone knew he'd been to Soler's flat. Bora went to untie Pardo, and took a different route to Cziffra's place.

Cziffra was not in. Elbows on her desk, a red pencil in her mouth, his secretary said she didn't believe he'd be back soon.

"Later today, then?" Bora asked.

"Not today. Are there any messages for him?"

Bora answered no.

His next stop was at the Seminary of Santa Clara, towering with its twin steeples over a compound of churches and convents just over a mile in length. Bora spent close to thirty minutes speaking to a priest in the courtyard, where an ugly statue of the Sacred Heart formed the centrepiece and the flower beds needed watering.

Sunlight lanced the streets by the time Pardo ambled up the climb to the public garage. Sudsy water trickled down the cobblestones, and when Bora came close enough he could see the source of the flow. The Ansaldo sat in front of the garage, where the albino was washing it with water and a soapy rag.

Bora dismounted, glanced inside the car, and without a word walked into the garage.

The man called him back. "Can I help you with anything?"

"I'll help myself."

The old Fiat the albino had been working on late at night and the car with the missing windshield were gone. In the small office, the ledger lay on the worktable. Two new entries concerned the repairs just done, and the latest, dated this morning, recorded the return of the Ansaldo at half past nine the night before. The distance travelled was eleven miles.

Bora leafed through the ledger until he reached the middle, where the central seam ran through the binding and the right page belonged to the same sheet as the left one, with the stitching between them.

Two by two, he began pairing the pages, right and left, checking the entries for continuity. The second half of the ledger recorded transactions well into July 1937. The first half listed entries of the previous months, going back to the summer of 1936. Bora found no discrepancy until he tried to match the page of 12 July with the corresponding page in the first half of the ledger, where the entries of October 1936 were recorded.

The bottom of the left page dated 7 October itemized repairs made on a truck, but the right page didn't match the entry. In a different ink and different hand, the next record was of a rental on 10 October, and a paint job on the same day.

Why had it taken so long for him to understand? An entire sheet had been removed from the ledger, so that no traces of torn paper would remain along the seam. While the latest entries seemed consistent, in fact a page earlier in July was missing. Gone with it was a specific mileage, and a specific signature.

Bora left the garage with the ledger under his arm. "*Hola!*" the albino shouted. "You can't take the book away from here!" He let go of the rag and tried to grab the horse's reins.

Bora vaulted into the saddle and touched Pardo's flanks with the spurs, startling him into a nervy canter that jostled the albino out of his way.

EL PALO DE LA VIRGEN

It was seven o'clock by Brissot's wristwatch when Chernik, Bernat and the couriers got back from their night in Castellar.

Walton saw them enter the house, but made no effort to come away from the fountain, where he was doing his washing. Nearby, Brissot squeezed a blue shirt over the muddy ground that surrounded the cement trough. Bernat joined them shortly afterwards. As he started to soak his peeling face and neck, he asked, "Who gets to do the cooking tonight, Mosko?"

"You do."

"Again?"

"Again."

Dripping wet, Bernat left.

Walton fished his soapy shorts from the fountain without rinsing them. "If Marypaz was worth her salt, she'd be doing the fucking chores around here."

Brissot draped the wet shirt over his arm. "I don't mean to sound unsympathetic, but I'd rather hear what Almagro told you last night."

"Before he went gallivanting to the Widow Yarza, you mean?"

"Whatever. What did he have to say?"

"Rumours. There's gossip in Teruel about Lorca's disappearance. At least one Fascist source expresses the worry that he might have been kidnapped by 'roaming Reds', and there's even talk of a ransom. If the information leaks out of the province it'll be known that his 'death' in Granada was a sham on our part, and everyone will wonder why."

Brissot stomped his sandalled right foot in the mud, at the risk of soiling his shirt again. "Ha! And surely the *cenetistas* will claim they saved him the first time around! Just as I thought, Felipe: we waited too long. We must spread the news that Lorca was killed by Fascists, straight away. It's far too late to have a real effect, but it's something. At least we'll be able to show people his remains when the time comes."

Walton cocked his head at the faint drone of a single-engined airplane. It was very high up, and the sky was already too bright to see it. "I was starting to miss the little bastard," he grinned.

At quarter to eight the couriers were ready to head south via the Sierra Camarena. Walton had been drinking coffee with Almagro by the open fire, watching Marroquí cosy up to Marypaz as he'd done last time. Marypaz laughed and swung her arms childishly.

Almagro noticed where Walton was looking. "We're not due back for some time now, Felipe. It's off to La Puebla de

Valverde and then to Barracas. If I hear of anyone headed this way, I'll pass on what's being said about Lorca."

Walton had time to drain his tin cup without a word before Marroquí clambered over like a young goat, smiling. "What are you old men waiting for?" He grabbed his backpack from the fireside. "I'm ready to go."

Walton squinted. "Do you like her?"

Marroquí's shoulders rounded instantly, a clumsy boxer's reaction to a blow. "Me?"

"You."

"Well, it's not like …" Marroquí tried uselessly to make himself small or apologetic, or both. "I'm sorry, Felipe."

"Don't say you're sorry. I'm just asking you if you like her."

"I can't say that I don't. There's nothing wrong with liking a girl, is there? No harm done."

It struck Walton how easy it was to challenge a younger man. "Marypaz is her own woman," he said. "To me, what she does is her own business. I don't own her, and she doesn't own me."

Almagro was obviously uncomfortable with the exchange. "*Ehi*, if it isn't eight o'clock already!" he exclaimed, sounding surprised. "Time to go, Marroquí."

The three of them started up the broken path that led away from the camp. Walton felt like he'd won something, but he wasn't sure what. It both pleased and annoyed him that Marroquí kept to his side, smiling humbly.

"You're a real comrade, Felipe."

Walton stopped where the trail became steeper and the thorny bushes struggled to survive on both sides of it. A grey tailless lizard sought the safety of a flat rock as the couriers put down their sacks to shake hands with him.

"*Salud*, Felipe. We'll see you next month."

Fuentes held Pardo by the reins as Bora dismounted. If he noticed the faded bloodstain on the lieutenant's sleeve, he showed no reaction.

Bora dipped a ladle in the barrel of stale water. He sipped from it and poured the rest over his head and shoulders. "You wouldn't think there's enough grass left in the valley to catch a spark, but I ran into two patches of wildfire on the way back. Scared the wits out of Pardo, because the flames were sweeping across the road. Is the colonel in?"

"He's in."

"Get me a clean shirt first, Fuentes, and see that Pardo gets watered."

Serrano, smoking in Bora's room, paid as little attention to Bora's clean shirt as he did his weariness. He used a dainty pocketknife to open his wife's letter, and read it at once. "My wife finds you pleasant," he observed without looking up from the paper. "Personally, I do not believe that pleasantness is a virtue as much as an expedient. She is more generous in her judgements than I."

Despite the heat, he looked impeccable, so much so that Bora began to apologize for presenting himself to Señora Serrano in a filthy uniform. The colonel cut him short. "I know you go off to execute orders from German intelligence, Bora, so the state of your clothes is hardly my wife's primary concern. My nephews and I will be leaving within the hour for Teruel. Send in Sergeant Fuentes to do my packing, and have our mounts readied."

By half past two Serrano and the Requetés were gone. To make sure they'd left for good, Bora waited until three to reclaim his room.

The colonel's cigar smoke had left behind a noxious spoor. Bora's few things – books, a backpack, drawing pads – were stacked in a corner and none seemed displaced. But because he'd been wondering about Lorca's "Ode to the Most Holy Sacrament of the Altar" ever since hearing Señora Serrano mention it, Bora reached for the poetry book and searched through the index.

The four poems had been censored in black ink by Serrano's German-made Pelikan pen.

> *You were alive, my God, in the monstrance*
> *Speared by your Father with a spike of fire*
> *Pulsating like the poor heart of a ...*

Bora wasn't sure, but the next word might be "frog".

Sulkily he put the book away. Now he'd have to take Niceto's offer and keep the book, or else make a fool of himself.

He'd been standing at the window looking at the distant fires when Fuentes knocked and walked in. "Sir, Tomé is downstairs saying he's to report to you."

Bora stayed turned to the window. "Send him up."

Fuentes hesitated, obviously in disagreement with Bora's command. "He's supposed to report to you, then."

"Yes, yes." Bora turned on his heels. "What's with you, Fuentes? Send the man up."

Moments later Tomé came into the room with an expectant look on his face. Bora gave no indication that he'd noticed it. He lifted the field glasses to resume his survey of the fires, and although Tomé stood there like a cat hoping to be fed, Bora made him wait.

Even through the lenses, the sole evidence of the fires was white smoke, billowing where the grass grew thickest.

"I want you to be ready to escort me in fifteen minutes. I'm going to the brook for a swim," Bora said, glancing over for a moment without lowering the field glasses.

"*A sus ordines.*"

"That's all." From the absence of any noise, it was obvious that Tomé had made no move to leave. Bora overheard Fuentes clearing his throat next door, where he was supposedly reclaiming his own space. "All right, Tomé, you're dismissed," he said.

"*Muchas gracias, mi teniente.*"

No sooner had he gone than Fuentes stood in his place, impatient to say something. Bora kept looking through his field glasses. On the ledge a solitary cicada made an inordinate amount of noise, the early afternoon sun blazed, and still Fuentes stood there. "All right, Fuentes. What's it going to be?"

"Sir, I don't know why you had to go asking Tomé."

"It's none of your business."

"Couldn't I come down with you to the brook?"

"I don't want you. I want Tomé."

EL PALO DE LA VIRGEN

By evening the fires had travelled across the valley, leaving behind wrinkled black trails like pencil marks. Now that the sun had gone down the charred stubble had become less visible; in the darkness, if they didn't burn themselves out first, the fires would start to glow.

Walton smelled ashes in the air and said, "It's going to rain." Around him, men sat on their haunches on the terraced space where Chernik was cooking soup in a kettle. "When I get this pain in my neck and shoulder, it never fails to rain."

Brissot tasted the soup and made a face. "Too much salt."

"Not for me. I like it salty," Chernik said. "What is it, Felipe, you've got war wounds that predict the weather, like an old-timer?"

"They're not war wounds."

Chernik turned to Walton with a conniving look on his sallow, hairy face. He asked, in English, "Where was it, Detroit?"

"Washington. The Bonus Army March."

"Were you with the veterans or the communists?"

"Both." Massaging his neck, Walton wondered why he'd brought up the issue. He didn't want to remember Anacostia. "Compliments of the US army."

With a twig Bernat scratched his right ear. "I thought you were in the US army."

"Not five years ago."

Beyond the open fire, Brissot surveyed the small group with his arms crossed. "The army charged protesters and burned down the shanties of some 20,000 veterans, Bernat. Isn't that so, Felipe?"

Walton tilted his neck slowly to ease the pain. The smell of smoke had reminded him of Anacostia, that's what it was. He neither answered nor looked at Brissot.

"I reported on the march and the Anacostia shanties," Chernik intervened in Spanish. "The paper didn't pay my way to Washington, but I got there on my own before 15 June. Damn, it was a great article on the passing and killing of the bill! When I went back to Chicago they gave me a promotion and fired me." He stretched to stir the kettle, grinning at Walton. "Four years in the newspaper's shit pile, and I still managed to cover the Chester strike last year and make headlines: ONE DEAD AND FORTY WOUNDED IN PENNSYLVANIA: POLICE CRACKED SKULLS, KEPT ORDER. Well, soup's ready. Bernat, where are the others?"

"Marypaz is inside. Maetzu, I don't know where *he* is: he said he was going to keep watch on El Baluarte. Valentin is on guard duty, and Rafael is with him."

Chernik started passing around bowls of bean soup. "For two people who tried to kill each other, they're getting along fine. Last night Valentin got Rafael laid with the Widow Yarza."

"How would you know?"

Chernik laughed. "He told me. Rafael came too fast and got his pants wet and had to hang around her house until they dried up."

"Don't put any oil in mine," Walton told Chernik. "It's your turn next, Bernat, so eat quick and go relieve Valentin."

Bernat filled his mouth with soup. "I don't have to. Valentin wants to keep watch an extra hour."

"What for?"

"Search me. I guess he wants to keep company with his new-found friend."

"Tell Marypaz to come eat, then."

RISCAL AMARGO

Tuesday, 20 July. Evening, at the post.

I don't know what possessed me to go down to the brook with Tomé. I had good reasons for doing so – if Tomé was ever to open up, he'd only do so away from the others – but there's no explaining any of it to Fuentes, who appoints himself the guardian of every young officer and probably drove Jover to get himself shot!

Thanks to his horror stories about snipers, Tomé was jumpy and overly watchful all the way down to the brook. What's worse, he only started to relax when I took off my shirt and got into the water (I kept my army shorts on). The water is low and tastes like mud, and there's no swimming to be had, really: you just sink into it and get out again.

Casually I told Tomé that I'd heard him play the guitar, and agreed with Niceto that he plays very well indeed. "I'm not bad," he said, and when I added I'd heard he'd won prizes, he said he'd won one, "when La Barraca came to Tarragona three years ago". I knew a little about La Barraca from Niceto. It was Lorca's travelling theatre group before the war, an attempt to reach the masses by celebrating Spanish folklore and history. Still, I let Tomé explain it to me. It embarrassed me beyond belief that he'd furtively picked up my bar of soap and was smelling it, facing away from the water. When he saw me watching, he acted as if he was just removing bits of dirt from the soap. He said that people came all the way from Almería and Jaén to hear the performers, and the poet García Lorca was one of the judges. This, too, I'd heard from Niceto. "Lorca gave me first prize for playing 'Los Cuatro Muleros'," Tomé said. "You know the song: they rewrote it as 'Los Cuatro Generales' when the war started." I mentioned I know the tune (meanwhile, I was struggling to unbutton my shorts to wash them; God knows what impression I was giving).

The idiot didn't take his eyes off me all the while. "The original words are different," he said. He sang under his breath, "Of the four mule drivers / who ride into the fields / he of the dapple mule / is dark-haired and tall." And then he actually said, "*Como usted, mi teniente.*" I was well beyond embarrassment at this point, and itched to strike him. But I attempted to laugh it off, saying, "Like myself? Like half of all Spanish men!"

Joking helped, I think, because he changed the subject immediately. The other judge, he said, was a Teruel man, who now serves in the city government. "A real patriot, that one. He argued and disagreed over every prize." I asked if he was another poet. "No, he runs a pharmacy on Calle Nueva." Don Millares, I thought. *That*'s interesting. The same man who knew where Soler was hiding, and who speaks so contemptuously of him! I tried to get more out of Tomé, but this piece of news seemed to be the only information he had to give. When I walked out of the water, he stood up with the strangest expression on his face and said, "Already? You haven't even been for a swim!" to which I answered that there was too much silt, etc. and put my shirt back on. He actually mumbled, "I'm sorry if I did something wrong."

All this without my saying a word about his staring or about the soap. He was so craven that it made me sick; I don't know what kept me from smacking him. I said I didn't know what he meant, that the water is getting too low for swimming, and that was all.

As we were climbing back to the post, he said that L. had told him, "You have a good voice, you know the tunes. But you won't succeed beyond Aragon, because you have no *duende*." The judgement seemed to grieve him: "*Porqué no tienes duende.* That's what he said, *teniente.*"

In other news, I'm trying to make sense of what I have learned in the last two days from Soler (he didn't tell me everything), Señora Serrano and the priest at the seminary. Who searched Soler's flat, and why did they remove the text and sketches of *The Miraculous Horseman*? Is it (as Soler himself admitted) because it features characters identified as *mariquitas* and others called *seminaristas de niña*, which I take to mean "girlish seminarians"? Why didn't Luisa Cadena tell me that Lorca had had his bags packed until I pressed her further?

I'm restless, crave action and can't keep still. Tomorrow I plan to approach the Red camp by way of El Baluarte, until

I find a good perch to take some photographs. The trick is going to be keeping Fuentes from tagging along. It's getting too dark to write without a light. Not looking forward to the night. I feel muddled and cannot get Remedios out of my head.

EL PALO DE LA VIRGEN

Fuentes insisted on coming along, making no secret of the fact that he thought it a bad idea. They had to clamber up the Riscal side of El Baluarte from the sparse cedar grove that reeked of human excrement and swarmed with flies. Bora merrily led the way uphill, ignoring the litany of Spanish profanities that came each time Fuentes risked losing his grip because of the rifle he carried. "We're almost there," he said when they were only a third of the way up. The odour of burning grass still filled the air, and when he turned the valley was a cauldron of brilliant haze. The fires created a single line across the arid land, beyond which all was veiled and unseen.

Fuentes laboured at Bora's heels. "Almost there, *mi madre*. Don't we have to find a way down to the other side first?"

The sun was rising by the time they crawled over the hump and found enough space to rest. The granite incline, no more than fifty feet wide at the top, divided the ledge, rising up almost vertically to become Mas del Aire, an impossible climb from here. Where it bulged and then tapered to rejoin the lower face of the sierra, the ravine separated it from the valley, the brook and the mule track.

On all fours, Bora preceded Fuentes to the eastern rim of the crest. The breeze carried impalpable cinders, like dead moths; below, El Baluarte dropped away with enough shelving and craggy projections to allow a descent. It bulged at an irregular sixty-degree angle, with a manageable foothill; the climb from the Red camp to the sierra seemed almost comfortable. Horses and supply mules must be able to negotiate it far more easily than from Riscal. On its portion of the ledge, a tumbledown, whitewashed house sat against the sierra wall, flags limp by the door, iron patches glaring on the roof.

"Well," Bora said, "there it is."

Fuentes kept his thoughts to himself. He started down with the clumsy agility of grizzlies Bora had seen as a child at Leipzig Zoo. They had lowered themselves from cleft to notch, hanging on to jutting, glass-sharp rocks to reach cramped footholds that just allowed them to crouch side by side and look out with the stone affording them some protection.

Bora focused his field glasses on the rangy man sipping from a tin cup by an open fire. Even from a distance, the American they called Felipe seemed mature, self-assured. His gestures were spare, which to Bora was always a sign of inner control. Just now, Bora would give anything to be thirty or even forty.

Fuentes said, "See down there, *teniente*? There's a woman at the window."

A woman. Bora's lenses searched the facade. The girl leaning with her elbows on the windowsill was young, plump, common-looking. Tanned, not fair. Hair black, not red. He breathed out in relief.

"The one by the fountain with a moustache and glasses is another foreigner," Fuentes added. "In Castellar they say he's some kind of physician."

On the threshold of the house a man squatted scratching his head, a rifle leaning against his left thigh. Bora took a couple of photographs before saying, "I don't see any outbuildings. Do you suppose they store their ammunition inside?"

"Maybe, unless they stack it somewhere in the walled-up space at the back of the house." Fuentes was crouching with his knees nearly touching his chin, pointing. "See the almond trees? In between there's a horse pen or something."

Bora watched Walton head into the house. "They're flying two flags. A mixed group of anarchists and communists. I wonder which one the American belongs to?"

"They're all Reds to me, *teniente*. Did you see the gun emplacement way up there?"

"I saw it." Another photograph followed. "There's no radio antenna on the roof."

"No damn weathervane, either."

"They have plenty of water, though." Bora handed the field glasses to Fuentes. "Look at it flowing." Below, after stopping to talk with the man on the threshold, the American had joined the bespectacled fellow Fuentes had called a physician. "Can you tell how many are keeping watch?" Bora asked.

"No. I only see the one by the door."

Bora took another photo before putting away the camera. He rose slowly until he stood with his back to the rock. "We're still too high, and the angle is not good." He showed Fuentes an exposed, rugged perch several feet below, and started moving to the right to climb down to it. "I'm going over there to get a better shot of the enclosure behind the house."

At the camp, watching Brissot deftly manoeuvre the razor over his own chin, Walton asked him, "Is Maetzu still on El Baluarte? I thought I told him to get down from there."

Brissot wiped the blade on his trousers. "He's been there all night and won't come down until he's good and ready."

"I'm taking Marypaz to Castellar. If we run late, make sure Maetzu is accounted for by noon." Glancing away from the rugged side of the granite hump, Walton shook his head. "I'd like to know what he's looking for."

"*Get down!*"

The rifle shot struck so close to Bora's head that sparks and stone debris flew into his face. The sky and mountain surged and sank before him. He thought he'd lost his hold and was falling, but it was Fuentes shoving him down. Bora felt the other man's bulk, his protective hands and elbows. "Stay down!" Bullets flew overhead, gashed the rock. Fuentes' knees, in the small of his back, clamped him down. He felt a stab in his groin from a rock beneath him. Bora fought to free himself enough to reach for his gun, and struggled out from under the sergeant.

"He's to the left, look out!" Fuentes was positioning himself to take aim at a point along the same side of the massif, where the flank widened towards the valley. "To the left, there!"

Bora looked, incredulous. The shots came from no more than an extrusion of the rock, a narrow bulge which was allowing the attacker to shoot with the sun behind him. Squatting beside Bora, Fuentes kept firing with the steadiness of a hunter, one crack after the other. Bullets came ringing in return, ricocheting at random, smashing against granite, scoring the rock with a clang like metal bars being struck. Bora caught the split-second glimpse of a rifle barrel and fired. Everything left his mind for that single point in space, compressed, circumscribed, lethal, where the sniper fire originated and became a target. It awed him how quickly his fourteen bullets were spent.

And all the while out of Fuentes' mouth flowed a stream of obscenities, in which he could make out words like *mierda* and "He can see us clearly!" One, two shots burst into sparks when they hit the granite just below the place he was aiming for. "We've got to pull back, *teniente!*"

Bora started shooting again. "It's more like *climb* back! Hold the line!"

"*What* line?" Fuentes drove another clip into his rifle and fired. "We've got the sun in our face! If we don't pull back, they'll figure out which rock we're on and let us have it!"

Shots were already coming from below. Bora saw men aiming this way, ineffectually; still, it was crossfire. For a minute or so crazed non-stop firing was all there was, a cat's cradle of bullets hitting and ricocheting from all sides, and then Bora realized the sniper had stopped shooting only because Fuentes had stopped aiming at the sniper's nest.

"Did you get him, Fuentes?"

Random shots were still coming from below. Fuentes wheezed, and his face was a mask of grimy sweat. "No, he's out of ammunition. *Ándale, teniente*, let's go! Up, up, up!"

Bora managed to empty his clip on the shooters below before Fuentes goaded him up the rocks roughly, with the brutality of a policeman.

Maetzu regained the low ground shouting like a madman. Walton and the others saw him come bounding from El Baluarte with his rifle held aloft. "Get me more rounds! I'll finish them off if you get me more rounds!"

"Who was it?"

"They'll get away, they'll get away! Somebody get me more rounds!"

Brissot held on to his rifle when Maetzu tried to grab it from him. "Whoever it was, they just made it over the hump. They're gone. What do you say, Felipe?"

Walton holstered his gun. He searched the mountain crest from under the shield of his cupped hand. "I say they're gone."

Alongside Maetzu, Chernik's small frame vibrated with anger. "Seems to me they're asking for it!"

"That may be." Walton confronted Maetzu's seizure-like fury and the men's dark faces. "If they meant business, they could have taken us out from where they sat. The worst mistake we can make now is to attract attention to the sierra while there's real military action being planned."

Chernik kicked the dust in a rage. "Are we going to let them get away with it?"

"They didn't get away with anything, and we're sitting this one out. Everyone, settle down. Even you, Iñaki. We're waiting this one out until the time comes."

Maetzu cried out like an animal. He swung his rifle over his head by the barrel and flung it into the air, where it rotated two or three times before crashing to the ground near Brissot.

CASTELLAR

It was at Brissot's insistence that Walton waited until the afternoon to leave the camp. A haze heralding the rain had covered the sun by the time he and Marypaz reached Castellar, and the heat was all the more oppressive for it.

Yellow butterflies laced forlorn cabbage patches and dusty chicory sprigs along the road, where Marypaz wandered, dragging her feet. Walton tried to reach for her braid, and she swung it away from his hand.

"Are you going to tell me why you want to see the Widow Yarza, Marypaz?"

"Don't start that again. I said I was going to see her, and that's all I'm saying. Why don't you go and smell Remedios' doorstep instead?"

Walton ran the inside of his thumb along the sweaty

underside of his rifle strap. "I have business in Castellar too," he said, and lagged behind until Marypaz was well ahead of him, reaching the end of the street and going down the steps to the widow's house.

Like a jolt, as if it weren't obvious, the idea raced through him that Marypaz might be pregnant. In minor shocks, he felt trapped at the thought of what lay ahead, which doors might be forced open then. Would Marypaz ...? Damn it, *would* she?

Soleá Yarza was the resourceful kind. There was more to her and her golden rings than an easy lay or a dutiful midwife. Anxiously Walton reached the end of the street and crossed the fig orchard, where he found a discreet place to sit behind a low wall. It was shady, and far away enough for Marypaz not to see him when she came back out.

He had to wait for an hour, during which he counted the stone chips in the wall and lost track of the constant procession of ants to and from a dead grub. A weaker tribe of ants was kept away from it, tiny insects that resorted to scrambling here and there on the ground in meaningless clusters, like football players planning a move. The minute ants also trailed up the grey bark of the fig tree. In the thick of the matte leaves, some figs were ripe and others still very small, knobbly, hard and bright green.

In Pittsburgh he'd waited for his wife to come out of countless doctors' offices', and for abstruse strings of Greek or Latin words that meant she would never get pregnant. How he'd listen with a straight face, all the while cherishing the selfish reassurance of his masculinity. *It's her, not me. Nothing to do with me if she can't:* I *can. If I want to.* Walton remembered secretly blaming his wife, disguising his lack of desire for children as concern for her. You're young until you have no children: then you're the older generation. There are no stages in between.

From the canopy of the tree, a drop of gummy juice rained onto his hand from one of the ripe figs, and Walton understood what it was that the tiny ants were scrambling for in the dust.

Spain must look like that from a distant planet: big ants, small ants, dead grubs. He dangled his finger near the ground to attract the ants to the drop of juice, thinking that his political anger had become little more than an insect's automatic reflex. His motivations – the Great War, poverty, an intelligent man's disgust for injustice – were about as irrelevant as the reasons the grub had died by the fig tree.

And yet men like Maetzu could go crazy playing the game. Walton could still see him grabbing the red-black POUM flag from the door and scaling El Baluarte to plant it in the spot where the Fascists had been caught in the crossfire, as if he were purifying the place or claiming it back.

Finally, Marypaz left the house. Walton saw her start back down the road, braid swinging. He considered going after her, but there was no way to keep an eye on Marypaz, and the Fascists had no quarrel with the likes of her. Still, he let a few minutes go by before going to the widow's house.

"Well!" She opened the door wide to let him into her kitchen. "If that's what you're afraid of, she isn't pregnant. Come in, Felipe."

Relief set in so quickly that Walton found her familiarity irritating. Weighed down by walnut-sized gold baubles, her earlobes hung at the sides of her head, the holes in the flesh stretched into gashes. She must be waiting for a man, because she certainly didn't dress up for other women.

Turned three-quarters towards him, her head slightly back, chin up, she struck a pose resembling that of the flamenco dancer on the postcard. Shiny black curls were pasted on her cheeks, and Walton remembered that when he first came to Spain he'd kissed a woman and discovered they were held in place with sugar water. She said, "She's built to make children, that girl. I'd think you'd want one or two." She suddenly burst out laughing, as if she had read his thoughts. "Why, you didn't realize that was what's been making her crazy the last few weeks? She came to see me two weeks ago, but I couldn't say for sure then. How stupid men are."

"There's nothing stupid about it." Walton didn't move from the threshold. "These aren't the times to start a family."

She shook her hand in a tinkle of bracelets, meaning "maybe", and sat down at the kitchen table. Her dress was cut low at the front, and moles showed on the solid flesh of her breast, right where the cleavage reminded him of a pig's ass. "So, was it Marypaz you came to ask about?"

"No." The half-light in the shuttered kitchen reminded him of his bedroom in Pittsburgh before dawn, and his wife waking him up for work, shaking him with jellyfish-cold hands. Perhaps it makes no difference if a man has sons or not: life itself makes you weary. Again, he felt older than his years. He said, "If you see any of the Fascists —"

"Why in the world would I want to see any of *them?*"

Walton felt himself growing annoyed again. "Soleá," he continued, "you're a good-looking woman. Where I come from, good-looking women are sought after. In case you see any of them, tell them that if they stick to their side of the mountain we'll stick to ours, and nobody gets hurt."

Perhaps in response to the flattery, the widow's expression changed. "What is it? Have you got something bigger planned?"

"I don't know what you're talking about." But then Walton recalled that Almagro and Marroquí spent the night in Castellar. Here, most likely. "There's nothing planned," he insisted, adjusting the rifle strap on his shoulder. "I'm just *carrying* this."

"Well, it's men's business." For a pleasant change, the widow seemed in a hurry to get rid of him. "I have a friend coming," she said. "But before you go, here's a confidence of my own. One of your boys – I don't know which one – stole a ring of mine, and I'm telling you nicely: you get it back for me, or else none of yours gets any more from me."

Walton was taken off guard by this, but Soleá Yarza's conciliatory expression belied real mistrust, and her threat would carry weight with the men. He said, lamely, "How do you know it's one of mine?"

"I know."

A northerly gale was raging by the time Walton returned to camp, and the evening sky looked like curdled milk. The fires were burning themselves out in the valley under a pall of static smoke. The smell of torched grass in the dark seemed close enough to taste the ash, and when the wind dropped, the fires glowed like a remote line of battle.

When he joined Marypaz upstairs, she said nothing and he said nothing. Getting ready for bed, he discovered a small ant in the rolled cuff of his shirtsleeve, and crushed it with his thumb.

In the morning, the weather was stuffy and overcast, and the red-black flag was gone from El Baluarte.

RISCAL AMARGO

Thursday, 22 July. At the post. Hopefully about to rain.

Here's a real question. Why in God's name did I study philosophy instead of engineering or architecture or some other useful skill? Colonel Serrano is right. Schooling has only made me presumptuous, and will not serve me well in the army, which is what I will do for the duration, as far as I can tell. It makes me agonize about every little thing, nearly as much as religion.

For example, chastity is out of the question, but continence is another matter; a matter to be striven after. Continence, desire, moral stance, political choice, love of justice, war: all of them I embraced with great trepidation, knowing how antithetical they can be. I wish I could go to sleep for ten or fifteen years: not think and not feel for that amount of time, and then wake up wiser.

In fact, I can think of nothing else but Remedios. I haven't had a night's sleep to speak of ever since I met her. Met her? What's wrong with me? Why would I put it that way? It's high time that I consider the meaning of this kind of intimacy. First in Italy, then in Germany, now in Spain … Whether or not I initiated it, I was shamelessly willing in all cases. I wonder how silly I really got with the girls in Bilbao, though I expect I was also pretty good, or so they said.

Last April I was relieved that Dikta was not a virgin because I'd have felt much guiltier otherwise – not obliged to marry her, because she isn't interested in getting married – despite having a fiancé, or at least someone she's lived off and on with for the past year. Still, I plan to propose to her when I go back (Nina would hit the roof if she knew).

But Remedios is the one, she is the one. No one in my life will be able to equal the level of intimacy I reached with her. I'm not in love with her, of course, but aspects of her are buried so deep inside me that I will never be truly free of them. I carry Remedios inside me, and she knows I do.

Bora looked up when Fuentes double-knocked and asked for permission to enter. Slipping a sheet of blotting paper into his diary, Bora closed it and set it aside. "Come in, Fuentes. What is it?"

"I was wondering if I could speak in confidence, sir."

"*Seguro.*" Bora capped his pen. "Close the door and sit down."

Fuentes shut the door and took his place in the chair facing Bora. He had his policeman face on, small-eyed, tight-lipped, and threw a positively critical look at the red-black flag furled in a corner of the room. Bora wondered what he possibly could have to say that was of a private nature.

Outstretched thumbs touching, he spread his hands on the desk. "I don't know how to start, *teniente*, but it comes down to this: I honestly can't remember a day in my life when I've been what you'd call scared, even though I've had my hairy moments and close calls."

"That's good," Bora said.

Fuentes appeared unmoved by the endorsement. "More times than I can count I've been plain angry, because younger men in the Guardia Civil didn't know what they were doing."

"I see." Bora felt a vague intimation of warmth in his neck, which meant blood was working its way up to his face. "What does that have to do with me?"

"I also have sons of my own."

"Look, Fuentes —"

"Please let me finish. I can't blame you for us being caught out in the open; I know reconnaissance is part of the job. But, *Cristo Rey*, I think you've got much too much energy for a time of stalemate. The brook, the photos, and now this." Fuentes motioned with his head towards the flag. "You don't want to hear about Lieutenant Jover, but it isn't like you won't have other chances to get yourself killed. I think ... Well, frankly, I think you ought to calm down."

"You think *what?*"

"Calm down. I think you ought to go to Castellar."

"What kind of stupid nonsense! Why should I go to Castellar?"

Fuentes didn't take his eyes off Bora. "We're all grown men here. We can take care of ourselves for a few hours. Before Lieutenant Jover came, we managed for six months without officers."

"And what does that mean?"

"It means that you can go to Castellar, or anywhere else you please on the sierra."

"I have no duties to discharge on the sierra."

Fuentes' stare had taken on the patient quality of a card player's. "In the Guardia Civil we always make a point of familiarizing ourselves with the surroundings. There's much to be learned away from one's post. Look at the colonel's example. He took his nephews all over the sierra."

Bora tapped his pen on the table. He felt he was visibly blushing, which infuriated him. "I have strong reservations about leaving the post without an officer in charge."

"Then you ought to consider who you leave the post with, even if it's just to go down to the brook." Fuentes thrust out his jaw. "I'd hoped not to have to say this much, but you're asking for it. This is a band of mostly ignorant men, with no sense of respect for their officers. I'm only looking out for your good name."

Bora put his pen down with a forcibly calm motion. "That will be all, Fuentes."

"I'm sorry I had to say it."

"*That will be all.*"

Clumsily Fuentes stood up from the chair and let himself out of the room.

Bora remained where he was, sitting with the diary in front of him and Aristotle's small dog-eared volume open to Book

Three. He'd rather be angry, but what he felt was a rancorous, floating sense of disconnection. The only weight anchoring him came from the rectitude of his youthful mind. And the anchorage was insufficient for the task at hand.

The Greek text on the left page curled into a crowded, graceful blur of ancient inanity, while Fuentes had spoken as though he either knew nothing, or knew too much. *Damn Greeks and damn Spaniards, they can't leave damn well alone.*

The page read, "Yet Virtue is born out of will, for Man does all out of will: thus Vice is also voluntary."

Is that how it is? Bora swept the book off the table. *It isn't. Damn Fuentes, it isn't.* He felt something inside, imminent like the approaching rain: an infinity of possibilities, all equally conceivable. His rectitude could be unanchored by simply saying, *So be it.*

MAS DEL AIRE

Bora went around the building to find her.

Remedios was squatting by the door of the chapel, head low. She was separating handfuls of weeds – limp, fuzzy leaves – into small equal piles. Her hands and her forehead in the frame of red hair had the shimmering paleness of the inside of a shell.

"*Buenas tardes,*" he said.

She didn't look up at once. "*Hola, Alemán.*"

Bora went to crouch with his back to the chapel wall, watching her. The smoke-scented north wind had dried the perspiration on his brow. He felt damp in his clothes, but the wetness was pleasant. Fish must feel so strong and alive when they slip between rocks, whipping among water plants. He rested his head against the wall, closing his eyes.

Remedios was entirely silent, and no rustle came from the parting of the leaves. He listened to his heartbeat slow down as he caught his breath, a steady rhythm inside the slippery self that swam in his clothes. The sun trailed a warm tongue on his bare knees, on his bare arms. Behind his head the wall felt strong and secure, like a thing he could lean on forever.

Remedios began to hum. The low rising and falling of her voice a few steps away, the wind and sun, the awareness of the immensity of the summer sky gaping above him: all made Bora want to stay here forever. It was a perfect, perfectly balanced moment of certainty. Having come here to see Remedios of his own volition, rather than because of anything Fuentes had said, he was grateful to be crouching next to her, hearing her hummed song.

When he opened his eyes again, she had finished dividing the bundles of weeds. As before, no word was spoken of lovemaking, yet Bora was absolutely sure that it would happen. It was so easy with her. Aristotle himself would smile if he saw her. Confidently, he watched her lay the leaves on the ground. They were the same hardy sprigs growing in the rubble of the wall, and once laid out he knew what they were.

Remedios smiled. "*Sierven para refrenar la sangradura.*"

Nettles. Bora remembered nettles from his childhood: not that they stemmed bleeding, but the welts and blisters resulting from taking a wrong step among them. She picked up a bundle and extended it to him.

Bora had been taught to grasp nettles firmly to avoid their sting. Stretching out his hand, he thought of the thorns that had trapped him when he'd first sought Remedios.

"Gently," she said.

The leaves touched his palm, and he was tempted to clutch them but listened to her and simply cradled them between his fingers. Remedios watched his hand, how he fought the temptation to close it into a fist and kept the hold even and slack.

She pulled back her hair, baring the fragile shimmer of her temples and neck. Turning a little, she faced him fully. "I'm glad you came, *Alemán*."

The nettle juice on his palm and wrist felt like green fire. Bora did not move a muscle. "I've missed you these three days, Remedios."

"*Verdad?* You don't mind that I've given you nettles to hold?"

"No. Because I know why you're doing it." Though the blistering pain in his hand caused his wrist to tremble slightly, Bora kept control of himself.

Kneeling in front of him, Remedios reached for his face with her small unblemished hands; as if moulding him, she ran her thumbs over his forehead and down from his temples, where the cheekbones were prominent under his youthful skin. She said, "I can see your skull. *Que hermosa calavera tienes.*"

Bora drew back at the words, cautiously. Her stroking aroused him, and the indirect mention of death aroused him even more. "It doesn't scare me, Remedios." But when he tried to kiss her she teasingly slipped away to push the sun-scorched leaf of the chapel door inwards.

Bora stood, aware of the burn on his blistered hand and the shrill cry of birds overhead.

God love you, Remedios! She waited on the worn threshold in her cotton dress, draped by the wind so that it showed the outline of her legs and the place where the flatness of her belly curved into a delicate mound.

When she disappeared inside, Bora felt a curious instant of agony and longing, which was both a fear of letting go too soon if she touched him, and superstition that the chapel's threshold separated two worlds. More than it had the first time, crossing it would mean losing himself to his anxious blood; and to the door that must give way, skill and desire represented small keys in an immense lock. *In church, Martin?* They were childish, distant voices. He pushed the chapel door wide open to follow her across the ancient sill. *In church?*

The opening of the door sent a glorious burst of light into the whitewashed space. The walls lit up and danced with it as Bora stepped inside. Across the floor, high beds of dry grass were heaped everywhere, pale and scented, letting out a fine sprinkle of seeds or green pollen into the sunbeams.

Chaff spiralled, weightless, as Remedios unfastened his gun belt. Bora had never let anyone even touch it before. He drew back against the wall, and flinched when she reached for the well-sewn edge of faded cloth below.

"Remedios, *no me toques.*"

The Holy Ghost soared on the wall in his faded blue halo. A single small moth flew into the light and seemed to catch fire. "Remedios, *no me toques,*" he repeated, but Remedios' hair was like a flame that would consume the tinder-dry grass all around.

Without kissing him first, she nestled the cup of her fingers between layers of cloth without touching the flesh. Bora, who had steadied himself to avoid buckling, dug his head into the white wall. Not looking, not looking, in awe.

Dikta's hand had fondled him through his uniform breeches at the army ball: not held him, not moulded itself to him, not comforted that most sensitive, despairing part of his body, in which courage and terror always seemed stored.

But Remedios, Remedios … He heard himself groan the way wounded men groan, and while he'd pulled back from Dikta for fear of defiling himself, he heard himself say, "Remedios, don't take your hand away." *You heal all that ever hurt me, or ever will.*

All resistance gone, he felt as light as the fine linen Alejandro Serrano had never worn, as weightless as the cinders meandering outside. They had to come to it. Soon the grass was bed and meadow and a nest without edges. She sank in it as in water. Swirls and eddies, gentle swells: in the middle of them, her shell-white flesh lay dazzling in the light from outside.

He trembled at the crudity of his need for her, bending low until his mouth met the surface of her belly. He was in church, he thought. He was in church, and all the while he passed his tongue round and round the small dip of her navel, and below it, where the sun lit a copper fire of thin tangled hair. His fairness, his colour, a sister to his brother-hood. He'd taken communion with the same scooping reach of his tongue.

EL PALO DE LA VIRGEN

The horse pen steamed behind the house, and the sun, having broken out of the haze, was now again covered, penny-red and small. It was already pouring down north of Teruel. Ragged curtains partitioned the furthest reaches of the valley.

Walton's neck hurt. Now that the wind had fallen, every-thing was still and like a picture: grass smoke waiting to be doused by the coming showers, skirts of rain hanging behind it. His own pain was fixed like a nail at the nape of his neck.

Inside, Maetzu's recriminations at the loss of the flag had the monotonous rambling of madness, to which Brissot's voice only said "yes" and "no" and "we must wait." From the door-step, Walton spat in the dust, creating a curd of saliva and dirt.

In Eden Mills, this was the time for the rich to rent cot-tages and invite poets to visit the lake. Had he gone back there after the divorce, he'd have avoided Guadalajara, two wounds and Marypaz. *You can starve anywhere,* he thought, *even without being shot at.* In Spain the bonus for bringing down an enemy plane would buy two cars back home, though being killed by one would bring nothing. *So a plane is worth two cars and an endless number of men. There's wisdom somewhere in there.*

Maybe lying down would help the pain.

When he entered his room, Marypaz was standing by the bed with her back to the door. She was wearing one of his shirts and seemed to be adjusting the front of it.

"Hello, Marypaz."

His greeting startled her into turning around. She'd wedged a pillow into the elastic of her briefs, secured by a string on her belly, and was trying to button his shirt over it. Its bulk reached under her breasts and swelled the cloth to straining point.

Walton stared at her. "What are you doing?"

"I want to see how I'd look pregnant."

"What?"

Marypaz turned sideways, holding the small of her back, pushing the bulge forward, leering at her reflection in the windowpane. "Maybe I'd like myself this way."

"Don't be stupid."

"Why, what's it to you?"

It was absurd that she was smiling. Walton felt the pain in his neck stab him when he walked over to her. "Take that thing off, Marypaz. You're being ridiculous."

"Am I? I'm going downstairs with it."

"You're crazy." He tried to grab the pillow from under the shirt. "Take it off. Take it off!"

Marypaz fought back. She freed herself and started for the door, but Walton was quick and caught her. He felt the pillow under his fingers and was close to yanking it out when she dodged him again. He heard the pounding of her bare feet on the wooden steps and went after her.

At the foot of the stairs, Bernat stared, round-eyed. Rafael, who'd been round-eyed ever since making love to the widow, dropped the cards he had in his hand.

Walton jumped over their heads to reach Marypaz, clumsy, bare-legged and heading for the door. "I've fucking had it with you, Marypaz!"

"No, I've had it with *you*!" Encumbered by her bulk, Marypaz put her head back in to yell at him. "*Puerco, putero!* It's me who's had it with you!"

Chernik was returning from his watch. She ran right into him, scuffled with him, kicked him and dropped the pillow at his feet in the process. He led her back inside by the wrist, telling her, "You just can't go out like that, Marypaz." An astonished look was on his face, and until he heard Walton shout, he seemed uncertain whether he should laugh or worry.

MAS DEL AIRE

The Holy Ghost was a white blotch on blue, trying to detach itself from the wall. Were it able to do so, it would have a short flight in the twilight, like a paper dove on a sagging wire. Bora could close his eyes and see it, a swinging blur of God seeking the chapel door. It was starting to rain, and the evening sky through the doorway was empty and wide, like a fading cut-out of the infinite: the Holy Ghost would fly into it, and wet its wings. *Poor Lord. Don't go,* Herr Gott: *you are made of paint, and would dissolve long before getting to heaven. The angels wouldn't be able to gather your milky drips in the rain.*

"Remedios, why did you teach me?"

"*Porqué eres digno.*" Arms circling her knees, Remedios sat up in the scattered grass like a dove watching him. Her nakedness and his own made him drunk; he wanted to stare at her and away from her.

"How? Why am I worthy?"

Remedios didn't say. Bora started to gather his clothes, but was trembling too much. These were no longer his clothes; they belonged to someone else who'd come here and shed them like a flimsy cast-off skin, leaving him transparent like the weather when rain is imminent. A stunned suspense, all potentiality, like the breaking point of birth. The khaki clothes belonged to the time before Remedios' door, to the *other side.* He felt them under his fingers without putting them on, kneeling with the coarse cloth gathered to the shadow of his groin, unwilling to forsake transparency, unwilling to go back. Back? There was no going *back.* No, unwilling to go *out. All outside of here is opaque. The Holy Ghost itself is scared to leave.*

In the scented shade, Remedios sat. Hers was the body out of which he'd come transparent, naked, weeping tears. New.

She birthed me, he thought. *This young woman has just delivered me. It took hours of opening. We were one, and it took hours. Callow and covered in moisture I came out at last between her smooth thighs, fearing I would die in the passage. Not wanting. Crying. Now bits of dry grass cling to me with the varnish from her womb, and we are not one. How will I live apart from her?*

His teeth chattered as he stumbled, seeking his gun belt. "I have to go."

In the dusk, less and less visible to him, Remedios' girlish body remained in the scattered bed of grass, and Bora couldn't bear looking at her because he couldn't bear to leave.

"Why am I worthy, Remedios?" His gun was heavy like the opaque world outside.

"Because you will suffer much." She stood up at last, reached the door of the chapel and remained there, her small figure framed by darkness against the damp coming of night. The Holy Ghost flew over her and set itself free.

Bora had no doubt she was telling the truth.

"*Alemán*," she said without turning. "Spend the night."

EL PALO DE LA VIRGEN

Rain curdled the dust at first, like spittle. It tapped on the metal roof next, then drummed on it. It pelted the window, lashing at the panes. The fires in the valley must have gone out. Weighed down by water, a quilt of ashes and smoke on the blackened grass must be turning to mud.

Lying on his bed, for the last hour or so Walton had been telling himself he'd have to find something to fix the ramshackle window before it flew open. At last he stood to rummage through a heap of equipment in the corner, but only because he was tired of thinking about it. He didn't give a damn about the rain, the bed could always be moved away from the window, and in the end, he didn't really care if the world drowned.

All he could find was a folding shovel, the same one used to bury García Lorca ten days earlier. Ten days. It seemed like much, much longer. To one who's already dead, it's forever. Walton jammed the shovel's handle across the window sashes and went back to bed. Folding the pillow in half under his aching neck, he felt his anger brim over at the memory of Marypaz wearing it over her belly this afternoon. The crazy bitch. Now the men actually thought she was pregnant.

As for her, she'd gone off before the rain started, and hadn't returned since. To spite him, she'd emptied the last of Walton's American liquor over the bed. The mattress reeked of alcohol even though he'd turned it over, because the horsehair mattress was soaked through. She had also shredded the paperback Lorca had given him in Barcelona. Walton had only managed to salvage the frontispiece, where Lorca had written a dedication to him. The tall, thin capitals of his signature were all that remained, penned high above the lower-case letters.

You don't know how dead you are, Federico, he thought. *And, Marypaz, you don't know how done we are with each other.*

Pain burrowed into the nape of his neck, eating at him. *There's a joke in it somewhere, not just a lesson. If you pinch your neck here and here, it hurts more, which makes it hurt less. That's the joke.* The pain made him wince and turn away from the rain-stained windowpanes. *And here's another joke. You're closer to Adam than you think, Philip Walton: you're longing for Eden for the first time in your life.*

RISCAL AMARGO

Friday, 23 July, at the post.
Martin-Heinz Douglas Bora, late of Leipzig, died and went to heaven.

7

No forgetting, no dream:
Crude flesh. Kisses bind lips
In a tangle of new veins
And pain will hurt without end
And who is afraid of death shall
Carry it on his shoulders.

FEDERICO GARCÍA LORCA, "SLEEPLESS CITY"

RISCAL AMARGO

23 July, at the post, continued. Afternoon, pouring.

I am convinced, after yesterday, that what the Church says is ontologically true (that God instituted matrimony), and I will add that it is an ideal condition of existence. Having spent an entire night in a kind of matrimonial state, I am determined more than ever to marry. Which is, I suspect, my own inhibited way of saying, "Screw continence!"

I can't get over my good fortune in coming to Spain. This great country in great peril is my destiny. I don't care a whit if I "will suffer much", as Remedios said. Yesterday was worth far in excess of all that's headed my way. Remedios knows, I'm sure, but I had to tell her I'm not afraid. And, quoting Lorca,

I will not say, man-like,
The things she told me.
The light of discretion
Makes me politely quiet.

Later, same place.

Fuentes is a good man overall. Reasons: I didn't return to the post until late this morning (and then only because I had to), and he was in a state. He thought I'd been killed. He was braving the rain below Castellar, having apparently checked with certain women in town to see if I was or had been there (poor Fuentes). While it was coming down in buckets, we met as much by chance as is possible these days, me slipping and sliding along the mountainside that had turned to a waterfall, having nearly broken my handsome skull (Remedios' words) three or four times returning from her house. He realized I'd been to her – to the *bruja*, no less, and in such spirits that he couldn't doubt what had happened – and yet he was so embarrassed at being caught looking for me, he couldn't think of an excuse. Whether he was looking out for me because he fears the loss of another officer (as if we lieutenants were important to anyone other than our mothers) or not, it's funny (and touching, too), that he is so concerned about my welfare. I think he blames himself unnecessarily for Jover's death.

He still can't swallow the matter of the anarchist flag (but that's the policeman in him), knowing that I crawled back before sunrise on Wednesday to take it away from the Reds. It was too good an opportunity to pass up, though I could kick myself for not having taken along a scrap of paper to write a message to leave in the flag's place. American Indians indulged in this sort of daring, and called it *coup*.

What the men think of my overnight absence on the sierra, I don't know. I'm sure Fuentes is taking care of my good name, which for him means that I am sexually active with a girl. As for calming me down, I slept for six solid hours after coming back.

Sitting in the corner away from the broken window, Bora reread the entry by flickering candlelight. Over the roof, right above the small room, the weathervane moaned in the rain. Bora's eyes followed the lines on the diary page as if trying to learn from them where he stood with women after Remedios.

There had been a time during lovemaking when he'd wanted to die. Die, not live. To sink from an extremity of pleasure to no more need for pleasure, to no risk of having pleasure denied to him; slipping out of his carnal self into her and abiding there forever. He knew now that he'd craved the unspoken thing man craves after he's born, and by then it's too late; tonight, this thought made him lonely and insecure. He wrote, underlining each word, "the sheltered dusk of not being". Remedios had borne him out of the very memory of that formless safety, and he couldn't help his longing.

EL PALO DE LA VIRGEN

On Saturday, the ceiling in Walton's room began to leak in earnest. It had been a blemish at the joint of two planks at first, like the wood was sweating, then drops yellow with resin had gathered in the fissure, growing pear-shaped at the tip of a splinter and dripping. Eventually the seepage turned into a string of water. Walton had moved the bed twice before reaching to wedge a rag in the crack. Marypaz was still gone.

"Shouldn't you go and check on her?"

Walton was using a knife to stuff the rag between the planks, and didn't look at Brissot. "Why?" He was as aware of her absence as anyone else, but this awareness had not turned into any desire to go and look for her. He kept working. Drops of water from the thrusting blade trickled down his wrist. It surprised him a little that he didn't care about

301

what happened to her. Without her, he bought himself a small piece of freedom.

Brissot chewed on his pipe. "Well, if you're not going to look for her, I will."

Walton faced him with a first nip of annoyance. "She's a big girl, she knows what she's doing. If I go looking for her, she'll come back."

It wasn't clear what the Frenchman thought of this statement. "She's one of us," he said. "Go and look for her and let her know you want her out of here."

The piece of advice energized Walton. It was still raining, but felt as if the clouds had lost their taste for it. As if they, too, were rags stuffed in the sky, letting the drips through. By the time he reached Castellar, the dirt had turned to mud around Soleá Yarza's house.

This morning she was wearing neither jewellery nor curls on her cheeks.

"So, have you brought my ring back?"

Surprised, it was beyond Walton's ability to come up with a story. "I will. Have you seen Marypaz?"

"Why, are you looking for her?" The satin robe Soleá Yarza had on did nothing for her, and wasn't particularly clean either. She took two steps towards a chair, but didn't sit down.

"No. No, I just want to know where she is."

"Well, that's good, because she's gone." The words came like the sound of scissors through cardboard, a soft cutting sound.

Walton felt sudden hope, but not enough to keep him from asking, "What do you mean, 'gone'?"

"Marroquí came for her." Wrapped in her flimsy satin, Soleá studied his reactions with a little smile. "I don't know if they'd planned it or he just happened to come back from wherever he said he was going. Fact is, he knew she was at my house, and came for her with a packhorse. They left together yesterday morning."

Walton let out a sigh that emptied his chest. With it, his wet shoulders and neck relaxed, as if tightly knotted ropes had frayed into strands of loose fibres, never likely to tighten again.

The widow tapped her knees, watching him. "The way they were going at it Friday night, I think she left for good." Under the robe, Walton reckoned, her hips were twice as wide as his, muscular hunks of flesh wrapped in satin. "By the way, a Fascist sergeant came looking for the German on Friday. He thought he'd be with me, I guess. 'Have you lost him?' I said. The man blasphemed so strangely, and the way he said *Cristo Rey* just made me laugh. Before he left I told him what you said, about keeping to their side of the mountain." Walton must have looked unenthusiastic at hearing the news, because the widow started to fiddle with the front of her robe, loosening it. "Now that she's gone, aren't you going to feel lonely, Felipe?"

Lonely? Now that Marypaz was out of the picture, he was thinking of Maria Luz de Nuestra Señora de los Remedios, who lived at Mas del Aire and was better known as Remedios.

CAÑADA DE LOS ZAGALES

The clouds withdrew on the day of St James, 25 July. By four in the morning, the drainage from the sierra had lessened to dribbles, and the brook ran engorged with a silty discharge, dragging along torn branches and shredded foliage. All memory of the grass fires had vanished: smoke, glimmer, the sweet odour of seared leaves.

Bora went down alone, and after bathing he climbed the bank to the place where he'd found Lorca's body. The sky was pale, as it had been that day, with a single star banking westwards. A planet, most likely Mercury or Venus, arching downwards. Past the sodden cane grove, he reached the bridge over the brook. It was narrow, with no parapets to protect it from the churning water; from here the reeds and canes would hide the bend from a night traveller.

In the dark, a car would not speed on gravel. It would brake on the bridge, and for the curve beyond. They could have ambushed Lorca's car here, unless Lorca had been forced to ride with them from the start. If the Ansaldo had been used for the trip, who had rented it, and who had driven it back to Teruel? Had there been one car, or more than one?

Even after his talk with Soler, Lorca's last moments in Teruel remained unknown. What other reasons might there be for having torn pages from the ledger, if not to conceal traces of a night trip? Bora walked back from the bridge. If only he'd paid more attention when he first found the body ... Were there other signs, elusive signs that time would quickly erase? It was possible the Reds had watched him turn the body over, check its pockets. Coming down from their camp wouldn't take them any longer than it did him from the post, although hauling a dead body uphill must have involved a considerable effort.

Bora shivered in his wet clothes. Colonel Serrano blamed the murder on the Reds. Leftist sources had kept mum about it so far. What made him think he would be able to uncover the truth?

Lorca's death was like the ugly red vase in the Abwehr office, its hidden blue side tucked into the niche and wholly invisible. Bora crouched down, touching his hand to the gravel that had been bloody that day. Closing his eyes, he tried to rebuild the scene in his mind. A car travelling here from Teruel. The brook and canes rustling like silk in the dark, a riot of stars rimming the sierra. Jover's blood calling to Lorca's yet unspilled blood. The thought of someone sitting in a back seat, smelling of medicine, came to him and slipped away, and so did his recollection of Soler surrendering the key to his apartment on the palm of his hand.

MAS DEL AIRE

"Remedios, you don't make love the same way."

"I never make love the same way."

Walton pulled up on his elbows, freeing himself from the tangled sheet of her bed. "Don't play games with me."

"I never play games either."

Without his watch it was hard to tell the time, but it was still dark outside her window. He'd come before midnight, so it was two, maybe half past.

He stared at a spot where he'd pressed his face into the pillow during lovemaking and his spittle had drawn a round coin. The wet was drying up already. "Has anyone else come to see you?"

Remedios smiled, her lips curling without baring her teeth. She sank her head into the pillow and smiled.

"You're not soldiers' flesh, either."

Walton watched the way she teased a strand of her hair round and round with two fingers, into a red curl over the bedsheets.

Remedios looked around the room, oblivious to him; the whites of her eyes, nearly blue, were like half-moons sinking. Walton smelled the bundles of herbs on the wall as if they'd just been hung there and were letting out their scent for the first time tonight. He sensed her detachment and resented it, but didn't want to argue yet. Angry and wanting to know more, it took an effort to put it the way he did. He said the words in a slow superstitious way, as if spelling them out would disprove them: "It's the German, isn't it?"

Droplets of sweat bloomed on Remedios' flesh, the moist whiteness of a bruised flower.

"Isn't it?"

She didn't say a word. Walton's own weight, half on her, half on the mattress, seemed suddenly leaden to him. Some inner structure, sturdy until now, wanted to buckle and he wouldn't let it. Details of the pillow – its weave, creases, the immaterial play of shadows in the folds – resembled a landscape unknown and impossible to explore. A broken geometry. "Is he any good?"

"Good?" Her voice was as new as the landscape, the voice of a person living in a place he'd thought he knew but was somewhere else entirely. "All men are good with the right woman."

"You know I'm good."

"Well, he's good too."

"Not better."

Remedios laughed. He'd never seen or heard her laugh. The arch of her teeth, the pinkish inside of her mouth, all new, all new. The sound rising from her, rippling and low, all new. The only known thing about Remedios at this moment was how against the white of her skin the red nipples on her little breasts seemed raw.

Walton leaned over her. "He's not better."

"He's younger. I taught him things."

"It's hard to be better than I am, Remedios."

"Yes, it is."

"Is he better than I am?"

She would say no more. Walton recognized her way of cutting him off by avoiding looking at him, as if they were not in the same bed or even acquainted with each other. It made him insecure, and he loathed the feeling. He was angry enough to feel the veins in his neck beginning to swell, and he lay on his back to regain some control over himself.

Whore, whore. The room seemed to go red, like a great heart or bowel. He felt himself sinking as though he were being pumped through or digested, estranged from his own still-aroused body. He'd often worried about Brissot, who never ventured this far up in the sierra. Now he had found out it was the German. The German. Fuck and damn the German. Walton had to close his mouth to avoid panting. "Remedios, *eres una coja.*"

"*Gracias.*"

"If I see him come up to your house I'll kill him."

"And I'll let him know ahead of time. I'll dress like a weathervane and go and tell him."

"'Dress like a weathervane'? What the hell are you saying?"

"I'm saying what I'm saying because I don't like jealous men."

Walton lay back, still. Far from collecting himself, he was fighting a raving morbid curiosity to sniff around the room for evidence of the rival, to catch a whiff of the bed and her body.

Remedios brought a curl of red hair to her lips. "He says I make his blood laugh."

"His blood laugh? He's as crazy as you are." Suddenly sure of himself, Walton took her wrists. "Let me show you how I make your blood laugh."

She didn't react when Walton straddled and then entered her. He was still erect, and already moving fast. "What do you do with him? You've got to tell me at least what it is that you do with him. You've got to tell me." And he dug deep into her, shaking the frame of the bed.

"We do this."

"This hard?" Walton felt the ache start in his loins, his muscles burning with the rude plunging motion into her.

"Harder."

Walton grabbed her by the shoulders, frantic to have an orgasm but unwilling to sell himself short now. He paused to catch his wheezing breath, sweat gathering in a pool between them. "Not harder. I don't believe it."

"Much harder."

Her words enraged him, but he was a good lover and kept at it, pulling her towards himself by the small of her back, kneading his hands into her flesh to get her firmly underneath him.

"Harder than this? Harder … than … this?"

Remedios had closed her eyes. Her teeth showed between her lips, but it wasn't a smile. Walton was afraid for a second, but she felt stiff, not limp, so she hadn't passed out. Her body was rigid and tight around him, closer and tighter until he felt the pain and tried to pull out, but he couldn't. He pushed down to get deeper, but this too was precluded, as if a door inside her had shut and her inner walls were closing in to trap him. "Remedios," he groaned. "What the hell …"

She didn't open her eyes. Her arms stayed stretched down at her sides, her thighs like marble, hard and cold, impossible to straddle. Only in her throat there was the beating of a vein, rapid, like a bird's heartbeat. Walton felt the pain affect his erection; he suppressed a groan and let go, feeling himself grow small, narrow and limp enough to slip out. He was too angry and sore to speak, lying face down on top of her, nose in her pillow, ashamed and angry.

Remedios stroked his head. Despite his anger, his need for comfort was so great that he sought the side of her face and kissed her.

"What did you teach him, Remedios?"

Remedios spoke in his ear, touching his lobe with her lips, then she lay back. "He cried after I taught him."

"Teach me."

"No."

They made love again, silently, and then he stood up and got dressed without washing. Walton left without saying goodbye to her, and Remedios went to the well to pour water between her legs.

RISCAL AMARGO

25 July. Afternoon, at the post. The great feast of Santiago and St Christopher.

I am put in mind of the epistle from 1 Corinthians 4:9 "Brethren, I think God hath set forth us apostles, the last, as it were men appointed to death …"

What I learned four days ago at the seminary in Teruel is no great help at this time. I went because of what I overheard Millares say at the bar, hinting at some sexual misbehaviour on Soler's part. Not a subject I could directly bring up in a religious institution, but the priest – a Father Iginio, S. J. – chose not to show me the door when, solely based on the authority my uniform gives me, I asked if Francisco Soler was a graduate of the seminary (a safe way of broaching the subject). Thanks to the impassive face I'm learning from Fuentes, the priest admitted that Soler had been a *student* there instead of asking me why I was seeking the information. The distinction made me understand I was on to something. "But did he actually graduate?" I insisted. To make a long story short, it seems that Soler attended the seminary, being expelled during his second year for "disciplinary reasons". I thought it interesting that Father Iginio would remember the name of a student who had been drummed out of the seminary years earlier: how serious had the incident been if it had resulted in that kind of punitive measure? I kept the pressure on. All I managed to get out of him was that there was another boy involved, and that he, too, was expelled. No details, no comments.

When it was the priest's turn to ask about me, I told him I am a foreign legionnaire fighting for the preservation of religion in Spain, a Roman Catholic whose errand has nothing to do with politics. He seemed satisfied with that explanation, although I suspect that if I try and spring any more questions on him in future, he won't be anywhere near as forthcoming.

EL PALO DE LA VIRGEN

It was a clear daybreak on Monday when Walton returned from Mas del Aire. He went straight to bed, and slept late into the morning.

Over and over, he dreamed of riding home from work in a bus that took every wrong turn and never reached his destination. The city was part Pittsburgh, part Washington, part a faceless derelict suburb. Dark unnamed streets bent around corners and crossed railroad tracks, passed through abandoned industrial yards or ran straight along streets lined with dimly lit drugstores and shops. Past the tracks where shanties had mushroomed on Sylvan Avenue years earlier, the sandy slope crowded with privies had become a yellow wall, shadowy and without end. The bus went on forever, and never reached home.

When someone stormed into his room, Walton's immediate reaction was to grab his pistol from under the pillow and level it at the doorway. "Stop the fucking bus," he mumbled. Then he recognized Rafael, and lowered the barrel.

The youngster was out of breath. Tramping upstairs after him, Valentin showed his face next. Both looked exhausted and anxious.

"Felipe, the grave —"

Walton jumped out of bed. Fully awake now, he groped around the floor for his clothes. "The grave what?" He dressed himself furiously, yelling at the boys. "What are you idiots telling me? When did you go to the grave?"

"We ... went to the grave as soon as it was light enough to see."

"To do what? Damn you, what's wrong with the grave?"

"It's empty."

Walton slumped back onto the bed. "What?"

"It's empty."

Brissot came into the room just in time to hear Valentin say, "It really is, Felipe. I was so sick of hearing about Rafael's rosary, I talked him into coming with me to look inside the grave. He sewed the body into the sheet, didn't he? Who's to say he didn't lose the rosary then?"

"I didn't want to do it," Rafael moped. "He made me do it."

Brissot interrupted him, staring at Valentin like an owl mesmerizing a crow. "Let me understand. You two went to the grave and actually dug into it?"

"All the way. There's sticks and rocks and branches inside it, but the body and winding sheet are gone." Valentin showed Brissot his bloody fingers. "We got so desperate, Rafael and me, we started rooting around in the ground like hogs. It's gone, Mosko."

Walton now sat lacing his boots, regaining control. "Valentin, Mosko, you're coming with me to the site. Rafael, you stay."

They took rifles and extra ammunition and left within minutes. From the camp, Muralla del Rojo could be reached by a shortcut across the steep face of the sierra looking west towards San Martín. Burdened with equipment, they spent nearly an hour climbing. Walton was the first there, and he only gave himself a moment to get his breath back before running to the gravesite. After last night's bitter lovemaking, or perhaps the strenuous hike, his hands and legs trembled as he stared into the hole, enlarged by his men's panicky search. All around lay pebbles and gnarled branches that had been used to create volume by those who had removed the body.

Brissot stumbled up and Valentin came last, blinking spasmodically. Brissot took him by the arm. "Was there evidence that someone had been here?"

"No, not a thing. It had been raining, but it was nothing like the storm of a few days ago. I'm telling you, Mosko, we didn't realize anything was wrong until we started digging out branches."

Walton took a stiff step back when Brissot joined him. Squatting by the hole, the Frenchman ran his hand through the loose dirt, back and forth, like a housewife checking the temperature in a bathtub. "You boys had it in your heads to search a decomposing corpse?"

Valentin tossed back his greasy hair. "The way I was looking at it, we wouldn't have to. Rafael gets scared so easily, he'd realize the rosary didn't mean that much to him, and stop complaining."

Walton heard every word as through cotton walls, bits of sounds his mind had to stitch together to understand. The tremor of his hands was the only outward sign of a reaction, even to him. When Brissot approached him, he struggled to look at the doctor.

"The soil deep inside is drier than I thought, Felipe. How did the grave look when you came a few days ago?"

Walton's tongue felt like a piece of leather he had to unglue from his palate in order to speak. "Undisturbed."

"So it probably *happened* before the last rain."

At the foot of the grave, Valentin counted on his bruised fingers. "That means some time between Tuesday and the end of Thursday."

Brissot ignored him. "If they re-stacked the stones, it means something. If they had just wanted to dump the body, they'd have done so."

"No." Walton moved his head stiffly from side to side. The desolate incline and the stone crags, as secluded a place as he'd been able to think of, was not isolated enough, not safe enough. Until now, no culprit had been mentioned, but only because it was obvious to everyone, and the fact called for a reprisal.

There was still a tremor in his hands, a small frantic motion he'd seen in old men. He must avoid thinking of the German if he wanted to keep his anger down enough to reason logically.

Brissot crossed his bulky arms, frowning. "Let's face it, Valentin is right. It must have happened between Monday evening at the earliest and Thursday night at the latest."

Walton glared at the grave. Clasping his left wrist, he was able to keep both hands from trembling, and the partial sense of control helped him. "Yes. Or much earlier than that."

RISCAL AMARGO

There were no outward indications in Serrano's behaviour that anything was amiss. The colonel arrived on Monday with news that the battle for the town of Brunete near Madrid was over and won.

"Our tanks pursued them and crushed them," he told the gathered men. "The enemy had to turn the machine guns against his own in order to slow down the rout. Colonel Barrón controls the field all the way to Villanueva." With a gesture he prevented whatever show of enthusiasm the men might have in mind. "One does not cheer when Spaniards die, whichever side they fought on." And he looked unkindly at Bora, who was the most unlikely to express his emotions.

The temperature had abated after the rain; still, the sun on the ledge was dazzling and the men stood in it as if purblind. Briskly Serrano crossed that splendour to reach the post, ordering Bora to come inside as he did so.

Unrequested, Alfonso's dog limped ahead of Bora, who said, "*Márchate, perro,*" patiently dodging him. Serrano headed upstairs; there must be more to tell about the victory at Brunete, or some other matter entirely.

"Open your trunk," Serrano ordered as soon as they reached Bora's room, gloved hands on his belt. Bora wondered why, but did as he was ordered. It all came back to him: army school inspections, and his boyish anxiety that he would be found inadequate.

"Now empty it."

Again, Bora obeyed. He took out a set of colonials slightly less faded than the one he wore, and two pairs of riding breeches and tunics. He was beginning to suspect what this was really about, and how Serrano's attendant – he couldn't imagine Señora Serrano having done so – might have told the colonel about the bloodstain. Since returning to the sierra he'd washed the tunic in cold water and soap until the stain had gone, although that sleeve was now perceptibly more faded than the other.

Serrano would not touch the clothes. He instructed Bora to hold the first tunic up for him to study it. "The other one," he said afterwards. "And now the breeches."

When the inspection was over, Bora set the bundle of khaki cloth on his cot. Serrano continued to stare into the trunk, where the linen remained that his wife had given Bora. Bora went into a quiet fit of anxiety until he realized the colonel did not recognize the handiwork. All he wanted was for him to take his linen out and show him what was underneath.

At the bottom were a small framed picture of Bora's mother and a pebble he'd picked up on the street when he first entered Bilbao.

Since the situation was anything but calm, Bora grew uneasy when he heard Serrano speak in a calm voice. "Yesterday a mounted army patrol was on duty along the Villaspesa–Castralvo cart road when the stench of carrion led them to a ditch in the neighbourhood of the Ermita de Santa Ana. There after a brief search they found the body of a man shot at close range, a bullet having entered his skull from behind. The decay and damage to the corpse's face, plus the absence of documents, did not allow them to identify the man. Other than abandoned farms and sheepfolds, the sole residence in the area is the *huerta* Enebrales de Vargas, to which the soldiers removed themselves to interrogate the occupants."

Bora concentrated all his efforts on trying to understand what Serrano was saying, as if he spoke in an unknown tongue. Like a deaf man, he found himself nearly lip-reading the colonel.

"… Professor Augustín Vargas and his wife, confronted with the slippers removed from the body, recognized them at once as belonging to Francisco Heras Soler, architect, who had been visiting the *huerta*. They then proceeded to inform

315

the soldiers that a Foreign Legion officer had last been seen with the victim on Monday 19 July."

From the sudden spasm under his ribcage, Bora knew he'd been holding his breath.

"Without prompting from the non-commissioned officer leading the patrol, the Vargases provided a description of the legionnaire. The rest, Lieutenant, I would like to hear from you."

The *rest*. Bora remembered few times in his life when he had failed to answer a direct or indirect question. Soler's death encompassed and entangled everything else. Bora felt the snare closing, and coming up with an answer for Serrano was far down his list of priorities.

"Is that what you were doing during your last errand? Tramping around Castralvo?"

Unwisely, Bora tasted just enough sarcasm in the colonel's voice to rise to the bait. "I met Señor Soler at the Vargas place."

"Why? What business did you have with him?"

This time Bora kept his mouth shut, as if he could ignore questions, orders and anything else coming from Serrano.

"I asked you a question, Lieutenant."

"Although the colonel disputes the matter, I am under orders additional to his own, and am not obliged to report everything I do to the colonel."

"That may be, but I'm giving you a direct command."

"By the colonel's leave, I'm disregarding it."

Serrano's perfect silhouette seemed to sway under the impertinence. "I do not know what else you do in Spain or what activities you engage in when you leave this post, but I have reason to believe you killed a Spanish civilian, and demand to know the circumstances of the killing," he said heatedly, further mispronouncing his accented German.

"That's preposterous."

"Not in the eyes of the Spanish army."

Bora felt the irresistible sentence fly out of his mouth. "The Spanish army! *I* think the Spanish army is deliberately obstructing the investigation of Lorca's death."

Bora was staggered by the lightning speed at which Serrano's hand rose and landed full force on his face.

No adult had ever struck him before, neither his indulgent mother nor his disciplinarian but remote stepfather. Bora was so unprepared for the sanction that he lost all sense of judgement and place. "I also think you have no right to rummage through my books and blot out what you don't like about my private readings, which are none of your military business."

The words fell into a void. In front of him, Serrano's face was altered, frozen; contempt, regret and national hostility were all apparent in his gaunt features. Bora dreaded to think what his own posture expressed. A moment later he was apologizing; he didn't know whether he spoke in German or Spanish, but it was a young officer's grovelling formula of submission, none of which Serrano acknowledged.

EL PALO DE LA VIRGEN

Walton sent Valentin ahead via the shortcut, and with Brissot took the longer way back. He needed time to collect himself. For the first half of the descent from Muralla del Rojo he had wound down from rage, to brooding, to an indistinct attempt to choose the means of action. When they were about twenty minutes from camp, he said, "He's bedding Remedios."

Brissot glanced at him, sunlight glittering through his eyeglasses. "What?"

"She told me he is."

"Who? Who is? I don't know what you mean."

Walton felt as though he'd just woken up: just back from Remedios' house, just finished dreaming about dark streets and the dirty yellow wall. The episode at the gravesite was like an intrusion, a dream within a dream, or the only thing that *was* a dream: because he had ridden buses through dark streets, after all, and had made love to Remedios until yesterday. He sensed a benign stupidity, as though he'd gone past the edge of consciousness into something like a pond of lukewarm water. In the middle of it lay a kernel of anger, black and ominous, harmless for now, but there was no telling what would come of it if he picked it up.

"Felipe, what's wrong?"

Walton stopped walking. At this point, the incline grew rougher and steep, but he found a rock stable enough to sit on. "I'm going to kill the sonofabitch." He clasped his arms tightly around himself. "The German, who else?" he said, feeling that Brissot was making no effort to understand. "The motherfucking German! He's been to her, and she's taught him *things*."

"'Things'?"

"Things, things! Lovemaking things. She taught them to him."

For the first time in eighteen years, it was happening. A tremor of muscles that he suppressed by clutching his wrists until the veins in the backs of his hands bulged like knots. Walton watched the black kernel of hate emerge from the calm pond. It made him atrociously angry and sad for all that had happened to him since the beginning of time, an explosion of blackness that he'd be killed by. All that had gone wrong in his life so far summed and multiplied into an immense blackness; he lost his vision for a moment, as when he'd passed out in Guadalajara, but but this time he simply folded inwards, his shoulders collapsing forwards.

"*What* things?" Brissot insisted.

"Don't you get it? She taught him how to keep coming without letting his seed go."

"Well, that's a good trick. It'll make him popular with girls." Brissot laughed unconvincingly. "Is that what this is all about? I thought it was about Lorca's grave."

Walton did not react. Once he'd confessed what had been eating away at him, the kernel of anger was shrinking again, slippery and small like a tadpole, nearly impossible to hold. Weariness followed, as if he'd lifted a massive rock and now even the infinitesimal weight of that tadpole could break his wrists. He let his hands dangle at his sides. "I swear I'll kill him."

"Maetzu would have done you the favour a week ago, if you'd let him."

RISCAL AMARGO

Monday 26 July. Afternoon, at the post.

Too ashamed to describe this morning's run-in with Colonel Serrano. He left without speaking a word to me, and now I don't know what to expect in terms of military sanctions. What is certain is that I would have never acted so unforgivably with a German officer. If Father ever found out! But it's done now, and whatever comes, I'll have to take my medicine, and like it too.

Soler's death is something else I can't reconcile myself with. It's bad enough that the army found out about my visit to the Vargases and that I was one of the last people to talk to Soler (not the last one, obviously). Aside from my imperfect Spanish, my height makes me recognizable, although I never gave Soler or the Vargases my name. I expect I could have

319

denied being at the *huerta* that day, but I saw no reason to lie, and Colonel Serrano is not above taking me there to confront the old couple.

Anyway, Soler's murder resembles Lorca's: but was it the same gun, the same hand? And why was Soler murdered? Someone other than the Vargases must have seen us together. Most likely the killer, because he was shot soon enough after my departure to make the Vargases suspect me.

Was Soler killed because I interrogated him? Was someone afraid he might have said something incriminating? How does the tampering with the ledger fit into all this? I'm starting to have an uncomfortable feeling about it all. What I said to Serrano about the army obstructing justice, and his reaction to my comment, only weakens my position as an investigator. Poor Soler, who was so afraid of me!

I don't have enough to go on and doubt that I ever will, unless Lorca himself lends a hand from beyond the grave.

Herr C. owes me some real pieces of information. No more stories about red and blue vases and vague intimations. I'm beyond "observational judgement", and if I'm to get to the bottom of this I need access to Lorca's file, to Soler's file (if there *is* one), and an explanation of the events in Granada a year ago. That is, unless the colonel lands a blow on my other cheek.

The double knock on the doorjamb was accompanied by Fuentes' matter-of-fact voice.

"*Teniente*, there's a boy who wants to speak to you. Says the priest sent him."

Bora looked out of the window. Below, a twelve- or thirteen-year-old boy stood under the combined watch of Alfonso and his dog. "All right," he said. "Have him wait there. I'll come down to meet him."

It was the same twiggy, locust-like boy who had accompanied the priest on the day Bora had first heard Remedios' name mentioned. Contrary to Fuentes' report, he actually said nothing at all; he simply pulled out of his pocket a folded piece of paper, which he handed to Bora.

Bora unfolded it at once. It was light, yellowed, with a thin red edge, the paper used for missals – probably an end leaf. The pencilled handwriting was unsigned, but clearly from the priest. Bora read quickly, skipping words to get the gist of the message:

"... he demands that you meet him tomorrow at noon in the cemetery at Castellar. Since he will not employ an armed escort, he expects you to abide by the same rule. If your answer is 'yes', let the boy know."

Bora had to be careful not to let out an irresponsible whoop. He glanced over his shoulder to see if Fuentes was around, but Fuentes was celebrating the victory at Brunete by having the men exercise in the murderous sun on the ledge.

"Tell the priest 'yes'," he said.

The boy didn't move. "I've got to bring the letter back."

Bora noticed the postscript at the bottom of the note: "Please return this so that I may dispose of it." He handed back the paper, which the boy drove into the pocket of his adult-sized trousers. He tackled the incline like a two-footed goat, bounding from rock to rock until he was out of sight.

The American wants to meet me. To think how much I've been wanting to meet him *these past two weeks!* Bora felt his critical sense and common sense and every other militarily definable sense fall off like needless ballast, and derived a heady lightness from the process. With a few strides, he reached the well at the side of the house. He looked into it, even though this morning it had been as dry as ever. A round eye of unblinking blue reflected his shadow at the bottom of the deep shaft. From its hidden spring in the sierra, water had come at last and mirrored the sky, darkening it into a colour Bora had not yet seen in Spain: the colour of a winter sky. "Another sign," he said out loud. He hauled up water to drink and wash his face, a flavour pure and cool after the stale water in the barrel and the silty spurt from the rock.

There were contentious and practical reasons for a confrontation with the American. Bora had no doubt that the offer, however unexpected and dangerous, was Lorca's way of reaching over from the other side to help.

CASTELLAR

Walton waited where he could clearly see the measly cypresses and cedars flanking the entrance to the cemetery. In the midday heat, the shrubs let out an embalmed odour; insects buzzed inside them. The German opened the gate, pausing as he opened it.

"Down here!" Walton called out in English.

The cemetery was no more than fifty yards across, and the newcomer approached him directly. "Hello," he said, stopping two feet away. "You wanted to meet."

Feeling himself under scrutiny, Walton was quick to initiate his own appraisal. Six foot two (or more) to his six feet, well built, lean. Young. Bright eyes. *Guapo*, as the Widow Yarza had said. It was annoying and obvious why Remedios liked him, at least physically. Well, damn him. How had he asked her …? When and how often had he gone to see her? *Sonofabitch*, Walton said to himself. Remedios preferred this German sonofabitch to him. He hadn't given an army greeting, and Walton wasn't about to give one either. "We've met before," he said instead, in a wry voice.

Bora ran his eyes over Walton's mixture of civilian and army clothes. He was straight-backed and a little contemptuous. "Do you hold a military rank?"

"I'm a major, Lieutenant."

A nod of acknowledgement from Bora was all Walton got – no other recognition of his higher rank. "I understand this meeting has nothing to do with military matters."

Again Walton noticed the way he pronounced the word *militree*, like the British. The scene by the brook came back to him in an irritating flash. "Right." Try as he might, he couldn't separate his assessment of him from the thought that Remedios had taught him *things*. Did the German know? He was also evaluating Walton, but smiling at the same time. Even if Walton hadn't already known the other man wasn't Spanish, he'd have guessed from his blonde body hair and the whiteness of his teeth; his front incisors were too close and overlapped slightly, a flaw that bordered on curiously charming. Had they been hounds, Walton thought, they'd be snarling and smelling each another. As it was, they simply stood face-to-face like adversaries waiting to catch the other off guard.

Bora was the first to look away, sweeping an unaffected glance across the cemetery. "Well, Major, I'm here. They say you go by Felipe. Is that what you wish to be called?"

"No. Walton's my name."

"Bora is mine. Have you been in Spain long?"

"Not long. And you?"

"Not long."

Just then a distant shot startled them, and both demonstrated their unease by turning towards the sound in alarm. No volleys followed, and Walton noticed Bora was the first to relax.

"Let's walk, Lieutenant." He started in a diagonal that led between the graves to the slope-roofed porch where tombs were stacked like headers in the wall. There were two such porches at the sides of the cemetery, and it was to the one left of the entrance that Walton went. As they walked past a cement cross, he brusquely came to the point. "You've been making inquiries on the sierra regarding a burial."

Bora did not so much as alter the rhythm of his walk. "Nobody in Castellar seems to know anything about a burial."

"I haven't asked you to come here to play games." Walton stopped in mid-stride. He'd last used the expression with Remedios, and righteous anger choked him.

"And I haven't come to be interrogated. *I* have questions." The way Bora said it, the controlled urgency of his tone, struck Walton as unrehearsed, naively betraying other interests, in fact.

"The grave is empty," Walton charged. "I know you're involved. Somehow you found the grave and removed the body that was inside. I want to know why."

This time Bora lost his cool enough to step into a sorry-looking bush that bordered the grave ahead of him. "I don't have to tell you anything, Major. If that's why we're here, we can end it right now." For all his bluster, he sounded imprudent or uncomfortable at disguising his feelings. "I thought perhaps it was about the matter of the flag," he added.

"The flag? I couldn't give a damn about the flag. And it's nothing to do with my gun, either."

They stared at one another across an untended grave. Walton was at this moment so obsessed with Remedios, he feared the German would mention her.

Bora said, coolly, "So, you must be wondering instead if my men killed García Lorca."

Walton was entirely taken aback. He felt as if the two of them had been dropped from a height, to a place where words were naked and newly important.

"If I knew who had killed him, Major, I wouldn't have taken the trouble to meet you."

Well, the sonofabitch. "What makes you think *I* know anything about it?"

"García Lorca wasn't coming to see *us*."

Preceding the American, Bora reached the porch and sat on its shady cement step. Where the walls met, the corner of the porch swarmed with green flies. Their hum sounded ominous in a cemetery, although they probably fed on decaying flowers and plants placed on the graves.

"Suppose you start by telling me what you did with the body," Walton said.

Behind Bora, the tombs were stacked six high, their ends sealed with marble plaques. On some of these, the lettering identified the dead as having fallen "for God and Country". The eternal lie governments indulge in, Walton knew. "*Por Dios y por España*" was the local version, and surely there was a German variation on the theme. Bora sat, seemingly ignoring the question. "I intend to discover who killed him."

The brash statement outraged Walton. "Is that a fact?"

Bora raised his eyes to meet Walton's. "I'm not sure I can figure it out on my own."

The American stood in front of him. Days of resentment were coming to a head. He stared at the wholesome tautness of Bora's face and neck, the vigorous, untouched looks of one who had grown from a privileged childhood to boyhood and was now a man. A *young* man, which made a difference to the way Remedios looked at him.

Before Spain Walton hadn't thought much about ageing, or about comparing himself to others. Today forced him to confront those issues. Bare-kneed and clean-shaven, Bora faced him with the satisfaction – there was no doubt about it – of having taken Remedios from him, the *older* man.

Instantly Walton was beyond prudence and back to his unformed murderous reason for coming here. He imagined levelling a kick at Bora's chest or face, in partial retribution for this encounter.

As if sensing the threat, Bora rose to challenge him, inch by inch. "On second thoughts, Major, I believe I can. You're welcome to tell me what you know, but I don't really have to reciprocate, because I'll figure it out anyway."

Walton began to laugh. "*I'm* telling *you* nothing." Seeing Bora unfazed by his laughter was another mortifying reminder of the age difference. "And about the grave ..." He straddled the ground among the sun-wilted shrubs. "I could thrash the answer out of you."

"Really? Forgive me, Major, but I'm quite a bit younger than you are." Bora smiled his half-amused, half-insolent smile. "And I don't think a cemetery is the appropriate place to fight it out." All the same, he started to tense around his neck and jaw, readying for a fight.

He had no time to do anything more. Walton landed his right fist on Bora's face, surprised at his own speed. The shock of his knuckles striking bone travelled up his arm. He could not ward off a blow to his shoulder, and when he aimed a second hook, he only glanced the German's cheekbone, and the excess energy propelled him forward. No blow came in return; instead, he felt a brutal shove as Bora forced him towards the centre of the graveyard, the two men now chest to chest. He hated the German's unafraid arrogance, his unwillingness to brawl. Walton stumbled, found his footing, and began to fight in earnest, using the crude techniques he'd learned in street riots: a hot-headed sequence of quick, bitter, short blows without thinking, without covering himself enough to avoid a heavy uppercut to his chin. It hurt, and he threw a wild punch; Bora lost his balance and stumbled backwards, but wasn't hurt enough to fall, or even to groan.

Walton grunted, kicking out this time, but the German grabbed his foot. Suddenly the bright sky was flying at him and Walton found himself lying flat on his back. He twisted to get up, felt the weight of the other man on top of him and the risk of being pinned down. There was blood on his hands, although he couldn't tell whose it was. No pain registered, although he was receiving and landing blows. Then he was up and pushing Bora back, back, over the cement step. Against the corner of the wall where the green flies buzzed, he struck hard with his fists and knee and Bora groaned after all, doubling over but not crumpling, in pain now; but so was Walton, and when another blow came it was like an explosion in the pit of his stomach. The breath jetted out of him and he groped for the wall to keep standing. He saw out of the corner of his eye Bora staggering away from him to the sun of the cemetery and stumbling towards a gravestone to sit on: blood was pouring from his nose, and for a moment or two he did nothing about it, letting it run down his chin. Then he untucked his shirt and wiped his face with it.

For the better part of a minute they remained where they were, Walton getting his breath back and Bora tending his nosebleed as best he could, head tilted back against a marble cross.

"I believe he was killed in or near the car that brought him here," the German said. The bleeding had not stopped, but he sounded singularly amenable given the circumstances.

"How do I know you're telling the truth?"

"Learning what happened is more important to me than your opinion of my sincerity. I want to know who did it, and you probably do as well."

Walton discreetly unbuckled his pistol holder, a motion that made his ribs and back ache. *I'm still angry,* he told himself. *I'm still good and angry.* "Were you the first to find the body?"

"I think so." Bora spoke with his face in the bloody hem of his shirt. "I found a spent shell nearby, so he must have been shot there."

Walton pulled out his gun three-quarters of the way before sliding it back in and turning around. "*One* shell? There never *were* two shots, then."

EL PALO DE LA VIRGEN

Chernik, who was keeping watch at the edge of the camp, stared as Walton strode past him.

On the stifling ground floor of the house the odour of burnt onions was overpowering. Brissot was playing solitaire with both decks of greasy cards while the others dozed on ragged army blankets by the back door, where a waft of stale air came from the horse pen.

"Well, did you kill him?" He was the only one who Walton had told about the meeting, and had advised against it.

"I beat him to within an inch of his life."

Brissot looked at him doubtfully. "Obviously within that inch he managed to give you a black eye. No. You never wanted to kill him."

Walton glanced at the tidy arrangement of cards. He hadn't felt anything wrong with his eye until Brissot mentioned it. Now he noticed a stinging throb in the upper lid, as if grit had lodged underneath it. He grabbed a water pitcher from the table. "In the end he told me nothing and I told him nothing."

"You were up there a long time for two people who said nothing to each other."

"I didn't spend all the time there," Walton lied. He poured water into the palm of his hand and cupped it against his right eye. "I went to Remedios afterwards."

"Hmm." Brissot stood up from his chair. He removed Walton's hand to look at his swelling eye, a physician's response. "Any impressions of the man we're facing?"

Walton stepped away from the scrutiny, tight-lipped with pain. "Army school prig," he speculated. "I bet he hasn't got any combat experience worth a damn. There's nothing to report. It was a waste of time."

"Maetzu left camp in one of his moods. He may be 'looking for blood' in Castellar."

Walton did not mention that he'd heard a shot while in the graveyard. He avoided a confrontation by going upstairs, despite the oppressive heat under the metal roof. In his room the bed was still where he had dragged it away from the leak in the ceiling. He sat on it to take off his boots.

Nothing to report? He and the German had squatted against the wall in the fly-ridden shade of the porch to talk warily for a long time. After Bora had washed away the blood with water from his canteen, they'd done nothing but talk. Walton could count on the fingers of one hand the times anyone had listened to him so attentively. He'd been tempted to feel flattered but had resisted it.

When he had probed him by asking, "What's in it for you?" Bora had looked genuinely surprised.

"*In* it?" he had repeated. He had a deep voice and pronounced words with terse clarity, like a soldier. "I hadn't thought about it. Peace of mind, I expect."

"You said you'd never even met Lorca."

"I never met the Generalissimo, either. But I'm here."

And then it'd been Walton's turn to say something memorable: "I was García Lorca's friend."

Take that. There are different ways of landing a punch. Walton grimaced when he tried to open his eye fully. The bed still smelled of liquor. Since Marypaz left, he'd lain in it every night with his boots on, leaving muddy tracks on the bare mattress. He searched for the tobacco pouch in his breast pocket. The last pack of cheap Italian cigarettes he was keeping to one side for night-time smoking, when he couldn't roll a cigarette in the darkness outside.

Forget Marypaz. It was all about Remedios. Remedios had taken more than she'd given him, sucking him dry. She let him make love to her like it was a concession. She'd never said the word "love" once, not even the way women do when they want a man to come. Now Marypaz was gone, and Remedios too was gone, as if her bed had floated away to an unmeasurable distance, visible but not reachable. She'd lie in it, white and small, with the handful of red between her thighs, that tight void that sucked the life right out of him.

Somewhere into the equation fit Bora, who had spoken about Lorca as if he had a right to know what Walton knew. He'd only agreed to meet again because, because … He liked to think it was because neither man wanted to give up, and because he might yet extort from Bora the new location of the grave.

But beneath this there was more. It was dark and filthy at the bottom, a degraded curiosity he hadn't satisfied, so he needed to go to Bora again. As for himself, he'd conceded that he felt bitter about Lorca's death. The German would realize that much, if he hadn't done so already.

Walton flicked the cigarette butt out of the window. Unless he saw and smelled more, his anger towards Bora risked changing in its intensity. Not diminishing exactly, but taking the colour of contempt, old wartime hatred, becoming more diffuse and less personal. Already Walton caught himself disliking not just Bora but all young men, Marroquí and Rafael and Valentin included, as if he'd never been one of them and their masculine stupidity and eagerness were unfamiliar to him. It needed to be broken in all of them, that assurance of youth.

He'd never felt secure. No one had ever given him anything, not even Remedios.

How could the German called Bora possibly have the arrogance to say, "Help me discover who killed him"?

RISCAL AMARGO

Tuesday 27 July. Afternoon, at the post.

Met the American! His name is Philip Walton, and he may have given me the greatest breakthrough in my investigation so far. Here's the summary: he knew Lorca well; he heard from an informant about a car with three passengers and two shots fired; he suspects I was first on the scene (I confirmed this). According to Lorca, he added, his cousin Antonio Cadena had been edgy and afraid recently.

Much tension between us from the start. Acted upon it. Told Fuentes nosebleed due to sun. Ended up talking about Lorca more freely than we'd intended, as if we both needed it. On edge at the thought he'd bring up Remedios … I think I'd have killed him then (he did pull a gun on me at one point and thought I hadn't noticed). Balance of the encounter: Walton self-assured, concise, impressive hard-bitten sort. Likely agnostic. Seems unflinching in the face of danger. Bora self-contained, circumspect, smacking of European and army biases. Better uppercut (if that's what it was). Planned another meeting for tomorrow morning, with the understanding that military business between us will continue unaltered.

In unrelated matters, Fuentes reported that due to the victory at Brunete Colonel Serrano has countermanded my orders confining Aixala and Paradís to the post. Aixala has been to Castellar and back already. Paradís is still out.

Bora resorted to his sketchbook to transcribe his conversation with Walton, quoting verbatim whenever possible. When Fuentes showed up on the threshold he distractedly replied, "Yes, yes," and "I'm busy," to whatever the sergeant said.

Fuentes wouldn't budge. "Busy or not, *teniente*, you'd better hear this."

It took them under half an hour to reach Castellar, a record time even for two fit men. Bora had never seen more than three locals together in one place, while this afternoon a cluster of onlookers watched and waited.

Paradís' body had been moved to the side of the road. A coarse piece of fabric lay draped over his head, and Bora thought it was dark red until he realized it was soaked through with blood. He warded off a grisly urge to look under the cloth.

"They got him in the left temple as he walked out," Fuentes said. With a slow gesture, he pointed at the blood on the step, starting at the small house in the fig orchard. "The widow inside says she didn't see who fired the shot. That's possible, because it looks like it came from a marksman's rifle. Could have come from a long way off."

"Get her out here."

Soleá Yarza emerged in her blue robe, a tacky pastiness on her face. Her ropy black hair bristled with cheap celluloid combs at the sides of her head, like fish gills. Bora, who had never met her before but like everyone else had heard of her, laid a quick, astonished look on her shabby person. She stared at him, trying to keep the blood and body out of her peripheral vision by contorting her head and neck in a strange position. A stance of avoidance and fear of what had already taken place.

Any suspicion Bora might entertain about her fell before the woman's terrified response, because any of them – including Fuentes, who was a married man; including *him* – could have been cut down walking out of any woman's door. It was raw and real, a reminder of men's fragility, shatterable at any time: Fuentes keeping on scanning faces and the land, rifle in hand; the old men gawking; and he, Bora, acutely aware of the danger they were in. And Soleá's turning away, the averting gesture of her open hand, reminded him of the verse in *The Odyssey* where the faithless handmaidens are brought in after the slaughter of the queen's suitors and ordered to sponge their lovers' blood before being hanged by the palace wall. *And there they hung like doves*, Bora quoted to himself. The pity he had felt for Lorca's body on the mule track returned, a creature's sadness for his own mirrored mortality. The sadness and mortality of things.

"I was in the house; I didn't see anyone." The widow began to weep.

"You may go back inside," Bora said.

Paradís had no one to claim him. Fuentes suggested that they bury him at once and be done with it, though Bora insisted on getting the priest. When the priest sent word that he was not well, Bora stormed to the church himself and came back with the old man glumly tagging along. A *mulero* and a cart were secured, and they headed for the cemetery. Its wall was visible not far from the widow's house, among fantastically twisted fig trees, and having just met Walton there, Bora had a peculiar feeling of déjà vu. There, Walton had hinted that a *mulero* had witnessed the murder. In return, Bora had confessed his admiration for Lorca's poetry. Edgily they'd begun to talk, revealing just enough, holding back just enough, posturing to avoid giving in. Bora remembered saying, "I am freer to move than you are. You may have more information, but it won't get you anywhere. You must help."

"Bury him here," the priest said, craning his wrinkled neck and indicating an unkempt patch among some old graves, close to the spot where Walton and Bora had wordlessly fought over Remedios as men always fight over women. Bora felt wayward and exhilarated at the notion that his blood would still mark the slab where he'd sat.

"Me? I haven't been to Castellar in a week," Paradís had said. Now he'd be here for much longer than that.

EL PALO DE LA VIRGEN

In the afternoon, Walton woke up covered in sweat after a bad dream. He must have slept long enough for his eye to swell. He could open it now, but it felt cottony and sore. Swinging his legs off the bed to stand, he stepped on a loose floor tile, a reminder that he ought to push the bed back into place now that the rain was over. In the dream, the German had told him he'd burned Lorca's body. No doubt the grass fires and the smell of overcooked onions had played a part in it, mingling in his memory.

"What if I told you that we had buried him in Teruel?" Bora had in fact asked him.

"I wouldn't believe it."

Walton pushed the metal bed across the floor, dislodging the loose tile in the process.

"Felipe," Brissot's voice called from the top of the stairs. "Maetzu is back."

"Well, what do you want *me* to do about it?"

"He killed one of the Fascists in Castellar. The man was leaving Soleá Yarza's house, and Maetzu knocked him down from five hundred yards away."

For an appalled, gleeful moment, Walton cherished the animal hope that it had been Bora. Defiance, triumph and a spot of regret were added to the mix. But Brissot added as he walked in, "That's the shot you heard from the cemetery."

"Ah." Walton knelt to joggle the loose tile, which came out. "What the hell …?" A small square space now gaped between the floor and the ceiling of the room below. "Fuck," Walton said.

Tucked inside the hole was a bright piece of cloth, which he recognized as a kerchief he had bought for Marypaz in Barcelona during the spring and hadn't seen her wear in weeks. It was red, with black and yellow swirls and flowers. He reached for it and felt before he pulled it out that something was wrong. He was sure of its contents even before undoing the bundle. His watch, Brissot's lighter, Rafael's silver rosary, Chernik's pen. Marypaz's gilded bracelet. The last piece … the last piece had to be Soleá Yarza's ring, a hefty gold band with a filigree pattern of leaves.

Walton's left eye watered if he closed it, so he stared at Brissot in spite of the pain. "What was she trying to do, Mosko? Under my nose, under your nose … She almost got Rafael killed over her joke!"

"It wasn't a joke, Felipe."

"No? What, then? Letting me go crazy looking for stuff hidden under my own bed!"

Brissot lifted his lighter from the small pile and put it into one of his many pockets. "If you cannot get it into your head that she was craving attention, there's no explaining it to you," he said sternly. "The positive thing is that without the story of Rafael's rosary you'd have never discovered the empty grave."

"For all the good that's done me! The German sonofabitch wants me to believe they hauled the body to Teruel."

Brissot quickly suppressed a sneer. "I thought you hadn't spoken to one another."

"So what? It was a lie, wasn't it? I don't need you telling me how to act with a sonofabitch half my age."

Brissot shuffled away in his sandals to avoid an argument, adding, "Are you going to tell the men where you found these things, or just leave them casually lying around? They were in *your* room. And when push comes to shove, everyone liked Marypaz."

Walton heard the peevishness in his own voice. "That's because *you* miss her."

SAN MARTÍN DE LA SIERRA

Sunrise was still some time away. After the rain, the residual moisture in the lower sierra and the valley had condensed in an immense billow of fog, frothing up to the edge of the rocky spur where the chapel perched alone.

Bora waited in the muffled silence, and although he strained to hear human sounds, Walton approached so stealthily that he was only revealed at the last moment. Caught off guard but unwilling to admit it, he immediately went on the offensive: "Your men killed one of my men."

"We also killed the lieutenant before you," Walton rejoined.

Only then did they reluctantly exchange a sullen army salute.

"It wasn't an act of war, Major."

"Everything between us is an act of war. There's nothing you can do about it."

Bora rested his back against the chapel wall. The spur where they sat unbeknown to others sank in the swell of haze two feet below them. Walton's black eye was a more visible reminder of their last encounter than his own bruised jaw. What formality was possible between them, given what they had shared sexually? In his longing for Remedios it all seemed sinful, intrusive and unavoidable.

We're not here about Remedios. I ought to be talking about García Lorca, or anything else that will lead to the subject. Across the small space that separated them, Walton's long Anglo-Saxon face had a day's growth of dark beard. Minute wrinkles embittered the sides of his mouth, and formed an untanned web at the corners of his eyes, one healthy and one battered. He smelled of cigarette smoke. Even in the open air, Bora recognized it, and wondered with inopportune self-consciousness if Remedios liked that smell. In the end, he said, "You served in the Great War, I expect?"

Walton nodded. "Western Front."

"There were ... splendid episodes in that theatre of operations."

"Oh yes? It was nothing but shit."

"Well, strategically at least —"

"Spare me."

A pebble rolled out from under Bora's foot, and he caught it before it sank in the fog. "I thought it admirable, how you defined yourself yesterday."

Walton turned to him with an annoyed smirk on his weathered face. "What a classist statement! Why, should I be ashamed of calling myself a *peasant*?"

"That's not how I meant it. People generally try to aggrandize themselves."

"Because they care for this life."

"Because they hold it in regard, yes."

"And you don't."

Bora tossed the pebble into the sea of fog. "On the contrary."

"You're in the wrong business, then."

"Or in the right one."

No mention of Lorca yet, but this was the ceremonial stage of their discussions, necessary if a deal was to follow. Walton sat with his knees drawn up, doubling up his shaggy figure, his blue eyes firmly on Bora. Bora resented his grudging, tactless attention and said, much as one nudges a sleeping dog, "I take it you don't care much for life."

For nearly a minute Walton simply sat, the nape of his neck against the chapel wall as if he could push the brickwork back. Halfway through that interval the sun rose. Bora tossed pebbles with increasing energy, awakening small echoes under the brightening fog.

Walton did speak eventually, although his first words were mumbled and lost to Bora's ear. "It's a hallway with doors, right and left. Think about it. You open, look inside, stay a while, shut them behind you. Right, left, right, left. Some of them you slam. You lock some others. Nothing's prearranged. You get sick of choosing and shutting doors after so long."

Bora mulled over the meaning of those plain yet troubling words. Not for the first time, he asked himself whether he had uselessly complicated his life. The unadorned idea of doors as Kantian "free elective will" had the advantage of simplicity. "Surely you get pushed through some of the doors," he said, tentatively.

"Do you really believe that?"

"One could argue that free will isn't absolute."

"Nothing is. Once you get that into your head, philosophy becomes pretty useless."

"Then you shouldn't subscribe to any ideology."

"Who says that I do?"

With the edge of his hand, Bora swept away a crowd of small rocks, sending them into the void below. "You must be in Spain for some reason other than greed."

Walton laughed. "Greed *is* an ideology. Didn't you know that? It's called capitalism."

He sounded strong, physically and of character, secure in himself. Like a man who'd suffered. "I envy you," Bora admitted without lying. Then, to make himself clear, "I envy that you were Lorca's friend. And I envy your age, your experience."

"Are you *crazy?*"

"No. I feel extremely awkward with men more experienced than myself."

"What a fool."

Walton's dismissive tone irked him this time, or else Bora was tired of preliminaries. "Francisco Soler is dead. Were you aware of it?" he asked.

With sunrise, the great swell of fog took on a gauzy sheen, a veiled incandescence that would soon make the world glow around them.

"When?"

"Last week. He was shot in the head shortly after I questioned him near Castralvo. Someone went through his apartment in Teruel looking for something, I have no idea what."

Walton let him wait, rolling himself a cigarette. He lit it and gulped down the smoke before saying, "All right, Lieutenant. Tell me what you know, and I'll tell you what I know." He took on a pragmatic lack of expression, an embittered face that smoothed itself into dispassion. Before Bora had time to reply, he slipped in, shrewdly, "If you think she likes you, you're mistaken."

Bora found it inadvisable to smile. "Maybe. I like *her*, a great deal."

MAS DEL AIRE

Black cotton stockings were all she wore; dipped in darkness from mid-thigh downwards, her body emerged like the dawn.

"… So we're not doing it because of him, or because of her?"

"*No sé*, Remedios."

"You *do* know." She knelt in the middle of the bed holding up her hair with one hand, like a mermaid in a milky sea. "She has another. No?"

"Not any more."

"She has another, *Alemán*."

"You're just saying that."

Gracefully Remedios lay down on her side. "She'll keep him until you come back."

Was it really about Dikta, or Dikta's lover? They'd been kissing on top of the sheets, Bora still completely dressed, Remedios wearing only her black cotton stockings. Kissing her with his clothes on pushed him to the edge of pleasure and punished him, and having said that he would not make love the pleasure was rimmed with pain, like a burn. Lorca's words haunted him:

> *Limpid pain, always alone.*
> *Oh, pain of the hidden stream*
> *And a faraway dawn!*

He lay on his stomach beside her, watching Remedios as one watches a delicate colour respond to the light, absorbing and reflecting it. She folded her hands on the pillow and rested her face on them; her crisp ruddy hair fell over her cheek, veiling her left eye. The other shone like a star.

"You said I would suffer, Remedios."

Her beautiful eye opened slowly, a crescent limning the blue-green of her iris. Bora prodded her gently, a slipping over of his hand to touch her shoulder. "Remedios, am I going to die?"

"Who isn't, *Alemán*?" Her waist, her hip … a curve like a snowdrift he could huddle against and be safe.

"You know what I mean. Am I going to die in the war?"

"You shouldn't be asking."

"But do you *know*?"

"Maybe."

"Then you have to tell me."

Moist from kissing, Remedios' lower lip had a delectable, fruity redness. In a gesture he was learning so well, she pulled back the hair from her face, baring the fragility of her neck and the meander of her small ear. "What good will it do?"

"Plenty of good." Bora grazed her lip with the tip of his finger, remembering the taste of it in his mouth. "Seriously, Remedios: it'll do me plenty of good."

"Will it, *Alemán*?"

"It'll do me plenty of good."

"No."

He turned sideways to face her. Remedios was holding her small breasts pensively. He longed to reach down to that cradled roundness, but he felt the question's urgency. "Yes, Remedios. Yes, yes."

"And then what?"

"Then I'll know how to act."

"If I tell you either way, you'll do stupid things. Then you'll regret that you know and wish that you didn't."

He'd gone too far to back down now, though he was starting to feel afraid. As if they were handsome bodies belonging to others, he saw the tanned skin of his knees meet the black-sheathed whiteness of her legs. "I won't. I promise I won't regret it."

Remedios sighed again. She lifted her hands to him, slowly. "This is all I'm telling you, *Alemán.*"

He looked at her outstretched fingers. "Seven?"

"Yes."

"Seven what? Months, days? Years?"

"That's all I'm going to say."

"And Felipe?"

"Felipe, too."

Bora turned on his back, silently swallowing. The sweetness of the kiss in his mouth was all he felt he could depend on. "Let's make love." He began to take his clothes off without sitting up, stripping anxiously, his eyes closed.

"You're regretting it already." Remedios' voice came to his ear, sadder than he'd ever heard. "Don't say no. You are, I can tell. You're counting and regretting it."

"No. No. I don't regret anything."

TERUEL

In front of the Hospital de la Asunción, at the Bank of Spain's end of the square, troops were lined up when Bora arrived in Teruel. Tassels dangling brightly from their side caps, in their brown uniforms they resembled clay soldiers with wicks stuck into them. Complete with military band, they faced the church of San Juan, ready to celebrate something or other, more likely than not the victory at Brunete.

A group of officers in dress uniform – ties, white gloves and leather gaiters – smoked cigarettes on the church steps, waiting for the ceremony to start. They looked over when Bora passed on horseback. He saluted them, and they returned the greeting slowly, resting their gloved hands briefly against their temples. Captain Mendez Roig was among them, and acknowledged Bora's greeting with an additional curt nod of his head.

The streets were more animated than usual, but Cziffra's storefront remained secluded and in the shade at this early hour. A fanfare was blaring from San Juan's square as Bora tied up Pardo at the end of the street. Cziffra himself stood behind his secretary's desk with one hand in the pocket of his linen suit, and for all the coolness of his expression Bora had no doubt he had a pistol in it. "Not going to the parade?" he asked, as if testing a boy on a school subject.

Bora took the garage ledger from his canvas bag, and handed it over without comment.

They stood there for some time, during which bugle calls and shouted orders distorted by loudspeakers created a far-off confusion of sounds. In the niche, a plaster bust of Wagner in his limp pancake hat had replaced the ugly red vase. Cziffra's summer suit was blurrily mirrored in the window; the shot pane had been repaired.

"Well, we did hear about Soler's sorry end," Cziffra conceded with jovial indifference. "The thought did cross my mind that you might have pushed your questioning too far. But if you say that wasn't the case, all the better. Being an assassin requires more training than you have. Naturally, Serrano will have to follow through with some sort of sanction against you, but it won't be for dispatching Soler. To

343

top it all, you contravened all orders by meeting Felipe, the American. It seems curious to me that you came to blows with him. Blows seem a brutish method of settling political differences between officers. As for what came out of the second meeting, you may or may not be on the right track."

"But do I have your permission to go to Alfambra?"

"Yes. Ask the Guardia Civil for transportation. In case you're planning to visit Luisa Cadena, let me dissuade you. She received the news of her relative's passing. I doubt she wants to see you, or any other uniform."

"I have more questions for her!"

"You'll have to do without them."

"What about the file on Lorca?"

"Later." Picking up the anarchist flag Bora had brought along with him, Cziffra freed it from its string bundle with a dainty pair of scissors. He unfolded it. "So, this is the trophy. How interesting. You had better leave it here while you travel north." He slipped the flag into one of the mysterious drawers of his desk. In its stead, Cziffra pulled out an envelope. "This came for you." He proffered an opened but uncensored letter. "In English, from your mother. She still doesn't seem to know where you are."

Bora hastened to read it.

… things are much the same here, my darling. Our J. H. Voss translation of the *Iliad-Odyssey* with its Genelli plates received flattering reviews in the *Literarisches Zentralblatt*, and we are confident the Bora Verlag will outshine Brockhaus and Baedeker this August.

On 8 June, your father and I went to Frankfurt for the premiere of our friend Orff's *Carmina Burana*, a "musical-ized drama", as he calls it, and a piece like no other: you would love it, and we must catch it together when you return.

You'll be interested to know that a young lady telephoned to ask about you. Her name is Benedikta von Coennewitz. I know her mother slightly from my tennis class. She apparently met you at an army reception during the spring. She wanted to know if you were 'back from Italy', so I assume you told her that you are abroad on manoeuvres. She sounds charming. Your father – you know how he is – made some gruff remarks about the young lady's grandmother and great-aunt. She seems perfectly lovely, and after we chatted for a while I invited her to tea next Thursday. I thought it inappropriate for me to ask her, but are you quite close to her? She mentioned you have only met twice, yet she speaks about you rather *en famille*. But here I am, at forty-three years of age, fussing like my Victorian grandmother! I'm sure that she is perfectly lovely and just very much enchanted with my wonderful son.

Cziffra made a wry face. "Speaking of wonders, I wonder what your mother means by 'gruff remarks'. If her father is the same von Coennewitz recently appointed German consul in Milan, the young lady's parents are in the process of divorcing and quite Protestant." Outside, the military band struck up a paso doble with vim. "Frau von Coennewitz, if I'm not mistaken, is openly living with a *Schutzstaffeln* colonel these days … something I wouldn't tell your mother. And I take it that you're closer to this perfectly lovely casual acquaintance than your mother suspects, though your stepfather seems to have a clearer idea of the matter."

"I plan to marry her, if I go back."

Bora was surprised at having said the words. Marrying Dikta? Was this what he'd been thinking of? It was one more step towards making it necessary to ask her. *Dikta, who has dimples when she smiles, and a vacuous look when we make love.* Other than that she rode well, wore beautiful lingerie and had attended Swiss schools, Bora couldn't say much more about her. Yet he had been thinking about her differently ever since meeting Remedios, as if Dikta could become Remedios somehow. He was enthralled at the idea of marrying without having worked out the details: his parents' opinion, his career, the fact that he hardly knew her. As if knowing someone too well decreased the chance of intimacy; the less he knew Dikta, the more he could ascribe to her qualities that she might or might not have. In the end, he loved those qualities anyway, or rather his idea of them: the sort of girlfriend and wife and bedmate who would bear his children. He felt warm and affectionate towards Fräulein Coennewitz and unready for her to say no. *She will simply have to say yes when I ask her.*

Cziffra eyed him amusedly, and handed him another open letter. "*This* came for you too."

Dear Horseman,

How's *Italy*? The last time I was there, I bought a very charming mantilla to use on cool summer evenings.

Father was just appointed consul to the Italian government, but Mother and I are going to America for two months. I always wanted to see New York and all that, and Mother is dying to shop on Fifth Avenue, even though we realize it is plebeian and their clothes are hideous.

I was in Hamburg over the weekend, and had a long conversation with someone. He didn't seem very happy, and finally I had to admit I'd met this dashing cavalryman from Leipzig and fallen for his tan. His intellect too, I think, though we girls are ambivalent about that in a fiancé. He put on a silly scene, and I'm afraid I won't be interested in seeing him any more. Which leaves a vacancy that may interest a man presently touring *Italy*.

A kiss like the kiss you know.

Dikta

PS. I met your mother. Nice. I can see where you get your good looks.

On the evidence of patriotic strains drifting over from the south side, the celebration was still in full swing as Bora left Cziffra's office. The streets all emptied into San Juan's square, and sunlight ran through them like quicksilver. Ahead, the slope of Calle Nueva, ending in the *paseo* and Guardia Civil barracks, ran like a waterfall to the bright river valley below.

The thrill of reading correspondence from home wore off quickly in the lonely streets.

Bora cautiously led Pardo by the reins. When he walked past a narrow alley and recognized Don Millares standing by the entrance of his pharmacy, gleaming like a white whale in his immaculate shirt, something like an intimation of danger forced him to look back, as if he'd stumbled into the sights of an unseen weapon and needed to seek cover. All Millares did was withdraw into the shade of the doorway, like a sea creature swimming away from the light.

Was he on edge after Remedios' prophecy? Seeing Captain Roig's superb, groomed figure at the end of Calle Nueva heartened him. Roig must be Cziffra's agent, of course. Uniforms understand uniforms. Why else would he have taken time away from the celebrations to keep an eye on him? Roig looked up the street, towards Millares, and then crossed the street in a few strides. He was standing at the top of the Moorish stairs that led to the train station when Bora reached the door of the fortress-like Cuartel de la Guardia Civil.

8

If death is death,
What will be of the poets
And all that sleeps
Unremembered?

FEDERICO GARCÍA LORCA, "AUTUMN SONG"

CASTELLAR

The Widow Yarza didn't want to open the door. Even after Walton showed her the ring through the slats of the shutter she simply said, "I see it. Yes, it's mine. Toss it in."

"Let me in, Soleá."

"No. Give the ring back. That's all I want. I'm letting no one in."

Walton pocketed the gold band. "Let me in for five minutes and I'll give it to you." From within, he heard a clatter of pots and plates. On the steps leading to her door, traces of blood were still visible, in line with the faraway perch where Maetzu had stood to fire the deadly shot. "Soleá, let me in. If you don't, I'll give the ring to Remedios." The clatter indoors increased, but that was all.

How many times had he left Remedios' house so drained and unsettled that anyone could have mowed him down on her doorstep? There might be a blessing to that kind of death, the *unexpected* kind, so rare for a soldier. He'd have never been afraid had he not expected death in Soissons, or at Guadalajara. Death had not come back then, but only because he'd run from it. "Should I give the ring to Remedios, Soleá?"

Lorca had been given time to fear death, and so, apparently, had Soler. Christ. Better, much better being broken like the stalk of a plant when your mind is elsewhere, your eyes are elsewhere, and your body doesn't know anything.

"If there were three men in the car, there may have been *two* murderers," Bora had told him by the chapel, throwing rocks into the fog in a curious show of energy or displaced anger. "Do you really have no description of the car?"

"I never saw it," Walton recalled answering. "Anyway, even if a car had come from Teruel, it doesn't mean that it returned there."

Bora's arm had stopped in mid-throw. "It must have done. It *must* have done, or else I'll never find out what happened."

The key turning twice in the lock alerted Walton to the fact that the widow had made up her mind. She peeked out. "Put it here." Her hand showed through the crack.

"Not until you let me in."

Sulkily she opened the door enough for him to squeeze through.

In the kitchen, he noticed that in place of her wedding picture she'd put a holy print with an angel leading two children across a rickety bridge. There was a candle lit on the shelf below it. "Well," she grumbled. "Now give it back."

Walton returned the ring. Once she had slipped it onto her middle finger, where she wore a similar one already, she said, "I want to know which one of your men took it, so I don't let him come here any more." Even as she spoke, her chin began to tremble, and her nerve left her like air out of collapsing dough. "It doesn't matter, I don't want to know." Holding her shiny temples, she sat down at the table. "I haven't slept a wink since it happened. The moment I close my eyes I hear the shot and see the blood seeping under the door. For two days I couldn't eat; I threw up everything I put in my mouth, everything. My cousin has to come and stay with me as soon as it gets dark, but she's scared too."

"When the Fascists came to retrieve their man, did they say anything?"

"What was there to say? The German stepped right into the blood and then went to wipe his boots with fig leaves. He got the priest to bury the man."

"He said nothing about getting back at us?"

Wearily Soleá Yarza smoothed her apron. "No. But he did stop by on the way back from the cemetery."

The idea of the German making advances to the widow after burying one of his men was ludicrous. "To do what, Soleá?"

Toying with her salvaged ring, she acted like someone who hasn't decided whether to feel flattered or offended. "He asked if the man had paid what he owed me."

TERUEL

It took the Guardia Civil the better part of one hour to secure a vehicle, and the round trip to and from Alfambra lasted two. By three o'clock Bora was back in Teruel.

The squares and sleepy streets had returned to normal. Only the soldiers still loitering in twos and threes along the *paseo* gave a clue to the morning's celebrations.

At her desk, Cziffra's secretary wore a pink blouse. Bora wondered what she was typing and how credible this tile factory front really was. Leaning on her typewriter, the secretary glanced up when he stopped in front of her, and said, "Herr Cziffra is with someone. Please come back in an hour."

Bora did not press the matter. He'd left Pardo in the Guardia Civil stables while he was in Alfambra, so he walked to the seminary in the north-west of town. Standing beyond the post office and the church of Santiago, the religious school, with its walled perimeter, would make a solid redoubt. The impression was strong enough for him to make a mental note of it, in case Teruel became a battleground. Soon after four, he found himself once more in the yellow room with its faded rug and framed posters, reporting to Cziffra.

"Antonio Cadena never made it to Alfambra." As he said it, Bora saw the minute change of expression on Cziffra's face, enough to show that he was in fact surprised. "He was not even expected at city hall there."

"Ha." Cziffra pulled the anarchist flag out of his drawer and gave it back, watching Bora tie it up again into a compact square. "So, what does it mean?"

"Only that Cadena didn't go to Alfambra. It'd be helpful if we knew the exact location and the circumstances of his arrest."

"I expect I can find that out." Noiseless in his canvas shoes, Cziffra left the office, presumably to have his secretary place a telephone call somewhere. When he returned, any hint of surprise had left his face. He was unflappable again.

Bora kept at it, a bit anxiously. "If the local authorities gave you incorrect information concerning Cadena's arrest and he didn't in fact go to Alfambra, he might still have been in Teruel that evening."

Cziffra sat on the corner of his desk, dangling his foot. "Are you suggesting he planned to accompany Lorca out of Teruel? Would Lorca mistrust the *Abwehr* after all we did for him in Granada, and trust his socialist cousin?"

"After speaking to Luisa Cadena, to Soler and Walton, I believe he'd try to get away by any means possible. He'd told Walton the Cadenas feared for him and for themselves. That's why I wanted to see Luisa."

"And you believe what this American tells you, because he was 'Lorca's friend'! He may yet fire a bullet into your skull, the way your man died in Castellar."

"Well, what difference does it make? I'm not serving any purpose on the sierra other than this investigation, sir. If I get killed, I get killed."

Cziffra's eyes narrowed, but if he meant to scold him, or to smile, he did neither.

Restless in front of him, Bora was tempted to share what he'd learned at the seminary, but it seemed to have little relevance, so he said instead, "By the way, when I met your agent at the barber shop, he communicated nothing to me."

"That's possible."

"This morning I saw him again on Calle Nueva."

"That's also possible."

"It impressed me that he left the parade early, being in his dress uniform."

"Dress uniform?" Cziffra was on the verge of wiping his neck with the handkerchief, but changed his mind. "What dress uniform? Whom are you talking about?"

"Why, Captain Mendez Roig."

Cziffra wedged his handkerchief back in the pocket of his linen suit. "My agent's name is Millares, not Roig."

"Don Millares?"

"The fat one, yes. The pharmacist. How could you possibly not have realized? I told him to keep an eye on you whenever you were in town."

For all the oppressive warmth in the room, Bora felt his hands go cold. Millares who had spoken disparagingly of Soler, who had hinted at Soler's hideout. Who had sat as a judge of La Barraca and disagreed with Lorca on the music prizes. Millares, who was "a real patriot", as Tomé put it, and who gossiped in the barbershop that Cadena had not returned home. Thankfully, Cziffra's secretary put her boyish head through the crack in the door at that point to say that the call was in.

Cziffra was gone for several minutes. "Well," he quipped upon his return, "this is an interesting turn of events. Early on the morning of the thirteenth, Antonio Cadena tried to run a roadblock near Muel, nineteen miles south of Zaragoza. Such were the circumstances of his arrest. And if you're wondering about his car, he was shot through the windshield of the Fiat 509 he was driving. That doesn't help you at all, does it?"

Bora did his best not to look disappointed. "I thought the Cadenas didn't own a car."

"The 509 is an inexpensive model. He might have borrowed it from a friend." Cziffra leaned against his desk, arms folded. "Anyway, it pokes a hole in your theory that he drove Lorca out of town in the Ansaldo."

Bora felt he should stand his ground this time. "That was never my theory, Herr Cziffra. After speaking to Walton, I postulate that someone in a position to alter the ledger rented the Ansaldo and drove it for a distance consistent with a round trip to the sierra. Also, that a car with three men in it – one of whom was possibly Lorca – was at the foot of the sierra on the night of the murder. I can say nothing more. And as for Cadena getting himself shot over a hundred miles away, I have no idea. May I be allowed to see Lorca's dossier now?"

"There's nothing in there you need to know for the time being." Cziffra walked around the desk to fish the garage ledger out of his desk and pass it to Bora. "You can take *this* back."

The Mudejar towers of Teruel took in the sun like the masts of a sinking ship, yet their intricate brickwork also made them resemble fantastic sleeves, as if the town was stretching brocade-covered arms to the sky. A fence of dark clouds, risen sometime during the day, set a boundary to the west.

The moment the sun dipped behind them, the red crowning the towers would vanish; the streets, already dressed in shadow, would settle in coolness. Occasional churchgoers, mostly women with rosaries twined around their wrists, met Bora along the way. Caps boldly askew, red tassels drooping, the last of the soldiers swarmed towards their barracks. They stiffly saluted the Legion's uniform and hurried on.

By a convoluted route that took him by the Renaissance arches of the aqueduct at the edge of town, Bora went to the public garage. No one, as far as he could tell, followed him there. A car with a high cab was parked in front of the building when he arrived. The garage itself was empty. The albino was mopping the floor, spreading an iridescent mixture of oil and suds. If he was tempted to ask Bora for the ledger, he didn't show it. His rosy face barely turned towards the German, and his posture, hunched over the mop, was reticent and defensive.

From the entrance Bora asked, "Is the proprietor back from his honeymoon?"

The mop made a circular motion, melting a violet swirl in the yellow, oily water. "He sent word that he's going to stay with his in-laws a while. Try his aunt next door."

The house door in question was ajar, but Bora still knocked before stepping inside. A pleasant old woman peered at him from the top of a steep flight of stairs. "*Qué quiere usted?*"

Bora explained the purpose of his visit..

"… The Ansaldo? Who rented it on the twelfth?" She repeated his words. "Come up."

Bora made up some spur-of-the-moment story about army bookkeeping. In the low-beamed kitchen, she scanned a calendar on the smudged wall over the stove.

"Ah, well, that was the Monday before the wedding. I let my nephew do the accounting, you know. I only give out the key or take it back as it's needed." She detached the calendar from its nail and brought it close to her eyes. "Two people came looking for the car that day, and we had to turn one down. That doesn't happen often. Anyhow, yes. My nephew always jots the name down on the calendar. The former mayor rented it, God have mercy on him."

"Cadena?"

"Yes." The old woman showed him the calendar. "He came first, and spoke for the car. Here's his name, here. Poor man. Had her filled up, paid beforehand ... Now God's taken him, and with a young family to look after!" In the dim kitchen, Cadena's name was a scribble on the page. Bora stared at the calendar without touching it.

"Did he return the car?"

"The car came back, didn't it? He borrowed it in the afternoon for an overnight trip. Alfambra, I think he said. We were expecting him to return it in the morning, but when I got up at four, the key was already in the basket. See, there's no army account to settle for the twelfth."

Bora reached for the calendar. "The month is nearly over, and tomorrow is Sunday. May I have the July page?"

"*Prefiero que no.*" The old woman hesitated. "Someone already stole our ledger. As it is, my nephew will be furious when he comes back. If I give you the page, we won't have any record at all of the July rentals."

Bora rummaged inside his canvas bag. "I need it." He took out a drawing pad and tore a strip of paper from it. "It's only a few names. I'll copy them out here for you with the dates."

Saturday 31 July, Teruel. 10 p.m.

I'm so close to finding out the truth, I can't stand it. By the time I finished today's errands (Alfambra, the seminary, the garage, a failed attempt against Herr C.'s advice to see Luisa

Cadena, securing an army guide to the place where Soler died) it was too dark to ride back to the sierra. Tomorrow at seven it's off to Castralvo with an army escort. Presently I'm writing in the Hotel Aragon on the *paseo*. Not a prime location, with the bus station to the right and a cinema in the back, but it befits this bizarre form of warfare to commute to town and meet with the enemy in a cemetery. There's no question that there will be an offensive of some kind soon enough, and then, *Gott sei Dank*, farewell to these strange comforts. High time, too.

So, Antonio Cadena did borrow the Ansaldo, but he never returned it. Where did he go? The round trip to Alfambra is 33 miles, while the odometer showed 43 miles. Besides, at the time the car was returned (before 4 a.m.) Cadena was about to run into a roadblock in Muel.

But why would Cadena say he would go to Alfambra and then go somewhere else? More importantly, how would he have ended up driving a different car and trying to evade armed soldiers? Most importantly of all, *who* drove the Ansaldo to the sierra and returned it to the garage?

Millares' name keeps cropping up. His vicious gossip in the *confitería* (I'd never have found Soler or thought about the seminary without those hints) betrays huge contempt for the likes of Soler ... and Lorca. It's no coincidence that Soler was eliminated right after we met. Given the political leeway Millares enjoys (and perhaps his work with Herr C.), he could have easily tampered with the ledger and secured a key to Soler's flat. Of course, the next question is why he would kill Lorca. Politics? Morality? A grim doubt crosses my mind that Herr C. may be playing cat and mouse with me and be somehow behind all this.

Having failed to meet Luisa Cadena, my best bet is to secure one more meeting with the American. Incidentally,

I must absolutely overcome the compulsion to confess to older men, as I did at San Martín. The only consolation is that Walton – whether to brag or because he felt he ought to share – spoke at length of his friendship with Lorca, and how both of them visited a rural place near the Canadian border called Eden. How fitting! He came close to pronouncing Remedios by name. I'll never do the same in front of him. The fact that she never mentioned Walton tells me that she doesn't care about him. It's important to me that she doesn't, although I'm not sure why.

EL PALO DE LA VIRGEN

Valentin's broken tooth showed in his smiling mouth, and he flipped back his wild hair with a satisfied, defiant toss of the head. "Who's laughing now?" He ran his eyes over the disbelieving faces of the men around the table. "Who's a fool now?"

Rafael had nothing to say. He furtively kissed the cross of his rosary and placed it around his neck. Chernik's attention was still on Walton, whose explanation everyone had just heard. In the middle of the table, Marypaz's red kerchief caught the last light of day coming from the door.

Brissot joined the group while Walton, rolling his sore neck at the head of the table, tried not to feel inexorably trapped.

"Goes to prove we can't even trust one another," Maetzu charged.

Walton felt the stab of the words, but still carried on massaging his neck. Maetzu had been agitated ever since hearing about a coming battle, and impossible to live with since the flag had been stolen. His going off to shoot the Fascist in Castellar had stemmed from that grim restlessness. Sucking his drawn cheeks in and accentuating his pointed, bristly chin, Maetzu spat on the floor. He glowered at Walton, which the American at first took for an accusation of complicity with Marypaz. But Maetzu cared little for material objects.

"Are you talking *to* me or *about* me?" Walton said. "I found the stuff and gave it back."

Maetzu, who'd been leaning against the wall at the foot of the stairs, left his post with a shove of the elbows. Still keeping his eyes on Walton, he slowly passed by the table where the rest of the men sat, and walked out. Chernik left after him, and one by one the others sought the open air too.

Munching on his unlit pipe, Brissot stayed behind. "I bet Maetzu found out you met the German," he commented.

Walton eased the sting of his swollen lid by closing his eyes. "What's that to him or any of you? I'm the head of this outfit. Until that changes, I deal with the enemy as I see proper, whenever it suits me."

"Does that mean you met more than once?"

"On Tuesday and Wednesday."

Brissot sat up. "What for? Don't you know how it makes you *look*?"

"I think he's actually going to find out who killed Lorca." Walton pushed himself back in the chair and rocked defiantly on its back legs. "He agreed to inform me of the results. We have a truce going between us."

"A truce with a Fascist. An *agreement* with a Fascist! The same man you were supposed to kill? This time it won't be just Maetzu, Felipe. If the rest find out about it, it's not going to sit well with any of them."

"As if I give a damn what *they* think." Walton kept his eyes closed. If he didn't look, the odours in the room – sweat, onions, sweet figs – were the sole obstacles to believing that he was elsewhere. Hell, elsewhere was always where he wanted to find himself, so he belonged nowhere. At about this time of year, he thought, the bogs near Eden Lake turned thick in the summer heat. Roots and wattles and buried rotting leaves drank up the water, until the swollen roots turned from spongy turf to felt.

Fancy thinking of that.

Many times he'd wondered what it was like to be one of the animals that stumbled in, or one of the leaves or pine cones that fell into the bogs from above. How you would sink, not fast but just as surely beyond salvation, all struggle made useless, bubbling under into the weave and fabric of organisms that do not breathe, turning from living matter into peat. Life turned into roots, stopped forever. *Philip Walton*, he thought, *you're sinking now. You've been sinking all along, and it's a matter of figuring out how deep you've gone. Up to your waist, maybe. Your feet are already part of the earth.*

Bora, stupid eager sonofabitch, had said at one point that sometimes the flesh-and-blood person gets in the way of the *real thing*, and that he, too, knew Lorca. By that time, the sun had turned the fog before them into a yellow wall of vapour.

It had been easy for Walton to counter the argument. "Well, you didn't. You read his works, period. He'd despise anyone of your political colour."

"Would he? You liked his poetry because you liked the man. I'm closer to Lorca than you are, because he carried the grief of Spain. I'm here because of the same grief. Having read his poetry, I can see Spain's grief clearly, and understand why our cause needs to succeed."

Now, with Brissot reeking of sweat and smoke two feet away, and hundreds of miles of Spain around him, Walton recognized that he was more than halfway down the bog, and there was no springing this trap. Having walked into it consciously, he had to acknowledge that the bog now held him captive. The younger animal – twitching with impatience, smelling of spring – sat by the bog watching him go down, doing nothing to harm or help.

Brissot said, "Maetzu is keeping an eye on you, Felipe. Next time you meet the German, he'll kill him."

Walton opened his eyes wide. Was it possible that the bog was treacherous enough to take the young animal, too?

TERUEL

It was the wind that woke Bora, even though he'd been tossing and turning with strange dreams and had just emerged from a disturbing one, whose details were dissolving in his mind like burning negatives.

Through the shutters a capricious westerly came, after buffeting the high riverbank of the Turia, along which the *paseo* ran. It was pitch-dark, so dark that even the spaces between the slats were not distinguishable. Bora sat up in bed, fully alert. The room stank of mice. A strange odour, one he knew only because he'd noticed it as a child in the sickrooms of a consumptive schoolmate, and someone had told him that tuberculosis had this smell.

In the privacy of his room, he could afford the luxury of sleeping naked, and the pleasant sensation of his waking body under the sheets put him in touch with his youth, his strength, his optimism. For a moment he appreciated himself without guilt, a young idealist embarked on a crusade, poised between intellect and physicality. A horseman, like the hard men in Lorca's poetry and the snub-nosed nameless Roman soldier.

He left the bed to open the shutters against the wind. He secured them to their external latches, looking out into the night. The elaborate stairway and the few buildings by the train station – no trains, no lights visible from here – were below. To the right, the small citadel of the Guardia Civil sat darker than night. Beyond were the river and the valley and the rim of mountains. It had clouded over, and you couldn't tell where horizon and sky met. The wind was scented, powerful. Bora leaned over the sill. Where in Germany would he be able to stand naked at the window?

"I want to know who killed Lorca as much as you do. That's the only reason I'm even talking to a Fascist," Walton had told him.

Bragging more than a little, he'd replied, "I will succeed in finding out, and share the information with you, only because you're wrong in thinking I don't care as much as you. I care more."

Now he was close. Now he was close, so close he could feel a small thrill. Although there was no stopping him now, he felt uneasy that he didn't know the specifics, and that something could still go wrong yet. Some vital piece of information on the periphery of his consciousness nagged at him and gave him nightmares. Walton had brought it up near the chapel of San Martín when their exchange had turned testy and complicit. But what was it? *In the morning I will present the evidence I have to Herr Cziffra, and demand that Millares be there to defend himself. A big piece is still missing, but circumstantial evidence ...* Walton had said something that fit, but whether out of forgetfulness or bias against the American, tonight Bora's conscious mind suppressed it.

A few drops of rain came with the wind. The storm was circling Teruel, slapping the bald hills to the east. It might reach as far as the sierra, ribboning the night, dissolving clay, washing the granite face of Mas del Aire.

Bora planned to climb up there as soon as his business in Teruel was done. Yet the last time at Remedios', after making love, he'd had the utter certainty that he would never see her again. It wasn't just her words, her whispered, ominous words. The premonition was so strong that all had gone cold around him, lonely, and she was like a small powerful flame in a frozen land. He'd said, "If I walked all day, Remedios, I would never reach the edge of your bed."

"Don't go away, then."

But the time for going away had come. He'd drawn a sketch of her face. "For me to keep you," he told her, and kissed the palms of her hands. In the end she too had said, "It's the last time, *Alemán*." And then he remembered that he had stood by the door sobbing, not because he was afraid of death but because he'd fallen in love and it hurt too much, and even now he couldn't think of it without feeling heartbroken. He had been in love with Remedios while he had thrown rocks at the fog, and as far back as the blows he'd landed on Walton, as far back as the moment he'd stuck a thorn in her door and heard the priest speak her name.

The damp westerly gusted, cool enough to raise goosebumps on his skin. Bora pulled back without closing the window. *I'll think of Remedios when I die.*

As he returned to the bed, the stale odour once again settled around him. Bora lay on his back, racking his brain to try and remember what Walton had said. He was at the edge of sleep again when swirls of recollection floated up at last, curling about like the oily pattern in the sudsy water at the garage.

"Major, did Lorca mention anything about those he was afraid of in Teruel?"

"About someone in particular, not just *all* Fascists?"

Bora recalled choosing to ignore the sarcasm. "Yes."

"He was scared of the Guardia Civil. Also the NKVD, they say, but I'd be surprised if the Stalinists had much influence in Teruel at this stage of the war. I'll have to think about this one."

"It's someone who can move around with impunity," Bora said. "A man of authority. Probably the same one who killed Soler, and Cadena comes into the equation somewhere, since he also disappeared. This Antonio Cadena, what kind of a man was he?"

"I only spoke to him by phone once, when Lorca and I met someplace. Cadena sounded like any other Spaniard. Scared shitless, if that makes a difference. That was the same day Lorca told me he'd been followed out of Teruel."

"By whom? Did he say?"

"Only that he wore a uniform. But you all wear uniforms: policemen, army and foreign legion," Walton sneered. "It could have been *you*, for all I know."

Bora sat up in bed with a start.

31 July, continued in Teruel. 11.45 p.m.

Nearly all I've come up with so far has been wrong. *Dead wrong.* Herr C. was correct about my wanting to fit the colours of the vase to a preconceived idea. Damn! Why didn't I think of it before? I've even had the ledger with me for several days!

Off to the garage first thing tomorrow, to collect the evidence that makes a fool out of me for my previous foolish assumptions (I might just as well admit Colonel Serrano is right about me too) and makes an unsuspecting sleuth out of Philip Walton.

Everything fits now, including the information I received today at the seminary and blissfully dismissed. I can't see the details clearly, but this is it. The crazy dream about the house in Trakehnen, with Lorca telling me I already knew the murderer's name ... all true!

Speaking of dreams, I half-remember the one that woke me up tonight: an army convoy in a place looking like Italy (it was too wet to be Spain). A treed canal or river to the right of the road. Opening a briefcase or other small luggage. An explosion. Windshield shattering, blood everywhere.

Nonsense. I'm confusing Cadena's fate with my concerns. Tomorrow is *the day*!

The morning was overcast, and the westerly still blustered through the higher districts of Teruel. Bora had been waiting by the garage close to fifteen minutes when the albino shuffled along, dressed in street clothes and munching on a piece of bread. Seeing the ledger in Bora's hand, the motion of his jaws halted long enough for him to resemble a colourless woodchuck caught feeding.

"When I first came to see you, there was a car without a windshield being repaired," Bora said without preamble.

Having swallowed the piece in his mouth, the albino pocketed the bread. "Yes. So?"

"Was it a Fiat 509?"

The stump waved in the folded, pinned coat sleeve. "That's what it was. *Teniente*, today's Sunday. I came to fetch something from the shop, but we're not open. If you've got business, either take it to the old woman, or else come back tomorrow."

It had totally escaped Bora's memory that it was Sunday, and that, barring this chance encounter, he might have waited here God knows how long for the garage to open.

"The ledger shows no entry for the Fiat 509 anywhere," Bora said. "I want to know who brought it in for repairs."

The albino fumbled with the bread in his pocket, an anxious irresolute gesture. "Look, I don't want any trouble.

The car came in, we found a windshield for it, we fixed it. That's all I know."

"Was there blood inside it?"

"*Bueno,* wouldn't you expect it to have some blood in it? The windshield got smashed somehow. There was none left by the time we got the car." The albino stepped forward, as if to ask for the ledger or grab it, but Bora slipped it into his canvas bag.

"To whom does the car belong, do you know?"

"No. An army private brought it."

Really. Bora kept the pressure on. "It surely doesn't belong to an army *private!* Who paid for the repairs?"

The albino glanced away uneasily. "I don't remember."

"Did the private pay for it?"

"Yes. No. We ... got an army voucher for it."

"And who signed *that?*"

"I don't know."

"Teruel's a small town, and you sure as hell know it, and you can take your choice and tell me now or I'll have you taken in and you can tell me then!"

"Well, what's any of this to me?" The albino walked around Bora to unlock the garage's folding door. "Ask for yourself, *teniente.* He's an army officer of the Comandancia Militar, Captain Mendez Roig."

Within minutes, Bora went from the garage to Cziffra's shopfront, finding it disappointingly locked. Wherever Cziffra lived his mysterious life, it was not there, because all the knocking in the world produced no response from within. Bora checked his watch, and saw it was nearly the hour appointed for him to meet the army escort to Castralvo.

He'd negotiated it the night before with a good-natured army lieutenant who had volunteered his services: "I was in that patrol. Funny, too, that we ended up going towards Castralvo at all, because originally we were scheduled to reconnoitre Villaspesa. Man, we went into the middle of nowhere. I'll take you there if you want to see where we found the poor fellow, colleague. What a mess he was! You've got to look hard for the spot now that the stench is gone. I'll meet you at seven on the viaduct."

No matter how urgently Bora needed to see Cziffra, he couldn't miss this opportunity. There was just enough time for him to retrieve Pardo from the Guardia Civil headquarters and ride up the Rambla de San Julián to the viaduct.

Like collapsing sand, a void gaped inside him when he reached the top of the street. Etched against the clouds of a sky that wanted to rain, Captain Mendez Roig stood on horseback in the middle of the spanning arch of cement and asphalt.

Pardo responded to the involuntary squeeze of Bora's knees by picking up speed and cantering towards the white army mount.

Bora was seldom lost for words, but this was one of those times. Roig's pockmarked, bloodless face had a Flemish quality of coolness and dispassionate judgement. Narrower than Cziffra's face, it was like a fox's or ferret's, intelligent and impenetrable at the same time. Cruelty sat no more on it than goodness, because either of them implied a moral compass.

He replied to Bora's salute with a faultless greeting. "My subordinate informed me of your request last night," he added. "I think I can be of service more than anyone else, since I was the one who led the patrol that day."

"*Le estoy á usted muy reconocido,*" Bora responded courteously, using the accepted formula of appreciation. The wind picking up under the viaduct sent moist buffets against the riders. No one, no one in Teruel or anywhere else in the world knew that he was going off alone with Roig on this first day of August 1937. He remembered Remedios' outstretched fingers, counting his lifespan. Seven. It had been much more than seven hours since then, and it wasn't even close to seven days. A faultless spirit inside him spurred him to go along.

SIERRA DE SAN MARTÍN

Walton knew the wispy clouds, like spittle across the sky. In Eden you could count the hours between those harmless shreds and the gathering of storm clouds. Twelve, fifteen hours at most, then rain would follow. It was already hazy near Teruel, perhaps raining. He left camp for Remedios' house out of habit, not because he needed her. Wanting and needing, he was finding out lately, were not the same thing at all.

Bora had asked for a third meeting. "I will have something to report, God willing," he'd said. The last part had been a strange expression for a soldier; Walton had found it humorous.

Going to Remedios now was part of reassuring himself, of re-staking his claim on her.

Walton was disposed to believe what Bora had said – that the Fascists had moved Lorca's body to Teruel – because it suited him and because his anger waned so easily, or kept turning into an unreasonable desire to laugh and strike out that ended in nothing. He was even inclined to believe, although not with admiration, that Bora had no other reason for seeking the murderer than his appreciation for Lorca's poetry.

Walton could climb this mountain with his eyes closed. Here dwarf plants and insects became scarce; just ahead, a flat rock resembled an old man's face. On the next toothed crag, the wind usually picked up. And Remedios' house, invisible until he hiked over the rim of Mas del Aire ... he'd seen a church like it in France during the war, run-down and with the cross askew on the roof.

Seven months in Spain. Ascending steadily, Walton couldn't strike a balance of the time he'd spent in Spain. He was becoming more and more convinced that no one can make a difference. His efforts and failures were like everyone else's, a hopeless mix, and there was no rhyme or reason why one side won and the other was defeated. Even politics, which had meant so much to him for so long, was turning out to be an empty bottle you put either goodwill or stupidity into. "For God and for Country" was just one label on the swill, but there were others no less dumb.

Having reached the crag where the wind picked up, Walton stopped to catch his breath. From the valley, not yet audible, infinitesimal against the wispy clouds, the airplane was approaching for its meaningless rounds, it, too, having become a part of the sierra. So small that an eagle could snatch it out of the sky.

When he reached Mas del Aire, the melancholy of his last meeting with Remedios returned, and Walton was tempted to turn back. Only the thought that Bora might be with her kept him rooted where he was, suddenly transfixed. New to him, this urge too lay at the filthy bottom, a part of his foul curiosity to seek the scent and sight of his rival. He approached furtively, stalking across the windblown upland towards the house.

High overhead, the small airplane went past, circling as though its only goal were to encompass as much sky as possible.

The door to Remedios' house was unlocked. Walton listened – no whispers, no sounds – before pushing it open. "Remedios?" What he would say to her, or she'd say to him, he didn't care. "Remedios?" He tiptoed inside, meeting a silence deeper than his own. There were no sheets on the bed. The bare mattress took up a huge empty space in its metal frame. The pillows were gone. Walton ran his hand along the rail at the foot of the bed, looking around. "Remedios, where are you?" A veil of dust covered the mattress, the floor and the few furnishings. It was like a house that had once been lived in, but years had gone by and now the objects within were skeletons of things, ghosts of things that were alive long ago. Walton felt around the room, groping like a blind man.

Often in Remedios' house he'd felt time stand still, that she was real only during the hours he spent here and would cease existing once he left. But she had been real enough to the German, too. Again he listened, tensely, for sounds in the small room upstairs, or in the chapel.

Come now. Remedios was simply in Castellar, or had gone to the sierra to gather plants. Somewhere real. Dust had blown in through the crack in the door, nothing more.

Why then did he feel the dismay of a broken spell chasing him out of her house? He fled, and superstitiously left the door open behind him.

Outside, the wind and sun belonged to the real world. Walton searched upstairs and in the chapel. Finally he started down the mountain, oblivious to the strained hum of the plane banking from the south. But from the change in pitch it was circling lazily, waiting to leave.

Or was it? There was no laziness to the sound.

Walton had just enough time to register the growl of a different, stronger engine before recognizing it. He turned around as the dive-bomber swooped down, screeching, first small and then huge and incredibly fast, cannons blazing from its crooked wings, landing gear extended like talons.

Under its deafening shadow, rocks and dirt burst in parallel trails of whipped explosions, strafing him.

"No!" Walton screamed the word, bolting with arms gathered to his head to protect it. He was in the open and there was no rock, no crevice, no shadow to beg for shelter. He ran and ran in wild zigzags while the bomber turned for a second pass, down the incline towards San Martín as if that would do him some good, fire and the unbearable din of death chasing him. Somewhere he fell or threw himself face down, hitting rock, dropping to a lower shelf where he scrambled at first, slipped and then lay still.

Holding fire, the bomber flew overhead churning the air, braiding a roar like a tail behind its blackness, ugly, ugly, raven-like, deathlike, seeking the sky over the valley. Like crossbones, white X marks showed on the wings when it nosed up to the left, and the square cockpit shone wickedly in the sun. Walton scrabbled for a piece of rock to hide under, dragging himself on his belly, on his elbows, face low to keep from seeing the plane. He could hear it bank tightly and turn south again. *Here it comes. Here it comes.* A sharp, straining curve. *Here it comes from behind.* Walton started digging. He clawed at the pitiless rock to find himself a hiding place, whimpering for a trench or foxhole in the dirt where none existed, and then bloody fear bid him run. *Here it comes!* Walton heard himself shouting death-denying words, not at all demented but conscious, because he was never as conscious as when he was mortally afraid, and everything made sense and had relative value compared to the only thing that counted: life, life saved, maintained, chosen above all else. He sprang to his feet and cried out wordless sounds – not death, not death, life! – as he ran, clear-headed, with a stark, terrific will.

What were they doing at the gun emplacement, why weren't they doing the only thing they were expected to do, firing at airplanes? In the dazzle of haste, Walton made out the outline of a larger rock and fled to it, shouting.

The plane soared, stalling like a black cross suspended, and then let go. As if a cord had been severed, it went into a nearly perpendicular dive, dropping, aiming for the gun emplacement at the edge of the mountain. Louder and louder it became, only at the last moment letting go of a single bomb.

Whether the anti-aircraft gun even tried to fire back was immaterial. The emplacement exploded under the direct hit. Ammunition burst sky-high, metal flew from the blast; blinding yellow and red blossoms shot open with the speed of projectiles; rocks sheared other rocks, pulverizing them. Swollen by debris, smoke rose and curled up in a stormy comma as the skinny black shape with upturned wingtips climbed with a squeal of its engine and left.

Walton lay stretched on his face, hugging pebbles to his chest. He'd torn his nails on the hard dirt. Jolts like electrical impulses running through a corpse shook his body, and he knew that uncontrollable trembling would follow. Tonight and the next night and the nights after he'd lie with his fists tight in a sweaty seizure-like rigidity. And though most of those who had known him at Soissons were dead, and his wounds justified his actions in Guadalajara, there was no hiding from Brissot this time.

Under the rain of splintered minutiae and ashen dust, his body felt withered, empty, all links between muscles and bones melted away, tendons like glue; his jaw hung slackly and he had to make an effort to close his mouth. He was overcome by a tremendous, back-breaking fatigue just getting to his knees; crawling was too much, so he simply cowered with his side against the rock, knees drawn up.

At camp, he'd say he'd fallen during the attack, fallen and got hurt. The small victory of managing to kneel and hold up his head filled him with a despairing sense of pride for not having lost his mind.

NEAR THE HUERTA ENEBRALES DE VARGAS, TOWARDS CASTRALVO

They'd come, barely speaking, to the place where the Rambla de Valdelobos, like all seasonal creeks, had dug a much wider bed than was necessary for most of the year.

The distance was now almost two miles south of Teruel, and there were no farms, no houses in sight. Bora remembered coming down this dirt road on a day so blighted by heat that blood had started pouring from his nose and he'd had nothing but his sleeve to stanch it. Today it was not nearly as warm, and yet he perspired heavily under the uniform. Roig, he noticed, tended to slow down his mount so that Bora would unwittingly find himself in the lead. Twice already he'd caught himself pulling away from Roig and made himself stop until the other man caught up.

"Did you know the victim?" Without waiting for Bora to reply, Roig voiced his own conclusion. "Obviously you did, or else why would you be interested in the grisly details?"

"I met him once."

"You met him *once*, and you're this curious?"

Bora faced a choice of answers, each one as good as the next, and gave none. He kept the reins gathered in his left fist and his right hand free. "I wasn't quite expecting to have the patrol leader as my guide, but I appreciate it. The man was shot once, was he?"

"Yes."

In the absence of landmarks, all looked flat and indistinguishable, a shadowless extension under the cloudy light. Bora recognized crossroads and turn-offs, however, and when they rode past the *huerta* of the Vargases, he felt a sting of remorse for having chased Soler from its safety. The walled space seemed easier to invade than the first time, even welcoming. The gate stood, still surmountable, as if to say *Stop here. Don't go, stop here. It's your last opportunity. Take it.*

Fingering the reins, Roig ignored the *huerta*, his eyes fixed on the road ahead.

Shortly the horses reached the dry ditch across the dirt road where Bora had held Soler at gunpoint and left him to return to Teruel. It was reasonable to assume that once alone, Soler would have wasted no time before crossing the road and trying to reach the *huerta*. The killer must have been too close for him even to have attempted it.

Bora spoke up. "How far from here is it?"

Roig contemplated him, as if he hadn't really been listening and needed to reconstruct the meaning of Bora's words. He indicated a blind curve ahead, where a rise of scruffy terrain flanked the road. "It's there, down a slope. We'll have to dismount to reach the site." Unexpectedly, he turned to Bora with a crisp smile. "We could smell rotten flesh from here. One of the men was taken sick. Why do you ask how far it is?"

"Because the ditch behind us is where I left him on the nineteenth."

Roig's smile remained fixed on his face. The blind curve seemed chiselled against the clouds, among sparse patches of hard-leafed scrub. Bora meticulously searched inside himself for a sense of fear, but all he found was an increased sense of vigilance which was wholly physical and not altogether unpleasant; the sense of an internal void, the feeling of sand falling through a timer, remained remarkably small given the circumstances. But all that could change in an instant. *Who says there aren't soldiers beyond the bend, or a sharpshooter stationed on one of the heights? All the evidence I've gathered is in my bag. My diary, the ledger, the anarchist flag. The sketch I made of Remedios. It'll be hard to explain to Nina how and why I came to this godforsaken place to get killed.*

Past the curve, the left shoulder of the slope narrowed to an eroded edge, to which Roig pointed. "Tell me, why all this interest in Soler?"

Having reached the edge, Bora dismounted to look down into the hollow. His heartbeat had increased to a steady dull race filling his chest, not irregular, just fast and getting faster. He removed his riding gloves and slipped them into his belt. "It isn't Soler that interests me."

Still saddled, Roig shifted his attention above and behind Bora, to the dry higher land. "*Y qué le interesa à usted, realmente?*"

Bora was tempted to look at him over his shoulder but didn't. "*Cosas.*"

"Things? What things?"

A cicada suddenly chirring on a dry stalk somewhere down the slope provided an opportune distraction. Bora envisioned the two or three seconds it would take his hand to reach and unlatch the holster on his left side. Pensively he stared at the scarified drop of land, sinking some twenty feet below into a trough-like depression. The stench of death was long gone. Still he couldn't help wondering whether these rocks, these thirsty shrubs were intended from the beginning of time to become his place of death. Like Jover, he knew now – Remedios had said so – that there was an as yet unrevealed place where his life would be taken. Sooner, maybe, than even Remedios had said.

Aware that Roig expected an answer, Bora made him wait. Then he said, "Horsemen interest me. Miraculous and otherwise."

Roig vaulted off the saddle. He, too, removed his gloves, but secured them to the space between the saddle and stirrup leather. "Why should you? What do you have in common with them?"

Motionless at the edge of the slope, Bora stood a few feet away and slightly ahead of Roig, but at such an angle as to keep him in his field of vision. "Other than that I'm a horseman myself? Not much." The crumbling rim under his feet had the colour of skinned flesh. His weeks on the sierra's heights rendered the short escarpment laughable; Bora could easily reach the bottom in a few bounds, but would not do so before or without Roig. Was this the place? *It'd be easy to kill someone here, push, and let the weight of death drag and roll the body down the slope. Easy, easy.* "For one thing," he added, "I'm armed." (*Remedios said seven.*) "I know where I am, and in whose company." (*Could she have been wrong?*) "Also, I left word of my destination." (*She could have been wrong.*)

Roig – Bora couldn't be sure that it wasn't just a misjudgement – had grown haggard under the shade of his visor cap, the shift in colour on his drawn face tantamount to a change in expression. His mouth, thin-lipped, monkish, became set and hard. Unquivering, drawn so it erased itself into a line, his mouth placed a seal of malice across that pockmarked pallor.

The cicada stopped chirring. An astonished silence followed, and then distant thunder, a sound like hoofs pounding dirt far away. Rain would come soon. Time was dangerous, like a short blade. Roig's voice came with dispassionate, surgical politeness. "I don't believe you told anyone about your errand. In any case, having come thus far, you should take a closer look at what you came to see."

Bora turned his face, then his whole body towards Roig. Unexpectedly, he felt as sure of his destiny as on the day he had looked down from Mas del Aire and sought the greatness and vanity of the world, the finite arrogance of it. The trap gaped ahead of him. Why was knowing that he would be shot the moment he started down the slope more important than the fear of it, more important than avoiding it?

There's a sharpshooter waiting for his signal across the slope, Bora thought. *He sees us and waits, finger on the small hook of the trigger.*

The thought exhilarated him, because he'd striven for lack of fear but now he was amazed that he'd even contemplated the possibility of fear. There was none. Pleasure and self-assurance in the risk he was taking with his soldering, yes. Trusting in risk at the potential cost of his life, absolutely. Fear, no. Holding Roig's stare, he wondered if this was what Niceto called *duende*, man's perfection in the face of and because of death. *No other perfection is possible.* The matter of his own end was surprisingly irrelevant, and Bora knew his face said as much to Mendez Roig.

For the longest deadly moment Roig's malicious mouth twisted in contempt, or bitter disappointment. His coolness discomposed, he turned away from the slope. With the motion, his shoulders lowered tiredly, as if a small piece had been taken from his haughty wholeness and the process were enough to affect him. Thunder edged the sky to the south.

Roig reached for the saddle and mounted his horse. "Let's go," he said, and waited for Bora to do the same.

On the way back they said nothing at all.

A small patrol of road police – the Guardia Civil Caminera – eventually fell in with them at the Villaspesa crossroads. Their bays rounded the curve at a trot, making the sound of bones knocking on the rock-strewn path, and would have ridden past if cries of "*Cho!*" hadn't curbed them in a pale commotion of dust.

"*Señor capitán, señor teniente.*" The corporal leading them brought his hand to his boiled-leather headgear, part helmet, part peasant hat. "With permission, you shouldn't travel without an escort. We've had reports of stray groups of marauders and Reds in the past weeks, and one never knows what may happen in the open country. Only a few days ago a civilian was killed up the road you come from."

Roig said nothing, disdainfully checking his mount.

"We thank you for the information," Bora said.

EL PALO DE LA VIRGEN

Nothing was left of the gun emplacement. Gouged out of the sierra wall, the site had lost all resemblance to the nest of stone where the two men had smoked and slept and heaped refuse for the past eight weeks. Of them, there was no trace. Flies would eventually find tatters of flesh and bloody cloth, but right now it seemed like an empty gum socket after a molar has been pulled.

Walton turned away from the wrecked mountain face, feeling physically ill. It was the second time he had tried to urinate, with no success, and his distended bladder was starting to hurt. Even taking a deep breath was difficult. Brissot wouldn't need to notice the tremor; he'd know as soon as he saw him. He'd be lucky if he succeeded in avoiding Chernik, who'd been a reporter long enough to have seen his share of frightened faces.

The rest of the men were unhurt. The horses and ammunition stored behind the house were safe. The worst damage to the camp was a boulder that had been dislodged by the explosion and fallen onto the roof. The sheet iron had caved in. Chernik pointed at it as Walton arrived. "Fell smack into the stairwell, Felipe. It's a miracle no one was inside. Holy shit, you should have seen it dive! It was a German machine, all right. I wish I'd had my camera when it hit."

Walton could see from the doorstep that the interior had been demolished. He kept his hands in his pockets, elbows close to his sides. "The other plane was a pathfinder. This one knew exactly where to strike."

Chernik went inside, rummaged and came back with a rickety chair. "It's like when the twister hit our hometown in '21," he said. "All we salvaged was a sofa, and my mother did the same thing I'm doing now: sat down. 'Might as well be comfortable in the face of disaster,' that's the way she put it. Were you at Remedios' when it happened?"

Walton wasn't listening. Hiding his agitation was difficult, and Chernik was already becoming inquisitive. Stepping away, he said, "The place is done for. Day after tomorrow, we move to the inner sierra."

"OK. But why not tomorrow?" Chernik called after him.

"Because I said so." Stepping away would take less effort than keeping Brissot from noticing the state he was in. *I won't fool him, so why try? I'll admit to some fear if it comes to it, and let the devil take what's left.*

He hadn't got five steps away from Chernik when he crossed paths with Valentin. Seeing him grin made his defences rise again. "What's so funny?"

The broken tooth showed like a fang in the gypsy's laughing mouth. "Mosko's glasses got broken during the attack – he can't see shit without them. He took me for Iñaki until Iñaki told him to go to hell from behind!"

Brissot can't see me. Walton's need to vent his amusement was obscene under the circumstances, but more than he could resist. *Hot damn.* He burst out laughing. *Scrape it all you want, there's still enough dirt left in the world for secrets to be hidden away.*

Herr Cziffra was having a cup of hot chocolate, the first visible sustenance Bora had seen him take. Lips on the cup's rim, he listened to the report of Bora's morning ride as if the heat of the drink were foremost in his mind.

It was raining outside, a tentative rain that would have to try harder to be convincing.

From behind his desk Cziffra said, by way of commentary, "Were you struck on the way to Damascus? Yesterday you were all blunders, and today, paradoxically, you see clearly through the biblical dark glass! Hot chocolate?"

"No, thank you."

"Everybody has hot chocolate late on Sunday mornings. Fried pastry? No? Oh, very well." Careful not to fog his glasses, Cziffra took a quick sip. "Let's hear these hypotheses of yours."

Bora amused him by asking for a blank sheet of paper and a pencil. "You found my misgivings about Don Millares naive, sir, but admittedly he had plenty of freedom to act, and he was deeply hostile towards Lorca and Soler. How was I to know when I saw him on Calle Nueva that the threat I perceived from him was not aimed at me, but at Captain Mendez Roig?"

"Indeed." Cziffra gleefully stirred his chocolate. "But you chose Roig over Millares, because he wears a uniform. What else?"

"Well, Roig rode to the sierra as far back as the fifteenth, officially on duty, most likely to check on Lorca's body. He found the body gone and Lorca's poems in my room, and may have sensed a connection between the two when I reacted to his presence. Millares can tell you better than I whether he was spying on me whenever I was in Teruel. What alarmed Roig was my plan to see the place where Soler had died, so he made sure he was the one who took me there."

Cziffra took a dainty bite out of a chocolate-dipped churro. "And you went, despite knowing that he was the murderer?"

"What choice did I have? It would have been dishonourable to pull back. I *had* to go." On the sheet of paper, Bora had drawn coin-sized circles connected to a larger one, in which he had written the name "Lorca". One of the smaller rounds read "Cadena". Pointing with the pencil to the latter, he said, "On the day I found Lorca's body, Colonel Serrano observed something to the effect that 'doubts and solutions begin at home.' That's certainly the case here. Walton mentioned that Cadena was afraid: sheltering a relative who was officially dead but still had powerful enemies put him and his family at risk. When I held Soler at gunpoint he admitted there were often arguments in the house, until Cadena and Lorca agreed it was better to part company. At this point, whether or not he knew of Lorca's connections on the sierra, somehow Cadena fell in with Captain Roig of SIFNE, who was all too familiar with Cadena's political past. I believe Roig terrified Cadena into action, making him believe that if he helped to secure Lorca's internment somewhere, any political risk to his family would vanish. Walton had no details, but I suspect it was Roig who tailed Lorca when they met in Valdecebro."

Seemingly having lost interest in his breakfast, Cziffra set the cup aside and looked at the third circle, which bore Mendez Roig's name. "We know what 'internment' means these days. What else?"

"As far as I can reconstruct, on the evening of the twelfth, Lorca leaves home. He says nothing to Luisa. To Soler, he says he plans to visit the sierra, although there might be an understanding between them that he'll try to escape Teruel. After all, you offered to have him escorted away from town."

"Not on that night. You were obsessed with the Ansaldo for a time: where does that come in?"

Bora drew two rectangles at the top of the sheet, writing "A" in one, and "F" in the other.

"The Ansaldo: Cadena hires it because he's agreed with Roig that he'll ride with him and Lorca to a place of confinement; he tells his family and the garage that he's going to Alfambra overnight, a routine trip for him, apparently."

Bora pointed to the other square. "The Fiat: I first thought the page stripped from the ledger recorded the Ansaldo's entry. Now I know the repairs to Roig's Fiat 509 were registered on it. On the fateful night, having induced Lorca to travel with him out of town, Cadena anticipates that after a moment of anguish his cousin will not oppose Roig's presence. Along the way, he plans to convince his cousin that internment is the best choice, and Roig tells him he will reassure Lorca. So Cadena remains in Teruel until evening, waiting for Lorca in an appointed place." Bora looked up from the sheet of paper, meeting Cziffra's bespectacled eyes. "What's important is to keep Lorca from travelling under your escort. Heartened by his cousin's presence, he might at first agree to be spirited away."

Cziffra leaned with his elbows on the desk to see what else Bora was sketching. "So far so good. What then?"

"Well, Roig has a more permanent solution in mind for Lorca. Cadena is a witness and has to be brought along. Roig comes to the appointment in his Fiat, probably driven by an orderly who knows to keep his mouth shut. That's the small question mark in the circle here. And it's into the Fiat that they suddenly push Lorca. Roig forces Cadena to drive. There must have been an interesting conversation going on, reassuring in some ways and dreadfully threatening in others. Cadena now fears for his own life as much as for Lorca's, but there's nothing he can do. The Fiat takes off with him at the wheel, Lorca seated in front alongside him, and Roig, possibly but not necessarily displaying a weapon, in the back seat. The other driver follows in the Ansaldo."

"What does *not* follow is why they'd drive to the sierra, of all places."

Bora rested his pencil on the zigzag line marked "Sierra" at the lower edge of the paper.

"Faced with internment or worse, Lorca may have pleaded for the alternative of being allowed to disappear on his own and suggested the destination he meant to reach all along. Did Roig deceptively agree, seeing it as the perfect spot to dispose of two corpses? We can only imagine what was going through Antonio's terrified mind at this point. The two cars reach the lonely bend at the foot of the sierra, where they stop. What happens next is conjecture like the rest, but probable. Roig forsakes all pretence and puts a gun to the back of Lorca's head. Cadena ... well, either he tries to intervene and there's a scuffle, or he tries to save himself."

Cziffra stared at the ceiling. "There's a difference. Which reaction do you subscribe to?"

"I'd like to think he tries to help."

"Go on."

"Be that as it may, a shot is fired inside the Fiat and kills Lorca where he is, seated in the front seat. Walton's informant spoke of a 'muffled shot'. Blood flows straight down Lorca's back. Next, Roig orders Cadena to remove the body with the help of his driver. They drag Lorca to the verge of the road, and some confusion ensues." Bora drew a short arrow from Cadena's circle. "*I* think Cadena tries to escape. A second shot is fired at him – the shot in the open air, whose shell I found – but it misses its mark. Cadena scrambles back to the Fiat and takes off. He doesn't stop until he reaches Muel, over a hundred and twenty miles away, when he unwisely tries to run through a roadblock."

"I'm surprised he got that far."

"Well, he did. The soldiers manning the checkpoint fire against the car, shattering the windshield and wounding Cadena. It must have taken some doing, but as a member of SIFNE Roig manages to retrieve his car, no questions asked. I saw the Fiat being repaired in the public garage in Teruel. Had I known the role it played in all this, I'd have searched it for the bloodstains I didn't find in the Ansaldo."

"Roig and his driver were lucky they brought the Ansaldo along, or else they'd have been stuck in the middle of nowhere." Cziffra fastidiously checked his immaculate clothes for chocolate stains. "I know the rest. They toss Lorca's belongings in the bushes to stage a robbery. But why undo Lorca's clothing?"

Bora looked away. "The lieutenant who discovered Soler's body shared a detail Roig and Serrano left out. Namely that after shooting him in the head, they undid his trousers and fired a bullet into his genitals. A signature, perhaps, or a form of contempt."

Cziffra pulled the spoon out of his cup and rested it on the saucer, concave side down. "You're fortunate that Roig didn't kill you."

Bora doodled around the central circle. "Something, perhaps overhearing the *mulero* Walton spoke of, keeps Roig from inflicting the same on Lorca's body. He leaves in the Ansaldo with his man, and in fact the reading on the odometer is consistent with a round trip to the sierra. Then he has to wait until news comes of Cadena running into one checkpoint or another, so sure that will happen that he doesn't bother to pursue him. Once he recovers his Fiat, Roig disposes of the ledger page detailing its repairs and the rental of the Ansaldo."

"Ah, but there's a fly in the ointment. The *mulero* mentioned only one car!"

"There's room off the bend to park a car, even a good-sized Ansaldo; the cane grove screens it from view. At night and with its lights off it'd be invisible to a distant observer. And on the subject of cars, may I know who was supposed to provide the escort for Lorca, and by what means?"

"No."

"Was it Millares?"

"You should know better than to ask me the same question twice." Having taken the pencil from Bora's hand, Cziffra tapped it on the circle bearing Soler's name. "What else about him?"

"Poor Soler. He was probably shadowed from the day of Lorca's death. They searched his flat for letters or evidence of his relationship to Lorca. When we met near the *huerta*, Roig was close enough to see us. The meeting convinced him of two things: that Soler had to die, in case he said anything about Lorca's (or Cadena's) fears, and that I was involved in the investigation somehow."

"Why wouldn't he have killed both of you there and then?"

"I could say I'm not as easy to kill, Herr Cziffra, but I actually believe Roig feels no innate antipathy towards me."

"Nor have you directly accused him yet." Cziffra took a long sip of hot chocolate that steamed up his glasses. "Still, you haven't answered this: why would Roig kill Lorca and Soler?"

Bora did not answer at once. He folded the sheet of paper, studiously pressing down the crease with his fingernail. "That is something I had to reconstruct piecemeal. Before meeting you yesterday, I returned to the seminary, where I first heard about Soler's misbehaviour and expulsion. Father Iginio wouldn't give me the time of day, so I had to go to confession in order to approach someone else there. As luck had it, I found a former Tercio chaplain on the other side of the

384

grid. He was receptive to the extent that he absolved me from sins I'd doubted would be remitted, and saw nothing wrong in telling me that the other boy expelled from the seminary with Soler was called Mendez Roig. According to the chaplain, a teacher at the time, Roig was not charged with any misconduct, only implicated because of his friendship with Soler. Both were sent packing, however." From the middle point of the crease, Bora again folded the paper, one side at a time, into equal triangles.

Cziffra watched his motions. "Really?"

"Really. Interesting, but of no great use to me until, in the middle of the night, I recalled Walton saying that Lorca had been followed by someone in a uniform. Why couldn't it have been Roig? And then there was the Fiat 509 without its windshield in the garage. You heard by phone that Cadena was shot in a Fiat 509. That it belonged to Roig only made my conclusions inescapable."

"That's circumstantial evidence, not a motive. Unless you infer that Roig had a passionate hatred of Soler and homosexuals in general for causing his dismissal."

Starting at the centre of the crease, Bora folded the paper down the middle, backward this time, forming two trapezoids which he bent into sharp wing-like shapes.

"*The Miraculous Horseman*, Soler told me, was in the same vein as other recent plays by Lorca, provocative enough to include same-sex flirtation. Some of the costumes Soler was designing included 'girlish seminarians' and '*mariquitas* in uniform'. It may have had nothing to do with Roig, but Roig – who, as other Nationalists in town knew, was aware of and tolerated Lorca's presence – must have scented the subject of the play and felt personally outraged."

"There might have been more between the two seminarians than even your priests suspected."

"You may wish to ask Don Millares about that. He seems much more interested in the subject than I."

Cziffra reached for the paper plane in Bora's hand and sent it flying nose-down across the room. "It all goes to prove that even in the Abwehr we may strain at gnats and swallow camels." Out of his desk he pulled a manila folder marked MENDEZ ROIG, FIRMÍN, which he handed to Bora. "Born in Alcañiz in 1903," he quoted from memory. "Graduated from the General Military Academy in Toledo in 1925, commissioned as second lieutenant at twenty-two, just in time to join the fight in Morocco against the Riffs. Not a bloody word about his younger days."

Bora read from the folder. "It does say here that he displays 'staunch opposition to all forms of left-wing activism and fanatical contempt for sexual deviance'."

"Don't you?"

"Not if it means 'summary execution of prisoners suspected of inversion, as evidenced by incidents in Tétouan and Badajoz'. Lorca's entire life was an outrage for Roig. Add to it his involvement in left-wing propaganda ... The only detail he ignored is that Lorca was working for you. But I'm sure he removed from the body those papers about the defences around Teruel – the ones you concocted to deceive Walton."

Cziffra simpered. He reached into the same drawer and pulled out a manila folder marked JÍNETE. "Here, I know you've been itching to take a look."

Eagerly Bora opened the file. "Where is the rest of it?"

"The rest of it?"

"There are only two pages in here."

"That's all there is." Dunking the tail end of his churro in his cup, Cziffra took a bite before speaking. "Lorca never worked for me. He probably never would have done, and I certainly would never trust someone like him."

"But you led me to believe —"

"Nothing. You chose to believe what fit your mindset or served you best. As for saving his life in Granada, well, we have our weaknesses. Murdered poets make for bad public relations." Cziffra chewed the fried cake, swallowing politely. "Put all you reported in writing and it will join the two pages in the JÍNETE file."

Bora returned the folders to Cziffra's desk. "Do I have your support in filing official charges against Captain Mendez Roig?"

"Absolutely not."

"Am I to seek Colonel Serrano's, then?"

"Out of the question."

"*Someone* must confront Roig with the evidence!"

Cziffra stood behind his desk. A look of annoyance had come upon him, reproachful more than dismissive. "And do what? Prosecute him for killing Federico García Lorca?"

"I don't see why not. There's still rule of law among us."

"Consider this: you'll move on to your next military duty, allowing *him* to assume that you informed Luisa Cadena, so he can vent his anger against her and her children. How irresponsible can you get?" Cziffra seemed suddenly disinclined to give more time to this encounter. "Truly, Lieutenant, you have lost your sense of proportion. You may admire Lorca's poetry and regret that he came to such a sad end, but don't forget he was just a queer."

Bora knew he was raising his voice, and his effort to control it only half-succeeded. "If redress is out of the question, I consider myself at liberty to walk out of here and kill Roig myself."

Cziffra's face underwent as much of a transformation as Bora was ever to see in him. Red blotches formed on his cheeks, bright like bruises. "Serrano is right; it's not just brainless insubordination you're guilty of. Except that I'm no Spaniard. I don't take any lip from subordinates, and don't give a damn about your baronial stock either. Take off your pistol belt and leave it here when you go. If you're to be this much of a problem, you can forget about working in Intelligence in the future and about glowing performance reports, I assure you. The gun, Bora."

"Herr Cziffra, I don't —"

"It is *Colonel* Cziffra to you, and there's nothing more to discuss. Your gun. The clip, too."

Bora went only as far as unlatching his holster. He was sure he looked as mortified as he felt. "I'd rather not turn in my weapon, Colonel."

Cziffra let him agonize for the better part of a minute, clearly enjoying whatever satisfaction there was to have. He remained deaf to Bora's pleas, ostentatiously locking away the files. "I don't need your grovelling apologies, either."

"Will you then at least bear in mind that Roig knows I'm on to him, and may try to act upon it?"

"Well? To quote your own words, if you get killed, you get killed."

Bora tried not to lose hope. "I cannot go back to my post unarmed!"

The mention of the post seemed to distract Cziffra from his displeasure. "You're not going back to the sierra."

Bora felt his stomach tighten as if to ward off a physical blow. He understood well there was no negotiation here either. He watched Cziffra take out of his desk a typed sheet of paper. "It's the copy of a reassignment order from Colonel Jacinto Costa y Serrano."

Wretchedly Bora handed over his pistol belt. "Where am I being sent?"

"North of here. Belchite."

"Oh, for the love of God. What am I going to do *there*? It's more dead than the sierra!"

Cziffra looked as though he found some humour in the matter, because he made an indulgent gesture indicating to Bora that he could keep the Browning. "You should have turned the other cheek to Serrano. At all events, the assignment at Belchite might be livelier than you think, sooner than you think. That's where the Reds are due to strike next."

CAÑADA DE LOS ZAGALES

The sky was as pale as dust. Haze made it look like a canvas tent stretched above. Along the mule track, the canes rustled like crumpled paper. The water in the brook was low and made no noise at all.

Walton came early to the meeting place to scope it beforehand; the German, however, was now running late. Ten minutes by his watch, enough to irritate him. Slipping on the gravel bed, he walked to a spot where he could squat and wash his face. The swelling in his eye had subsided; still, he wiped it gently. When he held it out, his hand trembled a little; he concentrated, and controlled the tremor by stiffening the arm. At last he'd been able to void his bladder, and had even managed to sleep for an hour or two on the mattress salvaged from the ruins. Brissot, who stored his political propaganda upstairs, was too busy digging through the rubble to pay attention to Walton's or anyone else's state of mind.

A swishing sound in the cane grove caused Walton to rise quickly and turn, gun in hand, expecting Bora to appear. But across the mule track, the feathery heads of the canes barely nodded in the breeze. Walton put away his gun. The next thought in his mind was that Maetzu was crouching by the bank, waiting for the German to show up.

"Iñaki?" he called under his breath, and the lack of an answer didn't mean that Maetzu wasn't there, ready for the ambush. After Brissot had warned him about it, for a moment Walton had considered sending word to Bora to cancel the meeting. His own laziness had stopped him taking action on Brissot's warning, and if Bora chose to come, it was at his own risk. Death was in this place: Lorca's, the *mulero*'s. It might be the German's turn, and there was no stopping it.

As for himself, death was somewhere too, but he had put aside any fear of it for the time being. He was as incapable of predicting when that fear would be needed as he was of controlling it once it took hold. Bora had said, "I envy you"! Standing on the mule track, Walton kicked pebbles around. The younger man's incomprehensible admission flattered him, although what there was to envy, he didn't know. *Age? Can you be so dumb as to envy age?* Experience? He'd had a bellyful of that, and there was nothing to pine for in that department either. *What can you say about a man who couldn't make it in Eden, and couldn't make it out of Eden either?*

Walton paced slowly. He was closing the chink in this door too, not out of indifference, but out of awareness that giving the key to Bora had been his contribution to solving Lorca's murder. *It's just as well.*

When they had parted ways at San Martín, Bora had come up with an unexpected request. "If your men should kill me, would you afford me the courtesy of a decent burial?" Because Walton had answered neither yes nor no, he'd indirectly, politely pressed the matter. "Would you like me to promise the same for you?"

To this, Walton recalled grinning in contempt. He had said, "Sure," knowing that promises are as good as scribbles on a cold windowpane. *No, worse than that. Boys are liberal with promises, love, curiosity; they swear and poke into doors, fuck, go on to the next thing. Whether they're from Eden or any other place on earth that isn't Eden – like Germany – they think themselves smart and hard-assed and immortal enough to mention death seriously, but only in passing.*

Speaking of promises, Bora was not about to come, the sonofabitch. Walton kicked the gravel. Waiting, clenching his trembling hands into fists, he only wished the German would show up so that he could say that he wasn't disappointed, that the fact Bora hadn't kept his promise meant nothing to him, that nothing really meant anything to him any more.

There. *And you'd do well to envy me, boy, because I took idealism and optimism and whatever other phoney piece of lead tying me down and tossed them away. As for dying, I died a thousand times, and there was no one to bury me. You, you are weighed down more than you know; it'll take you years to dig the lead out of your soul if you live that long.*

"You like Lorca?" he'd said to Bora. "Go back and read Lorca where he writes that 'a door is not a door until a dead man is carried out of it.' The sum of what you envy is all there: age, experience, life. All of it. The rest is commentary."

Rain was starting to fall out of the pale sky. Walton waited ten minutes more, letting water come down on him like a sad blessing, and then climbed back to camp.

POSTSCRIPT

SKAŁA, NORTH OF CRACOW, SOUTH-WEST POLAND

Thursday, 7 September 1939.

This is the first chance I've had to sit down to write since we crossed the Polish border on the 1st. Plenty has gone unrecorded in the past several months, so some catching up follows.

16 August 1939.

Drove to Halle, where Dikta was staying with friends. Decided to marry on the spur of the moment. Father displeased at my "marrying without thinking", as he puts it. Nina disappointed at not being able to organize a big wedding. Brother ecstatic at the thought that I got away with it and am now a married man. Spent two nights with Dikta before boarding the train to join my company (promoted to captain 12 August). Unfortunately a hotel, little privacy, still ... I'm head over heels. Bless Remedios tenfold for teaching a silly *Alemán* what it is to love a woman.

1–5 September 1939.

With my 1st Cavalry Brigade, 3rd Army (under General Feldt). Mounted reconnaissance duties, well in advance of the troops. My spoken and written Russian is coming along, and will come in useful soon. Life is starting to look like the dream two years ago, on 20 July: after we cut the Polish Lancers to pieces at Frankowo and Krasnobród, I saw many a fallen enemy alongside his dead mount. What senseless resistance they put up against our tanks! I remembered Lorca's words about the black horse carrying its dead horseman, and thought that the horseman's song ends here, come what will.

Later in the month.

Awful reports about our treatment of Polish Jews. I'd be disinclined to believe them if I didn't know better. On my own authority, I contacted the Army War Crimes Bureau, since the *tu quoque* rule of reprisals hardly applies here. We'll see what good comes of it.

And since I haven't written about the matter before, I might as well record how things went in Spain after I left the sierra for Belchite on 3 August 1937.

Herr – or rather *Colonel* Cziffra – was right about my assignment. The Red siege of Belchite was a nightmare that lasted until 6 September: no water, no food, a desperate situation. I made it out of there by the skin of my teeth before surrender, and rejoined the forces in Teruel. There I just traded one siege situation for another, and God keep me from having to go through the likes of it again. We lasted in -30 weather until 8 February 1938 (the last of us holed up among the dead and dying in the seminary, the one that had looked like a fortress to me back in July). In the fierce fighting for Concud, so many died that the piled corpses were doused with fuel in an unsuccessful attempt to dispose of them. We heard that half-starved dogs came in packs to feed on human flesh.

In Teruel death stared us in the face. The buildings around us were pulverized; we melted snow to drink and chewed on frozen stalks from the flower beds to keep our hunger at bay. It might have been *duende* that got me out of the trap. Under continuous fire, a few of us slipped out of the city before the Reds overran it at around 14.00 hours on the 8th.

By then, Nationalist battalions around Teruel, which needed twenty or so officers, were down to four or five, so I was granted more responsibility than I ever had dreamed of. We kept our spirits up and went at it like furies between the 18th and the 19th, when we retook Santa Barbara Hill and the cemetery. On the 22nd Teruel was ours again, and for good!

While the "Te Deum" was sung in the cathedral, I went looking for the unrecovered bodies of my men, many of whom had fallen taking the square. During the siege (this, to quote Colonel Serrano, is how incestuous civil wars are) I'd heard that we'd been facing Red units previously deployed on the Sierra de San Martín, and that Major Walton – under his battle name Felipe – was among them. Preliminary interrogations of prisoners revealed that he was missing in action, presumed dead. So, faithful to our mutual promise of a decent burial (even though later on he must have believed I had chosen to keep the result of the investigation from him), I secured the assistance of his second in command, a French physician by the name of Brissot.

At first Dr Brissot refused to accompany me, although I suspect he knew I'd met Walton on the sierra. He looked miserable and exhausted, and I no better, because in Teruel we all got lice and canker sores and so much else they glossed over in army school. Only after I repeatedly expressed in French my sympathy about Walton's death did he agree to my request.

In the rubble of Teruel, Walton's body lay in the Calle de Villanueva, behind a ruined yellow wall. A bullet had gone clear through his neck. Killed him instantly, I think. Recalling the impression I'd had of him as a man steeled to danger, I was glad in a way that he had been aware of his approaching death. Brissot said Walton had fought alone behind that yellow wall, having been cut off from the rest. He held the street single-handed for the best part of a day, against all hope. An impressive show of manliness, deserving of something better than death!

I wonder what Walton's thoughts were as he crouched by a wall the colour of fear, knowing that he'd die soon. I wonder if he thought of Remedios when the bullet struck. In any case, I'm sure he was unafraid to the end. That men, enemies included, should display such courage, is an example I have carried ever since Spain.

On that day, I told Brissot that I couldn't promise a decent military burial for all his men (not even for mine), but would secure it for Walton. He saw I was moved, and I think had less respect for me because of it. This chapter of my life began and ended with burying a man, I realize now, one of the rituals that set us apart from animals. Poor Walton. Poor Lorca, poor Jover. How final are your deaths.

Often I think of what Remedios predicted, and how Walton died seven months after she spoke to me. She was right; I counted the days: first the seven days that followed her words, then the seven months that led to February, when I came very close to fulfilling the prophecy. But here we are in 1939, and the next possible deadline (seven years) is 1944. The war will be over long before then, so perhaps Remedios was mistaken after all.

There are times when I wonder what Mendez Roig is doing. How, since he was never punished and must have gone on to better things, he can live with himself. I wonder what happened to Fuentes and the other men, whether Colonel Serrano will ever tell anyone where García Lorca is buried.

I have seen the grave in my dreams, suspended between

the sierra and the sky, remote, and I feel the grief you can only feel for someone whose death you mourn not having known him, more intimate because it is not altered by the reality of a friendship. All is possible in this sympathy; no misspoken word gets in its way, no falling out, no disappointment. Sometimes I think we can only love, only hate, only mourn this way. Love, hate and grief are fragile and have a way of not standing up to reality.

10 October.

Tomorrow I am to be detached in Cracow, *uralte deutsche Stadt*, as we like to think.

Billeted overnight at a farmhouse near Miechów. A weathervane on the roof moaned all night, and I lay in the dark thinking that daytime would come and I would be at Riscal Amargo, with the beams criss-crossing the ceiling, the broken window, and Mas del Aire touching God. In the morning it was rainy, and definitely Poland. Tomorrow after my official entrance to this "ancestrally German city", our horses will be stabled more and more often, as we gradually convert to mechanized reconnaissance.

All I seem to remember tonight of Lorca's verses, as I write in this requisitioned room, are three verses, which sum up more than ever what his writing meant to my younger self:

> *Tender and distant voice poured into me*
> *Tender and distant voice tasted by me*
> *Tender and distant voice that fades away.*

Yes, the horseman's song ends here, and something else – something else, unclear, that I want to call glory but is already so visibly made of blood – has already begun.

AUTHOR'S FINAL NOTE
AND ACKNOWLEDGEMENTS

The history books tell us that Federico García Lorca was arrested and executed by Franco's troops in the summer of 1936, at the beginning of the Spanish Civil War. His body, however, was never recovered, and his place of burial is at best uncertain. The characters in my novel (with the obvious exception of Lorca) are fictional. What is true are geographical setting, battles, political organizations – and, generally, the entire background of the plot.

While working on *The Horseman's Song* I became indebted to many university colleagues, researchers, journalists, musicians, actors, flamenco dancers, literary critics and military advisers, in the United States as well as in Europe. There are too many to list by name, but I warmly thank all of them. Without their help, *The Horseman's Song* would never have seen the light.